Blood Moon Yellow Sky

Yellow Sky Coven Book 1

by A.M. Burns

Copyright 2016 © MysticHawker Press
http://www.mystichawker.com/

ISBN: 978-1-945632-04-4

Cover design by Melissa Kary

Dedicated to:

Justine Bagley the woman who helped me discover so much about the world and helped me to understand there's so much more out there than I ever imagined.

And

My mom and dad who gave me the love for science fiction and fantasy. They taught me to read and from that point, there's been no going back. THANKS!

Chapter One

I FOLLOWED the elf down the street, careful to stay far enough away that he wouldn't spot me. The teeming afternoon crowd made staying out of sight easy, but tucked within the bustling throng, it was impossible to get a bead on him without drawing attention to myself. My assignment was to take out the elf, Carmichall Mac Ghille Mhicheil—Mickey, in such a way the other members of his group would get the message, but as always, I had to keep knowledge of the magical world from getting out to the mundane world. My stakeout started two days ago. He was part of a group of elves who decided exposing the magical world would help their cause of balancing the world's rampant financial inequality. From posts he'd made online, his group was determined to show that magical creatures existed, and some of us held a lot of power in the financial world and control over the humans.

His information was both right and wrong. A large number of the longer-lived beings, like myself, had vast fortunes which contributed to the financial aspect of our world. Most of us couldn't give a rat's ass about the mundane world as long as we weren't directly affected. The group I work for, The Coalition of Magical Creatures, is a vast group of beings who are determined to keep the magical world, a world where most humans would feel like little more than apes, in the shadows where it has been for thousands of years. The general public didn't need to know about the existence of like vampires, shifters, sorcerers, elves, fairies and dragons.

The crowd started to get on my nerves. I wanted the elf to move on to wherever he was going. I suspected his destination was a rally that had been entrenched for a couple of weeks in front of the Tulsa County courthouse. Psychic intelligence from the Coalition precogs said he was going to do something this afternoon. Coming out at the rally would definitely make the statement he intended. I wondered how many of his magical friends would back him. There were more than a few in the community who were tired of toeing the line the Coalition forced on us, keeping us out of view of baseline humans.

Mickey rounded another corner, getting closer to the rally. A large homeless woman pushing a shopping cart crammed full of her life's odds and ends cut me off. I sidestepped her. Crowds get to me. They always have. Nearly two thousand years ago, when I was a lad, we didn't have crowds like we have now. Even as a druid back then traveling with my father to all the villages in England, we never had more than a hundred people around at one time. I hate big cities. They encroach on me in ways I can't possibly explain. I wanted to get this done and drive back to my secluded Colorado mountain valley, ensconce myself in my library and wait until the next time the Coalition needed me to deal with threats to the magical world. I'd just started going over a series of scrolls saved from the Alexandria Library when this call came. I keep hoping to discover how to breathe fire and these scrolls may hold some answers. At the very least they were the first new dragon artifacts I'd run across in nearly a hundred years.

The elf entered the park where the rally was going on. Noise from the crowd assaulted my senses and Mickey disappeared into the throng. A makeshift stage had been erected in the center of the park. I tried to figure out where to go to get the best shot. Across the road, a small strip mall held an antique store. Its proprietor had set out sales flags obviously hoping some of the rallyers might come over and spend a bit of money. The roof of the place would provide me a perfect line of sight to the stage.

Blood Moon Yellow Sky

Taking the long route, so I wouldn't have to deal with the crowds, I walked around to the back of the strip center. After a quick look to make sure no one was watching and using a touch of magic to disable the closed-circuit cameras scanning the back parking lot, I easily jumped up to the top of the building. It would've been so much easier to fly, but the dragon form I inherited from my mother would attract too much attention and I didn't feel like expending the energy to shapeshift.

Settling in next to the air conditioner, I scanned the rally crowd. I took a deep calming breath and called up my mage sight. An alarming number of magical creatures filled the park. The magical aura of several werewolves and cat shifters shone above the normal auras of humans. Something I couldn't identify at this distance moved through the crowd, touching people. It might have been some kind of empathic feeder who would get a charge off of a riot, if one broke out. Carmichall Mac Ghille Mhicheil moved through them like a dancer. Elves are graceful no matter where they are. Sunlight glittered off his long blond hair as he walked up the short steps to the stage. People clearly expected him. A big guy in fatigues said something into the microphone before handing it over to Mickey.

This looked like the time he was going to out everyone. In my mind, I pictured the German sniper rifle in my truck a few miles away. It was close enough I could bring the weapon to me with a thought. The rifle appeared in my hands as Mickey took the microphone. He provided an easy target. Almost too easy, but I took the shot.

Chaos exploded in the park, as Carmichall Mac Ghille Mhicheil's brains decorated the elm trees behind the stage. The elf's first words had not even come out of his mouth before my bullet struck him. People scattered screaming from the park. I tracked several of the magical creatures as they dispersed.

Sending the rifle back to the truck with a thought, I pulled out a handful of business cards. They're simple, reading only Tal O'Duirwood, Enforcer, Have a Nice Day. I got down and around the building in seconds and into the crowd. It felt like swimming upstream as I waded through the masses. Finding the other magical creatures wasn't difficult. I didn't say anything as I passed them. I just handed them a card. Faces paled as I walked away. My reputation's good.

The little empath turned out to be another elf. Her, I slammed up against a tree. "Look, this is a warning. If anyone else is working with Carmichall Mac Ghille Mhicheil to expose us to the world, let them know that the Coalition is on to them. I'm never far away." I handed her my card and patted her on the head as she fainted. Her glamour flickered. I thought about picking her up and carrying her out of the park until she woke up enough she could hold her human illusion together. An invisibility spell was easier. Propping her up against the tree so she would be a harder for park goers to stumble over, I wove a magical field around her to render her invisible. The spell would break when she woke up. I left my card in her hand.

My truck, a black Pathfinder, waited a few blocks away in a crowed parking garage. I got in and rolled down the windows to let some of the autumn heat dissipate. I pulled out my laptop so I could send my mission report. Trying to keep it short and simple, I pulled up my email and sent the message, "Target no longer an issue. Reputation spread."

As soon as I hit send, before I could turn the truck on, another message came through. I groaned as I saw it was another assignment. What was the magical world doing these days that it needed me on duty so much? When I signed up with the Coalition about a hundred years ago, when it was just forming, I rarely had to leave my mountain. Nowadays I spent way too much time out in the world dealing with situations no one else could handle. I prefer to be left alone to my peace and quiet.

Turns out I was needed to help handle a growing vampire problem in a small Texas town. According to the email, a woman there, Geraldine Beggay and her students, all witches, had applied for membership into the Coalition about the same time as vampires appeared. J.P. Montgomery, my boss, wanted me to go and observe them. I wasn't to do anything, just see how they handled the situation, then I'd let J.P. know how they did and if they were good enough for membership into the Coalition.

My blood ran cold as I read the last part of the email. The vampire leading the trouble there was my ex-lover, Estaben de'Oro, or Steven Goldson as he was now called. I hadn't seen Estaben in over a hundred and fifty years. He hadn't been a powerful vampire when I drove him out of Colorado. How could he be gathering followers enough to trouble an entire Texas town? His most ambitious thought back when I knew him had been how find someone to feed on.

I stared at the screen. I met Estaben de'Oro back during the Spanish exploration of the New World. I'd been with him when vampires attacked in the South American jungle. It was because of me he survived. I knew enough vampires back in Europe to get him through those first few years. We'd been lovers for over two hundred years before he pissed me off by making another vampire and they'd gone on a killing spree. I'd been alone since then, keeping to myself in my mountain home. It'd been lonely, but it was safer that way, at least for me. Estaben taught me that. Of the many loves I had in my long life, he'd left the most scars on my heart. Emotional attachments weren't something I cared to indulge in any more. There were still ancient magical secrets for me to explore, and they didn't cause emotional pain, sometimes physical pain, but that was easier to deal with.

My reply was nearly as short as my mission report had been. "On my way." I knew J.P. would get me all the data he had on Beggay, her crew and the situation. If I dropped down to Oklahoma City and caught I-40, then I could be in Yellow Sky, Texas in about six hours, just in time for sunset.

Realizing it might be a longer assignment than normal, I sent J.P. another email asking for the Coalition to set up housing for me. I could bring a few things in from my place in Colorado and feel more at home for a bit while I watched the situation there work its way out.

Emergency vehicles roared pasted the parking garage as I pulled out onto the street. I wondered how many people the authorities were calling in. Sirens had been blaring for several minutes while I sat in the truck. Most of the traffic headed toward the park, so the roads were fairly clear as I headed toward the highway and Texas. More than anything, I wanted to head back to Colorado and leave the whole mess alone, but I'd helped create Steven Goldson. I had to see to the problems he created. Reading ancient scrolls could wait. Learning to breathe fire could wait. Even dragons have to prioritize things sometimes.

Chapter Two

LOCATED IN a small strip center along one of the major streets in Yellow Sky, Halfling's Hideaway looked like your average independent book store. On one side was a women's accessory shop, and to the other side, a malt shop. The store itself was fairly bright and cheery. A painted mountain on one of the large pane windows looked out into the street with the store's name spelled out in dark rocks. Various book posters covered the other window. Announcements adorned the door, making it impossible to see in without someone opening it. Being early in the day, the foot traffic was minimal.

I parked my customized black Pathfinder in a busier parking lot across the street from the store. The Pathfinder straddled the fence between being nondescript and looking a bit too government. It had a state-of-the-art GPS and a built-in wireless Internet link. I'd thanked myself for the Internet link many times already while I watched the shop. It helped me keep in touch with the office and my researcher, Beth, a sweet little tiger shifter who sent me several updates as she located more info on the group I was supposed to contact.

It was interesting how the store was apparently a hub of magical activity, but you couldn't tell it from the outside. Even I had difficulty feeling the carefully-cloaked underlying buzz of magic. The people who went in were another issue entirely. Several times, I watched people with a bright glow of untrained magic go into the store and come out a few minutes later carrying bags of undetermined contents. Most interestingly, no obvious non-humans had gone in. There had been one man, I think it was a man, that went into the women's accessory shop and then into the book store before hopping a bus with bags from both. He hadn't felt non-human, but his willowed appearance begged to differ.

So far, I hadn't seen the woman I was looking to contact. I reviewed the files I had on her. Geraldine Beggay was fifty-five years old. Her parents had been teachers at a ranch devoted to boys that were in trouble with the law. She was the first girl to graduate from there. It seems she met an old Indian shaman there and he taught her to control her natural magical abilities. The files indicated he applied for membership, but during his trial, he failed and died. She disappeared from our view at that time. Beth sent me state, county and city records. There is no record of her ever having married and the only mention of her in the police files was as an informant, someone they went to when there was no one else to turn to. It looked to me like she'd been using her gifts for good. It sounded to me like her early life on the ranch for boys helped her decide to take a liking to this group of young inexperienced mages.

The files on her students were sketchier. Alexander Biff Carlson, twenty-five, seemed to be the leader of the group and owner of Halfling's Hideaway. He graduated Yellow Sky Community College with an Associate degree in business with a 3.5 GPA. He still lived with his parents. His picture, taken from a college yearbook, was pleasant enough. His red hair and vivid green eyes caught my attention. Having grown up on the English isles, I had a soft spot for redheads.

Stanley Robert Belsario, twenty-eight, was a college dropout from a military family who somehow ended up in Yellow Sky. During his early years, his family moved around a lot. He had a juvenile rap sheet longer than my leg, but since coming to Yellow Sky, had either managed to stay out of trouble or evade the authorities. It could also have been Beggay's influence with the local police protected her students.

Next on my list were Charles Allen and Bernadette Angela Colfax, twenty-three, fraternal twins, of a divorced mother. Both attended West Texas University in Canyon about fifteen miles south of Yellow

Sky. Both had scholarships and neither seemed to have a job. Charles was on the Dean's list for his excellence in computer science, but Bernadette was barely keeping her grades up enough to get her law degree. There was a minor charge of shoplifting on Bernadette, but Charles was clean. Several companies were fighting over Charles and he'd be able to write his own ticket in the future. Bernadette seemed destined to be an ambulance chaser.

Twenty-two-year-old Terry Wesley Holloway had gone to high school with Charles and Bernadette, was an average student, with a squeaky-clean record. He currently attended to the local tech school and had a part-time job at a computer repair counter at a large electronics store. Larry Christopher Holloway, nineteen, brother to Terry. Currently not enrolled in school, he worked at the book store with Alexander. Another squeaky-clean record, but then their father was a cop and cops have ways of covering things up. Twenty-one-year-old Janie Hillary Miller appeared to follow Bernadette around, as their rap sheets were identical. She was also pursuing a pre-law degree at West Texas University.

So far, while I'd been watching, Alexander and Stanley had gone into the store and at that point, only Alexander was there. It was as good a time as any, for me to get a look inside of the place. I sighed and closed down the laptop before getting out of the truck, then walked to the corner so I could cross the road legally. The afternoon breeze was blowing, but then I already noticed that the wind always blew in Yellow Sky. Thankfully, the dust wasn't kicking up. As I drove in the previous day, an incredible dust storm blew up just as I reached the city limits. I hadn't seen a dust storm like that since the dust bowl days of the 1930s. The cloud tops had to be seven to eight hundred feet tall, very impressive.

Shaking dust storm thoughts from my head, I stepped into the shop. Crossing the threshold was like wading through magical mud. The shields around the place didn't try to keep me out exactly, but my magical sensitivity made entering an interesting, almost birth-like experience. Once clear of the shields, the calm of the place settled around me. My senses worked fine looking out through the shields of the shop. Apparently, they were designed to keep things out and from looking in, but not the reverse. The shields were the work of a major mage, not some little dabbler. Geraldine must train her students well. There was no reason to believe she hadn't helped in the construction of the field I walked through. A slight brushing of my own magic against it, showed several magical signatures in the shields, and as I got to know them, I'd be able to tell which signature belonged to which witch. I glanced about and noticed that magical signs and symbols, or sigils, covered the walls, but were hidden carefully by either a layer of paint or more posters. To my magical sight, they'd glowed a bit until I cleared the shield, and then faded down to a normal glimmer. Alexander would know someone magical just came in, if he were paying attention.

A quick glance at the shop's contents revealed an incredible array of items and literature held mostly on four-foot-tall shelves. A number of signs hanging from the ceiling informed people where to find the particular genre they sought, with the fantasy and science fiction section closest to the door. The main counter was located along the window and formed an L in the corner with the adjoining wall to the malt shop. There was only one cash register. On the far side of the counter, several racks against the wall contained candles and statuary. The metaphysical section was in that area, too. It was amazingly large for a small town. That must have been part of what drew the magical crowd into this store.

I started surveying the various idols and statues when a redhead appeared from under the counter. I almost jumped, taken by surprise for the first time in a very long time. I normally sense someone before they get that close to me. I looked into the deep green eyes of Alexander Carlson. The picture I had didn't do the young man justice, but then when did a yearbook photo do anybody justice? They were like ID cards and drivers' licenses, always an awful shot that you'll be remembered by and identified by for years to come. Looking at the real person now, I didn't think it possible for him to take a bad picture.

He looked like he should grace the cover of a magazine somewhere. He could make an incredible life for himself just on his looks alone.

"I heard the door, but didn't think anyone came in," he said. His accent was thicker than I imagined, based on his bio. The nametag on his tight black t-shirt said Alex. His eyes sparkled with curiosity at my ability to elude his senses and his smile showed a row of almost perfect white teeth that shone in the tan of his freckled face. Obviously something under the counter engrossed him to the point he hadn't seen his wards glow as I entered.

"I'm sorry. I was trying to be quiet." I lied easily as I felt my heart race more than it had in years. Something about him pulled at my soul. This young man had a kind of magnetism about him that I'd do well to avoid. "I hoped I could look around a bit before someone asked to help me."

"Well don't mind me then, just look about and holler if you need anything." His eyes glowed with a combination of intelligence and mischief as he settled himself down on the stool behind the counter.

"I'll do that," I replied, tearing my gaze away from his before I drowned in those beautiful green eyes. I didn't need this. I was nearly two thousand years old. I've had more men than I cared to remember and I'd sworn the entire thing off almost a hundred years ago after a really disastrous fling with a handsome English werewolf who was killed by some renegade vampires. That, coming on the heels of Estaben's betrayal, was almost more than my heart could handle. I decided then that all I needed was a good book and life would be fine. Now here I was, on a job no less, staring into the deep green eyes of some young mage who may end up dead by the end of the week. But, even I wasn't immune to the charms of an attractive young man. His face was very nice and he looked like he had a hard body. I turned my attention to scanning through the merchandise in the store, telling myself I had to focus and look beyond the siren song of those green eyes with their long lovely rusty-red lashes.

To this day, I'm amazed at the price some people will pay for things that won't matter in the big scheme of things. Now I admit to paying the value of a small country from time to time on a magical tome of one form or another, but really, the price they wanted for these books, most of which would not last a decade, was unbelievable. I suppose I should just view it as a form of entertainment for the mind and entertainment in any form has value.

Some of the statuary offered was fascinating. The bust of the vampire goddess was particularly interesting because there is no goddess of the vampires. But, if there was one, I doubt that she would have such profound cleavage or red bat wings. Any of the more extreme things that vampires are said to have done are not due to vampirism, but to a study of magic. Most vampires could only dream of such things as flying or shape shifting unless they studied magic before their change. Overall, more human mages could do things attributed to vampires than vampires could.

At the sound of the door opening, I turned my attention away from the statuary. Stanley Belsario walked in accompanied by Bernadette Colfax and Janie Miller. As they passed me, I caught the reek of pot smoke. The three of them had the afterglow of tantric magic about them, wrapped in a marijuana haze.

"You're early," Alex commented as they slid behind the counter.

"We wanted to practice a little magic that would take a bit, so we skipped classes after lunch and set to work," Janie whispered.

I studied the three of them, comparing them to the pictures from the files. Bernadette had changed the most. Her hair was now a bright blue with green highlights, and she had three earrings in the left ear and two in the right. A large silver pentagram hung in the center of her chest, almost buried in her cleavage. Janie also wore a pentagram, but only two earrings. Her blonde hair was halfway down her narrow back. Her eyes never left Bernadette for a second. It was easy to see where her interest lay.

Stanley changed in a more positive way. Not as scruffy as his prison shots, he was clean-cut with a neatly trimmed black goatee. A black leather duster hung straight down from his narrow shoulders, ending above a sleek pair of cowboy boots. He radiated magical energy that flowed strongly from the other two. There was a clear link between them that was almost impossible to miss. The link felt like one that had existed for some time and was maintained by constant closeness. They were a triad inside the little group that operated out of the shop. They could be the main circle of power inside the group, but somehow that didn't feel right.

Alex sighed and paused for a second. "You know Geri says you shouldn't be practicing tantric magic yet, particularly not with Hill. Her sexual energy channels are still forming."

"Makes the energy all the more sweet, my friend," Stanley said, in an almost lecherous tone. He cast a glance of possessiveness over the younger women, both of whom seemed to glow a bit more as his eyes passed over them. "So, what's on the agenda for today?"

"Geri wants us all over there after the shop closes. Something about preparing for this Coalition thing. I'll tell you more later," Alex said, nodding in my direction to let the others know I was there.

Stanley turned with concerned look on his face. "I didn't know anyone was here. I scanned as I came in and didn't feel anyone," He whispered to Alex. Had my hearing not been so keen I would have missed it.

I didn't even look up from the books. I dropped down into one of the chairs at the end of an aisle, slightly out of their sight and kept listening.

"Don't feel bad," Alex replied to Stanley, without much sympathy in his voice. "I missed him when he came in. He didn't set off any of the alarms, and I was busy under the counter so I don't know what the wards did. He's just not there. He may just be too well shielded for us to sense. He is really cute though, sort of a hot, sexy Celtic feel to him, around our age too. I'll mention it to Geri tonight."

"Let me try," Bernadette said softly. Then something pushed on my shields. Not enough to get through, but enough to let me know that someone was knocking. Luckily, I was prepared and skillfully pushed the energy to the side. It flowed around my shields quickly enough so it would feel as if I wasn't there.

"Damn," she muttered as she let up on her push.

"What Burn?" Janie asked, excessive concern clouding her voice.

"He's not there as far as I can tell. Do we know if he's human?"

That Bernadette questioned my humanity told me a lot about the teaching of Geraldine Beggay. Most minor mages and witches don't even know of, let alone believe in, non-humans. She must know the truth and be educating her students in it. I was also impressed with the caution she imparted on her students when dealing with unknown people. In some magical circles, such probing would be seen as rude, but being the dragon that I am, I would've done the same thing. It had kept me alive numerous times.

"From everything Geri has told us to look for, physically, the contact is human," Alex replied. "Beyond that I have no idea. I can't scan him either."

The door chime rang lightly.

To say that Charles Colfax didn't look like his twin is an understatement. A fair number of fraternal twins look a lot alike, and even try to look alike. From the pictures I'd seen earlier, I expected more similarities. Charles was a classic preppy college senior, almost like one of those that you see in the dramas on television. I honestly don't watch much TV, but I do try and keep up with the news and the pretty people always seem to pop up there. Charles kept his black hair short and had on a light blue polo shirt over a darker blue t-shirt. His khaki slacks were neatly pressed and his penny loafers brightly polished. He tossed a leather backpack behind the counter as he walked past the others.

"What's up guys?" he asked in a cheerful tone.

"Lower your voice, Char," Alex said in an almost normal volume. "We have a customer."

"Where? There's no one here," he said almost arrogantly without dropping his voice.

I decided the time had come to go. It was going to be hard to get much casual information out of them now they were starting to get a bit spooked by not being able to sense me magically. I wasn't about to lower my shields enough to let them, so I might as well go and see about finding their mentor. I stepped out into the main isle and walked to the door.

As I took the handle, I turned and smiled at Alex, getting a parting look into those green eyes. "Nice shop you have here. I'll be back." Everyone stared at me.

"Thanks for stopping in," Alex called as I stepped through the shields around the store, out onto the sidewalk and into the late afternoon light.

Chapter Three

DURING THE short trip across town to Geraldine's house, I thought about what I experienced at The Halfling's Hideaway. My exposure to young mages was limited to my days as an apprentice druid. Back then, it was common practice to give a young practitioner a good solid background in magic and then send them out to see the world with a more experienced tutor to watch after them, and make sure they didn't get into too much trouble. Once the initial journey was over, the studies of higher magic would begin. My own journey took me to the depths of the Black Forest in central Europe, into what is now Germany. I wondered if Geraldine would send her young students out into the world to find themselves and their places in it. But the world had changed so much. Where would they go? In my day, much of the learning was the journey itself. You learned when to use magic to help you and when to avoid its use. Every time you did something, even small magics, you risked being spotted by others and possibly burned at the stake, or at least chased out of town. Now, unless they were forbidden to use modern transportation, the journey would be easy. She'd probably have a new teacher set up at the end of the journey. When I went, it was with the hope the teachers would still be where my mentor had last known of them and they might still be alive. I sighed. Modern folks had it so easy.

The small house I drove past was rather deceiving. Many things about this group were not as they appeared. It looked like a strong wind could blow it over. The roof seemed to be at an odd angle and the windows were all mismatched. A small stained-glass window centered the bright blue front door. A perfectly tended small flower garden sat out front along the recently swept pathway to the porch. As I studied the house, I realized that as odd as it looked, it was actually in perfectly good order. None of the shingles on the roof appeared to be loose and it had a fairly recent coat of paint. Not that I found the almost lime green a pleasing color, but at least it was new paint. I realized that like a lot of people who lived in less savory neighborhoods, Ms. Beggay made her home appear less appealing to deter people from bothering her, while at the same time, keeping up the house to a livable level.

The small driveway next to the house held two cars. From a couple houses down, I sent the license plate numbers to Beth to have her run a quick check. She got back to me with her normal speed and efficiency. The first car, a classic red Volkswagen Beetle, came back registered to G. Beggay. The second car, a late model blue Ford Escort, belonged to Danielle Colfax. Why was the twins' mother here?

I sat for a moment debating whether to go in or not. The shadows were growing longer and if I wanted to have a good discussion with Geraldine before her students arrived, I needed to get it done. After circling the block again, I pulled up in front of the house and got out of the truck. As soon as I stepped onto the curb, the protections the witch had woven around her home reacted to my presence. The field actually stretched almost to the end of the block, effectively protecting her neighbors from things that might try to harm her. The shields had a different feel than the ones at The Halfling's Hideaway. They were lighter, more airy, while at the same time the sharp sting told me I passed through something major. The shields only had one signature unlike those at the store, but I noticed the similarities and acknowledged that Geraldine had a hand in the shields at the shop. I walked slowly toward the door, letting my senses adjust to the air inside the shields. It was filled with older magic than the atmosphere at the store. When I passed the edge of her sidewalk, I passed through a second layer of protections that wrapped around the property. The zap on this level was stronger than the last one. When I stepped onto the apparently-ragged porch, the final level of shields washed around me. It felt like walking through a waterfall, cool, almost inviting, but at the same time it held an element of danger, like it could wash me away if it wanted. I wouldn't have wanted to be someone who Geraldine Beggay wanted to keep out of her home. I had no doubt the feel wouldn't be something inviting, but something much more violent and extremely painful.

I stood there for a moment to get my bearings with the afternoon sun striking the back of my neck. Before I could touch the door, it swung open. A short woman with thinning gray hair stood on the other side of the threshold. She wore a simple blue kimono with small lotus blossoms on it. She smiled up at me, her worn face showing a profusion of laugh lines. "I presume you are with the Coalition of Magical Creatures. Please come on in. I've been expecting you." Her soft voice had a powerful command under it. Her gray eyes laughed at me. I have encountered enough beings with enchanted senses, I stop being surprised by the whole open-the-door-before-you-knock routine a long time ago.

I crossed the threshold without encountering further protections. "Tal O'Duirwood." I said offering her my hand.

"Geraldine Beggay. If you would please give me a couple of minutes, I am almost done talking with a friend of mine." She gestured toward an old but well-kept brown sofa.

"Of course, I have time," I replied, taking a seat on the overly-soft couch.

I strained my ears trying to hear what was going on beyond the living room, but somehow everything past the dark, panel-covered wall was beyond my hearing. I passed my time studying the artwork on the walls. She had an eclectic group of pictures ranging from modern fantasy art of dragons and sci-fi characters to old western paintings of cowboys, horses, and assorted landscapes. Most curiously, I saw no mirror in the room. The furniture was as eclectic as the art. There was a wing-back chair sitting alongside an antique wooden rocker. Neither one matched the old sofa. A large red and green Navajo blanket covered the majority of the oak flooring.

I pulled my attention away from my observations as I heard Geraldine and another woman come through the door. The other woman was tall and slender like her children; they all had the same high cheekbones and delicate nose. Her body language said that she was nervous about something.

Geraldine gave her a big hug at the door. "It'll all be okay Dani. I can't tell you it's just a phase, but Burn is a good girl and won't get into too much trouble with Char keeping an eye on her." I wondered if the twins were using abbreviations of their names for magical purposes. It wasn't uncommon for people to do that. Names have power in magic. I noticed it at the shop but didn't think of it until now. Char and Burn for magical twins had an interesting ring to it.

"I know Geri, I just wanted to talk, that's all. You have a good night," Danielle said releasing the other woman.

"You too, Dani. Call me if you need anything," Geraldine replied, closing the door behind the other woman before turning to me. "So Tal, please come on into the kitchen. I'm working on a bit of dinner before the gang gets here tonight. Plus, everyone always gathers in the kitchen."

I rose and followed her. "Was that the mother of one of your students?" I asked, trying to sound as if I didn't know.

Geraldine turned around and looked at me, her gray eyes blazing with internal fire. "Tal, please don't try and be coy with me. I figure you know very well that she's the mother of two of my students, the twins actually. I figure the Coalition gave you complete files on me and everyone around me as part of my application. I'm also sure you've already been by Halfling's Hideaway and met most of my students." She smiled slyly. "You see, as soon as you left, Alex called me to let me know of the attractive man who none of them could sense, who didn't set off the magical alarms. Somehow, I thought you'd be taller. At that point, I figured you were either the Coalition's observer, or our prey. I reviewed the files I received before Dani arrived and there is nothing in them about Estaben de'Oro being able to move about in the daylight. So, I figured out you were with the Coalition. Now I'm going to be honest with you, and I expect you to be honest with me." She turned around and finished the short walk to the kitchen.

I sighed. Something told me the woman was going to keep me on my toes. "I see my original assessment of your students is correct. You have trained them well. I'll be as honest with you as I can." There were certain things I'd have to keep secret from these people. At least until I was sure they'd be admitted to the Coalition.

The kitchen was as odd and assorted as the rest of the house. The wooden table with its mismatched chairs was an extremely large one for a woman who lived by herself. The rest of the kitchen looked like something a professional chef would have. The appliances were all of stainless steel, and a huge pot rack hung above a large worktop in the center of the room. An incredible number of herbs hung in bundles around the window that looked out into the plush green of the back yard. A small well-kept garden out back was visible through the window. A quaint picture framed by blue gingham curtains.

I seated myself at the table while Geri stirred a simmering pot on the stove. The woman was direct. I liked that. After years of dealing with people that spent hours getting to the point, it was refreshing to meet someone who could get to the point and expect me to do the same. "So, how much have you been told of my role in your trial by combat?" I asked.

She turned toward me with a wooden spoon in her hand. "You're here as an observer, unless we prove unable to remove de'Oro, at which point you step in and end his existence." She paused for a moment and looked me over. "What they didn't tell me is what you are. You look and act human, but no human would be able to hide so well from my students."

I sighed again. In all honesty, she needed to know what kind of back up I'd provide if she and her students should need me. There was nothing that said I shouldn't tell her, except the basic instinct to not reveal too much about myself, and that—as the last of my kind—I was a major Coalition secret. I looked into those piercing gray eyes and knew I had to tell her the truth, as she would know anything else for what it was. "I'm a half breed. My father was a druid in ancient England. My mother was a dragon."

Her grey eyes grew wide but her face remained impassive. Overall, it was the best coming out I've ever had.

"I suppose I should be shocked," she said. "But there seems to be more new things around every corner lately. So are there many dragons in the world?"

I shook my head. "To my knowledge I'm the last one. My existence is a secret in the Coalition."

"Why did you tell me?"She touched the spoon to her lips

I didn't want to tell her something in her gaze compelled me. But I couldn't think of a better option. "I felt compelled."

"Most people tell the truth in this house." She nodded and turned back to the stove. "So do you know this Estaben de'Oro?"

I sat there and stared at her back as she stirred another pot from which rose the smell of cooking vegetables. I tried to think of what to tell her, just the basics, or all of it. It was hard to believe that a human witch could be this intense, or get to me this fast. Then mixed with the aromas of the cooking, I caught the smell of a dog, but there was no evidence of dogs in the house or yard. I studied the woman before me. The smell was coming off her as she waited for my answer. Then I realized that she was sniffing the air, not the pot she stirred. I shifted my vision to mage sight and saw the overlay of a coyote shining out of her. "I know Estaben. Are you a lycanthrope?"

She turned to face me and I was suddenly looking into the blue eyes of a canine. "I see that the coalition wasn't aware of that," she chuckled. "Of course it's a recent addition to my life." She came over to the table, sat down and placed her spoon on a spoon rest that sat on its edge. "Stan had stumbled onto a werecoyote who was selling peyote to the local drug community. We decided to try to convince him to leave town. What was supposed to be a little pressure to get him out turned into a heated battle. I managed to keep any of the others from being injured, but I was scratched fairly badly. Nothing we came up with would stop the infection from setting in. But I was able to find some spells to help me maintain control when the first change hit me on the full moon last month. Since then, I've pushed out my new senses and gotten control of the change. I've actually managed to do a full change without the moon being full."

I'd talked to a few werefolk over the years and the couple of them that had been mages before being infected with the virus had an easier time getting control of the changes. Based on what I'd already seen and suspected, she'd gain complete control of her changes rapidly. The werefolk were different from shifters like myself who were born with the ability. Lycanthropy is a magical disease for which there is no cure. Luckily, it's mostly limited to predatory animals, or there would be a lot more in the world and everyone would know about it. "So how are your students taking the change?" Of course this also explained their comment about non-humans.

She smiled. "For the most part they think it's cool. There've been a couple of comments about taking advice from a coyote. But then, I'd expect no less from my gang, being pranksters themselves."

"Do you think this will cause a problem with you removing Estaben?"

"I'm hoping it'll make it easier. It definitely makes tracking things easier. It's also giving a little more life to these old bones. My arthritis disappeared completely." She flexed her fingers with a wily grin

"So tell me what to expect from your students. What are their strengths and weaknesses? And are you aware that some of them are experimenting with tantric magic?" I carefully kept the conversation away from my knowledge of Estaben. The longer I had before being totally truthful there the better. Most people would jump to the conclusion that our past relationship was a problem in me being able to assassinate him if need be.

"For the most part they're coming along very well. Alex is the best of the group. He doesn't indulge in any of the recreational substances that Stan and some of the others like to use. That gives him a much clearer mind and he's a faster learner and less likely to be caught addle minded. His control of magical energies is remarkable. He has almost reached the point where I have little left to teach him. I'll be sending him out into the world soon." She picked up her spoon and headed back to the stove.

"I debated with myself if that tradition was still followed. It's been a long time since I had any dealing with younger mages. And remembering my own journey of discovery into the wilds of Europe, I wondered if others still got the joys of finding new sights and experiences."

"I personally feel that it depends on the mage," Geri answered. "If someone has a lot of life experiences, sending them out's a waste of time unless you have a teacher in mind for them to find. If they've led a sheltered life, then they need to go out. Stan won't need to go out. His family moved all over the world as he was growing up and he learned at lot from all of that. Alex remained in the bosom of his family here in Yellow Sky the whole time. But then, most of his family has at least some PSI talent and that makes them very tight. I'd be surprised if his sister and brother don't end up in my tutelage before it's all said and done." She stirred the vegetables while she spoke, then pulled the pot off the stove and carried it over to the table.

"I guess offering you some vegetable soup is kinda silly," she said with a sly glint in her eye.

I returned her smile and chuckled. "I've never viewed it as rude when someone offers food. It's normally good manners. Thank you. But I don't have to eat very often and my preferences run a little more on the carnivore side of the spectrum."

She scooped the vegetables out of the pot and into a large porcelain bowl covered in Chinese characters of fortune and well being. "I need to get this eaten before they get here. They tend to stop before they come by as most of them find my cooking overly vegetarian and bland."

"I can't say I've ever met a vegetarian werecoyote before. You don't have the urges for meat?" Most werecreatures and shifters I knew followed a diet close to that of the creature they turned into. Thus, carnivores ate a lot of meat and herbivores ate mostly vegetables. Normally that was the hardest urge to overcome.

"I control the urge, but it's there. One of my email buddies says that if I don't eat meat on a regular basis then I might develop some health problems, but until I have proof of that, I'm going to eat the way I always have," she replied as she chewed the first bite of the vegetables.

"I doubt you'll have a problem. I've known a lot of folks who do things counter to popular belief and it works out great. You know there's a lot of evidence that wild coyotes eat seed heads and berries."

"Good," she said after the next bite. "So, tell me about Estaben."

I shook my head. It was a direct question and I felt the magic in the house trigger and push against me. I was ready for it this time. I'd see if I could work my way around the question. "I met him back during the Spanish exploration of the New World. We traveled together for a while."

She set her spoon down on the edge of her bowl. Her grey gaze locked onto my blue ones. "How close were you while he traveled with you?"

The pressure of the truth spells pushed against me. "Very."

"What made you part ways?"

"You probably noticed in his file that he's gathering humans around him and then turning a fair number of them into vampires. I don't approve of that now, nor did I in the past." The pressure of the truth spell let up as I continued. "The Coalition's concern right now is that he may be drawing public attention to the non-humans in this area. When too many bodies turn up, or too many people disappear, then authorities start to ask questions." A slight shiver passed over me, a warning that someone was watching me from behind. It was one of those rare times that I had actually left my back to the door in a strange place. I decided not to let on that I knew they were there. Geri didn't seem inclined to draw my attention to them. "Unfortunately he's been changing people since he got bored with a mostly solitary life at around two hundred years old. He made his first companion then. At some point, he realized if he made enough companions he'd never feel lonely again. About that same time, he also started to feel the power that having fledglings gives a vampire. That power grows with each new fledgling."

"How many fledgling vampires have you helped over the years?" Geri asked setting her spoon down.

"I've assisted many fledglings in getting through the first few years of their new lives after their sires abandoned them." I felt the folks watching my back more intensely now.

"So, you're a vampire?" asked Alex, behind me.

I turned and saw the seven people standing there in the doorway. I was amazed they'd all been able to enter without me actually hearing. But then I recalled not being able to eavesdrop on the conversation between Geraldine and Mrs. Colfax. I glanced at Geri and she nodded. They then filed into the room and gathered around the table.

"I'm Tal, and no I'm not a vampire. I'm working for The Coalition of Magical Creatures. I'm here to observe, and assist if need be." After many years of practice, it wasn't hard to pull off suave.

"Damn, you're not a vampire," Charles Colfax almost pouted. "I was hoping we'd get to talk to the one we're supposed to kill before we kill him."

I'd seen this type of enthusiasm before. Charles was a wannabe. There were lots of people in the magical community as well as some of the fringe communities that thought the idea of being a vampire was cool. They never stopped to think about the limitations. Funny I would've figured his twin Bernadette would be more the one to be the wannabe. Maybe after a few chats with me, he'd be convinced it wasn't the thing to be. "We can talk at some point over the next few days if you like, if Geraldine doesn't mind. I may not be a vampire, but I know a lot about them."

She rose to take her bowl to the sink. "I think it would be a good idea for you to sit and talk to all the gang over the next few days, but right now, I have things planned for them."

"One thing first, Geri," Alex said, his tone serious. "If Tal's not a vampire, then what is he?" His green eyes stared seriously at me, but his face was soft.

"Tal can explain more to you later, but for now let's just accept he's with the Coalition and let it lay," Geri said as she turned off the water. "Now, we have to get to work on some of our preparations and a little more study time."

I could tell she was about to ask me to come back later. I understood. She didn't know me other than as a member of the Coalition and would be reluctant to expose too much of her personal magic to me until she knew me better. "Before I go, I would like to get a feel for what Estaben has set up around here. Could you direct me towards any of the local hangouts where I might run into some of his people?"

She looked at me with a mischievous glint in her gray eyes. "Tell you what. Why don't you go out, get a bite to eat and then swing back by. I think Alex would like to run you around tonight and show you some of the spots around town where the non-humans tend to hang, as well as a couple of the gay bars as they seem to be where Estaben is getting a fair number of his recruits. I figure about now you're getting pretty hungry."

"Well, not …" A stab of hunger coursed through my body. I'd fed up less than a week ago and shouldn't need to feed for another week or so. What was this woman doing to me? First telling her my secret and now this? I didn't feel the use of any magic on me. I realized I had stopped in mid sentence and now all eyes were on me waiting for me to finish. "Now that you mention it, a bit of meat might not be a bad thing" It'd been a long time since I was this embarrassed. For some reason, Alex seeing me at a loss for words made it worse. I avoided his searching eyes.

Chapter Four

A QUARTER moon rose in the rearview mirror as I followed the busy highway west out of town. I was alone with my thoughts. It was unusual for the information I had on an assignment to be so incomplete. Normally the information on an assignment was complete within a couple of days. It should've included the knowledge of Geraldine's recent encounter with the werecoyote. Her change of species status automatically made her eligible for membership in the Coalition of Magical Creatures. However, it also made it so that her students would have to apply for membership on their own merits and not hers. I debated notifying Beth to see if she could get me more complete information but that would mean she would end up letting the Coalition know about the new intel.

I needed to decide how to proceed with this assignment. If I simply followed the orders, I could sit back and watch as Geri and her gang went after Estaben and hope they succeeded without my interference. I could notify the Coalition and they could decided how to proceed, which would probably entail me having to assassinate Estaben on my own. On the other hand, I could tell the Coalition nothing, assist Geri and her students while making sure the gang were the ones who looked to be knowledgeable of their craft and thereby eligible for membership into the Coalition. As each option went through my head, I saw Alex's green eyes. Why did those eyes haunt me?

I pulled the Pathfinder over to the side of the road and stared out at the cars passing by without really seeing them. I needed to run and clear my head. It was hard for me to find places I could safely fly without drawing attention to myself, so I usually opted for staying on land, or at least in shaped that wouldn't seem out of place. I stepped out of the truck, made sure it was locked and walked into the unfenced field next to the highway. Hunger called me, but with the thoughts of Alexander Biff Carlson going through my head, I really needed to run. I would prefer to fly, but a dragon showing up on local radar would have all the UFO nuts around pouring into Yellow Sky. One of the things I enjoyed living in the mountains was I knew where the radar would reach and where I could fly in certain valleys. Not being able to fly where I wanted was one of the things I disliked about modern technology.

So, I ran, slowly at first across the sage flats that ran parallel to the highway, then faster as the darkness of the open country closed in around me. The limitations of my human form began to irritate me as I ran, so I summoned the energy from the earth beneath my feet to shift. I didn't even pause as I ran. I just flowed into the heavily-furred form of the gray wolf.

The earth under my feet took on new meaning as I loped across the open prairie. I always enjoyed the change in perception. The view and feelings of the wolf varied so much from either my human or dragon forms. The world seemed so alive to the wolf. The wind carried even more scents and became like a living sea as it coursed over my form, singing down the follicles of my long shaggy coat. In the distance, coyotes warned their neighboring packs of my presence. A silent owl swooped down and snatched a small mouse before taking flight again before my charge.

Ahead, a tall butte jutted out of the desert reaching into the night sky. I raced up the side of it, my agile form easily finding footholds on the steep incline. I reached the top and paused for a moment to look back over my shoulder. The highway behind me was bright with the lights of the cars streaming past. To the east, the lights of Yellow Sky only covered part of the horizon. It seemed to scatter out across the landscape, but it did not cover the horizon as some of the larger towns did. It was large enough to hide in, but not large enough to get lost.

Blood Moon Yellow Sky

I sat on the top of the butte, staring at the lights in the distance. In that cluster of lights, an old love waited for me to help orchestrate his demise while a pair of green eyes watched my every move. What was I supposed to do? I was too old to worry about these things. Love and sentiment are for the young and foolish. I remembered something my father told me when I was about to leave his side and walk the world on my own. He called me into his workroom. I still recall that room, in fact I've tried to recreate just that room for myself many times. I failed to get it just right until I finally realized that each wizard had his own way of doing things, and I didn't need to be just like anybody else. Taliesin perched on an old stool before one of his boiling cauldrons mixing an ancient potion of some kind. He was the arch druid of England and by then, chief advisor to the king. He appeared tired that night, his brown eyes sad.

"Tal," he said with a little apprehension in his voice. To this day, I remember that shaky tone. I'd never heard before, or since. "I have one last lesson for you before you go and then you will carry all of my knowledge out into the world to pass on to your children and apprentices someday."

I forget what my response was, but his face stayed with me all this time. "You will live a very long time. Most likely, you will live until you decide it is time to let go. That is the way of your mother's people. This last thing is one of the most important things I have ever passed on to you." He sighed, then set down the large wooden spoon he was stirring with and took my hands in his. "My son, always remember, if you are to survive, then you must keep your mind open and learning. You must always keep your heart open and ready. It will not be easy this last part, I ask you, as there will be many who will be ready to step in and play with it. Always try to find companionship. Do not go through the world alone. But, you must be careful in your choice of companions. There will be those who will want to exploit you for what you are. I wish there were others of your kind for you to find, but I fear your mother was the last of the pure dragons in this world. I hope one day you will find love, the kind of love I had with her." With that, he asked if I had my things ready, called for his servant to bring my horse and sent me out into the world.

I saw him again many years later. We had come together and spent a couple of years sharing the knowledge we had both learned in the time we were apart. He was older then, the king he served had just died and the kingdom was in turmoil. Shortly after I left him again, he was betrayed by one of his servants and killed by religious zealots who had been able to overcome him. The age of Christianity had come to England and the druids were forced into the darkness of the forest. After that, I never had any human servants in my employ. I had also taken great joy in destroying that servant once I hunted him down. I remember finding him in the arms of the zealot he had betrayed my father for. They died in each other's arms; by their own religion, they had no hope for anything but Hell.

My father wouldn't have been happy with me looking out over the nighttime city in the distance debating love lost. I could hear him telling me to trust my instincts and follow my heart. But my heart had allowed Estaben to live that night long ago in the Amazon jungle. How was I supposed to follow it again?

Movement caught my eye. At the base of the butte, a small herd of pronghorn grazed. My hunger pushed thoughts of the heart out of my mind, replacing them with thoughts of the hunt. My focus narrowed on the herd passing the butte's base. The buck had gathered six does and four of them had young calves at their sides. Trailing the herd were two young bucks that the herd master would soon drive off before they could challenge him for the alpha position. I watched for a moment and decided one of the young bucks would taste excellent. They passed to the south of the butte and the wind carried their musk up to me. It pushed my hunger over the edge.

The jump off the top of the butte would have killed a normal wolf. As it was, the landing momentarily drove the air from my lungs. The nearest doe screamed to the others as they herded the youngsters into a circle ringed by the older does. One of the young bucks tried to join the circle, but was pushed out by the does. He ran around franticly while the lead buck tried to stand me down. The other young buck decided to stand with his father. This buck had what it would take to be the herd male, either of this herd or another. I dashed past them, toward the one that sought refuge. I dodged the doe's slashing hooves and pushed him to the point of panic. He took out across the sage flats toward the road. I followed. Behind me, the rest of the herd, pushed by the herd master, ran for safety.

I focused on the rust and white rump bouncing before me. It only took a couple of seconds to close the distance. He screamed as my dewclaw sank into his flank and I pulled myself onto his back. He tried to buck me off. But I held tight. I crawled across his heaving back to reach his neck. My massive jaws closed around the back of his neck, and with a jerk of my head, I severed the spinal cord. He fell to the ground. I rolled off, coming to rest a soft distance away.

His eyes still held life as I came back beside him. I almost felt sorry for him. But he had proven to me that he was not of alpha mentality; therefore, he was prey. One day, his father and brother would also lose that mentality and then they would become prey. Probably not my prey, but prey to someone or something.

There on the ground, with no one around to see, I shifted to my dragon form. My powerful jaws tore into the warm flesh. The blood flowed down my throat as I gulped large chunks of meat. I could've eaten the thing in wolf form, but it would've taken longer and Alex was waiting.

Chapter Five

WHEN I pulled up to the curb in front of Geri's house, Alex stood up from the old concrete steps. He'd obviously changed clothes and was now dressed for a night out. A tight light-blue shirt clung to his well-defined body. As he stepped into the pool of light cast by the streetlight, thick curly red hair peeked from two open buttons at the top of his shirt. His jeans looked almost painted onto his narrow hips revealing his above-average endowment. I sighed deeply as he stepped off the curb and reached for the door handle. The man was just too sexy for his own good, or mine.

"Hey Tal." He flashed one of his wide grins as he slid gracefully onto the seat. "Did you find dinner okay? You're running a bit later than Geri figured so I was beginning to think you got lost." He clicked the seatbelt and then turned to face me.

"I needed a bit of fresh air before dinner." I grinned back.

"Well at least the air around here is a lot fresher than some places."

I sighed as I put the truck in gear. "Not exactly as fresh as I'm used to."

"Where are you from exactly?"

"I have a big place up in the Rocky Mountains."

"Wow, I love it up in Colorado and Wyoming."

"It beats the hell out of most places on this planet." We stopped at the stop sign for the main street. "Where are we going tonight?"

"We discussed it and we think Mandalek's would be the best place to start. It's Thursday, so things aren't going to be quite as busy as they will the next couple of nights, but there's still the normal traffic. Some of the more desperate characters hang out there. We might even run into David Keyon there. If there's some kind of movement in the dark forces, he's sure to know something about it. David attracts darkness like fleas to a rat," he said with a chuckle.

"What's funny?" I asked glancing in the rearview mirror to make sure no one was waiting for us to move from the stop sign.

"Inside joke, if you know David. He's a wererat. The first magical creatures we ever met, although he's known Geri for years."

"So, where's Mandalek's from here?" I could have punched it into the GPS, but what's the fun of having a native guide if you don't make use of him?

"Oh, sorry. Turn right and then take a left at the second stop light."

I followed his directions and we drove in silence for a couple of minutes until we turned at the light.

"Just stay on this road for a bit," he said, looking out into the night.

"Okay. So can I ask you a couple of questions?"

He turned to look at me. "Sure, what would 'ya like to know? Of course, I get to ask you a few when you're done."

I glanced over at him and he had that mischievous glint in his eyes again. "How did you get into magic?"

He thought for a moment. "According to my mother, I've always been more than a little psychic. It runs in my family. My granny was always scaring my mother, aunts and uncles with her knowledge of what they were doing. So when I started showing a bit of talent early on, mom didn't do anything to try and stifle it. Then a few years ago, I ran into Geri at the local sci-fi con and she saw my potential. We became friends, and she started teaching me how to go beyond just the basic psychic stuff."

I nodded. "There're a lot of folks out there who get their start that way. At least your family had experience with it, thanks to your granny."

He chuckled softly. It was a very pleasant sound. "Yeah. They did. Okay, my turn. What are you?"

"I'm an almost two thousand years old druid," I replied as we stopped at another traffic light. I turned and looked at his face as he studied me.

His eyes were wide. "Wow, I figured you were about my age, around twenty five."

"Well I was in my early twenties when I stopped aging. Back then, we didn't keep track of age as closely as we do now."

"Hey, at least you didn't get stuck in the body of an old man, right? Better to be stuck at a time when you are all hot and sexy."

My heart raced a bit again. So Alex thought I was hot and sexy, he said as much to his friends back at the bookstore. I decided to let the comment slide past for now. I really didn't need to get entangled with this young mage, no matter how much my libido wanted to.

"Oh, turn here." He gestured to the right just before we drove through an intersection.

The tires squealed a bit as I hit the breaks in an effort to make the turn. The truck slid, but didn't flip as I spun the wheel. Alex slid slightly toward me before his seat belt stopped him. Damn.

"Sorry about that," he said after I had the truck going down the new street. "I forgot that you didn't know where we were going. We're almost there."

"That's okay, I have good reflexes. And the truck, although big, is still fairly maneuverable." I glanced his way to see him settle back into his place.

"Now for my next question. Is Tal your real name?"

I nodded in the dark. "Yes, it's the name that my father gave me at my naming ritual many years ago. I have gone by other names over the years, but Tal is my name. At the time I was born, most people only had one name and when you traveled outside of your village, you used the village as a surname. So I was known as Tal O'Duirwood."

"Cool. I like Tal. It's kinda exotic, but then in Yellow Sky, Texas almost every name other than Bubba or Billy Bob is exotic. See the purple sign ahead?" He gestured to the right.

A large purple sign towered over the other signs around it. It was for Vern's Beefy Burger. "Okay."

"Right past that is the blue sign."

A run down, droopy sign was missing the neon in half of it. It looked like Ma_da__k's. The pole leaned out over the street, threatening to crash into it at any moment. The parking lot was three quarters full with vehicles of various makes and models. I slowed and turned into the crater-ridden parking lot, then wove the truck through the small maze of miss-aligned cars into a parking place near the front of the building. I wanted us as close to the doors as possible, in case we needed to make a quick exit.

After turning off the engine, I turned to Alex before opening the door. "One more thing I need to know before we walk through those doors. Have you reached the point where your magic is reflex yet?"

"What do you mean?"

"Have you been in any situations where you had no time to think about using your magic and you had it there at your fingertips?" I looked into those green eyes, locked onto them so I could tell if he was telling the truth.

"You mean like when Geri was getting mauled by the coyote and I didn't even think about it and just let a leven bolt fly at him?"

"Exactly. If things get sticky will your magic flow or freeze?"

He took a deep breath. "I haven't had many close calls, but it's been awhile since I froze. Normally it's like a knee jerk, something happens, I respond without thinking it through and the right thing seems to happen for me."

I nodded and reached for the door handle. "Good." I tore my gaze away from those eyes and got out of the Pathfinder.

I'm not one for frequenting bars. In fact, the last bar I went into was a fair number of years ago. Even my enforcer work for the Coalition doesn't take me into bars on a regular basis. I normally just find somebody's house, pop in and assassinate them and head back to my quiet mountain hideaway. My views of the modern bar come mostly from the little bit of television news I catch. There you get such a varied idea of what things are supposed to be like that you never quite know what it is going to be until you walk in and see it firsthand. That said, I was still surprised as Alex led me into Mandalek's. Just inside the door, Alex stopped at a counter where a short squat balding man with large jowls checked ID. Alex and I showed him ours. Of course, mine was fake, standard Coalition issue for all of the immortals, giving my age at twenty four.

Just before we passed the inner doors, we walked past a bank of mirrors. For some reason, it surprised me that Alex and I looked like we belonged together. He was slightly taller and broader in the shoulders than me, but we could have passed for any normal couple of guys out on the town. True, my normal casual clothes were not as nice looking as his out-on-the-town ensemble, but we looked good together.

No TV can prepare you for the overwhelming push of humanity. The lights and music momentarily overwhelmed me and Alex seemed to sense my need to adjust. He stopped just a couple of steps into the bar. Blaring music made conversation difficult to consider. The bass on the speakers was set too high for my taste and thumped against my entire body like a hammer. The lights pulsed like over-zealous stars. As people sashayed around on the large dance floor, they seemed to appear and vanish within the swarm of humanity. The majority were men, but they were as varied as their vehicles in the parking lot. What amazed me was watching how they mingled on the dance floor. I watched a cowboy dance past with a slithering preppy in front of him thrusting skinny hips forward and raising narrow arms in an almost boneless sway over his head. A boy with a blue Mohawk danced in the arms of a man twice his age wearing an expensively-cut suit. I quickly realized it'd be difficult to distinguish predator from prey.

Alex touched my arm, bringing me back to the reality of him at my side. He pointed at a table just off the dance floor, but in a corner where we could watch the door. He gestured that I should go and he'd go get a drink at the bar before joining me. I nodded as he headed toward the bar. I watched as he moved effortlessly through the crowd. I noticed how he carefully avoided anyone touching him on the way through. For a psychic of any kind, a crowd like this would be difficult to deal with. Apparently, he'd done this many times before.

Blood Moon Yellow Sky

Using the strobe lights for cover, I used my draconic speed to get to the table before anyone else claimed it. I felt somewhat more at ease with my back to the wall where I could see people approaching. This also got me out of the direct line of the speakers and the sound dropped a bit. Before I got comfortable, an elegant blond young man in a t-shirt, purposely torn to expose his expansive, smooth, gym-toned chest, slid up to the table.

"So sexy, haven't seen you around before," he said. "Care to dance?" There was a hint of alcohol on his breath as he leaned close enough for me to hear him over the music.

I caught his brown gaze with mine. "You need to go home, alone." I forced my will into my voice, pushing the man away with it. "You really want to stop using steroids, they make your dick smaller. Stay away from the bars for at least a month."

The man's eyes glazed over a bit, then he stood up and headed for the door.

Alex appeared at the table almost out of nowhere with a glass in each hand. I flinched slightly.

"Didn't mean to scare 'ya. I just find it easier to move through crowds like this with an I'm- not-here shield. Sorry forgot to warn you about Flex. He hits any guy who's new and under twenty five that comes through the door." He set the glasses on the table and leaned close to me so that I could hear him.

"Not a problem. An I'm-not-here shield? What is that?"

"Basically it makes people not notice that you're there. It causes their conscious brains not register you, but their subconscious brain is aware so they don't bump into you. Really cool. It's one of the new ideas we came up with when Geri had us think of new and unusual things to do with shields." He pushed one of the glasses toward me. "I don't know what your drinking preferences are, so I got you water. I figured that was safe."

I smiled and lifted the glass to my lips taking a light sip. It was cold water, heavy with chemicals, not nearly as nice as what I was used to, but it would do. I nodded slightly. "Good choice. I prefer water."

He looked very pleased with himself. "Cool. So do we just settle in here for a while and see what happens?"

"Have you seen anybody you recognize? Maybe that wererat you mentioned?" I knew that the rat was not there. Even though the lights made aura reading impossible, wererats have a distinct odor about them even when they're in human form.

"So far, no one who I recognize. Give it time, the night's young yet." He lifted his glass to his lips. I could smell soda of some kind, but no alcohol. Good, he was planning to keep his wits about him.

I caught those green eyes as the lights flashed around us. "Then we wait."

We settled into an easy quiet, as quiet as anything can be in the middle of a loud disco-tech with men dancing and talking all around us. I watched the door for any sign of anyone who might be non-human. I knew from the files, Yellow Sky had a decently large non-human population. I figured it was only a matter of time before one or more arrived on the scene.

"So do you dance?" Alex asked leaning close to me again.

"What?" The question took me by surprise. We were supposed to be here to locate a contact into Estaben's group. Why was Alex worried about me being able to dance? It had been many years since I had danced, and the modern dancing I'd observed in the club left me questioning the thought behind it.

"Do you dance?" he repeated.

"Not in a very long time," I responded, my mind drifting back to the last time. It had been about the turn of the twentieth century. I went to an early meeting of the Coalition, and one of my friends talked me into going into one of the speakeasies of the time.

"Well, we should try while we're waiting for someone to show up. It will make us look less suspicious, don't 'ya think?" He smiled with a wicked twinkle in those damned green eyes. Then he sat bolt upright and focused his gaze at the door.

A small man entered the bar. He stood barely five feet tall. His clothes had a permanently-tosseled look and his stringy blond hair looked as if he hadn't washed it in over a week. There was a long scar down one cheek crossing over the high bridge of his pointed nose and ending under his right eye. Both eyes appeared bloodshot. I knew the look of a wererat. Even through the heavily-perfumed bodies between us, I caught the scent. He was so long gone. He had so little control over what he was that his animal side was almost in complete control. If he still lived as a human at all, he'd soon leave it for a life on the streets looking for scraps and begging out an existence.

"Be right back," Alex said, getting up from the table. "David just came in."

I nodded and watched as Alex slipped through the crowd heading off the rat who was heading for the bar. I found myself staring at the spot where his nicely-rounded butt vanished into the crowd. I mentally shook myself to remember I was work.

He returned a couple of moments later with the small man in tow. The man carried two drinks he sat on the table before he turned toward me. Alex began to introduce us as I reached for his hand in a polite gesture that if we weren't in public I would have forgone. The man's nose twitched and then his eyes got big. He snatched his hand back, clutching it in the other hand. His eyes flashed back and forth through the crowd and then came back to rest on me. I watched as all vestiges of humanity vanished from his gaze. I saw the animal take over, and watched as he shrank in size faster than I would've thought possible. "Alex no! Not you too," he whispered as his human mouth vanished, replaced by row of long sharp teeth.

"Alex quick!" I drew on my magic to stop him, but I was too slow.

A magical tingle rose as Alex also drew and miss his target when the large blond rat scurried across the dance floor heading for the door. Luckily with all the lights, music and general confusion, no one seemed to notice the exchange.

"Should we go after him?" Alex asked.

I sighed and shook my head. "No point now, he could be anywhere in a block radius and running fast." I gestured for him to sit back down. "One of the few things that can tell I'm not a normal human is a werecreature that is about to go into full animal mode. The longer a person is a wer the easier it is for them to lose themselves in their wereside. For all we know, I just scared him so badly he'll never be able to regain his human form. He probably thinks I'm a vampire, or worse."

Alex slid his chair closer to me so that we wouldn't have to strain to talk. "Do you mean that as Geri goes on she'll become more like the animal and less like the person?" There was no mistaking the worry in his voice.

I shook my head again. "Not necessarily. There are a lot of factors to take into consideration. For one, she's a competent mage. That means she's trained her mind and is in control of her body and the magical forces around it. That alone will help her fend off the worst of the animalistic urges that come upon her. Also she's a werecoyote, which is a higher animal than a wererat. A lot more thought goes into being a coyote than being a rat. Some of the higher predatory wers I've met are hundreds of years old and have complete control of themselves. With some of the species, wererats in particular, although possums and weasels are close, the progression to the animal state is almost certain and takes only a few months. I would figure that your friend was bitten about seven months ago based on his appearance."

"Nine, but then Geri tried to help him out the first couple of months. She's known him for years. Helped him get his first real job, but he quit it a couple of weeks back. We would've been out looking for him, but we've been trying to get ready for whatever the Coalition asked us to do to get accepted." He failed to hide his concern.

"I know a couple of spells that might help us track him down if he regains his human form. What bothers me is that he said 'not you too.' Have there been people in your circles who've been seen in the presence of vampires?" If the vampires were focusing on magical people, then this could be much worse than we expected.

Now it was his turn to shake his head. "Not that I'm aware of, but then if it's been in the last couple of weeks, we've been out of the loop. I'd like it if we could do something to try and find David. He needs the option for closure." His voice was heavy.

"Has Geri discussed with him the option of just putting him out of his misery? You realize that while he's in rat form, he can pass on the virus to anyone he happens to bite. And when he becomes a rat permanently that still applies." That was one of the biggest reasons there were more wererats than any of the other lycanthrope. Sometimes I wish lycanthropes had never arose and we'd just had shifters. Shifters couldn't transfer the virus to others. They were born that way and that was it. No one really knows where the lycanthrope virus comes from, but it was the bane of most shifter communities, and they shunned those infected.

He dropped his gaze to the tabletop and sighed. "Geri talked to him about suicide and how in his case it'd be acceptable. He's not the strongest guy at the best of times. He knew he couldn't do it. I'm not sure Geri could do it either. She's a soft heart and fairly attached to the little guy. Stan volunteered to do the deed, if we get our Coalition membership and can do it legally. Char and Burn suggested arsenic. Burn thought that it was real funny, arsenic for the wererat."

I put my hand on his shoulder. I wanted to draw my hand back, but I also wanted to draw the man into my arms. "If we can find him, after we get the information he has, I can do it with Coalition jurisdiction."

He looked up with a little water in those green eyes. "Thanks. That'd be good of you." He sighed again and I felt a little of the tension in him fade.

The lights went completely out on the dance floor for a second and a new song started up. Alex sprang up and grabbed my hand from his shoulder. "Enough. I love this song, let's dance." He headed toward the dance floor trying to pull me along.

"But I have no idea…" I started to say. An unaccustomed awkward feeling filled me. I was suddenly terrified I'd make a complete fool of myself.

"Don't worry about it," he interrupted "You can either follow my lead, or just let the music take you. It can be almost magical."

And then, we were on the dance floor. The sea of people closed in around us as Alex began to move with the music. All the time he refused to release my hand. We pressed into the heart of the dancers. Most of them moved in time to the music. Here and there I could see someone who obviously had their own rhythm going on in their head. The music seemed to take control as we moved closer toward the center of the dance floor.

Suddenly Alex stopped and I bumped into him as he turned to face me. He released my hand then and his dancing became more frantic. There was a bright smile on his face as his lips moved in time with the words of the song. His body writhed with the pulse of the music. I tried to get into it myself. The music moved across me like I was wading into the surf. I mirrored Alex's movements so I didn't just stand there in the midst of the dancers like the lone flower that somehow is not blown by the wind. Alex reached out for my hands and began to move them around between us. I relaxed and let him take control of my movements, merging with the music as the song changed.

A primal beat surged out of the new song. Alex laughed, then released my hands and moved in closer to me. Heat rose from him and he began to move against my body. I did my best to flow with him, so we looked like two lovers out for an evening of dancing. I felt a pull from him as his mind reached out for mine. It tried to illicit a response from my body. And before I could stop it, I felt a sensation I hadn't felt in a very long time. This human was calling forth energies I'd buried long ago. Hot primal need surged inside me.

I was about to head back to our table when he caught my hands again and pulled me tightly against him. He pressed his mouth against mine. With the intimate contact, lust and need poured off him. I couldn't help myself as long dormant feelings within me found an outlet. I wrapped my arms around him and returned his kiss with vigor. Urgency flooded through both of us. I tried not to think about what would've happened if we hadn't been in the middle of a dance floor surrounded by hundreds of people. He pulled back slightly to look me in the face. His green eyes sparkled in passion.

"Damn, you're hot," he whispered in my ear before sinking his teeth into it. Alex's mind sought to merge with mine. His needs and responses were clear to me. For a moment it was like we were on the verge of becoming one being.

Before I could respond, we both felt a vampire enter the club. Somehow we managed to work our way to the edge of the crowd. I stepped out of the sunken dance floor and back onto the main floor. I could see over the heads of most of the dancers. Standing in the doorway was a young vampire in classic Goth dress. Had he not been undead, he would have looked like it anyway.

Alex stepped up to my side and took my hand. "Do you think he knows we're here?"

I shook my head. I didn't want to remove my hand from his. "No, he's very new as a vampire. And he's hungry. At this point, the entire room looks alike to him. Everyone is just food. He'll most likely kill the first person he can get to leave the bar, probably in the parking lot. He may return for another, or he may hunt elsewhere for his next meal. I need to know his lineage and then I can tell if he is one of Estaben's children."

"How do we do that?"

"I need to taste his blood. Just a drop will do and I'll be able to recite all the vampires in his family tree. Blood is one of the most powerful substances in the magical world if you know how to use it." I pondered the best way to do that. I knew most of the vampire lines, and if as we both suspected he was from Estaben's line, I'd be even more familiar with the blood involved. It would be an easy spell for me to weave.

"Leave that to me." Alex draw power from the music in the air around us into his hands. He forced the energy into his right hand, flexed his fingers, and to my mage sight, a single silver dagger flew out across the room toward the fledgling vampire. As it nicked his arm, he slapped at it like a human might slap at a bug bite. But he was too late and the silver energy headed back to Alex. The luminescent dagger hovered in front of me and I saw two small red almost-gelatinous drops on its tip.

With my own energies, I tipped it up so that the red drops rolled off onto my tongue. As the first drop hit the damp skin, I drew on my druid magics to view the blood's history and the images began. His death was only a couple of nights ago at the hands of a man he thought wanted his body. He'd been drained and left alone. I focused on the vampire who sired him. I didn't know him, but I could see that his grandsire was Estaben's first companion. Beyond that I saw Estaben and the Incan priest who turned him those many years ago, followed by a rapid succession of feather-clad priests and priestesses.

Less than two heartbeats passed. I looked at Alex and nodded. "He doesn't know much, but there are some spells we can do to get more information than he knows he has. That and he needs some guidance right now."

The silver dagger settled on Alex's hand and slowly merged with his aura to vanish. "How do we bring him in?"

"How good are your telepathic command skills?"

"Best of the class." He smiled and something inside me fluttered. It felt like something that had been asleep in me for two thousand years, lost to me when my magical training had begun, was trying to awaken. Was this the feeling of finding a soul mate? I need to get back to my library and do some research, but had a job to do first.

"Good, follow my lead, and when we get him outside, take control of him so we can get him back to Geri's." I took his hand in mine and led him toward the vampire. This time, it felt like his hand belonged in mine. It was warm and comforting.

We avoided the dance floor and walked up to him just as he reached the bar. I stepped into his path, forcing him to turn toward us. "Excuse me, but we saw you come through the door and realized you were just what we were looking for tonight."

"We what?" His dark bushy eyebrows rose sharply, but this close, I sensed his hunger in ways his blood couldn't convey.

"Please let me start again. My name is Tom and this is Biff." I gestured to Alex. "We came out tonight to get into the pants of a nice hot guy. I believe you're just what we're looking for."

He glanced us over. He was obviously trying to decide if he could take both of us, but the thought of an easy double feast was too much for his hunger.

"A three-way huh? I'm Robert. I'm your man. So when do you want to get started." He was trying not to sound eager, but the energy of his hunger bubbled over in him, giving me a sudden urge to snap his neck and be done with him.

Alex stepped between us and took our arms in his. The movement interrupted my urge to do Robert harm. "How about right now, big boy." He smiled. The glint in his eyes was more lecherous than any look he'd used on me up to that point. He ran his hands along Robert's large smooth biceps. The vampire almost drooled on him. Alex led us through the club, out into the parking lot, and toward the Pathfinder. He gathered subtle power as we walked along and I watched out of the corner of my eye as he began to weave it around Robert with subtle grace and artistry.

"We're over here," he said, guiding us out into the darkest part of the lot. He brought us to a stop under a bright streetlight. Luckily there were no other patrons. He let go of my arm and turned to face Robert.

"I'd like a little taste of what is to come," he whispered as he wrapped his arms around Robert's neck and pulled his face downward.

Robert struggled to control his hunger. His hands tightened into fist and his body tensed. The energy coming off his felt like a tiger about to spring on a monkey.

Alex's power lashed out as their lips touched. It was bright and powerful, nearly blinding even without me using my mage sight. Even having heard Alex and Geri's report he was top of his class, I was unprepared for a practical demonstration of his strength. I was impressed.

Robert's eyes flew open for a moment. He tried to push Alex away, but he was new to his vampire strength and hungry too. Alex held them in place as he seized control of the vampire's mind. The mental tussle was brief. Robert's eyes glazed over and his body went slack.

Alex stepped away slowly, his eyes never leaving his prey. "That was harder than I thought. I've never had to touch someone before to take over, but then I've never tried to take over a vampire. He's still fighting. We'd better get him in the truck and get back to Geri's before he slips my hold." His voice was tight and controlled. I knew he didn't want to divert too much of his attention from holding Robert.

"You did great." I said. I wanted to take him in my arms to show him how pleased I was at his effort, but I knew that'd disrupt his concentration. "I'll bring the car around, you just keep him here." I used my speed, moving as fast as I could to limit the time I'd be away from them. Alex was vulnerable while he kept Robert under his control. I was at the Pathfinder in seconds.

They stood in the same pool of light as I swung the car toward them. Alex had his arms wrapped around Robert's neck, making it look like they stood there in the throes of passion. Alex opened the front passenger door then stepped aside to let Robert get in. He slid into the back seat, trying not to take his eyes off Robert for more than a split second. Sweat accumulated on his body from the exertion. I pulled back out into the street without a word and headed back to Geri's house.

Chapter Six

THE DRIVE back to Geri's seemed to take longer than the drive out to the bar had. Luckily, I recalled the route, so I didn't have to break Alex's concentration to find my way, but I had to ask for her phone number to call and warn her of our impending arrival with unexpected company. I glanced frequently in the mirror and Alex's face was still, and sweat covered his brow.

As I turned onto Geri's road, I saw several cars waiting for us. They left a place at the end of the walk so I could pull the truck up close to the door. Before I could get out and around to the back passenger door, Geri's front door flew open and people poured out into the night. As I opened the door for Alex, I quickly scanned the people surrounding us and realized it was just the gang. Although their faces showed eagerness to ask all sorts of questions, they remained quiet as they helped Alex get Robert out of the car and into the house. It was like they'd all done this many times before. They way they worked so effortlessly was impressive.

They silently led us through the living room, although their need to question hung heavily in the air. With furtive glances, we descended a narrow basement staircase. In the harsh basement light, a heavy, old, but still in good shape, barber's chair waited, bolted to the floor. Geri adjusted one of the many leather straps adorning it. Along with the leather, handcuffs and a good length of chain hung from spots around the chair. The chain was also linked to a large eye bolt sunk into the floor.

I glanced at Geri; she had this in place before tonight. Even with the help of her students, she couldn't have had time to install all that was here. It was very impressive. It wouldn't have held a mature vampire at full strength, but would do very nicely with this fledgling. This made me even more sure they'd had other people they'd questioned before. They operated more like a covert Coalition team than a group just applying for membership.

Stan approached and caught the clothes Robert removed at Alex's silent command. Once down to his underwear, Alex maneuvered Robert into the chair while the gang swarmed around it. Charles and Bernadette closed the leather wrist restrains after attaching the handcuffs. Stan wrapped the heaviest chain across his chest and linked it back to the eyebolt in the floor and Larry and Terry worked on securing his feet. Janie fastened the leather collar and smaller chain around his neck. If I didn't know the situation, the silence they worked in would have been eerie. It showed me how well this group worked together. I was going to have to say a lot of good things about this in my report to J.P..

Once they were done, Geri walked over, still in complete silence, and checked all the bindings. When she was satisfied that they were tight, she called on the magic that hummed in the room. It sent a chill thought me as a wall of protective magical force went up around the chair, preventing escape. It was then, I noticed the magic circle carved into the floor.

"Good job you two. Alex, let him go," Geri said.

Relief flooded Alex's features right before he collapsed. I caught him before he fell across the edge of the circle. One of the others, I'm not sure which one, showed up at my side with a folding canvas chair and I eased him into it. He was very pale and unconscious from the strain of holding Robert in thrall for so long. At my side, Geri took his left hand. When her power flood through him for a second, it brushed against me, leaving warm tingles in its wake.

"He'll be fine, just needs a bit of sleep and some food," she said. "Tal it'll be a few minutes before your prize here wakes up. If you'd please carry Alex up to the spare bedroom and make him comfortable there until we're done, I'd appreciate it. You're the only one other than myself who could carry him up the stairs without help. Hill will show you the way." She turned to her student. "Hill, the blue room, if you would. Alex is always more comfortable there."

"Sure Geri, just don't do anything cool without me," Janie said cheerfully. So Janie's secret magical name was Hill, I was going to have to pay attention to keep everyone straight. Burn/Bernadette was easy. Using the diminutive of Hillary took a little more thought.

I lifted Alex and started up the stairs with him. His body was limp in my arms, but the strong muscles in his back and legs felt nice against me. His head rested on my shoulder. It was all I could do to keep from taking a good deep breath of his red hair and the herbal shampoo he used a couple of hours before. That, along with the light cologne, combined for an intoxicating scent. The momentary fear I felt as I watched him collapse was pushed aside by the feeling of right about holding his unconscious form in my arms. I reminded myself I was not here for emotional entanglements. Once the assignment was over, I'd be leaving and the handsome young man in my arms would stay in Yellow Sky with his coven. I couldn't remember the last time I held another man in my arms like this. I enjoyed it while it lasted.

Janie, Hill as they called her, led us through the kitchen and down a short hall. I was beginning to think that this house was a lot bigger than it appeared from the outside, but hadn't encountered any magics indicating anything of the sort. She led me into a small bedroom and flicked on the light. Geri named this room correctly; everything existed in varying shades of blue. The headboard and bed clothes were a deep Navy. The walls were just a little darker than sky blue and the plush carpet a deep royal blue. Even the simple chair next to the bed had a deep blue leather seat. I wondered again about her taste in decorating, but understood the magics of energy and how color worked with that. Blue would be soothing and healing to anyone in the room.

Janie dashed ahead of me and folded down the bed so I could lay Alex onto the sheets. Before pulling the covers over him, I paused for a moment and pulled off his cowboy boots. I left the white socks on, but could tell his large feet were perfectly formed underneath them.

Janie stood silently waiting for me at the door as I pulled the blue sheet and comforter up to Alex's chin. I wiped the last of the sweat off his brow and then forced myself to straighten beside the bed before I gave into the overwhelming urge to stroke his hair and kiss his forehead. He looked very peaceful and extremely attractive lying there.

Janie frowned at me slightly as I straightened and looked in her direction. "What's your take on all of this?"

"All of this?" I responded softly heading out of the room, moving quietly to avoid waking Alex.

"Yeah. Us applying to the Coalition of Magical Creatures. You being sent here to watch us kill the vampire. Alex." She turned and strolled briskly down the hall.

I fell into step behind her as we entered the kitchen. "If you all have the skill Alex has, then you should be part of the Coalition. I'm an assassin and have killed a number of vampires and other magical creatures over the years. I've even had to take out the odd magician or witch once in a while, when one oversteps their bounds. You might view me as the magic police." It was an encapsulated version of what I really was, but I didn't want to take the time to explain it to her. If we were all successful we could tackle things like that.

"So, you think we can do this?" She turned, her delicate face eager for my approval.

"If you can keep things at the level Alex did tonight, then you have a *chance* of beating Estaben de'Oro. If you're not up to that level, then you can forget any chance of getting out alive. He's not the fledgling that we have downstairs. He has a coven of vampires under his control. You're going to need skill, knowledge and a lot of luck to walk away with your lives intact. But from what I've seen so far, you have a good chance." I didn't add that whether the Coalition liked it or not, I was going to do everything in my power to keep Alex alive. I realized that as I pulled the sheets up over him. If nothing else, Alex would live. Should anything happen to him, I'd kill every vampire in Yellow Sky with my bare hands. It would do wonders for my reputation and I doubted many vampires would even show their faces in Texas when I was done. I wasn't sure it was a good thing that Alex stirred such strong emotions within me. In many ways, it was like I was waking up from a long sleep.

We started down the stairs.

A scream ripped the air.

As our walk turned to a dash, I was careful to not charge over the young woman on the narrow stairs.

The scene in the basement was very similar to the one we had left except that Robert was now awake. He struggled against the bonds holding him to the chair and screamed for his release. Geri stood at the edge of the magic circle nearest his head.

She looked up at us as we stepped off the stairs. "Well, he's awake." She turned to Char, who sat at a laptop computer next to a half-full wine rack. "What can you tell me about him?"

Charles changed screens and turned toward her. "Well it looks like Robert Cooper has led a squeaky-clean life up until now. I can't find any police records and his driving record is clean. Not even a parking ticket. He's into internet porn, but then there's no law against that. He never visits the kiddie sites. He frequented adult chat rooms up until about a week ago, but he hasn't been back since he talked to someone called Fang. Their conversation was fairly standard for a quick trick. Based on those records, they met at a little hotel over on Nor'easter Dr. He hasn't even checked his email since he logged off that night. I would say Fang may have fanged him and that would be that."

"Sounds feasible." Geri responded. "Stan?"

"Based on the Coalition files, I'd say that assessment is fairly accurate. The magic related to the change is only about a week old, actually at this point, I'd say six days twenty-one hours. He probably died his first death about three in the morning last Saturday." He looked at me. Obviously, the Coalition thought it a good idea to give Geri and her brood a few records and some of the more complicated spells used to find out basic information on vampires. That also told me that if they failed their test, the Coalition was prepared to do memory wipes on all them.

I nodded and then turned to study Robert. He still struggled but he'd stopped screaming. His face contorted in a rage combined with a deep hunger that made him extremely dangerous to most of the people in the room. His smooth skin still held the tan he must've worked very hard on in life. His fangs were small as they flashed when he snarled. If he died last Saturday then he would've fed at least twice since then, maybe more. He hadn't managed to tear any of the leather straps so his strength hadn't manifested its fullest yet. Most fledglings don't gain their full strength until they survive the first month or so. Personally, I think it's almost a Darwinian thing. Those who cannot survive their first month shouldn't survive at all. He sniffed at the air inside of the circle, trying to get a scent of the people around him.

"How many have you killed?" I asked, keeping my voice low and steady.

He turned toward me. I could see the curiosity in his face about me, but his hunger controlled him.

I gestured for Geri and stepped away from the circle. She joined me by the stairs. "We won't be able to get any information out of him until his hunger is lessoned and he regains control. You or I are the only ones who can risk going in. He'll also find that our blood is stronger than that of the humans he's been feeding on. It will take less to fill him. But, if you're the one he feeds from, he may develop a taste for wereblood. That may become a problem for you brethren of the fur."

She nodded in agreement. "I'm new enough I don't need that hanging over me. Will you be okay?

"I've fed vampires before. The ones who enjoy my blood quickly discover it's one of a kind and not something they get unless I say they get it." More than a few times, I'd used it as a bargaining chip when I needed information out of vampires. The one time an old master vampire had tried to capture me so he could have a long-time supply of my vintage, I'd shown him the error of his ways in a way neither he nor his brood survived.

"Understandable." She stepped toward the circle and drew a long-bladed Kris dagger with a black handle. Power radiated off the narrow, curved blade. It was easy to see she'd used this knife for a long time and often. "If you're ready, I can cut you into the circle."

I took off my light gray wool jacket and rolled back the sleeves of my black silk shirt, then handed the jacket to Janie who reappeared at my side as I followed Geri back to the circle. She placed the point of the blade against the floor and slid it across the line, then slowly straightened, holding the blade in front of her. A seam of light flared where the blade passed through the barrier. When she reached a comfortable height, she began to cut horizontally to the circle on the floor until she had about a two-foot line and then she descended back to the floor. The others took up positions around the circle as she completed her doorway of light into the protected area of the room. The way they did it without speaking, told me this was also something they'd done before. I wondered again what they'd been doing here.

She stood up, bowed formally and gestured with her free hand to the doorway. "Pass freely into the circle. I'll release you when you're ready."

"Thank you." I said just as formally before taking a deep breath and passing into the circle that held Robert.

A slight jolt passed over me, and when I cleared the doorway, she closed it behind me. Robert struggled harder against the bonds as I approached him. He bared his juvenile fangs and hissed like a movie vampire. I chuckled. I hadn't seen a vampire do that in a very long time. I moved quickly, placing my hands on the sides of his head, forcing it back against the headrest. He struggled to tear at the bindings, but his strength was, as I suspected, barely more than that of a human.

With a touch of my druid magic, I reached out to him. "*Be Still,*" I commanded both verbally and mentally. He immediately went slack in my grasp. His mind still struggled but it would never be stronger than mine. My telepathic skills may be a bit lacking, but they were enough to still the mind of a non magical, fledgling vampire. I carefully only brushed his conscious mind.

I removed my hands from his head and lowered my right wrist over his mouth. "*Drink.*" His hands sought to press my arm into his mouth and his tiny fangs tore at my wrist, trying to get at the blood that coursed through my veins. "*Easier. Puncture, don't tear.*" He seemed to understand and sank his fangs into my bared wrist, easily finding the radial artery. He relied more on the suction of his mouth than his teeth once he punctured my flesh. My blood flowed into him and his hunger ebbed.

As he fed, I started to feel hungry. I'd need to eat again within the next twenty-four hours. I wondered what was happening that food ran through me so easily now. Something was wrong. I'd have to wait until the issue with Estaben was resolved before I had the time to sort it out, but it almost felt like someone was drawing energy off of me. But that moment, with the fledgling feeding from me, I didn't need to take time to think about that.

When the hunger no longer controlled him, I pushed his head back into the chair to get him to release me. His eyes pleaded for more, but he opened his mouth so I could remove my arm without doing additional damage. As I pulled away, I willed the skin around the punctures to close. Being a shapeshifter, I maintained full control of my body, closing small cuts was easy.

"Now that your hunger had been sated," I started as I rolled my sleeve down over my hairy forearm, "how many people have you killed?"

"Who are you and these people? Where am I? What have you done to me?" He didn't struggle against the bonds, but expressed his anger in his voice.

"At the moment, we're the ones who hold your life in our hands, young vampire." I tried not to sound condescending, but sometimes people need to feel that you might kill them.

"Vampire? Why do you call me that?" Fear crept into his voice, replacing the anger he'd just shown.

"You're a fledgling vampire. Surely your sire explained this to you." I suddenly didn't like the way this was going.

"What *are* you talking about? What does my father have to do with this?" His voice was now very shaky.

"Robert, what can you tell me of the past few nights?" This was definitely not going well. The sick feeling that he'd just been dumped onto the streets of Yellow Sky without any real knowledge of what had happened to him sank into me. For the past few nights, he'd been propelled by the hunger without any real thought of what was going on. The idea turned my stomach.

"I wake up after dark hungry. Nothing in the fridge looks good. So I go to the bar and have a couple of drinks, pick up a guy and we leave. I don't remember much from there. Then I wake up again the next evening. At one point I seem to have lost a couple of days. It's like after I gave that really hunky guy a blow job, I woke up a couple of days later. What does that have to do with vampires?"

"He's telling the truth," Bernadette said, from outside of the circle.

"How do you know?" I asked, ignoring Robert for a moment.

"See this rune here?" She pointed to the rune of truth carved into the floor between the rings of the circle. "It's not flared red once while you've been talking to him. As far as he's concerned, he's telling the truth."

I nodded with understanding. They'd cast a truth detection spell on the circle. Either Geri or one of her students came up with very good magical ideas. I'd have to be careful when they started asking me questions. "So either he's not remembering what happened to him, or someone's interfering with his memories. I can resolve that." I reached out with my will again as I laid my right hand against his forehead. The spell for memory was a simple one that I learned in my early druid training. I risked meddling with something his sire might sense, but it might help us get information we'd need. His eyes flew wide as my skin touched his again. "*Remember all.*" It was a very mean thing to do, but I didn't want to take the time to help him reclaim the memories the normal way. And there are times when I can be a real asshole. J.P. and some of the other older members of the Coalition said it came from being as old as I was. Most of the other immortals I'd run into over the years had been assholes too. I just try not to do it too often.

He moaned as all the memories flooded back to him. He saw his own death and those he caused. He sank into the chair. His body racked by sobs. I watched as he shook within the bonds, tears flooding down his cheeks, smearing his makeup, and I realized he was the real victim in all of this. I saw two choices, well three really, but I didn't need a fledgling to show the correct ways to be a vampire. The last time I took pity on a fledgling and helped them through their first few years I hadn't gone well. I gestured for Geri.

"If you would please reopen your circle my lady?" I made the formal request.

"But of course my lord," she said with a slight smile as she sliced the door into existence again.

"Charles, can you find any personnel files or psyche reports please?" I asked the twin waiting patiently at his terminal watching the proceedings with great interest. Having him do it would be faster than contacting Beth to see what she could find. If Charles couldn't find anything then I'd call her.

"Geri?" he asked quietly, careful not to let his obvious eagerness to please me override his natural need to get her approval.

"Good idea," she said, as she again completed her door in the magic circle.

Once I cleared it, and the opening closed again, I motioned Geri to follow me upstairs leaving the gang to guard Robert. I paused just off the stairs. "I need your opinion here. I'm supposed to just be an observer in all of this, so this is something you and yours should decide, but I can decide for you if you want."

She nodded and motioned me to the kitchen table. She went first to the cupboard and got a couple of cups out, and poured some tea from the glass pot that simmered on the stove. The pot seemed to always be there, always ready to provide water for tea. She wasn't the first witch I'd met that crafted magic to make her life easier.

She sat the fragrant mug down in front of me before speaking. "So, as you see them, what are our options?"

I sipped the warm, tart tea. There was a bit of cinnamon in it, with some clove and allspice and a few things that I felt like I should know, but couldn't easily place. "Well, he's obviously been changed without being aware of it until now. That goes against all of the socially-correct things any modern vampire stands for. His sire doesn't appear to take any responsibility for his upbringing. If we're lucky, he won't even sense what we're doing. Our first option is to try and find an elder vampire to take him under their wing and teach him. One of the other options is to let him go and let him figure it out on his own. That'd probably be more trouble than it's worth."

"Not to mention, I don't need that in my town, too many bodies laying around for my taste," Geri added grimly. "That'd draw way too much attention from the local police, even with Larry and Terry's father doing what he can to keep the non-human and magical community off the official police radar."

It was good to know someone kept things on the down low with the police. I'd remember that in my report to JB. "Well, the only other option is to kill him now. I doubt we can get any good info out of him, other than a description of the man who did this to him. We'd put him out of his misery and prevent a possible menace from prowling the streets of Yellow Sky."

"He's young. Are you that ruthless?" She set the cup down and studied me through the steam. She was trying to get a feel for me.

"I can be when needed. That is why I'm one of the Coalition's assassins. I can do what I need to do. Part of it's my magical training, helps with the logical thinking; part of it's the understanding of nature, and part is just being old enough to know when to take the steps to keep things running right." I kept my response as honest as possible.

She nodded then knocked back the last of her tea. "I can respect that. It also helps me to trust you. Let's go see what Char's found and get the gang's input on all of this."

Chapter Seven

AS WE descended the stairs, the gang was still positioned around the circle enclosing Robert. His sobs had slowed to the point they no longer racked his body. With the back of the chair facing me, I couldn't tell if his tears still fell, but his breath was still heavy and catching. Although I didn't show it to anyone, I was concerned about the future of this fledgling vampire. I got a good vibe off him. I secretly hoped Geri's crew would decide against killing him. But this was their test and I'd abide by their decision.

"Geri, we've got something here," Charles called us over to the computer.

He moved to the side and I saw he had several browser windows pulled up with different information on them. The first one was Robert Cooper's employee file from the telecommunications firm where he worked. Charles found records from tests they administered when he first started the company. He scored highly on them all, but overall they meant nothing to me. "Okay, what are these tests and what do they mean?"

"This first one is an honesty test," Charles explained reaching past me to gesture at the screen. "It says that he's basically an honest person. Anyone who knows how to take these tests can get a false positive without trying too hard. This second one is a logical thinking test. It judges a person's ability to think logically, based on the company's perception of logic. Overall, companies use it to see if he'll fit into the corporate structure. Two companies can use the same test and decide that different answers are correct. As far as we're concerned, this score doesn't mean a damn thing. Now this is an IQ test he scored a 140. That's real good. On this test the average person is a 95. Burn and I both scored about 155. Your average chimp can score about 30."

"Okay, so we know that he passed an honesty test that's easy to falsify, he fits in well with his company, and he's really smart. Not as smart as you are, but smarter than a chimpanzee." I condensed his assessment, careful to keep my voice in the hushed tone Charles had used. "What else do we have?"

Charles reached around me and moved the mouse to bring one of the other windows to the front of the screen. "Here's the latest psyche test from his doctor. It seems he's being treated for clinical depression, but then so are most of the people who have normal corporate jobs. Other than that, he was pronounced sound."

"That's good. Once out of Corporate America he should regain his sanity," Geri surmised. "I've seen it before."

"But here is an interesting note." Charles scrolled down to the most recent notes made the Monday before. "It says here the doctor recommended him to Estaben. No last name as far as Estaben who, or where. Could this be our vamp?"

"That's possible. See if you can search through the doctor's other records and see if there are other notes like that," I suggested. "Anything else on Robert here?"

"That's all I have found so far. But I'll let you know." He slid back into place in front of the computer as Geri and I turned back to the vampire bound in the circle.

"Char, who was that doctor?" Larry asked coming toward us.

"Doctor Mike Hammed. Why?"

I made a mental note to have Beth get me files on Dr. Mike Hammed.

"I remember Dad saying something about a shrink that an investigation was started on the other day." Larry peered over Charles' shoulder at the computer screen. "Weasel do you remember the doctor's name?"

"Nope, but we could try and check dad's files when Char's finished," Terry replied, but didn't move from his place at the circle's boundary.

I walked to the edge of the circle. Robert composed himself while we talked about his mental state before the change. He looked more like a man than he had previously. Gone was the predator who walked into the bar and been lured out by Alex and I. Gone was the creature of hunger that raged against us. Now a man sat there and listened to us talk about his mental state with trails of blood tears down his face and bare chest.

"Robert, what do you think about all of this? Now that you know what has happened to you." I kept my voice a well-practiced neutral tone. Overall his answers would help sway Geri and the gang in their decision on his life.

"What do you think I think?" Robert asked. "I wish that bastard had thought to ask before doing this to me." He fought to keep his anger from showing, but the edge of it was there, which was perfectly normal given the circumstances.

"What would your answer have been if he asked before changing you?" Behind me, a ripple of tension flashed off Geri. She kept quiet, but from the change of energies coming off her, I could tell that this line of questioning made her nervous.

Robert paused for a moment, obviously thinking about my question. He let out a long slow sigh. "I really don't know. I never believed in vampires and witches before. I would've probably laughed in his face. My Goth thing is really just a façade to rebel a bit. Everyone needs an outlet, at least that's what my shrink tells me."

"And when he proved to you he was real and he could change you?"

Another long pause. Charles' mouse clicked as he surfed through the pages searching for more information. "I honestly don't know. But it's too late now isn't it?"

I just nodded. At least the rune in the floor hadn't flashed at any point during his answers. "Robert what kind of books do you read?"

"What does that have to do with anything?" he snapped.

I was wearing at his patience, but I had to find out what kind of mind we were dealing with. A person's mind has to have a certain set to it if he or she is going to survive as a vampire. If he didn't have an inquisitive mind, then it would be kinder to kill him now. "It helps us make a decision. Please answer my question." I tried to sound as patient as I could.

"I read a lot of different books," he replied. "It depends on the mood that I'm in. I read some fantasy, a little sci-fi, some mysteries, the right kind of romance, and tech guides. So what does that tell you?" Anger flared in his eyes. With all the emotional turmoil he was going through, the light meal of my blood must've been wearing off and his hunger was flaring again.

"It tells me you have an open mind and that you're adaptable. You might even be able to survive being immortal. What church do you go to?"

"I don't, I've never believed in deities other than a source of myths." His voice was slightly softer now.

"Good then you won't have anyone to be angry at about your situation. How about family and friends that will miss you?"

"I'm single, my parents died in a car crash a few years back and I'm an only child, my boyfriend left me six weeks ago and most of my co-workers could care less about me." He was back to sounding almost lost. There was also a tang of bitterness in his voice.

"I can see why your doctor recommended you to Estaben. Do you know who Estaben is?" If he did this would be too easy.

Lines of confusion crossed Robert's brow. "I know several, but none that my doctor recommended. My doctor never recommended that I see anyone other than himself."

"Did you ever find out Fang's name?"

"How do you know about Fang?" The anger crept back into his voice.

"We have our ways. Now did you get a real name on Fang, or did you just call him Fang while he fang banged you?"

"No I never found out his real name." This time, defeat clouded his voice. His chin dropped and rested on the top of his chest.

"How about a description?" It'd be harder to find him by description, but at least when we encountered the vampire, the gang would know him.

"I never even saw his face. He was already at the hotel when I arrived. He was waiting in the lobby with the hood of his sweat jacket pulled up. When we got to the room, he made me keep the lights off. He had a nice hard body. Smooth, and firm I think there was a nipple ring in the left nipple."

"That's not much to go on," Geri said from behind me. "There is a booming business in town with tattoos and piercings."

"Anything else you can think of that you felt or saw in the darkness?" I was seeing a definite lack of information here.

"No, he bit me before we got going very well. Although I do remember that as I was dying, he made a call on his cell phone. Somebody named Ssay or something. Then I remember tasting blood in my mouth, but I still felt like I was dying. I woke up three days later in my apartment starving." Recalling your first death is hard for any vampire. Red tears ran down Robert's gray-streaked face, but he stifled his sobs.

"So Fang had to get instructions from whoever he talked to on that call." I glanced at Geri who nodded in unspoken agreement that he had called his sire and or coven leader. "Robert, I have a very difficult question for you. Do you want to go on living the way you are now or would you prefer that we let you die your death for this lifetime?"

He didn't even really take time to think, he just blurted out his answer. "I'd like the chance to live this life, or afterlife as the case may be."

"Folks, let's talk upstairs if we could." I motioned toward the stairs.

Stan motioned Bernadette to come to him for a second. He whispered something to her. "I'll stay down here just in case. I think Robert's harmless right now, but one of us should stay down here. Burn can speak in my place."

Bernadette nodded as she passed me and hurried toward the kitchen.

"Good idea. We'll be right back." I said and followed Geri as the others vanished up the stairs.

The gang gathered around the table and sat waiting for me to catch up. I could tell by the looks on their faces that they never had to decide on a person's death before. Now they faced a grim decision and Robert's life swayed in the balance as did the lives of many others if they made the wrong choice and he wasn't the nice person he seemed to be. I faced this same decision every time I had to kill someone. In my time, I've killed more than a few fledglings who I felt wouldn't make good vampires.

"Gut feelings guys?" Geri asked as she seated herself at the head of the table.

"I say he's an okay sorta guy, for a dead blood sucker," Larry spoke up first.

"Yeah, we all know what it's like to have something happen and not remember it for a couple of days," Bernadette added with a chuckle.

"Burn we are talking about a major life change here, not a pot haze from some really good shit," Janie scolded playfully. I could tell her bravado was simply covering up the fact she was terrified of making the wrong decision.

"I've been trying to see his aura through the circle," Terry said from the far side of the table. "It seems mostly blue and silver. When the hunger was overriding him it was blue and red. Now it is a really dark blue, but still blue."

"You say his aura is blue?" I asked. It'd been a long time since I had met someone who talked about seeing auras. Most vampires lose a lot of their aura when they die. It gets turned inside out and only a slight bit is visible to the outside viewers.

"Right, and there is the silver in it too. Is that normal for a vampire?" He ran a hand through his long dark hair and seemed to study me more closely.

"The blue and silver are the vampire energies." I explained.

Terry pursed his lips. "That makes sense. So, if I can see someone's aura, I can tell if they are a vamp or not?"

"Of course, you just need to learn what the different parts of it mean. I'm sure Geri can tell you more, or I'll be happy to when we have more time. Your description of his aura is that of a vampire in transit. He could go either way at this point. He could go good or he could go evil. I think he's just right for a teacher to come along and work with him and get him on the right path." I'd have little trouble showing this young mage how to see the various nuances of auras and teaching him their meanings. Geri obviously gave them all a very good basis in magic. It'd reflect very well in my report to the Coalition.

"Are you volunteering to teach him the proper way to be a vampire?" Janie asked softly.

"No, I have too much to do right now. It has also been a long time since I took a fledgling vampire under my wing." Then it hit me. It had been right before Estaben went out on his own. We'd taken in a fledgling, David Cox. He'd been attacked in New York City by another fledgling. David adjusted well. But his sire hadn't and I had the unpleasant job of decapitating the idiot after less than a week when Estaben and I found him on a feeding rampage down among the poorer sections of the town. I don't even remember the poor fool's name. David's still a friend. He isn't a mage, but then I saw no mage talent in Robert. David was very well adapted and living a good life in New York still. He created a life for himself as a flamboyant young actor this time. He should be able to work Robert into his entourage, which consisted of artistically-inclined magical creatures of all sorts. "But I have an idea. If you want to let him live, why don't we send him to one of the vampires I helped raise a long time back who'd be a good teacher for him." I smiled slightly when I thought of David's face at Robert's arrival. The last time I talked to David, a few months back, he didn't have a partner and was more than a little lonely. The two would be a good match.

"Very good idea," Geri responded, from her seat at the head of the table. "Can you get a hold of this other vampire? Is he a member of the Coalition?"

"David's part of the Coalition and I keep his number in my phone. Give me a moment and I'll give him a call." I turned and walked toward the living room.

I glanced at the phone. There was a good enough signal in the house, which surprised me with all the shielding that Geri had over the place. David picked up on the second ring. He was surprised to hear from me. After a slight catching up, I told him what I was up to. He was worried about Estaben as they had been close the first few years of his change. He wanted me to try and talk to him before letting Geri and her students kill him. David always tried to see the good in people. I promised that if the opportunity presented itself, I would, but it didn't look good at this point. Then I explained about Robert Cooper. David listened and understood. He asked almost no questions before he agreed to take Robert on. I made sure David lived in the same apartment that he had the last time I was in New York. He did, and could be back there within ten minutes. I asked him to hurry and turned back to the kitchen.

Alex leaned heavily on the doorframe watching me. "So we're sending him to a friend of yours? Is this a close friend? And how are you proposing that we get him there?" A tinge of jealousy colored his tone, but I wrote it off as exhaustion. His eyes looked almost haunted. I wondered where he found the strength to stand there.

"David was one of the fledgling vampires I helped to survive years ago. We still keep in touch, as you will find that you do with the apprentices of yours in future years. And I was going to see if Geri knew and had taught all of you how to open a portal." I replied moving to his side. "Now I think you probably need to lie back down before you fall down."

He shook his head, but reached for my shoulder for support. "Too much magic going on. It's keeping me awake. Let's get this done and then someone can take me home so I can sleep in my own bed under my own shields."

I steadied him and sighed. "Alright, this won't take long. David will be home in a few minutes. I can open the portal and send Robert to him. Then, we can call it a night."

We walked down the hall with me supporting most of his weight. His feet seemed too heavy for him to lift. He was going to go on. I could see it in the determined set of his stubble covered, freckled chin.

I quickly explained to Geri what we needed to do. She'd worked a couple of gate spells in her day, but so far hadn't bothered to teach any to her students. They all seemed eager to learn and were happy they didn't have to kill an innocent vampire. The basic idea of the gate is fairly simple, open a hole in space between two points on the same or different planes of existence and then either go through yourself, or send someone else through. There are really no spells as such. We just called it a spell so that most people would believe it's more complicated than it really was. The really hard part's getting enough energy together to open and maintain the gate. If I was going through the gate with Robert, it would've been much easier. But opening a gate for a non-mage to go through was hard. I'd need to draw off of Geri and most of her students to hold it long enough for Robert to pass.

Once downstairs, we explained it to Stan and Robert. Robert liked the idea of getting the opportunity to learn about his new life and said that he always wanted to live in New York, but never had the chance to go there. I didn't bother to mention that it would also move him far enough away that his sire wouldn't sense him. To all appearances, he will have died. It wasn't at all uncommon for a fledgling vampire to die during the first few weeks of life, particularly one that was left on his own. Starvation was often the biggest problem.

First we brought down the circle that enclosed Robert. Then Stan, Bernadette, and Janie undid his bindings and handed him his clothes, while the others sat down on either the floor or stairs and began to relax, preparing to draw the power they needed. I sat Alex on the stairs and told him to stay out of this, just sit back and watch.

By the time we were ready, David had time to get home. I motioned Robert to stand next to me as I reached out and began to draw the power needed. I shaped the power from myself first, then reached for the energy coming off of Geri. It was a deep ochre, almost the color of Yellow Sky dirt, and there was also a slight musk to her power. Next I pulled in the triple energies of Stan, Bernadette, and Janie. They wove a strong thread of rose and yellow, lust and power. Charles's power flowed easily with the gold of intellect to it while Terry and Larry came in as brown and green. Alex reached out with a light touch of deep green, but I pushed him away gently.

Once the power flowed, I wrapped it into the form of a knife and made a slicing motion with my hand as I unleashed it. A gash in space appeared before me and heard the gasp of wonder from the people behind me as they saw it form. I thought of David's apartment in New York. There was a doorway where the Empire State Building was visible, many blocks over. I focused my energies on that and forced the tear in space to find its way there. It seemed to take forever before the view I remembered came into focus, but finally, the gate locked onto the doorway and solidified. No longer a simple tear in space hovering in the basement of Geri's house, the doorway stood open, waiting for someone to walk through.

David appeared in the opening. "You look well old friend. Is this my new charge?" he asked, looking Robert over from a distance. His short haircut made him look very young and his blue eyes danced with mischief as they inspected Robert's frame.

"Yes. David Cox, meet Robert Cooper."

"Well come on over here Robert. I can see the strain of this is hard on Tal and those friends of his back there."

He was right. The others were getting ready to drop. The energy coming off them was flickering as it dropped in strength. I pulled more from the world around us, hoping to bolster their faltering force.

Robert looked at me for a second then took a step toward the gate. He looked hesitant.

"It's okay," I urged. "Just step through and then you'll be in New York with David. Go on, there's nothing to worry about."

The energy from Larry ebbed and almost failed. Terry tried to boost his brother's output.

David stretched out his hands toward Robert. "Come on now, it's just one small step. Trust me, next time it'll be easier." He was careful not to cross the gate himself. The energy drain might cause it to collapse.

Robert squared his strong shoulders and stepped into the gate. The pull of power intensified as he passed over the thresholds and into David's apartment. I lost Larry and Terry, and very nearly Charles. "Good luck Robert," I called, as the gate crumbled.

"Thank you," Robert called back from the other side as it collapsed into the nothing from which it sprang.

"Goddess, that was intense." Geri said, as she lay back on the floor and closed her eyes. The others followed suit as I sat down in the barber chair for a moment. That had taken a lot out of me. I'd need to eat again soon, but I would hide that from the others.

After a couple of minutes, Geri ordered everyone to the kitchen for glasses of orange juice, then directed those that could drive to go on home and get to bed. She gave everyone but Stan the night off the next night.

I offered to take Alex home. He was in no shape to drive and had expressed an earlier need to sleep in his own bed. I understood.

On the drive to his parents' house, Alex's head lay back against the headrest, but by the time we pulled into the driveway, he'd shifted so that he rested on my shoulder. It felt warm and comfortable there.

"Well, here you are," I said softly, turning off the motor.

He looked up at me through drooping eyelids. "Thanks for the lift. One more favor, can you help me in? I'm not sure I can make it up the stairs and I don't want to wake anybody."

"Stairs?" We were sitting in front of what appeared to be a one-story house.

"I live over the garage out back. It was easier that way once my sister needed her own room. If you could lend me your shoulder, I'd appreciate it." His voice had very little life to it at all. He was worn out.

I brushed a lock of hair off his forehead. "Tell you what, I'll get you up there and see you to bed and you call me when you wake up and let me know you're alright."

"Deal," he sighed.

I wrapped a shield around us just in case any of the neighbors were watching, then raced around to the other side of the car. I scooped him up in my arms before he had a chance to get out. He nestled his head in the hollow of my neck and I walked around to the back yard with him in my arms. I didn't notice his weight at all, enjoying his presence there. He felt so right there. I began to wonder what it would take to keep him there.

Behind the main house was a large garage with a good-sized room above it. Stairs near the fence led up to the door. Alex reached for his key, but I used a small spell to unlock his door and it opened before us. I didn't bother turning on the lights. I carried him over to the neatly-made bed, sat him on the edge and pulled back the covers for him as he unbuttoned his shirt. With the sheets and comforter folded down, I reached for his boots and gently pulled them off as he worked his shirt out of his pants. I placed my hand against the hard hairy contour of the center of his chest and pushed him back against the pillow before he could reach for those painted-on jeans.

I quickly pulled the covers up around him, overcoming the urge to run my hands up and down that perfectly-sculpted body, letting my fingers play through the thick red hair. He smiled up at me as I straightened above him. "Thank you Tal," he said sleepily. His eyelids fell as the words left his mouth.

I watched as he fell asleep, reached down to brush the tangled red hair off his forehead, then bent over and kissed him softly. His scent filled me. I could stay all night and just drink in his aroma. I had to go.

I glanced at my watch. It was only four thirty in the morning. I still had time to kill something before dawn. It had been a long time since I had to hunt twice in one day. It had also been a long time since I forced myself from someone's bedside with a pang in my heart. I gave into my hunger as I drove away leaving Alex asleep above the garage.

Chapter Eight

SOMEONE OR something walked into my yard, shattering my sleep. My first thought was that something had just snuck in. My second was the realization that it was still daylight outside. Before sunrise, I'd settled down for the first long sleep in several days. After satisfying my renewed hunger on a deer south of town, I made it home as false dawn appeared on the eastern horizon. My temporary home was located in a nondescript, upper-middle-class neighborhood where most of the people worked hard to keep a perilous grip on a standard of living just beyond their means. There wouldn't be a lot of people around during the day, and even when they were around, they were too tired to notice anything out of the ordinary. My odd comings and goings shouldn't be noticed. Beth set the house up for me, as I drove in from Tulsa. I often wondered what I would do without her efficiency to back me up. She always seemed to find just the right place or the information I needed at the moment I needed it. Even though she wasn't a precognitive, she acted like it. More than once I'd wondered if she didn't have a partner who was.

The weak alarm spell I placed on the boundaries of the property the previous day sounded in my mind. I mentally reset it. I got out of the plush bed and walked across the floor to where the boxes with most of my magical tools sat and opened the box filled with crystals. At the top of the box holding the bare minimum of my great array of stones was the large obsidian viewing ball. In many books and movies, witches and sorcerers use crystal balls, but the object doesn't really matter. You can focus on anything. I know one eccentric old human that uses old hubcaps from early-model cars. It doesn't have to be a clear quartz crystal ball. Personally, I happen to like obsidian. It gives most people a headache. They just cannot attune obsidian's strong energies. I held the ball out in my left hand level with my eyes, relaxed and cast my mind out across the large yard to see what had invaded my space.

I almost missed him. He'd let his mind slip except for the basic ideas of his task. A large wolf, which in this neighborhood would've looked like a large husky, padded out from under the hedge that encircled the back yard. It carried the carcass of a much smaller canine in its mouth. He meant to leave it on my doorstep. It was a classic warning among the werefolk to a new magical creature in the area that they were there and not to bother them. I looked closely and realized the carcass had a pair of puncture wounds on the neck. A vampire ordered this wolf to make the drop. I could've destroyed him from where I was, but for the moment, I didn't want Estaben to think I was in town. Better to let them think I was a werewolf.

I moved quickly to the back door, shifting form as I went. Once again, I chose a wolfen form. I mentally opened the door as I charged out into the daylight of the back yard. The werewolf was on the other side of the swimming pool. He was a large gray wolf, with a long scar running down the left side of his face. This scar would also exist on his human face. Too bad he'd never get to use it again. He paused as I easily jumped the width of the pool and landed near him.

"I have a message," he growled, dropping the dead dog in the yard.

"Not interested in your message, but here's one of my own to send to the coward who used you as an errand boy." I responded in a mellow and civil tongue, but bared my teeth for show.

"What's your message?" he snarled, stepping over the carcass of the dog.

"Your body!" I replied as I leapt for his throat. I didn't believe in taunting prey with silly words. I liked to get right to the problem and go on. Plus, it was nicer to my prey if they didn't have to put up with more drama than necessary.

Blood Moon Yellow Sky

He rose up on his hind legs to meet my jump. I landed square across his broad chest and we rolled onto the dry grass of the yard. I regained my feet first and realized he might have some information that we might find useful. I recalled where I left my glassware and mentally summoned a beaker and cork to one of the benches near the pool until I needed it.

He struggled to his feet. His right rear leg lagged a bit. I might have dislocated it with my jump. He snarled again and lunged at me. I glided out of his way and caught his throat in my mouth as he shot past me. My jaws clamped down. His death was swift and anticlimactic.

As I felt the life leaving his body, I regained my human form and called the beaker to hand. The spell I used was an old one, known to many a voodon over the years. As I cast it, I reached out and caught his escaping soul in the beaker. The face that glared at me from within the glass was neither human or wolf, but a cross of the two.

"What have you done to me? What are you?" he demanded as I pushed to cork into the top of the beaker.

"Not much, just killed you and trapped your soul. Don't worry though, once I have all the knowledge of your thoughts, I'll release you and let you go to the rest you so greatly seek." I resisted the urge to laugh manically for effect, thinking it too bright and sunny for that.

Before returning to the house, I summoned fire to clean the carcasses from my yard. Although I was fairly sure the turkey vultures I'd seen from time to time around town would find them in short order, I figured there was less clean up this way. I also figured his disappearance would send a message to Estaben as surely as if I sent the body back to him, as I threatened at the start of the fight.

As I walked toward the bathroom, I glanced at the clock. Four o'clock in the afternoon. At least I'd gotten a good amount of sleep. It wasn't uncommon for me to go several days without sleep and then sleep for a day or more. Since my last sleep was only two days ago, the ten hours I got left me relaxed and revitalized, even after the magic I wielded the night before. Now I needed a good brisk shower. I sweat in my sleep. Dragon sweat can be extremely smelly and it can make a real stinky mess of things on hot nights.

As I turned on the shower, an image of Alex lying on the bed beneath me while my sweat dripped onto him flashed into my mind. I pushed it away. It vanished only to be replaced by thoughts of him in the shower with the hot steam boiling up around him. I didn't need this. Again I pushed thoughts of him out of my mind. I'd never had this much trouble putting someone out of my mind. Through sheer force of will, I managed to rinse off the remnants of my sleep and my conflict with the werewolf without further thoughts of Alex.

What I needed was to spend a while in meditation. I wanted to see if there were any spells working on me that I wasn't aware of which could cause my sudden increased need for food. I pulled the curtains and settled into the well-used, plushy, chair that I had found decades ago in a small shop in Denver. From the first time I sat in it, it had always been the most comfortable of chairs. I bought it immediately and hauled it home. I now took it with me wherever I went. It had a set of shields all its own and was comfortable enough I could sit for hours in meditation before feeling the least little cramp.

My mind drifted off into the ether, going through my standard checklist of things as I slipped into the meditation. I checked my physical body to make sure nothing was out of order. My blood was pure and strong. Barring any problems, there should be no reason for me to feed for almost a week. My muscles showed fine, no evidence of strain from my battle earlier. Then I checked the magical energies working around me, dropping my shields one by one and feeling them sink into the elements from which I'd drawn them. As all the protections fell away, I found nothing out of the ordinary. I checked everything I could think, but there was nothing new.

Then I moved beyond my own magics, feeling the world around me. A bright golden cord flared out of the astral plane toward me and embedded into my heart chakra. It had never been there before. With an experienced eye, I analyzed it. It wasn't woven by any magics I'd encountered before. Instead, it felt like it was part of me. When I compared it to my own astral cord, it was similar in makeup. My own magics carefully coupled with someone else's, perfectly woven together. I touched it with a careful finger and it hummed with a power that swept over me. It felt good. I felt lighter and more cheerful, like a butterfly emerging from its cocoon, realizing there was a bright sky above and no longer forced to crawl through the muck of the world. My fingers lay against the golden cord in an almost euphoric state. What would cause a daze like this? The darkness of the world seemed to fade away. There was only light. I felt complete, too. I'd never realized how lonely the eternal life of the last dragon was. Vampires gathered covens around them, staying in constant contact with others like themselves. Most werecreatures gathered in packs, prides or flocks. Mages wandered the world alone for the most part, seeking knowledge wherever they went but they came together from time to time to pass on the knowledge they'd gathered to others so that it wouldn't be lost in the turning of time. Then, they'd go off again for years on end, either locked away in their solitary towers and libraries, or roaming the world in distant lands. I was older than any human mage. They could live a long time by their standards, but not as long as dragon. I knew of only a few vampires older than myself that still sought companionship even for an evening or two.

I'd become the perfect assassin. I was alone and I had more knowledge than most beings ever thought existed. But I'd lived alone for a long time and had been alone for most of my very long life. Now this golden cord sang to me of completeness and wholeness with another, the power of two becoming one.

I didn't will myself to follow the golden cord. I moved through the vastness of the astral plane with the cord flowing across my palms as I held onto it in the effort to follow it to the other end. As I moved, the feeling of right grew stronger. Then I came to a wall with a coyote sitting in front of it. The cord passed through it and the coyote smiled as I approached her. I released the cord and my heart cried.

"Sorry Tal, that's as far as you go for now," the coyote said in Geri's voice, but not Geri's voice. There was the hint of deity in it. "I think you know already where this leads. It's not time. Soon, but not yet. Go back now. There's nothing wrong with you. This was meant to be. It's the thing most of us yearn for but know that we'll never find. You've lived long enough to know that you can be happy now, if you'll let yourself. Your true passions were locked away long ago. Far too long, you've lived with only knowledge to keep you going. Soon you'll reopen doors which were closed long ago. Go back now in peace and know that love awaits you beyond this wall that shall not stand long." She laughed then and I felt a lurch in my reality.

The astral plane vanished and I was back in my chair with my shields down. The sun had also gone down. I'd been lost with the golden cord for longer than I realized. Then I felt the first of the hot tears roll down my face. It'd been a long time since I cried. I let myself go and cried for the love that waited and the end to my loneliness.

Chapter Nine

"WOULD YOU please slow down!" demanded the voice from the beaker as we sped down the street. I ignored it as I headed for the next pothole, swerving to hit it squarely caused the Pathfinder to bounce into the air. Before pulling out of the driveway, I'd wrapped an illusion around the car to ensure that as long as I didn't hit anyone, no one would notice my erratic driving. I'm not a big one for torture, but I can be rather creative about pulling information out of a source when necessary. If I shook the bottle up enough, my messenger would be willing to talk and then I could send him on his way.

A message from Alex waited for me when I aroused from my meditation. Before calling him, I checked in with Beth at Coalition HQ to see if there was any new intel from the area and have her run a check on Dr. Mike Hammed. She informed me the number of missing persons in Yellow Sky was growing, as was the number of mangled or drained bodies. I gave her the information on Larry and Terry's dad being with the police and how he might be able to help with the cover up. She said she'd get that info to damage control and see what they could do. And she'd see what she could find on Dr. Hammed and check to see if any of his patients were on the missing person's list.

For some reason, I felt nervous calling Alex. So first, I called Geri to let her know about the werewolf. She was interested in interrogating the beaker-werewolf spirit but said she and Stan were working on something so I should come over after midnight with the others.

Finally I returned Alex's call. Hearing his voice made my heart race. The sensation was strange and almost alien to me. It made me wonder what other affects he was going to have on my life. He asked me to join him and the others at Char and Burn's house for a while before everyone headed over to Geri's after midnight. The drive wasn't far and I figured I'd make the most of it while I could. I'd pass the beaker around so each of the gang could shake it, just to keep things interesting for the messenger.

"Damn, could you hit it a little harder next time?" the spirit complained. "You can never understand how confusing and disorienting this is."

"Maybe in your next life you'll be a little pickier about who you work for," I snapped trying to sound rougher than I felt. The GPS indicated I needed to turn onto the next street and then the house should be about half a block down. I took the turn on two wheels tossing the beaker in its safely-padded box to the floorboard.

"Hey now! Why'd you do that?" the muffled voice came from the floorboard.

I just chuckled as the truck bounced back onto all four tires. Let me tell you, getting a Pathfinder to go around a corner on two wheels isn't easy, but after a little TV back in the 1980s, I found it was fun taking corners on two wheels. I screeched the tires as I pulled up in front of the small house. Just then, I realized Alex must have left his car at Geri's when I took him home last night. I had no idea which car was his, but I hoped he hadn't had a problem getting it back.

Grabbing the beaker off of the floor, I pulled the protective plastic bubble wrap off it and headed to the door, ignoring the spirit's complaints. The place was a small normal-looking house, with an untidy front yard. Broken steps led up to a white door covered in cracked paint. I knew from the files their mother worked hard to support them, but I didn't like the conditions I saw.

"Nice place here," the werespirit commented as I reached for the cracked doorbell button.

"It's none of your concern. I'm sure you've been in worse," I growled back as I poked the button with one hand while shaking the bottle with the other. Soft steps came to the door and a seeking magic passed over me before the doorknob turned. The door opened and Charles greeted me.

"Hey Tal," he smiled. "Sorry we started without you, but we didn't know when you'd get here. Alex'll be happy you're here."

"Don't worry about it." I stepped into the room. "Just hit a few bumps on the way here."

"Yeah the way he drives we're lucky we got here at all," the voice from the beaker complained.

"Hey, what's that?" Charles peered curiously at the vapor swirling around inside the glass.

"I call it messenger in a bottle." I grinned lifting the bottle a little higher.

"Guys, come look at what Tal brought with him," Charles called. "This is cool!"

"Great now I feel like a fish under glass," the spirit griped.

"Get used to it," I said, giving the bottle a good shake. "And quit your complaining. It's going to get a lot worse for you before it gets better."

"Wow," Terry said, as he got a look at the beaker. "What is it?"

"Looks like some kind of spirit trapped in a beaker," Alex replied stepping around the others staring at the bottle in my hand. My heart skipped when I caught sight of him. His jeans weren't as tight as the night before, but he wore another tight t-shirt covering his firm chest. This one had a stag on it with a Celtic knot pentagram in its antlers. A modern artistic rendition of the ancient god Herne, normally lord of the hunt, but sometimes of lust. He looked up at me and smiled. "So, where'd you get it?"

"Here." I tossed it to him. "Careful not to uncork it, but other than that, if you all could keep it moving I'd appreciate it. This is, or was, a werewolf who showed up at my place this afternoon. He came carrying a message from one of the local vampires. So far, he's a little reluctant to tell me who or where. I think we can shake him up a bit for a while and maybe get more out of him before we go to Geri's. "

"Yeah, Geri called as you pulled up. Said that we needed to be over by midnight. She figured they'd be done by then. That should give us a couple hours of game time," Alex said holding up the beaker. "Nasty looking freak isn't he."

The spirit glared at him. "I could say the same for you human."

Alex gave the beaker a good shake and smiled at it. "I think that if he's such a smart ass, we're going to enjoy shaking him all night." he tossed the beaker to Janie. "Here, bounce him around a bit. Let's get back to the game. Tal, you have a choice, you can watch, or we can give you a NPC to play."

"Okay, I know the basic concepts of the role-playing games, but what is an NPC?" I asked. The whole idea of the role-playing game was fairly new to me. In some ways it was too close to the way my life had been in the distant past, and there were a few things I'd just rather not revisit. I wasn't sure I was ever going to shake the smell of the Middle Ages.

"An NPC is a character that the Dungeon Master would normally play. We have several in this one." Alex explained, taking my elbow and steering me out of the room. I felt a slight jolt of electricity as his hand touched my arm. "I'm DMing tonight, and if you like, you can use my normal character who I'm dragging along tonight just to keep her going."

"Hey, it's no fair letting him play Pauleen," Larry objected. "He wouldn't play her the way you do and you'd have to prompt him on what items she has. Besides it would slow down the game."

"Topper might have a point there," Bernadette added, opening the refrigerator as we walked into the kitchen. "We've got a few hours before we have to be over at Geri's. Tal, would you be okay with just watching this time? If you're interested in playing, we can sit down later and roll you up a character, but right now trying to let you play would probably slow things down."

Alex released my elbow as I felt him bristle at Bernadette and Larry. "Look, if he wants to play, he can play."

"Alex, they're right and you know it," said Charles, accepting the soda Bernadette handed him out of the refrigerator. "Let's pull up a chair for Tal and get on with the game. Anyone else want anything before we get back to playing?" Everyone shook their heads.

"Alex, it's okay. I'd rather just watch to try and figure out how the whole thing works before trying my hand at it. Besides I'm horrible at dice." I tried to smooth over ruffled feathers. Truth be told, I was pretty bad with dice, unless I decided to cheat at it, which I only did when really necessary.

"Okay, I just didn't want you to feel left out," Alex replied, heading to the chair at the rear corner of the table. "I know it can be kinda boring just watching. You can sit over here next to me though. You'll have a better view."

"Of you." I heard someone mutter under their breath as we walked across the kitchen.

Surprisingly, the evening didn't drag for me. Actually, it went rather well for the most part and I found the little insights into the working of everyone's minds intriguing. I thoroughly enjoyed myself until something brushed the edges of my senses and the front door opened. Game play stopped as the gang obviously felt something enter the house. The room quickly fell silent. I knew there was another fledgling vampire to deal with. My hearing picked up the sounds of Mrs. Colfax giggling and talking softly to someone.

Janie sat the beaker on the table, the spirit mist still spinning around in it, and Charles and Bernadette moved to get up. Alex held a finger to his lips and shook his head. He gestured for the others to also stay seated. I nodded and tried projecting an I'm-not-here field around me the way Alex had explained it to me the previous night. Hopefully, no one who didn't know I was there would be aware of my presence. The giggling got closer. The male voice said something, but I couldn't make out the words. They'd be in the kitchen in just a couple of seconds.

Alex held up both of his hands with the fingers spread for a second and then held up two fingers. Gesturing to Charles and Bernadette, he made an exploding motion. He pointed at Larry and Terry then covered one of his hands with the other. For Janie, he made a quick gesture to the side, then pointed at himself and made a flashing motion. He made a general sweeping motion then pointed at the table before he rose and walked toward the refrigerator.

Mrs. Colfax entered the kitchen holding the hand of a tall dark-haired vampire. He was young, but not as young as Robert Cooper. He also was well aware of what he was doing. He smiled broadly, spying what he must see as easy prey at the table. I wished I could laugh. Here was an evil vampire about to get more than he bargained for on his menu.

Alex turned toward them. "Mrs. Colfax, I thought I heard someone come in. Nice night?"

She giggled again. This wasn't the same woman I'd met the previous day at Geri's. She was in the thrall of this predator. "Alex, nice to see you all staying in out of trouble. This is Ted." She turned slightly so that Alex could reach for Ted's hand.

"Hello Alex." Ted's voice held a slight pull to it. It'd take more than that to ensnare Alex's mind, but then Ted only saw easy prey.

"Hello Ted, you look like you could use a little light." Bright light burst around Alex. The extremely-focused aura flash seemingly poured out of his skin.

"Look out fool!" the spirit in the bottle pulled itself together enough to scream.

Ted let go of Danielle's hand and backed up, his eyes blinking, trying to get his bearings. Larry and Terry enveloped Danielle in a shield while Janie moved her out of the way. Power surged behind me as the glare from Alex wore off. Ted stood in the doorway of the kitchen blinking, rubbing his eyes, trying to see what was happening. Then the power behind me released. Flame seared across the kitchen, striking Ted in the chest. He screamed but couldn't move before the second volley hit, knocking him to the floor and completely engulfing him. Within seconds there was nothing left but the smell of burned flesh.

"That, you bloodsucking bastard, is why they call us Char and Burn." Bernadette growled while Charles dashed from the table to their mother.

"Damn, you guys don't mess around do ya?" The spirit in the beaker commented as the smoke cleared.

"No we don't," Janie replied as she picked the bottle up and shook it so that he spun on the table again.

The way the group had acted in the face of danger was fairly impressive. I had to smile at the way Geri had taught her students to work together. There was no doubt they could handle one, and probably two or three vampires, but our intel was there were a lot more in Yellow Sky and they'd need more than just a few small fire balls and quirky comebacks.

Chapter Ten

STILL DAZED by Ted's assault on her mind, Mrs. Colfax was fairly easy to manipulate. Alex gave her a slight mental push until the twins found her sleeping pills and put her to bed. Charles and Bernadette made sure the wards around the house were up to full strength. I sensed an alarm spell linked to them that would let them know if anything crossed their magics. We didn't find an extra car in the driveway so we figured it was safe to assume they'd both arrived in Daniel's car. We then piled into the truck and drove over to Geri's.

The gang was fairly animated as we drove, hyped up on the adrenaline aftermath of their short fight with the vampire.

"Wow, that vamp was an easy kill," Bernadette said proudly.

"Yeah, you guys hit him with your one-two punch," Janie agreed.

"The way he went up, this might be easier than we thought," Charles piped in.

I let them go on in that vein for a bit before I interrupted. "You guys realize that Ted was a fairly young vampire. Older vampires are harder to kill."

"Yeah, but will they be that much harder to kill?" Larry asked.

I nodded. "You bet they will. Not only that, but if you go charging in, the odds won't be in your favor. This time you were six to one."

"You're probably right, Tal." Alex said warmly from the passenger seat. "But hey, it's our first vamp kill."

I couldn't resist reaching over to pat his arm. "And you guys did an awesome job of it."

"Yeah we did!" Bernadette cheered from the back seat.

"Hey, Tal, can you swing through a drive through on our way?" Alex asked. "I don't know about everyone else, but that left me with a bit of a munch."

That idea brought cheers from the back seat, so we stopped at the next open drive through we passed. I wondered how they could put away so much food, let alone food that smelled as bad as what they ordered, but they inhaled it in the short distance to Geri's house. It reminded me of a wolf pack tearing a deer apart. As we pulled into Geri's drive, a shadowy form dashed across the street away from the house.

"That was David!" Terry cried, watching the shadow move stealthily down the street.

"Well I guess he hasn't totally gone over to the rat side yet," Alex replied as I parked the truck.

"Not if he's leaving Geri's. Let's get in there and see what he wanted. This night is getting more interesting by the minute," Charles said, opening the door. "Are you two coming?" he asked Bernadette and Janie, who had piled on top of each other in the back of the truck as soon as we got in, separating only far enough to feed each other fries once they had food.

Bernadette's blue and green head popped up over the back seat. "Look, killing vampires makes me horny. Besides, this helps me build up my energies."

I shook my head and followed Alex into the house, trying not to pay too much attention to how his firm round butt filled out his jeans. I wouldn't mind recharging some of my own energies with him, but we had more important things to worry about.

Geri and Stan waited for us at the kitchen table. Several piles of fabric lay in front of them. The piles looked identical except that each glimmered with slightly different energies.

"Way cool, you finished them!" Larry cheered and reached for one of the piles in the center. The energies of the cloth leapt toward him and merged with his aura.

"All we have left to do is cast the final spell on each of them and they're finished. That will only take a moment," Geri replied. Larry draped the cloth over his shoulders. As he adjusted it, I saw it was a cloak. "Besides each of us needs to be in them at the time of the last spell for it to work correctly." She turned to me, "Good evening Tal, I take it you have the spirit in the bottle we talked about earlier."

Terry held up the beaker he had been bouncing on the drive over.

"Good, we'll get to him later. Right now, I want everyone to settle down and prepare for spell casting." She gestured at the chairs around the table as everybody grabbed their particular cloak. Almost as one, they sat down and breathed deeply. I watched as what had moments before been a rowdy car full of college students turned into a group of quiet mages sitting around a table preparing for serious work. They all reached out and drew energies. Some drew from the air around us. A couple drew from the earth beneath our feet. I felt Charles and Bernadette reach out for the molten core of the earth further down, harnessing the fire that lay there. Water energy flowed up to help invigorate. For several minutes, Geri only watched. When she was ready, she rose from the table and her students followed her as she walked toward the downstairs workroom. They hadn't asked me to stay in the kitchen, so I followed Alex as he brought up the rear, turning lights out as we went.

The chair from the previous night no longer occupied the center of the circle. In its place was a small altar, laden with the accoutrements of spell casting. Energy already pulsed around the circle. An incomplete line of salt lay waiting for someone to close it and finish the circle of power. After she crossed it, Geri stopped at the edge of the circle and stood to one side while the others filed in after her, circling around to the left until they were all inside. I sat in the barber chair that now stood near the east wall. Once Alex was in the circle, Geri turned to the opening and completed the line of salt. As the last salt crystal fell, connecting the incomplete circle, it pulsed to my magical sight and then held brightly, protecting all those within its boundaries. Everyone then took up positions at equal distances while she stepped to the altar.

Geri lifted the athame off the altar and walked to the place in the circle where the door had been. She carved a couple of runes in the air then turned back to her students in their cloaks. "The foundation spells are cast, the cloth has been sewn by your own hands with your own sweat and blood. The crystals are ready for the final energies needed to activate your cloaks."

She picked up a small incense burner and lit a stick of incense. "May the air grant us the wisdom and knowledge needed to use our new tools wisely." She passed by each one, and as they held the cloaks open, she waved the incense around and under their cloaks. When she was finished, she walked back to the altar and lit a red candle. "Spirit of fire we invoke your passion, light our way as we use our tools, but should we ever misuse them, we invoke your power to destroy them." Again she moved amongst them, this time passing the flame around them.

Then she took up a small bowl of water. "Water, we call upon your fluid state to pass over us, allow us to walk among those around us as the stream passes by the stones in its middle." She sprinkled small drops of water on every one of them.

Finally, she held a bowl of salt from the altar. "Earth, sleeping place of our great mother, source of all our power, grant your strength to our tools in that while we use them, we remain grounded and never assume lofty ideas or be tempted to use them for wrong." She flicked salt at them as she passed through their ranks.

"Now everybody draw your energies through the cloaks and repeat after me."

Energy filled the room as they drew up their personal energies and wrap them about themselves and the cloaks. "I call upon the power of the light and the power of the shadows. While I will it, cloaked in this shell of fabric, no light shall shine through it or me, nor shall any be reflected. All shall perceive nothing as I pass among them. Like the wind, I shall be unseen, clear as crystal or pure water and illusive as smoke. By my will, with the blessings of the Gods and Goddesses, so mote it be." The eight voices intoned as they wove their power into their cloaks, as the final word was spoken, they all vanished from my view.

"Cool," Larry said off to my right.

"Tal, can you see us?" Alex called, his voice coming from where I'd last seen him.

"Not even with mage sight," I replied.

"Well guys, it seems to have worked like it was supposed to," Geri said from the center of the circle. "Now lower your hoods, and we'll open the circle and get on to the other business of tonight."

Almost reluctantly, they lowered their hoods one by one. The general look on their faces was astonishment. I knew from my own apprenticeship that when a magical tool works the way it is supposed to, it's a wondrous thing. My first magical tool had been a staff of fire. I still have it somewhere in a closet. Staves are just not something most people carry around nowadays.

Once they all lowered their hoods and stood visible in the circle again, Geri walked over to where the door had been, intoned a dismissal of the circle, and with her athame, cut a path in the salt. The circle fell back into the elements from which it formed. As one, everyone let out a deep sigh as the pressure of the magic vanished and the energies of the air around them returned to normal.

Geri stepped across the circle of salt and headed toward the stairs. "Let's talk upstairs."

I trailed after them as they followed their teacher. She moved her students along at a phenomenal rate. Most mages these days didn't get to the major stuff like magical tools until they were at least in their thirties. But then, most were not lucky enough to find a real teacher.

Geri directed everyone to sit at the table. With a look, Alex asked me to sit next to him. Charles had been planning to take that seat, but then moved over to the other side of the table next to Janie. Alex hummed with power as he folded his new cloak up into a neat pile. As I sat down, he touched my leg and a bolt of energy shot through me.

My stomach fluttered and power pulsed in my root and heart charkas. He looked over at me and flashed a soft smile that made those beautiful green eyes blaze. I returned the smile while I centered out the energies coursing through me and forced my heart back to calm.

"First, I want to know the details of what happened at the game tonight," Geri said calling everyone's attention to her.

Over the next few minutes Alex, Charles and Bernadette filled her in on their encounter and defeat of the vampire. Remarkably, they didn't embellish the details.

"Did your mother say where she met Ted?" Geri asked after they finished the tale.

"She said he was one of their regular customers at The Happy Hillbilly," Charles replied. "It had been a couple of nights since she'd seen him, but they'd talked before and had a few drinks after work. So when he asked her out to dinner tonight when she got off early, she didn't think anything of it."

"But she did say he'd been acting funny tonight when he showed up there," Bernadette added. "Never had anything to drink, but spent some time smelling the pretzels and nuts."

"Normal for a fledgling," I injected. "I'd say he'd probably only fed once or twice before and that was at his master's knee. He was different from Robert Cooper. Ted probably had a sire that oversaw his change and wanted him to actively recruit others to his cause."

"I agree." Geri replied. "It's unfortunate that we cannot question Ted and find out more about his sire and what's going on. Next time guys, try not to fry a potential source of information." More satisfaction than scolding colored her voice.

"The next one better not have his hands on our mother," Bernadette growled defensively.

"I didn't say that you shouldn't have defended your mother. Quite the contrary, I think you performed extremely well given the circumstances. I see Ted's death as unavoidable. And, you resolved the situation without Tal's help, which is even more important. Please try to remember that he's only supposed to be an observer, and not a participant in all of this."

"So, we rack this one up for experience and go on," Alex said with a nod. "What did David want, and how far gone is he?"

Geri sighed and shook her head, her mood changing dramatically in a split second. "David's fairly far gone. The poor boy wasn't cut out to be a wer, and now the sudden influx of vampires and werewolves is pushing at his sanity. His grip there wasn't very strong to begin with. I don't think he'll be with us as David much longer. Seeing you with Tal last night was almost all he could handle. As it is, after tonight he cannot seem to pull himself together enough to resume his full human form. At least I could understand him." She got up and walked over to the ever present pot of tea on the stove.

"He said that a lot of the rats are falling back to Magenta's place outside of town since it sounds like a pack of werewolves is working with the vampires," she said, returning to the table, her cup steaming with fragrant mint tea. "David was at the Huff and Puff Book and Novelties tonight. At that point, he was still able to pass for human and was out looking for a trick. He's never said for sure, and his alphas aren't saying either, but I think that he may have contracted lycanthropy there and has been searching for the rat who bit him. But that has nothing to do with tonight. He managed to stumble onto a vampire feeding off someone. The poor fool was already dead by then and it scared David out of his mind. He said the vampire would've caught him, but he shifted and got away as fast as he could. All he could think of was to come here and tell me."

"I checked the police scanner and the sheriff responded to a call down there," Geri continued. "So far, I've only heard about one body they recovered. I'd like to know more."

"Do you need me to tap into the police computer and find out what's up?" Terry sounded eager to help.

Geri took a long sip of the tea. "That's one of the things I have in mind. I want someone to go by the morgue and make sure the body stays there. Also I need another one of you guys to go by the Huff and

Puff and get a psychic impression of what happened and maybe who we're dealing with."

"Burn, Hill and I can get in and out of the morgue the fastest and easiest," Stan offered with nods from Bernadette and Janie. "We can make sure the guy stays dead and anybody else there does the same."

"I want to go to the Huff and Puff," Charles added.

"No Char, I need you to stay here and keep a telepathic link open with Burn so if they run into trouble, we can get to them quickly. You can also help Terry with the computer. I need Alex to go on that one, but would prefer not to send him alone," she said, taking another long sip of her tea.

"Tal could go with me, strictly as an observer. I'll do all the spell work," Alex replied eagerly.

"But he doesn't have a cloak of invisibility," Charles objected.

I chuckled, how little these people really knew about who they were dealing with. "Charles, I don't need one. I'm only seen when I want to be seen. That is true of most magical creatures. The human mind has a way of not seeing that which is out of the ordinary. You'll find that to be true when they deal with vampires, werekind, shifters and magic as well. How often do you hear about real magic when it happens in public?

"I remember one time that I had to actually do a public execution of a werewolf who was trying to run for office in a small town in Alabama. I could never get him alone, so I waited until he was doing an appearance at a Fourth of July celebration, and just took him out with a leven bolt in front of several hundred people. The papers the next day called it a freak fireworks accident. Most of them saw the bolt that was obviously not pyrotechnic in nature, but their minds couldn't accept that. It's second nature for me not to be somewhere. I haven't needed a cloak of invisibility in years."

"I remember that mayor thing." Geri said with interest. "For some reason even as an eleven-year-old school girl, it didn't seem right when I read it."

"So what about me then?" Larry asked looking young and dejected.

"I need you here with me, Char and Topper to keep in contact with Alex and Tal, and as back up for either group if they need us." Geri replied.

"What about me?" the spirit in the bottle whined.

Geri snatched up the beaker and tossed it to Larry. "Here, Weasel, keep our friend here moving until everybody gets back and we can shake some information out of him."

It was hard not to feel sorry for the poor spirit, but that's part of being a bad guy. You get caught, you get hurt. I knew he'd do worse to us if he had the opportunity. So off we went into the night, hopefully ready for whatever Estaben and his crew threw at us.

Chapter Eleven

ON THE way to the Huff and Puff Book and Novelty store, I called Beth for info. With her normal efficiency, she told me that the store had been in business in one form or another for over fifteen years. There were a number of murders there every year; most of them were never investigated very deeply. She provided the name of tonight's murder victim. Harvey Bates, age fifty six, had been found with his throat slit. She also let me know that J.P. wanted a report soon on Geri's progress. He was concerned about the growing civilian body count and wasn't happy.

The store sat off away from town in a cornfield with two large floodlights lighting up the sky. The three large red Xs on top of the building felt rather foreboding to me. They looked bloodstained. The parking lot was full on this Friday night. The signs out front promised naked dancers of all flavors, as well as movies, DVDs, CDs, books and adult novelties. Posters for various movies and products covered the outside walls, adding color to what looked like a rather drab, black building.

"Boy, the new place is sure taking a bite out of business here," Alex observed.

"What do you mean?" I asked as I parked the truck out near the edge of the parking lot.

"There was a time, at this hour on a Friday night, you couldn't find a parking spot here, but since the new joint opened up north of town, fewer people are coming out here." He reached across the seat and touched my arm. I felt another jolt like before. "So, how do you want to play it?"

I turned off the truck and sat there. "What do you see as our options?"

"Well, we can just walk in there together and find the booth where the guy was killed and see what we can get. Or, we can go in separately and meet at the booth, kinda more causal that way. Or we can go in stealth mode, sneak in and then get to work. I think that plan A is the best. It will take less energy and there is less chance of being interrupted." His voice held a suggestive undertone.

I shrugged. Here I was about to go into a place where sexual predators preyed on one another with a mage who was sending magical shocks through me each time we touched. He was supposed to open up and try to psychically see what happened at a fresh murder scene. And he asked me, how I'd like to do it. I pushed images of how I'd like to do it out of my mind. "I'm just here to observe, however you want to do it is fine."

"Cool, come on." He opened the door and swung out, then waited for me at the back of the truck. He took my hand and led me into the store. The energy was more intense this time when we touched. I wondered how long it was going to be until the astral wall between us was blown apart and our spirits became one. I forced my mind away from such thoughts and fought to focus on the job at hand.

As we walked in, the level of tasteless porn increased, posters advertising various movies and products plastered the walls. The posters varied depending on the genre of the movies in that section. Alex led us over to the section dominated by the gay movies. These posters mostly portrayed nearly-naked muscular men either singularly or in pairs. There were fewer movie boxes in this section than in the others, but then they probably had a lower calling for this type of movie than the mainstream straight porn.

Alex picked up one box and handed it to me. "I got a real laugh outa this one a while back," he chuckled.

I looked at the box. It was for Count Suckulala. The man on the cover was standing in the classic black cape tossed back over his shoulders exposing a highly-defined smooth chest with a leather cod piece covering his genitals while an apparently nude young man knelt at his feet looking up at him with rapt surrender in his blank eyes. I chuckled, shook my head and started to put it back on the shelf.

Alex pulled in close. "We could rent it and act out some of the scenes," he whispered teasingly. I must have blushed when I dropped the box to the floor, because he broke out laughing softly.

He picked up the box and set it back on the shelf. "Don't worry about it, Tal." His voice still had a lilt of merriment to it. "I won't force myself on you. Yet." He chuckled and moved further into the store.

I glanced around and only a couple of the other patrons looked away from the scene they'd been watching. I had to get a hold of myself. This hunky, flirty mage was trying to get the better of me. The worst part was that I wanted him, too. For the first time in many generations of human time, I wanted one of them for myself. I sighed and followed his tight blue-jean-clad ass into the back of the store.

Alex paused at a curtain in what appeared to be the back wall before pushing it aside and walking through. I followed a breath behind. As I passed into the dimly-lit hall, I felt a large number of eyes on me. I followed Alex down a gauntlet of men standing against the wall and in the doorways of the booths that ran up and down the hallway. Geri told us which booth David had found the vampire in and Alex walked right to it. I wasn't sure I wanted to know why he was familiar with the place. Not that I had any illusions about his purity, but I had developed a few fantasies. I tried to not look at all the men that haunted those booths. Most looked hollow. There was obviously something missing in their lives and they sought to find it here. Such places have existed for a long time. I remember the first time I ventured into one of the Roman baths. The scene had been much like this, only better lit and the men there were more open about what they did. Of course togas hid a lot less than modern clothes. Like walking into a room full of vampires, there were too many predators in a small place, everybody looking for the same thing.

Shaking off the past as I followed Alex around a corner. He was one of the better looking men in the place and several of the men reached toward him from the doorways. He moved easily away from them without a word or change of demeanor. He'd obviously done this many times before. I wondered if that was why he'd been eager to come here. Up a small flight of stairs and we were in a longer hall. Alex led us to a short hallway about halfway down the main passage. There were only a couple of booths here. The one with the number we were looking for had a red light above the closed door. I was surprised there was no police tape around the scene. Obviously, either the police were very expedient in Yellow Sky or they didn't really care about the death of a man in an adult bookstore on the edge of town.

"Looks occupied right now," he said with a sly grin, then reached for my arm, pulled me into the next booth and closed the door. He went over to the large television screen and put a dollar bill into the slot next to it. As the movie began to play, he took a seat on the couch.

"I'll check in real quick with Weasel and see how they're doing," he said. "Want to ride along?"

I shook my head. "I'll listen for the people next door to leave."

"Okay, I'll be quick." He relaxed and I felt his attention turn outward.

I listened to the movement in the hall and the sounds indicated several people moving around, but so far, I hadn't heard the door next door open and close. I pushed my own senses outward, brushing only one consciousness in the next booth, I pushed against it, sending waves of anxiety. Seconds later, the door opened, slammed shut and feet ran down the hall. I guess I pushed harder than I intended. Either that or people in here were a bit on the jumpy side and easily frightened.

Alex laughed a bit. "Scared him out, huh?" His voice startled me, I hadn't expected him to contact Larry that quickly and get back. "Weasel says everything's okay. Stan, Hill and Burn just arrived at the morgue, and so far, no problems. Topper got into the police system without anything happening and is getting the files right now. So let's get our info and get back to Geri's."

The screen went black and he stepped over to the door. "Let's go next door." He opened the door and I followed him into the hall. Surprisingly, no one stood there as we emerged and quickly entered the murder scene. This room was no different from the other. After putting a couple of dollars in the bill slot next to the screen, Alex sat down on the couch and closed his eyes. To my eyes, the couch was filthy in more ways than almost any other couch I've ever seen. I was glad I didn't have to sit on it. There are some things that even a dragon doesn't want to do.

Alex's energies reached out to the nether regions filling the space and sifted through the many strong emotions enveloping the place from the past. His mind searched for the information, wavering in the sea of emotions trying to find the death and its perpetrator. Suddenly he gasped and his hand grabbed mine where it rested lightly on the back of the couch. His grip was tight, and his nails dug into the back of my hand. He needed an anchor in the swirl of emotions he'd plunged into. I placed my other hand on his shoulder and poured power into him. He caught it and I suddenly felt what he felt, the tug of the lust, fear and shame that filled this room. I pushed at it, trying to move past it to find death. That too was there, not just one but several.

Together we struggled to keep them in chronological order. We sought to find the most recent. It was like trying to fast forward through several horror movies at once trying to find a specific scene. A young man died of a drug overdose, dropping his needle to the floor. A gun blazed in the darkness and a man fell over a chair that was no longer there as his wife turned the gun on herself. An old man grabbed his chest as a rent boy screamed for help. Finally a fresh scene loomed up that was new to the room. The victim, an older man, was happy with a handsome younger man who showed interest in him. He'd always had a taste for younger men and this one suited him well. The lust was strong. The picture of the killer was prominent in the energies put off by the victim.

He'd been a tall lanky blond man with blazing blue eyes and a strong nose. His crew cut added a feeling of strength and had been the factor pulled the older man to him. No words were exchanged. The young man's strong kiss and powerful embrace engulfed the older man. Death had been swift. The vampire tore out his prey's throat, but the lust didn't end there. The older man had been so enraptured by the attentions of the hunk, the sensations of his lips and tongue endured and provided an anchor in this world for the spirit, helping to tie it to the cooling body. He lingered on the rough hands that lowered him gently to the sticky floor. Harvey hadn't accepted death, and struggled in the light of his killer. He still tried to find a way back to the world of his killer. If left alone, there was a chance he might be able to find the last object of his lust.

Harvey's spirit latched onto Alex's energies. Lust and shame filled the room continuing to push at us as he fought to find a way to recapture his killer's light through Alex. I tried to push the spirit aside, but Alex panicked and the room began to close in on us. The tide of emotions flooded the room and swept us away.

Alex pushed back at everything, trying to shield himself from all the outside forces that pounded at him...at us. His shield pushed at our tenuous link and only our continued physical contact held it in place. I tried to strengthen his shields, to protect us and at the same time calm his mind, get him to focus again. I reached out for him by totally entering the astral with him. Here too, our hands linked as in the physical world. He was running. I stopped him. A myriad of emotions played across his features. He brought our linked hands up to his mouth and kissed my fingers. I couldn't pull back. The lust from the room and my own heart combined and the force was too strong. He moved his hands up my arms. He couldn't break the link. His astral hands moved up to my shoulders and he pulled me into an embrace, totally losing himself in the emotions permeating the room.

His kiss was warm and tender. We held it as our astral bodies sought to become one. I returned the kiss. I couldn't help myself. I knew this was not the time, place or conditions, but the lust was too strong. The feel of his body next to mine felt so right. It'd been too long since I held another in my arms for even a moment of passion. His body responded with a lust of its own. I glanced down, and hoped that the astral body was an accurate representation of the physical in this case. Then an idea came to me.

I surrendered to the lust from the room and totally opened the door to my own desires. The feelings I had every time Alex walked into a room. The pain I felt, leaving him alone in his bed last night. I pushed at him with all that lust as I crushed him to my body. My lust was stronger than that from the outside and pushed it back. Alex apparently saw my intentions and copied me. His intensity increased and was almost my undoing, but I kept one thought in the back of my mind. I wanted him somewhere other than this filthy couch in this place where the human predators prowled too close to us. The hope for perfection kept that strand of control thinner than a spider's web, but just as strong.

When the emotions retreated far enough, I pulled us out of the astral plane and back to our bodies. As the sensations of my physical body came back to me, I realized I was sprawled across Alex's lap. His regular breathing felt good through the fabric of my shirt and the heat from his body felt natural and very right. The next second, his breathing changed slightly as he emerged from his trance. For a moment, he lingered where he was, but moved one hand to trace the contours of my arm that hung to the floor. His body responded to the action, and to my surprise, mine did, too. I caught his hand in mine and held it close as I sat up.

I sat next to him on the couch for a moment in silence, still holding his hand. As in the astral world, he brought it up to his lips and kissed it softly. He looked at me with soft green eyes that held no mischief, only deep emotions. "Tal." He started, but I pressed our hands against his lips.

"Later." I moved in close and kissed him lightly on lips, his scent filled me. I wanted that aroma by me always.

I started to pull away, but he held me close and kissed me back with passion and need. Then he stiffened, and through our link, I heard someone scream in his mind.

His eyes flew open. "Stan and the girls need help!"

Chapter Twelve

WE RACED across town. If I'd been to the morgue before we would've gated there, but the closest I could get us was my rental house. It saved us ten minutes at least. The gate opened on the street out front as we roared from the parking lot at the porn shop onto the quiet suburban street. Alex directed me to the morgue. He slid across the seat and pressed in under my arm. It felt very natural. He was scared for his friends and I could help him ground those fears to keep a clear head. He didn't say much outside of directions.

"The guys and Geri are on their way too," he said.

We made another turn onto the busy street where his shop was.

"Do we know what's going on?" I asked.

He directed me onto the highway that ran through the center of town.

"All Char is saying is that he picked up the same scream I heard. It hit him harder because of the twin link he has with Burn. Right now, he's not getting anything through that link. He's trying not to panic, but it's all Geri can do to keep him calm." He shuddered under my arm. "Shit, another scream. Hurry! Char just blinked out. Where did Char go?" He voiced his unfiltered thoughts as he pushed harder against me. "Geri, where's Char? He did what? We're hurrying. Tal, drive faster! Geri just said that Char teleported. Something bad is happening to Burn and the others. We have to get there now!"

Time lurched and suddenly we moved much faster than the world around us. I thanked my draconic reflexes that allowed me to move the truck around the other vehicles that looked like they were all but parked on the road. I knew several spells that achieved the same affect, but this was no spell. At Alex's need, time slowed as we raced to save his friends. Like Char had just done, Alex found a new aspect to his personal psychic powers. He moved us into a different part of the time stream. We'd be there in seconds rather than minutes.

As I pulled up behind the hospital, we dropped back into normal time. I'm not even sure he realized he did it. A lot of people who discover new aspects to their abilities never realize what they've done until it happens again, or until they take time to analyze what happened.

Alex pushed me out of the truck and took off running. Luckily he'd thought to grab his cloak. I caught up with him and scooped him in my arms. "Wrap your cloak around you. I can move faster than you can, and you don't weigh anything to me. Basement I presume?"

He kissed my cheek. "Yes, thanks." Then he pulled his cloak about him and he disappeared from view. With his weight in my arms, his musky scent filled my nostrils, but other than that, it looked like I carried nothing as I ran. Not that most humans would see me as I ran past them. Luckily, late at night there'd be only minimal staff and few visitors in the hospital.

Running three flights of stairs was faster than waiting on the elevator. As I opened the door to the basement an aura of evil slammed my senses. Carefully, I set Alex down and he squeezed my hand before letting go. I could follow his scent, but I motioned him behind me. "No." he whispered, "You're the observer. It's my coven and best friends in there."

Before I could react, he raced down the hall to the door marked Morgue in big red letters. I followed, but didn't reach him before the doors opened. Just as I caught his scent, I bumped into him as I came into the room. He'd stopped in the middle of the doorway.

Chaos greeted us. Tables overturned. Big metal drawers mostly pulled out and instruments scattered about. More than a few bodies lay around like they'd been carelessly tossed by a very strong person. The scent of blood permeated the air. I quickly scanned the bodies. None looked like they belonged to anyone we knew. Most wore either nothing at all or green scrubs so common in hospitals.

I heard a tapping on glass and turned toward a window from what appeared to be an office set in the far wall. Stan and Janie were there, blood streaking their faces. They pointed upward.

I pushed at where I thought Alex was and jumped to the other side. My shove sent Alex out of the way as the vampire fell down toward us. I spun to face it as I cleared his leap. He was older than I expected, at least two hundred. He looked like his first death had been in his middle twenties. His long greasy brown hair was pulled back in a severe ponytail that snaked around as he moved his head. His tattered clothing indicated that things were not going to well for him. Could he be part of Estaben's coven? Before I could do anything, a leven bolt shot out from where I'd shoved Alex.

It knocked the vampire back, but didn't appear to do any other harm. "Great, another invisible mage." The vampire snarled.

Another scent hit me over the blood scent that covered the room. From behind one of the tables, the large form of a wererat in half rat form lunged at me. She was larger than most of the rats I'd ever seen. In human form, she was at least six feet five and now she stood right at six feet unless she stuck her foot-long snout straight into the air. She charged fast. I barely dodged her flashing claws. I pulled the silver dagger I kept in the sheath at the base of my spine just in case of such emergencies. Two wers in one day was more than I was in the mood to deal with.

The vampire sniffed the air trying to get Alex's scent just as another leven bolt came out of the office door. Stan's hands moved in the early stages another spell as Janie ducked down out of his way.

I couldn't spare much time worrying about them because the wererat was trying to get her claws into me. When she came too close, I thrust the silver dagger into her arm, and it struck a bone with a satisfying crack. She howled in pain and nearly tore the dagger out of my hand. She succeeded in laying her arm open from mid-bicep to elbow. She lashed out with her other arm and knocked me over onto one of the fallen tables.

As I stood up again, the vampire screamed in rage. A large red bubble enveloped him, holding him securely. The wererat saw the trap and turned to toward the door, jumping the distance in one easy graceful leap, landing in the room's entrance. She turned long enough to snarl at us, then swung the door open.

"Going somewhere, sister?" Geri growled. Her monster form was larger than her normal human form. She grabbed the wererat and threw her to the floor. Her muzzle snapped shut on the other's neck and she jerked once, severing her opponent's spine. The rat twitched, then lay still.

Apparently alone, Geri stepped on into the room, but I knew Terry and Larry were with her in their invisible cloaks. Stan and Janie came out of the office and moved toward us. Alex still had his invisibility cloak up.

"Stan, Hill, where are Char and Burn?" Geri asked as she resumed her normal human form. That her clothes appeared with her attested to her control over her changes and her status of a mage. Only a magewere or a true shifter can make clothing survive the change to and from their animal form.

"The vamps took Burn. We don't know where Char is. We thought he was with you," Fear clouded Stan's voice as he wrapped his arms around Janie.

"He was, until he teleported to wherever Burn is." Geri turned toward the captive vampire. "Maybe he can tell us where they were taken." She looked at me with the fierceness of a lioness defending her cubs. "Tal, how do we knock this guy out and get him back to the house?"

"That's easy, but first. Guys, is he the last one? Are you sure that there are no others around?" I asked Stan and Janie.

"Positive," Stan replied. "They took several corpses and Burn, then left these two to deal with us."

"Okay then, I'll gate us back to Geri's basement. We can return later for the cars. Alex, I'll need a little hand with this, I've already gated once tonight with the car, which isn't easy."

"Damn, you can gate that big Pathfinder of yours? I'm impressed." Stan said. "I thought that gating people was hard."

"Depends on distance a lot of the time and how familiar you are with the vehicle and the place you are going," I explained. "Also if you go through a gate, it's easier than if you're sending someone. I can do several short gates that I pass through a lot easier than I can a long gate that I just hold open for someone else. There are other tricks too that I can explain later. Like in most magic, adrenalin also helps a lot."

"No problem Tal." Alex said uncloaking. "I'm here."

At this point Terry and Larry also uncloaked, their faces pale and shaky. Obviously, a trip to the morgue with scattered dead bodies and missing friends was a bit more than they'd been ready to deal with. We stood in the middle of the torn up morgue with an enraged vampire snarling silently at us. They waited for me to make the next move.

"You guys are going to have to show me this silent trap spell. It's a new one on me," I said, reaching for Alex's hand. It settled into mine as naturally as if it had grown there. His energies and mine linked for the second time in one night. We merged easily as if we'd been doing it forever. I pulled him close as I opened the gate to Geri's basement. We stepped through together, following the others and the captive vampire.

Chapter Thirteen

ALEX AND I gated the gang back to Geri's basement. Fear darkened the captive vampire's eyes as it must have dawned on him who I was. My legend as a Coalition assassin had grown tremendously over the past few years. Once someone recognized me, it became difficult to ferret out my prey as they normally crawled into the smallest hole they could find and stayed there until they thought I'd given up. Now that he knew, his fate was sealed. If Geri and gang didn't kill him, I'd have to. We couldn't afford for Estaben to disappear on us.

Stan moved the captive, still bound in the spell sphere, over to the barber chair that held Robert Cooper the previous night. The sphere conformed to the chair as the two came into contact then shrunk, forcing the vampire to conform to the chair's shape. Janie moved in quickly, helping Stan bind the vampire physically. Even though the chair was no longer in the magical circle, the bindings would hold the vampire for the short time needed. Again, they amazed me with their ability to work in silence.

"Good." Geri said, as they finished. "We'll deal with him in a little while. Right now, we need to try and find Char and Burn. Stan, you and Hill try and locate Burn. Alex, you and Topper find Char. Tal, I won't ask you to give us a spell, but if you could help Weasel and me go through some of my books to find a spell that I know I've seen, I'd appreciate it."

"No problem, Geri." I replied as the others broke off into their pairs. Alex squeezed my hand briefly before walking to the corner of the room with Terry.

I followed Geri and Larry up to the first floor and into a room I hadn't yet seen. Geri's library held several heavily-laden bookshelves, two plush recliners and a small oak desk. She flicked a switch, turning on a row of ceiling lights that shined on the cases. Walking over to a shelf facing the door, she removed several leather-bound books. "I think the spell we're looking for is in one of these." She handed one to Larry and one to me. "See what you can find. I'm basically looking for a spell to pull them back using their psychic links to us."

With normal text, I generally speed read, which allows me to go through about three hundred pages in an hour, but it's not a good idea to do that with spell books. You can easily trip over things. After one experience blowing my eyebrows off while speed reading magic, I've never done it again.

I skimmed through the spells. This book was far more complex than I expected. Most human mages never get as far as the non-human mages in magic study due to age limitations. This book was one that I would've expected to find in either an extremely old human mage's care, a non-human mage, or a magical library where many mages had access to the books. In today's world, the only one I know of was in Scotland, where it was moved to during the Second World War when the Germans gathered much magical knowledge for the dark side. At the time, it was thought best to move it from Geneva where it had been for hundreds of years. As complex as it was, I couldn't find any usable teleportation spells that could pull the twins out of wherever they were. I did find the sphere spell they were using on the vampire down stairs, it was fairly simple. I was surprised I'd never run into before, or for that matter, thought of it myself.

"Nothing here," I said, breaking the silence as I closed the book.

"I think I have the right book," Geri said without lifting her head. She was already on her second book and scanning like a madwoman. She tried to hide it, but the loss of her students was hitting her pretty hard, and she wouldn't rest until they were back with her. Without question, Geri wanted all her coons up one tree.

"Good, cause it isn't here either," Larry said closing his book.

Neither Larry nor I bothered to get up, but watched in silence as Geri scanned. She slowed her page turning and we watched as she read over a spell twice. "This should work. Weasel, go to the storeroom, get the emergency locator kits for Char and Burn and meet us downstairs. Hopefully the others have made contact by now." She lifted the book from the table and headed out of the room.

I followed in her wake as she passed through the kitchen again and headed downstairs. Once more, the room lay silent as the vampire raged against his confinement. When I appeared, he became strangely still. Stan and Janie sat with their hands linked and eyes closed, their minds searching for the lost part of their triad. In the faint light, glistening tears trailed down Janie's soft pale face.

I glanced at Alex and Terry. Their search wasn't as focused, because their bond with Charles wasn't as strong as the triad bond. Their search was more like a fisherman casting a net. They knew who they searched for, but were having trouble finding him.

Larry appeared at the bottom of the stairs with two cedar cigar boxes. He handed one to me and gestured toward Alex and Terry. I opened the box and found a lock of hair, several pieces of cloth, a couple of samples of handwriting, a small zip-lock bag with nail clippings in it, and several dram vials of blood. Everything you'd need to find someone, or cast a heavily-focused spell on them was there. I touched Alex lightly on the shoulder to get his attention. He looked up, his green eyes weary. He reached for the box when he saw it and I moved back a step as he handed the lock of hair to Terry and took the bag of nail clippings for himself.

I glanced over my shoulder and saw Geri doing the same to the others. As she moved the box toward Stan, he shook his head briefly. "Got her," he whispered. Geri tensed and I knew she wanted to cheer.

"Can you move into the circle without losing her?" she asked

Stan nodded. Then without breaking contact, he and Janie slowly stood up as one, and moved toward the circle.

Geri hastily gathered things from the cabinet that sat in a cubby under the stairs.

"Would you like help?" I asked barely above a whisper.

"Watch over Alex." She looked up at me, her arms laden with jars, pots, and candles. She smiled. "Get used to it. You'll be doing it for a long time to come," she whispered and then dashed for the circle.

I went back to my place behind Alex. It felt much more natural and I could feel how he and Terry focused their search through the parts of Charles they now possessed. Still, they came up empty.

I turned, feeling the circle go up behind me. With Stan and Janie seated in front of the altar, Geri again laid the salt out around the edge of the circle. She took one of the vials of blood from the box, intoned a series of words over the small cauldron that sat next to the altar, held the vial up and tossed some herbs into the empty cauldron. She then picked up the cauldron and placed it between Stan and Janie who shifted slightly to make room. She reached into the energies flowing between the two of them and Bernadette and wrapped those energies into the cauldron. As the energies swelled around her, she raised the vial above her head then cast it into the cauldron. As the energies swirled even faster around her, Stan and Janie pulled with her and she shortened the connection between the three of them. Then, Bernadette lay in the circle with them.

She was naked and had long scratches down what I could see of her back. Her blue hair was almost purple with the amount of blood matted in it. She still lived, but she was badly hurt. Stan and Janie broke contact and moved in next to her. They placed their hands on her, drew energies up from the earth and a blue aura surrounded all three. They were trying to heal her. Stan jerked as a long scratch appeared on his neck above his collar as they tried to take her pain and wounds into themselves. That was always very risky. If the wounds are too extensive, all people involved can be lost. I was just an observer, but I suddenly realized, that if it were Alex in that circle dying I'd have done the same thing.

As I watched, Geri poured more herbs into the cauldron and tossed in a match. The cauldron blazed to life next to the three caught in the grip of the healing. Power poured out of the flames and Geri washed it over her students. Soon all wounds began to fade as she forced them along with the magic down into the earth.

Sweat covered everyone in the circle as Geri stood from where she'd fallen to her knees. She picked up her athame from the altar and dismissed the circle. The last of the magical energies flowed back to the earth.

Bernadette had fallen into a deep sleep that she'd need to complete the healing, the magic started. Stan and Janie looked like they were ready to fall over, too. I glanced back at Alex and Terry, they were still searching.

"Can you two help them get upstairs?" Geri asked Larry and me.

I nodded, crossed the boundaries of the circle and cradled Bernadette's limp body in my arms. She was covered in sweat, but her life force felt steady. She weighed less than Alex, and I could have easily helped with the others, but Larry went to Stan and Janie to stand between them as they wobbled on weak knees. Once he had them balanced with hands on either shoulder, I started for the stairs, heading for the room we'd put Alex in the previous night.

Stan and Janie stumbled several times behind me on the stairs, but Larry proved stable enough to get them up without dropping them. Once on the level floor, they moved more easily. We made it to the bedroom, and I lay Bernadette on the bed. Her skin was still pale and I gave her a quick once over for bite marks. I couldn't find any, and if any of the scratches were weremade then hopefully, the intense magical healing she'd just undergone would purge the lycanthropy from her system. Stan and Janie quickly disrobed, unmindful of Larry and myself in the room, and crawled into the bed on either side of her.

I touched Larry on the shoulder and gestured for the door. We walked out to the sounds of light kisses and heavy tears. I knew that soon the three would be in a much-needed sleep. The magic had taken a lot out of Stan and Janie, and the battering Bernadette had undergone would take time to totally repair. Through the strength of their triad, they'd survive and be stronger for their ordeal. Now, if we could only get Charles back.

When we returned to the basement, Geri readied the circle to try for Charles. Alex and Terry walked toward the circle and Geri motioned me to enter with them. "Alex is a little below his peak tonight after everything you two have been through. Can you stay in here and back him up?"

Like she had to ask. "Yes," I said, sitting down protectively behind him as she closed the circle.

The link to Charles was weaker than the link to Bernadette had been. Geri had to work hard to get it to the point where she could connect it to the cauldron. Alex pushed himself to strengthen the link with his friend. Sweat beaded on Terry's forehead as I added my strength to Alex's. Alex pushed out to get a better hold of Charles, but something in the contact didn't feel right. We felt Charles' pain. From what I could tell, he was not conscious as we touched his mind because our contact was met with a fog. Geri began to draw the power around the cauldron as she'd done with Bernadette, but it was weaker. I tried to strengthen the link, but it wasn't the same as the triad bond. Alex was there with me, pulling to get more of Charles to us. Terry reached out with us as the three of us sought to get a better hold. It was like trying to grasp a length of twine with heavy gloves.

Then, as Geri threw the vial of blood in the cauldron, another presence came to fight us. She was human. That much was blatantly clear. Her magic was powerful, but dark. She'd waited for the blood to be tossed and used the blood to her advantage. Alex screamed as she severed the link they'd formed to Charles and a flaming sword flashed down toward the link that still existed between Alex and Terry. I threw up a shield using Alex's energies augmented with my own. I hoped she wouldn't realize I boosted Alex. If she did, my invisibility in Yellow Sky would be neutralized.

Alex thrust Terry from the fray. He and I stood facing the sorceress with the flaming sword.

"Your friend is mine," she gloated. "I let you take his sister. This one I think I'll keep. There is such darkness in him, darkness even he doesn't realize he has." She laughed.

A katana of light appeared in Alex's hand. "He's one of mine, and I don't feel like letting him go just because you want to claim him." He charged. I carefully shrank my connection with him to make it invisible, but toughened it so she shouldn't be able to accidentally sever it and pumped all the power I could into him while making myself invisible on the astral plane.

His katana bounced off her hastily-erected shield. She lashed out with a bolt of energy, which I helped him deflect with the sword, but the shock sent shivers down his arm.

Then Geri was there. She smashed her coyote form into the shield, howling and scratching at it. Then she stopped and sat down and peered at the slender blonde on the other side.

The sorceress laughed again. "How sweet, your dog comes to your rescue. Lassie go home." She shot another bolt of energy directly at Geri. A rock rose out of the ground and deflected the bolt.

"You'll have to do better than that, bitch!" Geri growled. Larry and Terry appeared at her side, heavily shielded and carrying glowing swords of their own.

"I'm really not in the mood to deal with all of you right now. So, I'll say my farewells for now. Please tell Burn I'll enjoy Char." She shot a poorly-aimed leven bolt past us, then vanished.

Geri quickly pulled everyone back to the physical plane.

"Sorry to take so long getting there to you, but I had to let Weasel into the circle first. I figured we needed all the backup we had at the moment. But now we're going to have to rely on more mundane methods to find Char." Geri rattled as she prepared to bring the circle down, and soon, the real world rushed in along with the stench of charred flesh. The vampire in the chair had turned into a pile of ash. The sorceress' parting shot hadn't been aimed at us, but to the vampire we held captive. She destroyed him before he could give us any information. At least we still had the werewolf in the bottle.

It had been a long night already, and I was tired, hungry, and still had to get Alex home safe and sound.

Chapter Fourteen

CONSIOUSNESS RETURNED with a shock for the second day in a row. Someone's arm lay across my chest. I'd long ago got over the react-first response when awakened in such a manner. Instead, I took a long deep breath and a mental check from the previous night. Alex's scent filled my nostrils. I glanced down, and it certainly looked like his hairy arm. Then I remembered that Geri suggested that he stay with me while Larry and Terry stayed with her to watch over Bernadette, Stan and Janie.

Alex, Larry, and I took a cab from Geri's to the hospital. I hadn't felt up to another gate at the time. Once Alex and I retrieved the Pathfinder, and Larry had gotten Geri's car, I drove out of town again. I needed to hunt. I fed for the third time in two nights on a large deer just north of town. I hadn't needed to feed three times in two nights in a very long time. These people were putting me through the ringer. Alex fell asleep right after we got in the car, so I hadn't needed to explain my dual nature to him...yet. I distinctly remember putting Alex in the guestroom that was set up before going to bed myself shortly after sunrise. I glanced at the clock and it read 6:30. It would be sundown soon. I guess Alex snuck in sometime during the day.

I lay there just breathing in his scent. I was almost afraid to move and wake him, but I turned my head and gazed at him in his sleep. He looked young. His tosseled red hair looked more like he'd been in a strong wind and his piercing, often challenging, green eyes lay hidden behind long, lush, rusty-red lashes that many women would die for. Rapid movement behind his lids made me wonder what he dreamed. A heavy dusting of red stubble covered his cheeks and chin. I stopped myself from tracing a finger down his sharp cheekbone, but I couldn't resist gently laying my hand on his firm chest. It wasn't overly muscular, but no one would call him skinny either. He had the potential to have a large chest, but somehow he seemed perfectly sculpted this way. The dense hair was soft to my touch. I just lay there feeling his heart beat with my hand rising with his breathing.

We lay that way while I waited for him to wake up. He didn't move again, but stayed with his arm thrown across my chest while my hand rode his. I wanted to take him in my arms and hold him, but I was afraid to wake him. Even as my neck stiffened, I enjoyed watching him sleep too much for that. After the turbulent days we'd just survived, it was nice to just relax.

My memories reminded me of the heartache that could be waiting for me down the road, but if it meant moments like this, it was worth it. I was amazed I'd let myself go without companionship for so long. Books and teaching can only carry you so far. I was beginning to see that now. To really live, you needed companions, people around you who you could love and who loved you back. Gods, I really was falling in love with this handsome mage.

The phone rang, breaking my thoughts. I rolled over and snatched the receiver off the cradle as Alex muttered something behind me.

"Tal?" Before I could say anything, Geri's urgent voice was on the other end.

"Yes Geri, I'm here."

"Thank the Goddess. Weasel just woke up and had a dream that Alex was gone and no one could find him." The words sent a chill down my spine. "I promised I'd call you and make sure you were both alright."

Alex wrapped his arms around me and pulled himself against my back as I talked to her. Shivers shot through my body at his touch. It made me want to hang up the phone and just lay there with him holding me in his strong arms. "We're both fine. Just starting to get up and around."

"We are all about up over here. Larry and Terry's mom called earlier to make sure everything's okay with them. I'm getting ready to go over and see Charles and Bernadette's mother to let her know what happened. I want to assure her that as soon as Bernadette's up for it, we'll try again using the twin link between the two of them. I'm worried the longer we wait, the smaller the chance to get him back." She was babbling, definitely struggling with the potential loss of one of her students.

"Geri, would you like Alex and me to go with you?" Alex began running his hands through the dark hair on my chest, his touch leaving tingles as it passed.

"No, I'll be fine." Her voice nearly cracked.

"Geri, have you had any sleep?"

"A little, I've been pouring over the books trying to find anything that might help." Her shaky voice betrayed her feeling of failure.

"Geri, we did what we could with our resources last night. Everyone'll be stronger tonight, and we can start as soon as Bernadette wakes. I know a few spells that'll help without draining her too badly." Alex's fingers found my right nipple and he tweaked it playfully.

"I appreciate any help you can give. I was expecting vampires only, not werewolves and sorceresses too. I'm afraid we might be out of our league here." There, she voiced some of her fear.

"Geri, at this point, it might be a good idea if I got a little more active in all this. I think I should go from being an observer to an assistant for you and the gang." Alex gave a soft cheer behind me and kissed the back of my neck. It sent a major shock down my spine.

"Thank you Tal. With your direct help, I know we can do this." Her voice strengthened a little. "Is Alex where I can talk to him for a second? I'll see you two when I get back from seeing Dani Colfax."

"Sure Geri, he's right behind me." I smiled as I rolled over to hand him the phone. "Geri wants to talk to you."

He took the phone in his right hand, but kept the left wrapped around me. "Hey Geri. Doesn't sound like it's going great today, but with Tal's help, we'll get in there and kick some ass."

He paused while she responded. I heard her voice but couldn't make out the words. I made no move to shift out of his embrace, but pulled him closer to me, as our legs brushed I realized that he still wore his jeans. That was probably a good thing. We needed to talk a lot more before things went too far.

"Okay Geri, we'll be at your place in a little while. Should we eat before we get there?" He ground his body against me as she responded. A big smile covered his face and his eyes danced gaily.

"Sounds like a plan. See you guys in a bit." He reached across me to put the receiver back on the charger.

I rolled slightly so that he could reach easier. This put him lying across me. His weight felt good and our auras meshed naturally. He laid his head on my shoulder and took a deep breath. I could tell he enjoyed the feeling as well. We lay there for several minutes, just feeling each other. He turned his head slightly and placed a light kiss on my neck and then kissed his way up to my mouth. I pulled him in so tightly as we kissed that I feared for a second I'd break him, but his strong arms held me tightly as well. I think we were both afraid to be the one to back off first. I let up on my embrace enough that he could pull away if he wanted. He used the opportunity to run his hands over my chest again. I pushed his tongue out of my mouth with my own and felt the inside of his mouth. I caught his hands as they began to slide inside the shorts I had put on before climbing into bed.

"Not yet. We don't have time." I whispered in his ear as I nibbled on it.

"Ah, not even a feel?" There was a tease in his voice as his hand slid across the outside of my shorts. "Nice," he whispered.

I returned the gesture because I could. What I felt matched what I'd seen on the astral plane. "Very nice." I breathed into his ear. "But we need to get going. When this is all over, I promise you a night you'll never forget."

"Hopefully the first of many." He smiled before crushing his mouth to mine again. He pulled away more quickly this time. "I get the first shower. Unless you want to wash my back. It would be faster." He teased as he headed for the bathroom.

"You go ahead. I need to check in with the office." I called after him.

He turned on the light, but left the door open.

I rolled back over and picked up the phone. It'd be after dark in Scotland, but everybody should be awake and in the office.

Instead of calling Beth first, I called straight to J.P.'s office.

Tasha, his secretary, picked up. "Coalition, J.P. Montgomery's office, this is Tasha how can I help you."

"Hey Tasha, its Tal, is J.P. in?"

"Hey Tal, how's stuff in Yellow Sky? About got the whole thing wrapped up yet?" She was one of those secretaries who almost always sounded up and perky. It could be really irritating at the wrong time.

"Not even close."

"Sorry to hear that. Just a moment, I think J.P.'s available." She put me on hold. Classical music played this time. Last time I called, it was some New Age retro stuff that was supposed to be British tribal music. I'd been there; it wasn't British tribal. Not even close.

"Tal, how's it going out in Texas? Beth says there's a growing body count. Is the Beggay woman and her group going to be able to handle everything or not?" J.P. sounded gruff, but then a three-hundred-year-old alpha bear shifter couldn't help it.

"Yes, and I was wondering how old your info on this situation out here is?" I knew better than to sound angry over the phone with J.P.. He'd get defensive. If you're going to get defensive with J.P., do it in person and be sure that you can back it up or he'll rip your head off, literally. I saw him do it one time when I stopped by HQ and a junior field agent got in his face about the working conditions in an observation station for one of the African tribal units. I think the guy had been a vamp, but J.P. grabbed him after the guy started yelling and ripped the head right off his shoulders. Luckily, he's only had to do it twice so far. Most everyone has learned to stay out of his face with tones he might not like to hear.

"Let me see here." I could hear him accessing his computer. "By the cave," he swore under his breath. "Tal, I'm sorry. It appears that the intelligence on this one is a bit old. Last update was about six weeks ago other than what Beth added the past couple of days. Is there a problem?"

"Only a couple. First, are you aware that Geraldine Beggay is now a werecoyote?"

"Really? Why didn't she update her petition for membership? She's in. I'll get Tasha to send the information over to Kyle in roles right away. And send out the official welcome kit and instruction manual. What else?"

"She didn't update her petition because she wanted to make sure that her students made it into the Coalition as well. And as far as what else, does your info say anything about a sorceress working with Estaben de'Oro?" The sound of his heavy hands mashing the keys of his keyboard as he updated the files while we talked carried easily across our connection.

"No, according to our records there shouldn't be a sorceress working in that area. A couple of minor witches, and of course the Beggay woman and her people. Oh and a high magician, but he's of no threat based on his file. He's been strung out on something he brewed up years ago." There was no hiding the disdain in his voice that he felt for the substance abuse so common among many magic users. I always felt it was a way to help limit the numbers of the ones who wouldn't make good mages.

"Could you please find out if there is a sorceress that's not where she's supposed to be? Her astral form was blonde, buxom and carrying a mean flaming sword."

"I'll see, but you know how misleading astral forms can be."

I sighed. I reminded myself that he was a bear at heart, but not the teddy bear sort. "I know, but we can at least find out who it might be. And lastly, due to changes in the situation, I'd like your permission to be a more active participant in this whole thing and let me decide if the coven warrants membership once this is done. So far, what I have seen from them is impressive. Geraldine Beggay is a good teacher and her students are well chosen."

"I don't see a problem with that Tal. Sorry for not having more up-to-date intelligence on this one. I'll have a talk with the guys down in intelligence about that later. Heads may roll." He growled and then paused. "Tal, Tasha just handed me a note here." He paused again. "It seems that Marion Shearwood, you know that pretty little vampire who's had the crush on you for as long as I've been around, had a vision last night of you as a groom in a wedding. Do you know anything about this?"

I tried not to choke on the phone. Marion was one of the best seeresses around. She'd been an Oracle at Delphi, and had been after me for centuries since we meet around the time of the second fall of Rome. It always amazed me how blind some psychics could be, but Marion was rarely wrong. "J.P., I have no idea what she's talking about. Does it say if she got a look at the other groom?" I lied, I normally don't do that to J.P., but this was all getting a little too much for me right now. I did not need the whole magical community sending Alex and I down the aisle before we had even gotten past the case we were working on.

"Nope. I'll send her a message and let you know in email. If anything else comes up just give me a ring and I'll see what I can do. Let the Beggay woman know you can help and that she has been added to the roles of the Coalition. I expect her to fill out the updated data form I'm sending her in email."

"Thanks J.P.. I'll keep you posted as this goes along. By the way, do you have a damage control team ready just in case we end up with a high body count on this one?"

He huffed. "Try not to let that happen. But yes, I can have damage control on the way in a matter of hours. There's already a major viral outbreak planned for the area if we need it. We're all hopping you can prevent the need for that."

"I'll do my best, but we already have a growing body count. Estaben's acolytes are apparently on a spree changing as many people as they can. I have already encountered one orphaned fledgling vampire."

"Did you dispatch it, or what?" The growl returned to his voice.

"I sent him on to one of the fledglings I trained years ago in New York. He's in good hands with David." I knew David would do the best he could for Robert.

"Ah yes, David Cox, good choice. I'll see that our roles officer in New York contacts them and gets him registered at once. Anything else tonight, Tal?" The overwhelming sound of dismissal filled his voice.

"No J.P., that should be all for the moment. If anything else comes up, I'll call, or have Beth let you know. Thanks." I tried to sound cheerful, but I really hated being dismissed.

"I know you'll handle the situation properly. Goodnight, Tal." J.P. hung up.

I sighed and lay back on the bed, listening to Alex in the shower. I smiled envisioning the water cascade over his body. I heard the water turn off and resisted the urge to walk in there and watch him come out of the shower.

"Hey Tal," he called. "You off the phone yet?"

"Yes."

"Do you keep a razor around here? I don't want to dig around too much."

Another sigh escaped as I pushed myself off the bed. "Coming."

"Not yet," he laughed.

Where was my nice quiet life in the mountains with my library?

Chapter Fifteen

WE ARRIVED at Geri's just as she returned from speaking with the Dani Colfax. We'd stopped by Alex's to get some clean clothes and he took the time to pack a gym bag in case of a repeat of last night, or so he said with a smile. He made a show of changing in front of me, and though I refrained from making any comments, I enjoyed the exhibition immensely. He looked very nice in the skin-tight black jeans with the burgundy t-shirt under a forest green dress shirt. I wondered how many of his choices were for my benefit, but since I had no choice in the whole matter of a relationship with him, I relaxed. There was a lot to enjoy while he was around.

We took a moment to let his parents know that he may be out without warning and they might need to make sure the shop opened on Monday. We went through a drive-in burger joint to get him food that he devoured as we drove. I hoped that it'd be a few nights before I needed to feed again, but the way things were going, the odds weren't in my favor.

Geri watched us drive up, leaning against her Volkswagen while I parked. She looked like she'd been through the ringer. Her face had more lines than the night before and her gray hair appeared thinner.

Alex took her in his arms and gave her a big hug.

I patted her arm in an attempt to be reassuring.

"How did Dani take the news?" Alex asked softly.

From the streaked mascara, Geri'd been crying. "Better than I hoped. She just sat there as I explained what happened and shook her head saying she was afraid something like this would happen. She partially blames herself for bringing Ted home last night. I tried to tell her it wasn't her fault. If anyone is at fault, it's me." Her voice cracked. She laid her head on Alex's shoulder.

Alex tightened his embrace. "Geri, it's not your fault. It's no one's fault but Estaben de'Oro's. If he wasn't trying to do whatever it is that he's trying to do here, we wouldn't be trying to stop him. And if it weren't us standing here then it would be some other poor fool, or even Tal by himself. Together we have a *chance* of making sure that the forces of light prevail. Alone, we'd all fall to the darkness."

"Would someone get me a tissue, I think I might cry." A high-pitched voice mocked from above. As one, we looked up and saw the astral form of the blonde sorceress floating just above the rose bushes in front of the house.

"What do you want bitch!" Geri growled, stepping out of Alex's embrace and advancing toward the astral form, tears dried by anger.

"Just stopped by to make sure I had the right house and witnessed your little display. You goodie-two-shoes people are too much for me. That was almost enough to make me switch sides. Almost, but not quite. I'll let Chucky pooh know that you're already mourning him. I'm sure he'll be touched," she laughed and then vanished before Geri could touch her.

"Damn, this isn't good. She's figured out where I live," Geri muttered, as we headed into the house. "She got through the outermost shields. And she still has Charles."

"Do you have another place to do magic?" I asked knowing they probably didn't want to do magic somewhere they might be attacked while working.

"We have a couple of possibilities," Alex explained. He opened the front door for Geri. "We each have our own private working areas. There's the shop, a piece of land out in the country that Larry and Terry's folks own and they let us do things on, and there are a couple of spots out in some of the wild public lands that we use sometimes."

"What just happened?" Terry ran down the hall from the bedrooms into the kitchen.

"We just had a visit from the sorceress who has Charles," Geri said, settling into her chair at the table. "This house isn't safe right, now. How are Stan, Janie, and Bernadette?"

"Stan and Hill woke up right after you left," he explained, his voice taking on an almost frantic tone. "They've both showered and eaten and they're in with Burn now. Her aura's better, but she's still not awake."

"I'll look at her and see if we can move her." I said. "Alex, why don't you fix Geri a cup of tea? Then we can start getting things ready to move out."

"We need to move that fast?" Alex asked, fear touching his handsome face.

"I think so. If I were Estaben, I'd move as soon as I found out where my enemies were. So far, we have cost him one werewolf, one wererat and three vampires. We're definitely proving to be a threat. They may be on the way now." Gods, I was taking charge. "We'll need to move soon, but I think the tea will help Geri's nerves."

"I can fix the tea," Geri replied getting out of the chair she'd slumped in. "Alex run down to the work room. Get the emergency travel kits, all of them. Terry, go to the library and get the outdoor spell books, then set the trap spells around the place. Don't forget to grab that damned bottled messenger of Tal's. We'll need to deal with it soon."

"Sounds like a plan," I said. "By the way, where's Larry?"

"He's run to the house to get some clothes and let Mom see that we're okay," Terry replied as he headed for the library.

I walked to the room where we had left Stan, Janie and Bernadette. As I entered, Stan stood up off the edge of the bed where he had been sitting next to Bernadette. Janie laid on her other side.

"What's going on?" Stan asked

"The sorceress from last night has found the house." I didn't sugar coat anything. It was best if they knew exactly what was going on. "We're going to have to move elsewhere until this is over. Have we had any change in Bernadette?"

Stan sighed. "Well it looked like she might be waking a little while ago, but she slipped back into a deep sleep. It feels like she's getting better and her thoughts are no longer filled with the pain from last night." He looked down at his sleeping lover with concern in his eyes.

"That's good." To my mage sight, her aura was strong. It appeared that most of the physical healing had been done. Upon closer inspection, there were several cords running off her aura. The two strongest ran to Stan and Janie.

"Give me just a moment here." I said, before looking deeply enough to follow the other strands. I found the one that ran to Geri, and one to Alex, and then others to the rest of the gang. That left two strands that I couldn't account for. I pushed further down the largest remaining one and found her mother. That left a small almost unnoticeable strand. There should have been a large strand leading to Charles, but I couldn't find it. Then, I noticed a large but camouflaged hole in her aura where a massive cord had been yanked out. This had been her connection to Charles. Before Geri, Stan, and Janie had retrieved her, someone severed the link and patched it over so that we wouldn't notice until either Bernadette awoke, or someone did this kind of check. I looked back to the smallest cord and followed it as I had the cords in my own aura the previous day. It ended in a wall. I could guess what the wall protected.

I called my own astral sword, an astral embodiment of a sword I had carried centuries before, after it had been given to an ill-fated leader of the English isles. The sword of dragons flamed to life in my hands. I severed the cord, then released the sword and returned to my physical body.

As I refocused on the physical world, Bernadette's eyes flew open. "Where is Char? I can't feel Charles! Something has happened! *Geri*!" She sat up frantically. Her physical and mental voice echoed through the house. Janie tried to maintain contact, but Bernadette pushed her aside, almost tumbling her off the bed.

Stan took her face in his hands. "Burn, please try to stay calm." Calming empathic energies flowed off the oldest of the trio. "We're trying to find Char. We couldn't get him back when we got you back last night."

Geri rushed into the room. "I take it she woke up?" She too projected a calming air. "Burn, we're doing what we can. What can you tell us?"

Bernadette took a deep breath, and let it out slowly. "We were taken by surprise when vampires showed up at the morgue. They had some werefolk with them or they might've been shifters...I don't know. I was across the room from Stan and Hill and they got between us. One of their guys managed to get the drop on me. I remember being carried down the hall by one of the wers and tossed in a van with several corpses they stole from the morgue. I seem to remember Char being there somehow and, there was some blonde bitch who told me to sleep. Then I woke up here."

"Okay, here's what happened on our end," Geri started, as Janie and Stan settled in around the calmer Bernadette. "We got your distress call and headed out toward you. Part of the way there, Charles yelled something and teleported out of the car. Luckily, he wasn't driving at the time. When we got to the morgue, we found Stan and Janie. You and Charles were nowhere around. After we defeated the remaining bad guys, we got back here and used your link to Stan and Janie to bring you back to us. That tantric magic you guys have been working paid off in other ways. We tried to retrieve Charles the same way using Alex and Terry with help from Tal, but the blonde sorceress intervened and stopped us from rescuing him last night. You've been unconscious all day with Stan and Janie giving you healing energies."

"You woke up after I severed the psychic link that the sorceress had attached to you," I added for everyone to know.

"Good," Geri continued "Now, this evening I spoke to your mother and you are supposed to call her when you wake up. She's worried about both of you, but you can at least give her an update on your condition. Also, the blonde bitch paid us a visit in astral form. She knows where I live, so this house is no longer safe. We're going to get out of here as soon as we get a few things gathered up and can hit the road. Burn you need to get a bite to eat and call your mother. Actually, I'll get you food, you call her now."

"So where are we going?" Stan asked as he handed the phone off the bed stand to Bernadette.

"I was thinking that the rim would be a good spot. It is a nice night out and it's far enough out, no one should bother us. It'll give us time to think about what we're going to do. And we'll have enough energy there that we can tap into to get things done tonight, if we decide on something."

"Sounds like a good plan," Alex said, coming into the room. He walked immediately to my side.

I resisted the urge to put my arm around his waist and draw him closer. "I'd also advise that we take different cars and different routes out there so that we'll be harder to follow. All of us going out there in masse will leave one hell of a psychic trail."

"We have enough cars and able-bodied drivers. I say we travel in three groups," Geri thought out loud. "Weasel and Topper can come with me. Alex and Tal together, and Stan can take Hill and Burn. If anything happens to anyone, send up psi-flares and we'll come back for you. Stan, you take the short route down the middle. I'll drive the southern route and Alex, you two use the northern route." She finished off her tea. "I'll get Burn some food to take with her. Burn, call your mother. The rest of us will break the emergency gear into three sets, so that not all of anything is riding with one person." She turned and headed down the hall with Alex, Terry, and myself in tow.

"Good plan Geri," I said as we walked. "The only thing I wonder about is sending the triad off by themselves. Are they ready, in case of emergency?"

"Their bonds are tighter than I realized," she explained. "I think they'll be stronger together than if we separate them, and I'd rather have three cars instead of two, just in case." She rummaged through the cabinets.

"You know them better than I do," I replied as she took several power bars out of the cupboard.

"Run these down to Burn," Geri ordered. "They're the best we can do right now. We'll try and stop at an all-night spot I know on the way back. Here take this, too." She tossed me a large bottle of sports drink from the refrigerator.

I hurried down the hall and found Stan and Janie helping Bernadette dress. I handed the food and drink off and they said they'd be out in a minute. I went back to the kitchen. Larry was back, and Alex and the others had piled a stack of small wooden boxes and binders on the table and were shoving most of them into backpacks.

"Our emergency spell kits," he explained and flipped one open so that I could see the small vials of herbs, candles and other things that would be useful in spell casting. I guessed the binders were the outdoor spell books. I took the pack Alex was loading and held it while he piled a couple more boxes in along with two of the binders.

When we were done, the other two piles had also been put into the backpacks, and Stan, Janie, and Bernadette stood in the room.

"Okay, we're ready." Geri said. They gathered around her for a group hug, Alex caught my hand and pulled me in too. The energies were strong and pleasant. They felt like family and it had been a long time since I'd had family ties. My dragon mother died when I was born and my druid father died over a thousand years ago. Silently, I hoped this wouldn't be the last time this little family banded together.

"We all know where we're going and how we're getting there," Geri added. "Good luck and may Mercury speed us on our way." She picked up a big travel mug of tea she'd set on the table and swung one of the backpacks over her shoulder before she headed toward the street.

A howl rent the darkness as we stepped out of the door. All of the streetlights were out, up and down the street not a single porch light or street light shone. Another howl shredded the night.

"Crap, they're already here!" Larry said.

"Which of you is the best shot with a gun?" I asked as I raced to the truck. Thinking we'd be faced with more werecreatures, I'd packed a little assistance. I was tired of wasting good magical energies on werecreatures if I didn't need to. Silver bullets worked just as well with less energy expenditure.

I pulled the back door open just as the first werewolf loped into view. It was a large one. He chose to come in monster form, that in-between form not quiet human, but more than a little wolf, which offered high fright value. I grabbed the first pistol I'd stashed under Alex's bag on the floorboard. The werewolf had almost reached the car when I straightened, fired and splattered his brains halfway down the block. These new firearms with powerful ammo that delivered lots of punch beat the hell out of flintlocks any day.

Multiple howls erupted up and down the block as several more werewolves appeared from behind cars and hedges. I tossed the gun I had just fired to Terry as he stopped at my side. I also handed him a handful of silver bullets. "Silver, cover the others as they get to the cars. There may be vampires with them as well, silver won't slow them down much, so don't waste your shots there." Another wolf charged in full wolf form, leaping over the truck at us. Terry fired, catching it in the chest as it cleared the roof. "Good shot." I pulled out another gun for myself, and then I felt a chill I hadn't felt in a very long time. I looked up and the werewolf whose head I'd blown off stood up. The damaged head hung loosely over his right shoulder. The gore that bubbled down his chest from the open neck added to the horror of the monster form. We now faced zombie werewolves along with the live werewolves to heighten the fright value even more.

Zombies are nasty to deal with and the sorceress who can create them from a distance is very powerful. I was about to call a fire ball when one flashed past me, striking the werewolf in the chest sending it back down the road in a blaze of burning fur. I flash fired the one under my feet before it could get up.

Stan signaled to Bernadette and Janie that the car was clear and they piled into it. Geri set a magical shield around it that glowed with the silver dust she tossed from smoking hands. Then Stan backed the car out of the drive. Two wolves rushed it as it headed down the street. They screamed in pain as they hit the shield much like a cow hitting the cattle guards they put on trains in the old days. They flew to the sides with long burns striping their fur. Terry took out the one on the left while I took out the one on the right and Geri followed our shots with fire bolts.

Alex tossed his bag in the back seat of the Pathfinder and took up a position at my back. "I think there are only a couple more," he whispered.

"I agree." I counted three that I could sense. That didn't mean there weren't more, but that was all that I could detect. And so far, I couldn't sense any vampires. That surprised me.

"We're clear here!" Larry called from Geri's car after checking it for lurkers and tossing the backpacks into the trunk.

"We'll cover you then!" I hollered as they piled into the car. The werewolf behind the fence in the next yard decided to make his move at that point, looking like a creamy comet streaking over the fence. Terry saw the movement and fired out of the passenger side window, catching him in the shoulder and sending him rolling off the hood of the car. Geri slammed the car into reverse and the little red Beetle buzzed out of the driveway. Before the werewolf could get up, I fired a clean shot into his heart, tearing his chest neatly apart. Alex delivered the flaming coup-de-gras.

That left two more on the other side of the house. They were probably hoping we didn't know they were there, but too late. Werecreatures leave a distinctive magical feel. It was different from shifters or regular humans. I did a quick scan and unless someone or something was well shielded, these were the last.

I gestured for Alex to follow me, and we headed around to the where the wers were hiding. A burst of speed carried me around the corner before the first one could react. My bullet caught him square in the head. Unfortunately, the second one moved a bit faster than I planned, and Alex's fire bolt for the first one only singed the second. He caught me square in the shoulder, knocking me to the ground.

"Tal!" Alex screamed, then the weight of the werewolf lifted off me. It flew into the side of Geri's house, slamming the wall repeatedly.

I got up and laid a hand on Alex's shoulder. "I'm okay, and he's dead now. You pummeled him to the point that I don't think he'll be able to be raised either. We need to go."

Alex turned and threw his arms around me. "I'm sorry, I thought you were hurt and I just reacted. I know better than to do that, but I was scared you were hurt." His voice shook, tears threatening.

I returned the embrace, and kissed him. "You did fine. Sometimes we have to just react. It's okay, and so am I. But now, we need to be going if we are going to meet the others."

Energies washed over me as Geri reached out from a distance to lock down the shields around her home. Nothing would enter without her knowing about it, and even then, there'd be some nasty surprises awaiting anything that did. Alex straightened as he felt the energies too.

"We need to get, before we get stuck here or have to break something to get out," he said stepping out of our embrace.

I checked the car before we climbed in to make sure that nothing snuck in while we were busy with the other wolves. We were clean. I reloaded the gun while Alex climbed into the front seat, then I followed. Once the doors were closed and locked, he pulled me into another embrace and kissed me roughly. "I feel safe with you," he whispered before settling in next to me as I put the car in gear.

I wrapped my arm around his shoulders. "I'll be here for you. You watch my back, I'll watch yours and together we can get out of just about anything." I don't know where that came from, but it felt like the right thing to say as we drove off into the night.

Chapter Sixteen

WE DROVE in silence through the desert night. Occasionally Alex would give me directions, or let me know that the others were still alright, but mostly he scanned our surroundings in silence as we sped to our rendezvous point. He plastered himself to my side and stayed there. As we drove, the waves of fear coming off of him lessened. I should've been talking him through his emotions, but sometimes, dealing with one's fears is a very important part of growing up. A mother can tell a child there's no monster under the bed, but until the child looks and either sees no monster or confronts the thing in whatever form it might take, the creature under the bed is still to be feared. Alex and his group had faced things in the past, but from my understanding, nothing like this. Here were the monsters under the bed and they were something to be very afraid of. So, I just kept my arm across his shoulder and drove where he directed me.

Once the last of the city lights faded behind us, he roused slightly and kissed the curve of my neck. "There's nothing following us. We got away. Thank you for being here for me."

I ran my hand through his soft, thick, red hair. "Whenever you need me I'll be here." I said softly. "Is everybody else clear too?"

"Topper says there is nothing near them, but they're just clearing the last populated area. Hill also reports all clear, and they're ahead of us. The road they took intersects with the one we're on about ten miles down."

I grabbed his shoulder to keep him from sliding forward as I slammed on the breaks to avoid hitting a small herd of mule deer that bounded across the road in front of us. Before we started again, I pulled him close and kissed him. "You were very brave back there. Most people would've frozen. You know, that's what they're hoping.

That's why they chose the half form. It causes more fear than either of the full forms."

"The werewolves don't bother me. They pissed me off. But I've never faced a zombie before. I've heard of them. Most of the voodoo people stay out of our area, and the one time I went to Louisiana, I managed to avoid them. It's an abomination. Those poor souls should go on to their next turn of the wheel, not trapped here kept in rotting corpses. And how did she do it? In the little bit that Geri has told us about voodoo, the necromancer has to be close to the corpse to animate it. Even then, it has to have been dead a certain period of time." He shivered as I started the truck back down the road.

"I've been thinking about that. The only thing I can think of is she placed the spell on them while they were still alive just in case they were killed. Zombies are harder to destroy than wers. And, if we hadn't been prepared, they would've slowed us down enough for the whole pack to rally. The other question that I had is, where were the vampires? If she's aligned with Estaben it would make sense that there would've been vampires there too, but she only sent werewolves. We were also missing the other wers. We know that there are wererats working with them."

Alex stared out into the darkness for a moment before answering. "Maybe the vampires and other wers had something else to do, or maybe they don't view us as enough of a threat to send more than pack of werewolves."

"I guess Estaben is going to know I'm involved soon if he doesn't already. He'll acknowledge a threat then." I knew then what Alex was about to ask. It was the part of all of this that I had hoped to keep hidden as long as possible.

"Tal, what is your real relationship with Estaben?" his voice was even.

"Well, it all began a very long time ago on a long lonely ocean voyage to the New World." He'd asked the question, now I needed to let him know the entire thing, so as we drove toward the others, I explained how Incan vampires in the jungles attacked Estaben and how I helped him through his fledgling time. I told of my disappointment with Estaben's lack of magical talent and of our years of travel through South America in search of knowledge. I explained how we grew apart over time while I wanted to spend more time studying magic and he wanted to go explore the world. I told him of how Estaben left my side, made his first companion and then proceeded to leave a trail of corpses across several western states.

When I finished my tale, he sat there for a moment in thought. "So, will you be able to kill him, if it comes down to it?"

I nodded slowly. "Yes, I can. I realize he's motivated by power and he betrayed several of the principals I hold most dear. Due to my age and longevity, I've had many vampire friends over the years. Recklessly creating other vampires is something I don't tolerate. Most people aren't cut out for being a vampire, particularly most non-magical people. It's just too difficult a life."

"So you view it as a curse?"

"For vampires with no magic, it is. To be trapped by day, left to wonder the world by night and having to kill to survive, yes, it's a curse. Sometimes, most times nowadays, I think it would have been kinder for me to leave Estaben to die in that jungle. I thought I was in love and I knew how to keep him alive, so I cursed him to an eternity of nights. My love for him was not enough, and I know now I can never be happy with a non-magical partner." It all came out a lot easier than I'd been anticipating and I really hoped it didn't make me sound cold and uncaring. All in all, I was just being truthful.

"Together we can stop him. I promise to never betray you the way he has." He was very serious, and I felt in my heart he was right.

I pulled him as tightly to me as I could without breaking anything. "I know Alex, I know." At that point, I wanted to take this handsome man and vanish into the night, let the werecoyote and her brood of magelings battle the evil vampire and his cohorts as we disappeared into my secret mountain hideaway until it had all blown over.

"Hey, turn in at the top of the hill here," he instructed.

So wrapped up in my story and the little emotional display after, I hadn't realized we'd passed through the dark cut of a canyon and were now climbing up the far wall. The darkness of the place was almost as complete as my mountains and it had a peaceful power about it.

Near the top of the hill, with almost no warning, there was a turn to the left. I swung around, and as I pulled into the small road there, I had to stop suddenly to keep from running over the armadillo that ran for a hole on the other side of the road. Alex laughed, the sound was startling, but good after the past couple of days.

"Everyone almost hits Ole Speed Bump there the first time they come in, then you learn to watch for him. For some reason, he's always running back and forth across the drive, has been for years," he explained almost cheerfully.

"How nice for him," I replied dryly. I never liked taking a life unnecessarily, even something like a silly armadillo.

Where the drive widened into a parking area, the lights from the truck reflected off taillights ahead of us. Stan's car was the only one there right now, but the lot was designed to hold a couple of dozen. The triad was on one of the picnic tables that sat along the edge of the cliff. They sat close together with their backs toward the parking lot, looking out over the vista of the canyon we'd crossed. Stan sat between the two girls with his arms around their shoulders. They looked like bookends propping him up.

Alex and I got out of the truck and he dragged me over to the tall chain link fence that stopped people from falling off the edge of the cliff. The sky was clear, and there was no glow from the city. The moon had already set and someone had broken the single streetlight that stood on the edge of the parking lot. The effect was spectacular. The Milky Way lay before us with all of its shining stars. It looked like a slowly-moving river of cream with stars scattered throughout just for effect. Again I was reminded of my alpine valley home. Off in the distance a coyote howled, answered by another further down the canyon. Nearby a barn owl screamed into the night, warning the mice it hungered.

Blood Moon Yellow Sky

Alex put his arm across my shoulders and pulled me close. I let myself lay my head on his shoulder. It felt strong and steady beneath me. I always liked men who are nearly the same size I am so that either of us can fit onto the other's shoulders without trying too hard. Alex was a perfect fit for me and I for him.

We stood there for several minutes, just looking out over the darkened canyon, listening to the sounds of the night and taking in the way that the stars twinkled off the small stream down below. Then I caught movement down on the canyon floor. A line of ghosts appeared and walked across the canyon below us. It was a long precession of Indians, mostly women and children with a few older men scouting ahead. The older men flickered in and out of the moonlight as they sneaked down the creek bed. The women and children walked more slowly with only a few dogs dragging the travois loaded with their meager possessions. An overwhelming sadness floated up as they passed. We stood there and watched until they disappeared behind a bend in the creek.

"What was that?" I asked. A lot of Indian slaughters had occurred while white men pushed their way across the continent. The number killed in Texas alone was staggering. People today complain about the genocide that modern tyrants attempt, but they fail to see what their own ancestors did in the name of Manifest Destiny and imperialistic expansion. Whenever the explorers of the New World arrived, death followed in their wake for the native tribes, wildlife and lands. That was one of many reasons so many vampires traveled with explorers. They knew the body count would be high. When conflicts arose around me, I fought on the side of the Indians. More than a couple of times, I offered sanctuary to a tribe until the whites passed by. That also allowed me to learn from their shamans. The massive amount of knowledge lost from the tribes depresses me even now.

"That was a group of Indians that escaped the Calvary. They were part of a group led by Quanah Parker who met their end here after the Calvary stole all their horses and drove them off the south rim of the canyon. You can go down to that part of the canyon and still see the horses as they fall to their deaths along with most of the braves from the tribe. They sacrificed their lives so the women and children could get away. The Calvary hunted them down here in the months that followed, but some survived. Now they keep trying to complete their journey. On clear nights, you can see them like we just did. Even when you can't see them, you can feel them as they pass. This place is one we use to determine if a new person who says they're psychic really is, or not. If they cannot feel or see them, then they're completely head blind."

"Has anyone tried to let the tribe know they're dead and get them to pass on?" Most ghosts just needed to be shown the way and they continue their journey into the next life.

"Geri, Alex and I tried years ago, before the others came along," Stan commented. I hadn't even realized he'd come over. Alex was having a bad effect on me, dulling senses that should have alerted me to his approach. "They're so set on their course that everything we tried failed. We tried for a long time. A couple of times we got the scouts to acknowledge us. Once we even got the chief's first wife to acknowledge us and stop and talk for a few minutes. Unfortunately, we couldn't convince them to leave. Geri thinks that part of the problem may be that their men don't rest, either. They're still running farther down the canyon, and until they can be brought to rest, the women will keep walking their lonely nightly path."

"That makes sense, but it is still sad. They'll never rejoin the wheel of life until they can let go and pass on," I replied as the lights from Geri's Volkswagen crossed over us.

We turned and watched as she parked next to the Pathfinder and she, Larry and Terry piled out.

"Feels great out here tonight. Can I hope I missed the march?" she asked as she walked up.

"Just barely," Alex replied. "I know how much you hate it."

"I'm just frustrated that we can't help them move on. But no matter now, we have other things to worry about." She walked over to the picnic table where Janie and Bernadette were still sitting. "Our top priority is finding Char and either getting him back or at least making sure that he's out of the hands of the bitch. We still need to complete the mission for the Coalition...killing Estaben de'Oro. If we cannot pull Char out with the spell from last night using Burn as the focus, we're going to have to track him down. In doing so we should find de'Oro."

"Geri, if I may," I began and then waited for her nod. "I don't think that the spell from last night is going to work even with Bernadette as the focus. First, the sorceress should've adjusted her magics to block that spell. Second, when I woke Bernadette earlier, I noticed a patched hole in her aura where her largest psychic connection used to be. I found the one for her mother, and the ones connecting her to Stan and Janie. That leaves her connection to Charles. As twins, their bond would be the strongest. I think what we need to do is try and find out where Estaben has set up his base of power and work on getting in there so that we can disrupt that. We'll find Charles there. I'm almost positive the sorceress is working with Estaben."

"Makes sense. I know if someone used a spell on me once, they'd have trouble using the same spell on me again," she admitted. "But that means we're going to have to face down an unknown number of vampires and werecreatures to get this done."

"So, we need to go in with a lot of stakes and silver bullets," Terry grinned. "I guess that means that Weasel and I need to get into dad's gun case and get some decent ordinance to deal with these guys. Tal, how many silver bullets do you have?"

"More than enough to get done with these guys." I replied. In truth, I always traveled with more than I thought I needed just in case of situations like this. I probably had over a thousand silver bullets with me that would fit my pistols as well as some nine-millimeter and a few larger shells.

"So what else do we need to go in there and take on these suckers?" Larry growled. "Classic vampire stuff, holy water and crosses?"

"Probably work with what you're dealing with." I said. "Just remember that crosses and holy water don't work on all vampires. It depends on your belief in the holy object and what the vampire believes in. In your cases, I would recommend Celtic crosses. Most of the vampires you're likely to encounter are probably from a Christian background even if you're not. The belief that you have in the four elements can be your focus. Breaking out pentagrams wouldn't be effective for them and standard crosses aren't a good focus for you. All that you're doing is focusing faith energy here, nothing more. And your holy water would probably be best if blessed by Geri, all that is a charging of the water with intent for goodness."

"Okay then, so we have to gather a few things before we can get going on all of this," Alex said. "And we need to find out where Estaben is hiding. We still don't have any leads on that."

"Well actually we do." Larry pulled the beaker out of his backpack and gave it a good shake. "Don't we bottle boy."

I'd forgotten about the spirit in the bottle. In all the excitement of leaving Geri's, I'm glad that someone remembered to bring him along.

The werewolf spirit in the bottle looked out and bared his teeth.

Chapter Seventeen

WE SET the beaker on the picnic table while Geri rummaged through the backpacks the guys brought along from the house. She pulled out a container of sea salt. "Okay guys, everybody on the inside of the circle." She poured the salt around us.

While she created the circle, her students dug out a series of candles and placed them in the appropriate quadrants. I sat on one of the concrete benches and watched as they worked with practiced efficiency. It was obvious this wasn't the first time they'd worked at this particular site. Each one of them knew exactly what they needed to do. The werewolf in the bottle glared out at us through the glass but remained oddly silent as they proceeded.

The natural power of the place blazed in as Geri completed the casting. She tucked her athame back into its sheath that hung from her belt, walked over to the beaker, picked it up and carried it over to one of the unlit candles. "Now little spirit, we need to get some answers. You can answer our questions as we ask them, or we can light this candle and you can answer them once you get warmed up."

"What makes you think I know anything about Marcella?" he growled.

"Who is Marcella?" Geri growled back.

The spirit swirled around in the bottle agitated. I always love dealing with dim flunkies who spilled the beans without too much prompting. It always made working with them so much easier and really pissed off their bosses.

Geri shook the beaker. "Come on, who *is* Marcella?"

"Why should I tell you? What do I get out of this?" The werespirit snarled.

"You get released from this beaker and allowed to go onto your next life. You're already dead. So I can't threaten your life, but I hold your prison in my hands. If you don't answer my questions then I'll just let Tal go put you on a shelf of his library. Or, maybe the Coalition would like to put you in their vaults. I hear they have some very extensive vaults with all types of things in there." Geri shook the beaker again with a very wicked look in her eyes.

"Yes, I like the idea of the vaults." I added. "There is an entire section just for spirits of people we don't like who are never to be touched. Just think of it, locked away in a dark room, trapped in this beaker forever, never talking to anyone ever again. Lifeless. Formless. Just a collection of thoughts and memories of the life you had. If you tell us what we need to know, we'll let you go onto your rest."

"How do I know that you'll do that? You may decide that I haven't told you everything and keep me in this thing, then forget to set me free." His face faded in and out of the glass as the vapor swirled around.

"We're the good guys," Alex said. "We'll let you go when you've told us everything we need to know." He pulled out a match and handed it to Geri.

"Now who *is* Marcella?" Geri asked as she lit the match and moved it toward the candle.

"She's the witch that sent me to your house." There was a strange note of desperation in the werewolf's voice. I think he was starting to believe us about the torture.

"And why would she do that?" I asked as Geri blew out the match.

"That vampire guy she works with said there was a new player in town who needed to be told to stay out of our business." The wolf's face took on a more solid appearance within the confines of the glass.

"Okay, I've gotten that before. So where's his lair? I need to leave him a little message of my own." I sat down and rested my chin on my hands so that I faced the spirit head on.

"I don't know. My orders came from my alpha and he always had us meet him at a little bar on the far side of town. He always had that witch with him since we came here."

"What bar?" Geri asked taking another match from Alex.

"The Screaming Eagle."

"I know that one." Stan stepped closer to the table. "It's a small leather bar out on the boulevard, not a place most of us would go. They cater to a rough crowd. The police normally get called once a week down there to drag off a body or two."

"Where are you from?" I could get some helpful info from Beth if I could have her look up a particular town for wer activity.

"My pack is out of Big Springs, Idaho. Most of us came down here to go on one of our yearly boar hunts. But we end up on this job, protecting this new vampire who says he's going to change the world so the monsters can walk freely among the men. He talks real pretty and his sorceress is mean enough to make it happen for him." Suddenly, he was full of information.

I stared directly into the beaker."So what's your pack been doing while you've been in town?"

"The instructions for all the monsters are to make as many monsters as possible, especially if they can be mage monsters. That goes for wers and vamps. So we've been on a recruiting drive. Some come willingly, some don't." The spirit chuckled. "The head vamp, he don't care about the body count."

"So how long have you been doing this and how many have been changed?" Geri demanded. Her anger rose. She was hearing how big the problem was. The people of the town she felt was hers were in more danger than she'd dreamed and she believed we were the only things standing in the way of what might happen to those people. And now we discovered we were up against a lot more than we'd thought. She must be hoping we were enough to deal with it and at the same time keep the innocent body count from getting much higher.

"We've been in town two weeks. I've turned one a night myself. Killed a couple too. Most of the pack are doing the same. The vamps are busier, but then they have to train their new ones after three days, we can wait until the full-moon. When that hits, this town is going to be a howling good place to be." He laughed. It was the laugh of a cold-blooded killer who enjoyed what he did. If he was representative of his pack, it didn't look good. I knew some of the vampires would have the same mentality.

Geri paled. "My Goddess. How many of your pack came down here with you and your alpha?"

"Twenty five of the hardest werewolves that you've ever seen," The spectral werewolf howled. "Then of course there are those filthy wererats. I don't know how many of those there are. They've been here longer and a few of them are local. Except those whores on the outside of town. They refused to participate, something about being bad for business"

"I can see Cerebella refusing to let her rat pack help in this atrocity. But even still, twenty five werewolves infecting at least one person a night for two weeks, that means there are at least three hundred and fifty werewolves that'll make an appearance at the full moon which is in…" Geri glanced up for the moon that had already set.

"In about ten days Geri," Terry said reading her glance to the sky. "It was just a little off of quarter last night while we were on the way to your house."

"One thing at a time." I called their attention back to the situation at hand. "So is the full moon when this witch and her vampire are planning their big takeover?"

"First this little town and then the state by the next full moon, then the nation, and then within six months, the world." Had the werewolf been the mastermind in one of those cheap fictional books, he'd have laughed manically at that idea.

Personally, I didn't think it was possible for Estaben to have such far-reaching plans, but then, he'd always been greedy. If this Marcella fanned the flames of that greed, it might be possible. I'd seen it before, the old concept of with my magic and your might we can rule the world. A similar scheme in Spain had been what caused me to get on that damned ship to the New World in the first place. It had failed because of a peasant uprising. The would-be tyrants always forget the little people, and they're the ones who always bring them down. "So do you know how to contact Marcella?"

"Nope, she always goes through Tom, our alpha. Nothing happens in the pack without going through Tom, and she knows that. But he does everything she says."

"What does she look like?" I continued the questioning. I could tell by the looks on their faces that Geri and the boys hadn't expected anything that was on the level of saving the world. Things always had a way of getting bigger than anyone expects. If they hung around me long enough they'd learn that.

"She normally wears a glamour of a really sexy blonde." He wolf whistled, with a leer in his ghostly eyes. "Long legs that go on forever with really nice big tits. If you were into the girls, you'd go for her in a heartbeat."

"How do you know it's a glamour?" I ignored his jibe.

"She smells different than she looks. She smells like some fat old cow, but she looks all sexy and shit, so who cares what she smells like." He did another short howl at that, then lolled his tongue toward the bottom of the beaker.

"What does Tom look like?"

"Look for the biggest meanest werewolf around, that's Tom. Looks like a big truck driver, with a touch of gray hair at the temples." For the first time I heard reverence in the bottled voice, but then an alpha was supposed to command the loyalty and love of his pack.

"What does your alpha female think of all of this? Does she also follow Marcella's orders?"

"Cindy ain't here. Tom knew better than to bring her along. She'd kill that witch without thinking about it. Tom left Cindy watching most of the females back in Idaho."

Now this was useful information. I might even have time to get to Idaho in person. Maybe I could get Cindy down here to take out the sorceress for me. Also she could help prevent the infected people from changing. An alpha would have the power to influence the change of the neophiles his or her pack changed the previous month. In rare instances, with a bit of magical assist, they might even stop the change from happening the first time. It was a slim hope, but a hope.

"So then, any last words before we send you on your way?" I asked, in the slim hope he had a little more information. "Any messages for anyone?"

"Nope, I just want out of this beaker. Please, I'm ready to go on now," he pleaded.

"Nothing else you'd like to tell us that you think might be helpful?"

"No, I've told you everything that I know. Can you let me out now?"

"Geri, do want to give me a hand here?"

Her confused and scared look vanished with the hope of action. "What do you need?" Most people face the idea of saving the world better when they have something to do.

"I'm going to open a portal straight to the afterlife so that when we free…" I paused realizing I'd had this wolf in a bottle for a couple of days and never bothered to find out his name. "Hey I just realized we don't even know your name."

"Wayne." The werewolf supplied

"Wayne. When we free Wayne, he'll be sucked straight into the light, and we don't risk him getting back to Marcella and telling her anything that we might be up to. I need you to open the bottle. First shield yourself with the tightest shield you know. Guys, you need to shield too. There's always a possibility that this might not work the way it's supposed to and he gets out and away from me. He can't get out of the circle, but he might get into one of you. Just be prepared." There was also the possibility the pull from the other side might be a bit too strong for someone to resist if they weren't shielded first. I'd prefer not to have to stop one of them from being pulled through while making sure Wayne didn't stay on this side.

I took a deep breath and called on the power from the other side. After doing this enough times, like most magic, you don't need fancy words and motions to do it. You just extend a bit of consciousness and do it. A doorway opened between our world and beyond. I looked up and light in its purest form circled above us, just within the upper boundaries of the circle.

"Now Geri," I whispered.

Geri removed the cork form the beaker and the spirit flowed with an unseen force toward the glowing portal. He swirled briefly, like a dead goldfish flushed down a toilet bowl, then flew into the center of the light and vanished.

I took a deep breath and began to release the portal.

"Tal, don't let it go yet," Alex whispered in my ear.

I glanced around and a beautiful Indian woman stood just outside the edge of the circle, with her tribe behind her, all staring at the small portal.

Geri walked over to the circle and spoke to the woman in Cherokee. The woman responded. My Cherokee's a bit rusty. I haven't used it in conversation in a long time. It sounded like the woman asked what we'd done to the spirit in the bottle. Geri explained that we sent him onto his next life. The woman turned and spoke to the rest of the tribe behind her in a language that might've been a Sioux dialect, but I wasn't sure. The reaction was one of excitement from the children and the old men, but several of the women expressed concern.

She spoke again to Geri in Cherokee, explaining how they'd been drawn to the magic of the light. The light called to them, but they waited for their men who were trying to steal their horses back from the Calvary devils.

Geri explained to her that their men could meet them on the other side of the light. Maybe if they went into the light, their men would hurry to find them as they couldn't find them if they remained here.

The Indian woman again turned to her followers and explained the situation in their tongue. More of the women became excited. She turned back to Geri and agreed to let her tribe go through the light and await their men on the other side. They were tired of the endless walk they'd been on for so many years.

Sometimes ghosts begin to see their situation when the time comes for them to move on. Sadness darkened the squaw's face as she spoke of their endless march. I recalled Alex saying earlier how Geri'd been trying to get these spirits to move on for a long time. Maybe a small triumph now would give her the hope and strength to get through the coming challenges.

Geri agreed we could let them pass into the light. Then she turned to me. "So Tal, can you pass the portal out of my circle, do we bring them in, or do we take the circle down?"

"Let me try and move the portal out to them." I should be able to move the portal through the circle without disrupting it too much if Geri helped. "What we'll need to do is merge our energies so that my portal and your circle match. Then it should be able to pass out of the circle without too much trouble."

She stepped over to my side as Alex moved out of her way and placed her hand on mine. Her primal werenergies rushed in tune with the wild place we were in. I fed those energies into the energies of the portal. It grew slightly, which was fine. It needed to be a bit bigger for the Indians to step through without disorientating them too much. With our energies combined in the portal, I slowly moved its focus from above me to above the sidewalk outside the circle. For a moment there were two portals, neither strong enough to allow anything to pass through. Then the portal vanished from within the circle and relocated fully outside it. I pushed more of our power into it and made it big enough while reorienting it so the Indians could all walk in without having to stoop.

The lead woman smiled at us and then, without a word, led her tribe into the light. For several minutes they walked at their slow steady pace into the light. Finally the last of them moved off this plane and Geri and I closed the portal. Geri looked at me with tears streaming down her face and threw herself into my arms.

"Thank you."

Chapter Eighteen

DUE TO the increasing urgency of the situation, we decided it'd be best to base everyone out of the same place. The problem was Charles knew where everyone lived and where everyone liked to do magic. With so many unknowns factored into the equation of the vampires and wers, we didn't dare check everyone into a motel as it'd cause too much stir and be too easy for someone looking for us to track. It also created too big of a risk of innocents getting hurt if something happened. We couldn't move everyone over to my place, since either Tom, Estaben, or Marcella knew where my temporary residence was. In my eyes, that left one alternative. I didn't like it a whole lot, but to keep everyone safe I was willing to do it, just this once.

Every time I set up a temp residence, I always have a gate back to my place in the mountains. It's there so if things get messy, which they obviously do sometimes, I can go through, bring things back and not have to waste the time and energies setting the spell and keeping it up while I cross back and forth. It also helped with not having to rent a moving van, just activate and walk my belongings through a doorway. A long time ago, I had taken a black silk drape, cast the gate spell on it and then made it permanent. Now when I travel, I just hang the drape over a doorway and activate the spell. For the first time in many long years, my mountain library would host visitors.

It took a bit of talking to get Geri to agree to withdraw to gather information and strength before bringing the battle back to Estaben and Marcella. I also hoped that it'd cause them to let their guard down, thinking they had succeeded in driving us off. Finally, with the help of her students backing me, Geri agreed it was a good idea. I showed them the gateway, leading them through with Alex's hand in mine.

The gate was set to open into the front hall next to the coat closet. That way I had the same access as if I came through the front door.

This was the first time anyone had come through the gate with me. Alex gasped as he stepped through and into the long hallway. I guess the richness of it all surprised him. The few people who've seen it were amazed that I'd take the time to do such labor-intensive work. True, it had taken a lot of time. And the welding of the magics that went into it were as tiring as any physical labor, but the results, when done properly as I had, were breathtaking. There is also the fact that due to my youthful physical appearance, most people don't think I've had the time to do the years of work that went into the place.

"Tal, this is your home?" Alex's voice held the same wonder as his face.

"Yes, Alex, this is where I live most of the time. But this is just the main hall." I caught his arm and led him a couple of steps further in so the others wouldn't bump into him as they stepped out of the gate.

"Then I, for one, cannot wait to see this library we've heard about," Geri said as she and Janie stepped across the threshold of the gate.

"Then come," I said, starting down the hall as Stan and Bernadette cleared the gate in front of Terry and Larry. "We need to get some of you settled there. I need to confirm some of what I think will remedy the wer problem. You can look there, while I take care of some other things." I paused long enough to close and lock the gate so nothing could follow us. I'd let that happen once in my life and vowed it'd never happen again. Home invasion wasn't something I'd ever tolerate.

I led them down the long hall past the rooms I designed for greeting rooms and living rooms. I'd always collected things during my travels. When I built my permanent residence, I started getting things back, but even now, I still haven't made it back to all the places and retrieved all the items I'd collected and cached in various banks, homes and secret places around the world. Back in the days of my youth, travel was not as easy as it is today, so I was always very careful to sequester my things away where I thought they'd be safe, unless they were small enough to carry along. This was also true of many books that I had wrapped in oilskin and magic to keep them safe from the passage of time. When it came time to go back for the things I was amazed how many of them were where I'd left them, untouched by time or human hands. I'd lost a few items, like an old tome buried near a well in a small town in present day Germany. When I went back the well was gone and the whole area was now a much larger town, and where my book should've been, a large mansion stood. The really irritating thing was that I could sense the book was still there, somewhere under the foundation, taunting me. Due to the magical protections I put around it, I couldn't call it to me. Unless I wanted to destroy part of the mansion, the book was lost.

During the construction of my house, I planned each room out around a particular theme that I collected for. The formal greeting room was a formal Romanesque theme complete with a couple of pillars from the Parthenon standing on either side of the doors and actual benches from the Roman senate for seating. I didn't design it for comfort, but for effect. I heard several comments from each person as we walked passed its door.

The French doors to the living room had been pulled closed, but through the paned glass, the majestic stone fireplace partnered with a pair of modern recliners and matching sofa and loveseat. I spent more of my own time in this living room than I did most of the rest of the rooms other than the library and my workroom. I tried to keep it up to date. They could not see it yet, but there was even an entertainment center with big-screen TV. For almost two years in the 70s, I never turned one on, so I still don't know who shot J.R.

My kitchen was a little larger than Geri's. I don't do any cooking, but I had it ready for anyone that might need it. All it lacked was foods that'd spoil. Geri gasped as we walked passed. It sounded like she wanted to do a little exploring there. I guess it's hard to take the kitchen out of the witch no matter how advanced she gets.

As well organized as it was, my library would've been a librarian's nightmare. Most of my many shelves were fairly close together. A large table was positioned near the door and there were no other tables in the room. Even though it was three stories in height, I designed the place for one person, me. Whenever I wanted anything, I simply found everything that related to it, carried it down to the table and worked through the books, scrolls, magazines, manuscripts or whatever held the knowledge I needed. I directed Geri and the gang to the table as they stood wide eyed just inside the heavily-carved oaken doors.

On the basement level, the papyrus scrolls I obtained from some priests of a sect of Set that they claimed to have rescued from the library in Alexandria rested waiting for me to have time to study them properly. I'm not sure I ever believed them, but I secreted them away centuries ago only to have recently unearthed them when I had the means to properly protect and use them. Luckily, ancient languages are an easy thing to understand when you were around when they were used or knew people who were. I haven't quite unlocked the secrets of the scrolls, but at least for now, they were safe in protective cases in my home. The scroll on fire breathing that awaited my attention also lay in the case. It looked like it'd lay there for a little while longer. I hadn't gotten it long ago, it was a recent acquisition. Life had gotten busy since I'd gotten it. Somehow my life always seemed to get busy when I found something I really wanted to study.

"We'll need to bring in a few more chairs," I said as everyone gathered around the table. "I believe that there are some in the storeroom right outside the door here. I'd keep more around the table, but they get in my way so I only keep out what I think I'll need."

Terry shook himself out of the wonder of the library first. "I'll check," he said, stepping out of the room. His movement broke the others out as well. Alex, Stan and Larry set their backpacks on the table. Geri stepped forward to the first shelf of books, skimming over the spines.

"I'm sure that there's a lot of information here that we can use," she said. "The biggest catch is going to be finding it. I thought I had problems finding things in my library."

"Most of it's grouped alphabetically by subject then author," I explained. "Where books cover more than one subject, I've gotten more than one copy of the book. I know it sounds cumbersome, but it works for me." I gestured to the section on the first shelf that dealt with astral projection. "Upstairs, the magazines are alphabetical by title and in order by date," I added. "There are a number of binders on the first set of shelves that have a listing of subjects and which magazines have what in them. I'd advise using the index binders when looking up there or you'll take forever to find anything."

"So you found all these books by yourself?" Stan's seldom-used voice held more than a little wonder in it.

"Not totally. The Coalition provided most of the more modern books," I explained. "They have an arrangement with most of the book publishers to get their books sent out to me and most of the other members that have need of them. I'm sure that we can get that going for you guys too. Some of the other books have been left to me by people I've studied under who had no human students to leave them to. Over the past few centuries it's gotten harder for most mages to find students, so they leave their books to other mages so their knowledge and studies will not be lost for all time."

"Wow, I knew that it was hard to find a teacher, but it's hard for teachers to find students too?" Bernadette said looking down the second row of books.

"Harder than you might think. Not every town has someone like Geri or people like you that want to learn. Most mages have to be very careful in taking in students. In the past, many people have posed as students only to get into a mage's home and destroy them. Even mages aren't infallible judges of character."

"There are only a few places in the world like Yellow Sky," Geri added, stepping back over to the table. "Even though the Christian teachings run deep in the area, the natural energies of the earth still call to the potential mages. It was those energies that led Alex and Stan to find me and then the rest of you guys to find them."

Terry returned carrying several folding chairs that were circa 1945, but still in very good condition having only been used once in that time. He propped them up against the table. "So is there food in the kitchen? I'm hungry," he announced. A couple of the others nodded silent agreement. With the night we were having, a quick meal might be in order.

"Good idea, that'll give me an opportunity to give you a quick tour of the house so that you can find your way around safely while Alex and I are gone," I replied, walking toward the door. "If everyone'll follow me, we'll also take a moment and find you all places to rest. We may be here for a few days. I have an antenna on the roof that the Coalition put up that can send or receive almost any signal, so your cell phones will work here, except in the working chambers that are down below. It'd be a good idea if you contacted families and let them know that you'll be out for a while and not to worry. Let's get you all settled so we can get busy."

With Alex at my side, I gave the quick tour off the main hallway. Even though I was letting them in, I was still reserved about showing them too much. If we hadn't needed some of the information that was in the library, it's doubtful I would've brought them here. Luckily there were a series of unused rooms near the kitchen that had some of the military surplus cots I picked up on a whim years ago could turn into temporary bedrooms. Geri was delighted to find a closet full of old quilts I forgot I had. With a little help from Larry and Janie, she set about making a couple of rooms hospitable for them. Nobody really believes me when I say I haven't had guest in years, so when they really see that I'm telling the truth, they're amazed.

I left Alex, Stan, Bernadette and Terry in the kitchen trying to figure out the best way to turn the little bit of emergency rations I kept on hand and rotated out every two to three years, into a decent late-night snack. If they didn't have it worked out by the time Geri got there, she'd work it out for them. I hurried down to my private office.

I called the home office. Beth informed me J.P. wanted to talk to me and transferred me to his office without saying why. Tasha answered on the second ring. "Tal, J.P.'s expecting your call. Hang on and I'll put you through."

I'd called Beth on the way from the overlook to my Yellow Sky house asking her to follow up on what the werewolf spirit told us.

"Tal, I guess this means you have arrived home and got everyone moved in safely?" His voice was gruff.

"I've got everyone here with me in the library. We should be safe while we work this all out. What've you got for me?"

"Well, let's start with this Marcella Bovelwood woman. According to our records, she's a human woman, been around about 75 years. She studied under almost anyone who'd take her for years, but never stayed with one teacher very long. Record was two years with some fortuneteller in Houston. I've got people digging up more information on her, but right now, she has a major magical rap sheet. For some reason, she never set any of our alarms off because most of it was small stuff, love spells and money scams run on the elderly. She did try and get a coven together a few years back. They tried to raise one of the old Neanderthal tribal gods from around the central states area, but one of her people decided that it wasn't a good thing to do and caused the spell to go haywire. Our records end about five years ago. I'd say she found herself some magic item, a spell, or something that could bring her up to the level you described. I also wouldn't be surprised if she isn't working for someone. I've got Beth working on getting the info into an email for you now."

I didn't like the way this sounded. Too little was known about the woman. "I'll look for that, and let me know what else you find out. We've got to work on bringing the intelligence group up to standards J.P., what you're telling me I could've gotten out of the human intelligence groups."

J.P. growled. "Look, I've been threatening department heads for a couple of hours to come up with what I got. If I do much more than threaten at this point we could have even less."

Visions of a group of wererats cowering before the might of J.P. as he bounced the lead rat's head against the wall made me stifle a chuckle. "So what else do you have for me?"

"Well I had to get a hold of an old friend for this, but she owed me one."

"J.P., nice to know that you'd call in favors for me."

"Hey, at this point we're trying to save the world, so if some of my contacts in the shifterworld can be productive then so be it. This nice little werebear that I know, in the area of that pack, had a lot of information on them. They seem to be a pack of losers. The alphas have an almost human relationship and she rules the roost. Rumor has it he's split due to a little argument that they had over child rearing."

"So they're a true alpha pairing then?" Only alpha wers can reproduce biologically, unless they were shifters, but shifters didn't spread lycanthropy as easily as wers did. Most never worry about kids as it's normally so easy to transmit the lycanthropy to humans, why worry about having biological children?

"Apparently. They haven't bothered to register with us, but they both show up on the human welfare rolls. They've been getting state support for about twenty years now."

"Wait a minute, are you saying I am dealing with welfare werewolves here?" I suppose it could be possible, but it was mind-boggling. Why would werewolves need welfare? Even if they weren't good werewolves, they had a pack to support them.

"It would appear so. I personally don't know what the world's coming to. But anyway, it looks like a majority of their female pack members are also on welfare. I'd say the good people of America are giving these killers about ten thousand dollars a month. But my contact says she'll be happy to point you in the right direction when you get there."

"It'll be nightfall by the time I get there. The house here is the closest place I've been in the past few years to Idaho, so I doubt any of my gates there would be successful."

"Probably not, but that's all the info I have for you. I'll keep my folks on this end working on what they can and let you know if and when I find out anything else. From here on out, call me directly. I'll send things through Beth, but I'm handling things on this end for you. Tal I don't have to tell you how major this is."

"I'm going to leave Geraldine and most of her group here digging out information. What I need is a way to stop all the wers from turning at the full moon while at the same time taking out Estaben."

"Taking out the vampire shouldn't be too hard. Finding a way to stop all those new wers from becoming active will be a major trick. I'll put people on it from this end too. Make sure the Beggay woman has access to Beth before you go. I'll have a strike team standing by, in case you need them," J.P. mumbled. I heard in his voice that he'd do everything he could to make sure we had as much info as he could supply.

"Okay, I'll get on the road. I'll call if I come across anything else."

"Good hunting," he hung up.

His closing statements made a rumble in my stomach. I would need to feed, *again*, before the trip across the mountains to Idaho. I was about to give up on hoping to last longer than one night on a meal. This whole thing was already wearing on me and we hadn't even gotten to the major fighting yet. I'd better hunt, then gather Alex up and get going. At least in the mountains, on my land, I could hunt in dragon form and not worry about anyone spotting me.

Chapter Nineteen

WE TRAVELED through the night. By sunrise, we were part of the way through Wyoming. The twisting mostly two-lane roads, once we got off the miles of two track that made up my driveway, made for a slow go. Thankfully, the snows hadn't come early. That would've slowed us down even more. I made a note to myself that in the near future to take the time and drive through the area so I would be familiar with the current landmarks. That way, I could gate more readily and accurately to wherever I needed to go. I also cursed modern technology that made flying in dragon form dangerous. I didn't need the Air Force trying to shoot me down.

At my suggestion that he get some sleep, Alex curled up in the seat and laid his head in my lap. With a sly smile, he told me to wake him if I needed him and then drifted off to sleep. I passed the miles by stroking his hair as he slept. He seemed even younger with his head resting in my lap and his long lean body curled up in the seat. It was remarkable he could sleep that soundly as we drove. But I remembered back to my apprentice druid days when, after days of work, I'd fall into an exhausted slumber for almost a day. Even the other apprentices couldn't wake me. And then, there were the times during my travels that I had to catch sleep where and when I could. I guess that's what Alex did now. I was thankful for my ability to stay awake for long periods when necessary. I had the feeling it was going to be a while before I got the opportunity for a good long sleep. And with any luck, when it came, Alex would be there with me and sleep might not be the highest priority.

For a moment, the first rays of sunlight that reached over the mountain ridge to our east looked like a phoenix rising with the sun to sing the praises of the day. It lasted only a split second. The sun completed its climb over the horizon and the illusion was gone, just like the phoenix from this plane of existence.

As the sun rose, so did the raptors. Soon hawks and eagles sat on the phone poles and tall trees along the roadside. Some soared high above, catching the early thermals that drifted off of the black pavement in the fall morning. I watched the sky as much as the road while the miles passed. It'd been a long time since I took a relaxing drive in the mountains. I reminded myself that we were on an urgent mission, but I still enjoyed the sight of a golden eagle chasing a snowshoe hare across the road in front of me, grabbing it as it came up the bar ditch before it could gain speed across the meadow that led down onto the open plains beyond. The eagle and the hare both flipped twice before they landed with the eagle on top, holding its prize on the ground.

Openly flying down prey was something I missed from the old days. Watching an entire herd of deer or buffalo run in terror as you swoop down on them from incredible heights is a feeling like no other. Even in my remote mountain valley, I had to be careful. There was too much of a chance of being spotted on radar. I envied the eagle. Running my hand through Alex's thick red hair, I knew we were going to have to get to the subject of my species very soon. I wondered how he would take it. Sure with Geri as a mentor and being exposed to strange things with growing frequency, me being a dragon would only be another piece of weirdness. Would he be less inclined to continue our growing relationship? Would dating a dragon just be too weird for him? Our drive would be a perfect time. Who knew when we'd have time alone again before this was all over and something told me it'd be better if he found out from me rather than by accident.

The realization of how lonely my life was hadn't hit me until I found this small group of magic users. They were more than just a coven. They were a family, a family that welcomed me in with open arms. I'd never really needed that before in my life. Books and knowledge were enough, but now I wanted these people around me. I suddenly needed people. I didn't want o be alone anymore. Solitude can get old after a while and I was too old to endure it any longer. Looking at the handsome sleeping face in my lap, I resolved to tell him before we reached our destination.

I would've liked to go through Yellowstone to see what humans had done with it in the past fifty years, but I cut west so that I could go straight into Idaho. Using this path, I managed to get us to Pegram, Idaho right at lunchtime. I decided this would be a good time to wake Alex, check email and let him get a bite to eat. I'd had an elk from the valley at home. A little gas station advertising sandwiches occupied the intersection of two farm roads. At least I think they were farm roads, even though they were little more than two tracks.

As I pulled in, Alex roused in my lap. He looked up at me sleepily. "Are we there yet?"

"Not quite, a few hours yet, but I thought you could use a little food, and I need to check email and see if the information Beth is supposed to send me is there. I need some contact information for J.P.'s friend who knows this pack we're visiting." I resisted the urge to lean over and give him a good-morning kiss. Instead, I just ruffled his hair a bit before reaching around him into the glove box for a comb. "Here straighten up a bit and go on in. I'll get on with the connection out here and be in shortly. Just get me some tea."

He ran the comb through his hair to get it to settle down. "Okay, don't be too long." He smiled and I saw the urge for a kiss on his face, but he apparently had more common sense than that in this part of the country.

I fished the laptop out from the back seat and booted it up. The signal came in strong and I had several pieces of email from Beth. The first was the info on the pack she had put together for me. I scanned it and there was nothing new from last night.

The next piece was the contact info from J.P.'s werebear friend Suzzy Goodberries. I ran her address through my GPS and she was about five hours from where we were if the roads didn't get bad, but the weather forecast was for the first heavy snow of the season. I left her address in the GPS and jotted down her phone number. I'd try to call as soon as we got a little closer.

The last two pieces were a long piece about Marcella and her background, along with a link to a story from the *Yellow Sky Morning News* stating that there had been an attack by wild animals at one of the bars in town. The Rusty Nail had been overrun with wild dogs and no one had escaped unscathed. They found it miraculous no one had been killed. This made our journey even more urgent. The pack was out of control. I had to stop them before their mess became bigger than I could clean up and I still had Estaben to deal with.

I shut down the computer, got out of the truck and walked into the store. An old cowbell clanked as I opened the door. A quick glance showed me that the restaurant area was toward the back of the place. An odd assortment of animal trophy heads hung mounted along the top of the wall around the place. A large number of them were deer of various sorts but I also spotted a fair number of African antelope, an elephant, a couple of bears and one of each of the kinds of rhinoceros that existed in the past hundred years.

I spotted Alex sitting behind a mounted leaping lion that was poised to pounce on a gnu. He spotted me about the same time and waved. I hurried over, past the isles of meaningless junk food and pornographic magazines.

The waitress showed up to the table with his order as I arrived. Noting the glass of tea that Alex had obviously ordered for me, I declined her offer for food as I sat down.

"Well if you boys need anything else just let me know," she said as she went off to the next table.

I quickly and quietly let Alex know what J.P. had sent me.

"Should we let Geri know so that she and the others can head back and try to work things from there?" Alex asked, setting his hamburger back into the cardboard basket.

"I'd prefer they stay at my place and see what they can find in my books. I recall several things that could be useful. I just need them to do the research to locate them. Otherwise we may not be able to fix all of this by the full moon."

"Makes sense. So do you really think that this Cindy person will be able to help us?"

"By her very nature, she should be infuriated that another female is bossing her male around. What I'm hoping is that with her help we can at least eliminate the threat of the pack so that we can concentrate our attention on Estaben and Marcella. Actually I'm hoping she'll also take care of Marcella for us, but one of us might have to help her with that a bit."

"But won't we still have to deal with the pack's handiwork?" Alex chewed a bite of hamburger thoughtfully. Looking across the table at him, I felt the bond that had formed like it had always been there. He seemed to glow in my eyes. Even slightly scruffy from not shaving, he was beautiful to me. I fought the urge to reach out and touch that handsome face.

"That's part of what Geri and the others are looking for. If they can find what I need, I think with Cindy's help, I can undo what her children have done. But then we're still left with talking to the mother of the rats and getting her help too, and for all we know, Marcella has her in on the whole thing." I fought to concentrate on why we were here. I glanced around the room. We were definitely in an appropriate place for a hunting discussion.

"We've had the rats around a lot longer that the pack. I encountered the rats years ago." He finished off the hamburger. "We had a run in with one just after I started training with Geri. She was trying to start up a strip club on what used to be the main street in town. She called Geri to cleanse the place for her. Seems it was haunted by a couple of gunslingers that kept showing up and having a shootout in the middle of the evening every night and running off most of her customers. Everything went fine until Geri found out that she called the spirits and then lost control of them. She had some minor magical power and tried to do more than she was equipped to handle. Geri made short work of the ghost and then made sure that the rat left town. She left behind several girls that she'd changed."

"And they have become the mothers of all the rats in Yellow Sky," I said, finishing his thought. It was a classic tale. The mother is chased out of town and the children were left behind to wreck havoc. "And I take it these girls are the Magenta and Cerebella that Geri mentioned?"

"That would be them."

"Then when we get back to town, we'll need to talk to them." I stood up from the table. "I guess we need to get on the road again before we waste too much time." I knew that very soon I'd be telling Alex my secret. My heart beat harder than it had in a very long time. Secrets are very hard for dragons to let go of.

Chapter Twenty

I WISHED the road I drove down was one I knew well. I wanted to pull over and tell Alex my secret. Something told me it would be a good thing if we weren't in the car when we had our little talk. If he didn't believe me and needed a demonstration that what I told him was true, not being in a moving vehicle would definitely speed things along. We needed privacy for me to do that too. The last thing I needed right now was some yokel to drive by, see me in my dragon form and call the police. Or worse, get video and post it online. J.P. would have a fit.

We topped a rise and a spectacular vista opened up before us. Alex drew a deep breath. "Wow, that's incredible."

"Yes it is," I agreed. "One of these days, we'll have time and I'll show you some of the vistas around the library."

Alex didn't take his eyes off the scene ahead of us. "That would be great. As a simple Texas boy, mountains are just awesome. I don't think I'll ever get tired of them."

"I never have. I've been all over the world and mountains are still my favorite landscape."

"So that's why your place is in the mountains." Alex said, finally tearing his gaze off the scenery and looking at me.

"I love the view. Mountains also make me feel safer than other places." I spotted a small forest service road crossing our path. It looked like a Godsend and I turned, which made the GPS complain about my change of course.

"Where are we going?" Alex asked.

"We have a little bit of time. I thought we pull off up this road and stop for a bit," I replied. "Maybe take a short hike and get a feel for the energies around here."

"Cool. So how long do we have?" Alex watched the trees close in on the road.

"I figure we have about another hour of driving if the road stays good and about two hours of daylight." I scanned the road ahead of us for a good place to pull off. "We can stretch our legs for half an hour or so just to give ourselves a safety window. I hate being late."

"That looks like a good spot." Alex pointed to a wide clearing alongside the tree-lined two track. Moments later we started up the densely-forested hillside. We hiked for several minutes before we topped the hill and looked out over a small valley with a lake along its north edge.

Alex looked out at the scene, "Wow, this is so…so…"

"Beautiful." I supplied as I wrapped my arms around his waist pulling him in against me. It felt good holding him like that while he stared in wonder at the vista before us. For me, it was all the more incredible because he was there with me.

"Yeah, beautiful," he said, turning in my arms. He smiled at me and our lips met.

The feel of him there with me, held closely in my arms as a soft mountain breeze skipped over us, was better than any feeling I could remember. I felt complete. I had to tell him. I had to trust that he wouldn't run from me. I tried to recall anything that had terrified me as much as possibly losing this handsome man. I wondered if he felt the frantic beating of my heart as we kissed.

I took a deep breath. The moist taste of him filled my mouth. I squared my shoulders. I was Tal O'Duirwood, a powerful druid sorcerer, one of the most feared men in the magical world. I could muster up the courage to speak to this very handsome man in my arms.

My lips screamed at me as I pulled away from his face. "Alex," I began. "There's something I need to tell you." I kept my arms around him, looking up slightly into those luscious green eyes.

"Sure Tal, what is it." His voice was soft and lusty.

Part of me wanted to release him so I could pace. The bigger part of me never wanted to let him go. "You guys have all been very accepting of me without knowing exactly what I am. I told Geri, but she's kept it a secret."

He nodded. "We all know that you are a Coalition operative. We figure you're an immortal or something."

"That's a common misconception. I wanted to let you know all about me before we got too much further into this budding relationship." It took a lot of effort to get the words out. The next part would be even harder.

"Tal, I really like what I see in you. I don't think any grand revelation is going to change that." He brought my chin up so he could kiss my lips again.

My heart melted. Never in all my years had someone touched me the way this young mage did. I had to get this out now. "Alex, I'm half dragon." My heart beat wildly as he stood there staring at me. That second seemed to go on forever.

"A what?" His tone didn't change. He didn't pull away.

"A half dragon," I repeated. "My mother was a dragon and my father was a druid back in ancient England."

He tilted his head slightly as if he were trying to wrap his mind around the idea. "How did that work? Were you hatched?"

I chuckled. The few people who knew my secret had all asked that question. "No, my mother was of the higher race of dragons that could shape shift. She was a woman when I was conceived and when I was born. For centuries, the ancient emperors of China all had dragon blood."

He let go of me and took a couple of steps away. "Are there a lot of you?"

"Unfortunately, I am the last of the dragons—" I shook my head "—at least to my knowledge. Humans hunted us down. Every so often there are rumors that one of my kind has been seen somewhere in the world, but it's never been more than rumors."

Alex stared out over the small valley. "How many people know?"

"Not many. I'm the biggest secret on the planet. More people know where Jimmy Hoffa is buried than what I am."

Green eyes looked at me puzzled. "Who?"

I raised a hand. "It doesn't matter."

"So can you change into a dragon?"

"Yes." I nodded. "Would you like to see?"

His face lit up. "Sure would!"

He wasn't scared. Yet. I hoped he would still be interested in me after this. I hadn't been so scared before a change since my first time, back when I turned twenty one. "Okay, stand back a bit." The image of my dragon shape formed in my mind. The energy of the change surged outward. Seconds later it was done.

I towered over Alex. He looked up at me with more wonder on his face than he'd had when we first looked down into the valley. He reached out a large strong hand and touched my neck. Electricity passed between us as his skin connected with mine.

"Can you breathe fire?" he asked, continuing to caress my neck.

"No. I'm always looking for that secret," I replied telepathically since it was impossible for me to speak in a way humans would understand while in my dragon form. *"There's a scroll I just found, back at the library, that I haven't had time to study yet. I'm hoping it might hold some answers."*

"Wow. But you can fly?"

I flexed my huge black wings. *"Of course. Would you like to go on a flight across the valley? We have to stay low."*

"You bet." He looked around.

"Here, I can give you a leg up," I said, lifting my nearest foreleg so he could swing up and sit at the base of my neck, right in front of my wings.

He settled in with the natural grace of a born horseman. It'd been a very long time since I had someone ride on my neck. Estaben was the last person, after he'd become a vampire.

"Hold on to the neck ridge there in front of you. Now hold on tight." I launched myself toward the valley. I opened my wings and soared down toward the lake. The land passed under us in a rush. It felt good to fly. It felt great to share it with Alex.

"Wahoo!" he yelled as I pulled into a tight circle around the small lake. Joy radiated from him running through him into me. He'd taken my secret and found happiness in it. I felt happier than I had in several hundred years. I'd found my partner.

A shot rang out from the forest beneath us. A bullet flew past my right wing. I tucked and flew for the hunter running back toward the trees.

"Alex are you okay?"

"Fine, what the hell?"

"One of the reasons I don't normally do this outside my own lands, especially during the day. We've been spotted."

The hunter made it to the trees, running for his life as I swooped in to land at the tree line. The trees were too dense for me to go crashing through in dragon form.

"What're we going to do?" Alex asked, sliding off my neck without me asking.

As soon as his feet hit the ground I changed back to my human shape. "We need to catch him and make sure he doesn't tell anyone what he saw."

Alex's face paled. "We're not going to kill him are we?"

"Not if I can help it. Memory wipes work just as well as killing unless he's already told someone about it." Modern communication was another bane of my existence. Cell phones and instant messaging made it really hard to keep secrets in today's world.

I raced into the woods, chasing the fleeing hunter. Alex followed behind me, but he couldn't keep up with my supernatural speed. I caught the hunter before he made it to the next clearing.

"Stop!" I cried.

He swung around and pointed the gun at me. "It was a dragon, man. A real dragon." His hands shook as he spoke.

"No you just tried to shoot an eagle, a really large bald eagle. You realize that's illegal."

"No man, that was a dragon. I know eagles, and that weren't no eagle. Eagles don't have people riding them." The gun shook more. "Look I even got a picture of it with my cell phone."

I tried to catch the man's eyes, but his black baseball cap was pulled too low. The man kept the gun pointed with one hand and fumbled to get his cell phone out with the other.

Alex ran up to us. The man dropped his cell phone as he swung the gun toward Alex.

"You're the one that was riding the dragon. Mister, this guy here was the one riding the dragon."

"I wasn't riding any dragon." Alex's voice held a telepathic undertone. I suspected he was a stronger telepath than I was.

The man's movement became jerky. The rifle went off. The bullet struck the ground just inches from Alex's foot. The shock of it shook Alex's control of the man whose motions smoothed out again. I dashed forward, knocking the man to the ground. The gun fired again. The bullet harmlessly hit a tree. I wrenched the gun out of the man's hands and threw it to the side.

I held the man's face in my hands, pushing his baseball cap back so I could look into his eyes. They were a bloodshot blue. From the smell of his breath I knew he'd had a few too many beers. My mind forced its way into his and I found the memory of us flying. In the alcohol haze, I easily removed it and his encounter with us. I replaced it with a very lucky run in with a bear before I forced him to sleep.

"He'll wake up in a little while," I said as I turned to Alex. "Are you okay?"

He nodded, a bit paler than he had been moments before. "Yeah, I almost had him before the gun went off. Still not used to getting shot at." He smiled. My heart leapt at that bright smile.

"So we're okay?" I asked as I walked toward him. I purposely stomped on the hunter's cell phone as I walked over it. I couldn't have those pictures getting out.

"Yeah, we're great." He nodded.

I motioned for him to follow me back into the forest. We needed to get back to the truck and back on the road.

Once we were well away from the hunter, Alex had a few more questions for me. "So are you immortal. You're over what, two thousand?"

Shaking my head, I sighed. "Just shy of two thousand, and no, not immortal. Dragons can be killed. That's how they've been hunted to extinction."

"If you're here how can they be extinct?"

"I'm not a full dragon. I'm half dragon. The last full dragon died over a thousand years ago, as far as I know."

We started back up the hill toward the Pathfinder. "So is your human shape your real shape or does it change to what you want it to be?"

"My human shape is the same as it was when I first learned how to change into a dragon. Well, back then I had a beard and my hair was longer, but other than that, I look the same now as I did then. I stopped aging at twenty one." I didn't bother to tell him I was nearly a hundred before I realized I had stopped aging that fateful day.

"So if we're going to be together," he stopped on the trail and took my hand, "and I really want us to be together. Dragon or no, you are one of the most awesome and sexy guys I have ever met. Geri always said I'd never meet anyone in Yellow Sky. You had to come from somewhere else."

My heart pounded in my chest. Emotions rose up in me that I thought would never surface. Here was a man who knew my secrets and still wanted to be with me. I didn't know what to say.

"But if we're going to be together," Alex continued, "what's going to happen to me? Am I going to grow old and die? Will I just be a passing thing in your life?"

I looked into the vibrant green eyes and nearly cried. "There are spells and rituals we can perform that will tie your life to mine. You'll stop aging as long as I'm alive. I found them in some notes my mother left with my father. I don't know why she never used the spells. When we are sure we're ready, we can use them."

Alex caressed my cheek as I spoke and then kissed me. "Tal O'Duirwood, I already know how special you are. When we're both ready, we'll use the spells."

Wishing we could stay like that forever, I wrapped my arms around him and pulled him tightly against me. His body felt like it belonged crushed to me. I knew then, without any doubt whatsoever, that this man was mine and he'd be with me for a very long time. We stood there for several minutes kissing and caressing.

Chapter Twenty One

WE PULLED into the short driveway of Suzzy Goodberries' picturesque cabin as the sun dropped below the mountain ridge in the west. I called her number about half an hour before we arrived and she informed me that J.P. had called her earlier to advise her we were coming. She told me she was preparing a suitable meal for us before we headed out to meet the werewolf alpha female. The cabin itself was rather unremarkable from the outside, but perfectly suited to the heavily-wooded land around it. If I still had preconceptions about what people would live where, it looked like somewhere you'd expect a werebear to live.

Before we could open our doors and get out of the Pathfinder, the door to the cabin swung open and a short buxom blonde came barreling out to greet us. The chilling wind caught her long hair and it streamed out behind her like a horse's mane as she shot down the path toward us. She stopped just before the end of the path and, in an almost self-conscious gesture, smoothed her hair back before continuing toward us. "You must be Tal and Alex." She met us as we stepped in front of the truck. "J.P. gave good descriptions, but then J.P.'s always been good with descriptions. Aren't you two just the cutest couple? But come on in. Let's get out of this wind." She shook each of our hands before leading us back up the moss-covered path to the cabin's door.

Inside, it was larger than it looked; the trees hid the depth of it all. We walked into a large front room sparated off from the rest of the house by a half wall. Off to the left was the kitchen area where steam rose from several pots on the stove. To the right was obviously a sleeping area with a large lone-star quilt hanging on the wall above the bed. It all held with the perfect idea of what a cabin in the deep north woods should look like. The only thing unusual was it was only one story, but the beam-studded ceiling was almost ten feet high. Evidently, the designers built it to accommodate werebears in their monster form.

Suzzy led us back to the kitchen area that featured a small round oak table with four matching heavy captain's chairs around it. She'd set the table for two with a third place set with only a teacup. A couple of dishes piled high with food already waited on the table.

She motioned for us to take a seat. "Hope you don't mind having dinner first. I don't get much company from out of town up here. I love a good conversation. Catching up on gossip from the world outside of these mountains is always a great thing."

"Not at all, it'll give us time to get a little more information on the pack we're going to see." I replied as I sat down in the comfortable sturdy old chair.

She started toward the table with a steaming pot. "Of course, but first I want to get to know you two a little better, and what news do you have of J.P.? Is he still overworking himself? He looked terrible on the vid-link this morning. He looked like he's lost weight. We can't have such a fine strapping example of a bear wasting himself away."

"You have a vid-link?" I was astonished. I'd been trying to get one out of J.P. for years. They weren't really a video phone like the humans are working on. They're more a magically-linked camera that allows two people to see and talk to each other over any reflective surface, most of the time a mirror. J.P.'d been promising to get me one forever, but so far hadn't come across with one.

"Sure, had it for years, J.P. made sure I had one as soon as they'd perfected the spell. He always makes sure I have the latest in all the stuff that the Coalition puts out." She smiled while she came back over with another steaming bowl.

Now my curiosity was up. "So if I may ask, how did you meet J.P.?" It's not always in good form to ask a woman how she knows a man, but he was providing her with top of the line magical tech.

"Honey, I don't mind at all. Let's see it was back in the winter of 1915 I think. My clan was just getting ready for our annual winter festival and week of hibernation when J.P. came into town. He was working on gathering members for the Coalition back then. He joined us for our winter festival, then I offered to let him join us in the cave, and he said yes. He is really just a big cuddly teddy bear. So, he hibernated with us that year, and he comes back every couple of years to join in. He says we have one of the best caves in the world. I always look forward to him coming. He's said he might try and come this year."

"So, J.P. comes out here to hibernate? That's interesting." Bears are one of the few werecreatures that the animal side doesn't eventually take over most of the people that become infected. Some people think it is because they hibernate each year, not for months on end like regular bears, but for a week or so normally during the week of the full moon in December. That total immersion every year into the animal side helps them control that side whether they happen to be a mage or not. "How many are in your clan up here?"

"I am happy to say that we're the largest clan outside of the main clan in Russia, currently one hundred and twenty three. Most of us live within a hundred miles of here." She set the last pot on the table and took her seat. "Go ahead and dig in Alex."

Werebears were not one of the more populace wers, so to find that many outside of the original clan was amazing. Although they lived all over the world like most of the other wers, their form of lycanthropy didn't spread as easily as some. The only one harder to spread was weretigers. The werbears were the only wers that could trace their lineage back to a single cave deep in the steppes of Russia. The bear shifters, like J.P. could do the same. That was why a lot of people thought the lycanthropy virus was directly linked to shifters, even if no one could ever really explain why shifters could breed other shifters but couldn't infect humans like wers could.

I stared at the tea cup that held Suzzy's hot herbal tea. It wasn't normal for people who never met me to just offer me tea, particularly when they offered others a full plate. "Suzzy, what did J.P. tell you about me?"

Suzzy smiled at me in a warm motherly way. "Oh don't worry none, your secret's safe with me." She patted my hand as she turned back to the stove. That J.P. trusted her with my secrets told me a lot about how much she meant to him. I suspected there was more than she let on and decided not to pry.

"So, how well do you get along with the werewolf clan around here?" Although the dinner conversation and the insight into J.P. was interesting, I felt it was time to cut to the chase and try and get a little more information on what we were heading into.

"Well, I've always tried to have as little to do with Cindy and Tom as possible. They emigrated over from Germany I think. It might have been Hungary, or whatever they are calling those countries in central Europe right now. But that was back during World War II. They came in and took over a small ranch up here. They started out as ranch hands then changed their bosses and took over. Over time, they changed more and more people. At one point, they changed most of the reservation Indians under the age of twenty. That was when the elders up here started shooting their people on sight. Some of my folk too, until I went down and explained the difference."

"Are you saying the American Indians up here can see a wer for what they are?" I'd heard rumors to that effect. Most of the shamans I talked to always evaded the question, and trust me, no one evades a question better than a shaman.

"Yeah, they all seem to have that ability. I think it's the fact that most of the elders still follow the old ways and are in tune with the earth. Our alpha male goes to their sweat lodges all the time, now that we've made friendly contact. They're a really nice group of people. I wish all humans could be as accepting of the others that share their world."

"I agree. That's interesting about the local elders. So how many of the werewolves did they kill?" This was getting to the type of information that I needed.

"Over the course of several years, they killed quite a few of them. I'd say an easy twenty or thirty. But then they're able to change people so readily, it's never really a problem to them. I'd almost swear they're more prolific than any pack I've ever encountered."

"White trash is like that." Alex muttered in between bites of some very tasty-looking roast beef.

Suzzy chuckled. It was a deep brassy chuckle. "That's just what I always say."

"So are the tribal elders still trying to get rid of the pack?"

"No. Most of the ones that were alive when Cindy and Tom did the change on their younger folk have died now and the ones left really don't care that much. Things are bad enough on the reservation. The tribes really don't have time to go chasing after werewolves. We try to help them out a bit, but it's kinda hard for us too, way out here. Bears tend to be a little less social than some of the other wers. We like our isolation. But, it makes it hard to make money, until the internet came to town. Now a lot of my clan have jobs online that they can do from way out here."

"But the werewolves are content to take government money?"

She nodded her bushy blonde head. "Yep, they've always been ones for taking the easy way out." She glanced at the clock over the sink. "We need get on the road. I told Cindy I'd stop by to see her this evening around nine, and it is an hour's drive by the winding mountain roads. That's if we don't hit any snow or ice on the way. I try to be on time, even though I know she won't be ready when I arrive. That's her way of trying to appear superior to everybody."

"Did you tell her we were coming?" I asked setting my teacup down on the edge of the table. It had been a very enjoyable cup of herbal tea with just a touch blueberry or black berry and a little bit of honey.

"No, I just figured I'd show up with you two cuties in tow and kinda give her a little surprise." She grinned one of those grins only a wer can do that causes you to remember you're dealing with a creature of myth, and in this case, a predator to boot. To a human, it would've been a thing of nightmares.

Chapter Twenty Two

AS WE pulled through the gates of the ranch, it took me a moment to notice the wrongness. All along the winding dirt road that served as the main drive up to the ranch house, trailers lay scattered haphazardly. The trailers varied with the older ones nearest the road and the newer ones closer to the main house. They all appeared to be lived in and had a lot of old cars and trucks scattered among them. In the darkness, even my keen eyes couldn't tell how many of the vehicles were operational.

Wolves moved among the chaotic setting. The snow that began falling during dinner with Suzzy helped hide their movements. They paced the Pathfinder as I drove toward the house. If I hadn't been confident in mine and Alex's abilities to get us out of here if things turned nasty, I might've been worried. It would've made most humans nervous enough to leave right then and there.

Alex leaned forward over the seat. He'd relinquished his front seat to Suzzy. "You might be a white trash welfare werewolf if…" He chuckled softly in my ear.

"Careful young mage, their hearing is as good as either of yours, and it doesn't take much to set Cindy off," Suzzy scolded softly after allowing herself a deep chuckle.

I held my tongue but nodded in agreement. I'd never encountered anything magical, other than wererats, that lived this way. To think that a pack of werewolves actually lived out of trailers, had actually turned what looked like a once beautiful ranch into a dilapidated trailer park, was appalling. It was also unusual for wers to actually live this closely together. It showed me that Cindy and Tom Willowbranch didn't trust their pack members and kept them on a very short leash.

Normally a wereclan lived like Suzzy's and spread out over an area but kept in close contact with each other.

I parked where Suzzy indicated in the lineup of older pickups. Howls erupted around us when we opened our doors. They were all fairly high pitched for werewolves. It confirmed to me that most of the wolves were the females of the pack. Suzzy gestured toward the path that led toward the door without a word. I nodded and motioned Alex to follow her and I brought up the rear. They expected Suzzy, so she should go first.

The path up to the door maintained the general run-down look of the parts of the ranch we'd witnessed so far. Broken rocks along the path seemed to cry of a beautifully-cared-for trail at one time. Now weeds pushed up through the shale and cactus shoved the railroad ties on the edge into the walk itself. Off on the edges of the path, leaves from many autumns piled under the oaks from which they fell. The steps up to the porch wobbled slightly as we crossed over them. Refuse, ranging from broken furniture to piles of beer cans, covered the once-grand porch. It wouldn't surprise me to see a wererat in charge of maintenance of the place.

The claw-marked pine door opened and a slender woman with long greasy black hair stood there in a pair of ragged jeans and an oversized motorcycle t-shirt. "Greetings Suzzy Goodberries, Matriarch of the Bitter Tooth Bear Clan." The woman bowed low.

"Greetings Tamela Smith, handmaiden of Cindy Willowbranch, matriarch of the Bitter Tooth Wolf pack. May I introduce Tal O'Duirwood, agent of J.P. Montgomery of the Coalition of Magical Creatures and his consort, Alexander Carlson. They're here as my guests in your lady's territory tonight," Suzzy nodded slightly to the werewolf.

I can only hope I kept my outer façade holding. She'd just given our full names to the woman and named Alex as my consort. I wasn't sure if it was a good idea to let our feelings for one another out. So far we hadn't decided what the future held for us and here Suzzy was, having only known us a couple of hours, off and naming us married. I wanted to throttle the woman. I glanced at Alex. His face held a little more shock than I hope mine did. I caught his gaze and nodded slightly. He nodded back and didn't say anything.

"Greetings Tal O'Duirwood and Alexander Carlson." She nodded to us, but still did not move out of the doorway. The snow was beginning to fall heavier around us. "Suzzy, why have your brought this creature and his human," she sniffed the air, "mage to our house this night? You know that our alpha male isn't here currently."

"I'm aware of Tom's absence. It is your Matriarch that I've come to see, and as these two are no threat to Tom's claims, then they're safe to speak with her as well." Suzzy affected a strong air of command as she dealt with her neighbor's underling.

I now understood why she introduced us as consorts. If she hadn't, then they would've seen us as potential rivals for the alpha female's attentions, and therefore, a threat to the male's standing. But it was still a bad time in our blossoming relationship for people to be doing that.

"Please step inside, out of the snow," she said, opening the door wider so we could step inside. "I'll let my matriarch know of your arrival."

The room stretched the apparent length of the front of the house. The condition of the front porch continued to be reflected here as well. These piles were just a little newer. A variety of things cluttered the room. They all looked like they'd been pulled from various trashcans. There were several couches with long scratches down them where the fabric lay in shreds. A pair of recliners lay on their sides with similar scratches. One of those deer antler chandeliers that you can only find in this part of the country or in a store specializing in early country tacky provided the only light in the room. It had so many broken antlers that only two lights shone. Among the overturned and trashed furniture, I spotted several torn paintings. I began to think that someone in the household had a temper problem and desperately needed anger management counseling. That didn't help my hopes for dealing with Cindy in a polite and civilized way. Of course I was prepared to be nasty and uncivilized if I had to. It would help my overall reputation in the magical community stay intact.

Right after Tamela walked out, Alex stepped over to Suzzy and started to say something. She held her fingers to her lips and shook her head. He got the hint and stood there in silence. I realized when we walked in, Cindy was probably in the next room listening to everything we said. Like many of the other heads of clans, be they wer or vampire, she chose to emulate a royal court type of conduct. Well, I had more experience in royal courts than she could imagine. I could and would play her game as long as it suited my purposes. I just hoped that Alex was up to the challenge.

We waited nearly fifteen minutes standing silently in the room of wrecked furniture and trash, before Tamela returned. She held the door open and motioned for us to enter. "Please come on in. Cindy will see you now."

Once we were at the door, she began walking down the short hall that led deeper into the house. The signs of distress grew. Long scratches in the walls lay unfixed and here and there, torn-up pieces of the deep red shag carpet lay about. We walked carefully as not to stumble over the ruin that lay scattered along the hallway.

At the end of the hall, Tamela stopped with her hand on the doorknob. "Please be aware that our Matriarch was expecting only Suzzy Goodberries and not you other two. She has prepared as best she can in the short time she was given."

It was amazing listening to this handmaiden try and cover up the fact her pack lived a less-than-perfect life, and her mistress could care less about the way her pack's home appeared to outsiders. I'd met a large number of beings in my life, and it never failed to amaze me how trash tried to conceal the fact that it was trash. My already low expectations of what we'd find grew lower with each word the werewolf spoke and each second that passed.

Tamela opened the door into what looked like a living room with a pair of recliners at its far end. One was empty, the other held a slender blonde woman dressed in short cut-off jeans and a halter top. This was the first time I'd ever seen La-Z-Boys® used as thrones, but I guessed it worked in the given environment. Around the room, lounging on a variety of cushions, couches and chairs, were another twenty women, an old man and a dozen or so wolves. I felt the weight of all the eyes as we walked toward the chairs.

Tamela stopped six feet from the recliners and we lined up on either side of her. The woman in the chair seemed not to notice us, but I watched her eyes move ever so slightly as she slowly scanned Alex and me.

"Matriarch, my I introduce Tal O'Duirwood, representative of the Coalition, and his consort, the human mage Alexander Carlson. I believe you already know Suzzy Goodberries, Matriarch of the Bitter Tooth Bear Clan." Her tone was formal even if the surroundings were not. She gestured toward us. "I give you Cynthia Willowbranch, Matriarch of the Bitter Tooth Wolf pack, wife and mate of Thomas Willowbranch."

"Suzzy, good to see you again," said Cindy with a smirk, ignoring the rest of us. "I keep telling you that need to stop by more often. We ain't seen nearly enough of you these past few years." She stood and stepped toward Suzzy.

"Cindy, you know how it is when you are Matriarch of a clan, life can get busy. Even when you want to visit with your friends, it can be difficult. So how have you been?" Suzzy stepped forward and embraced the werewolf.

"Oh, you know how it is. The guys go away on a hunting trip and leave most of the girls to keep the home fires burning. Cubs to clean up after, new pack members to train, the usual," she sounded so casual, but her face moved nervously.

"That was why we've stopped by," Suzzy replied, as they stepped away from each other.

"You need help training your new clan members? I hadn't heard that the bear clan had any new members. Last one I remember was about ten years ago and you guys threw a party that rivaled one of ours. I'm in the mood for a party right now. Where's my invitation to this one?" Cindy seemed so pleased with her incorrect conclusion, she was almost cheery.

"Sorry Cindy, this isn't a social call. Tal and Alex have some information concerning your men's hunting trip." Suzzy was more serious than I'd heard her before. She took on a commanding role with the other werematriarch. It was the first time she'd used her alpha energies in my presence, and overall, it was fairly impressive.

"What have they done? They often go hunting in the fall. That's the normal hunting season for most of this country, ain't it?" she demanded as she turned on us. Her social tone threatened to slide away.

"If normal hunting involves changing as many people as possible into werewolves, then that *is* what they're doing," I answered her accusing glance in a steady, almost monotone voice. "If you think they are off stalking wild beasts in some distant wood, then you're mistaken."

"They're off hunting boar in Texas. Tom' d never set out to change anyone without *my* approval. I'm his wife and mate! He needs *my* approval of every new member he brings into the pack, just like I get his approval for the ones I bring over," she ranted. Her look had gone from one of pleasant denial to near panic. The shift in her voice was almost unnerving, and showed more than a little mental instability.

"Do you always know of your husband's movements?" I pushed.

"Do you always know what your pretty little human does? Of course not, but Tom tells me everything. I'm sure they'll be home any day with their trucks packed full of wild boar and maybe some good venison too." Her pale blue eyes were frantic.

"They lie." A large American Indian woman stood up from one of the couches we walked past. "They come into our home with lies, trying to tear us apart. They're afraid that our pack grows too strong. Even the bears fear our growing might."

"We do not lie. Over the past couple of weeks, the men of your pack have been ravaging the town of Yellow Sky, Texas. They're infecting one person apiece each night. When the full moon rises, over three hundred new werewolves will run the night. One of your own, a wolf named Wayne, told me before he went on to his next life," I explained. I hoped to talk some sense into these women, but by the frantic look in Cindy's eyes that would be next to impossible.

"Wayne's dead?" A small woman near the back of the room screamed and pushed her way toward us. As she cleared the front of the pack, it was obvious that she was beginning to show signs of losing herself to her wereside. Her brown hair was too thick to be normal human, her fuzz-covered ears were too long and her eyes showed the amber of her wolf.

I turned to her as she approached. "I am sorry, but he'd been sent to deliver a message to me, and in trying to get information out of him, I killed him." I bent the truth a bit. "He was following the orders of Tom, and Tom is being commanded by a sorceress named Marcella Bovelwood. She directs them in everything they do."

"Impossible!" Cindy roared as the other woman collapsed in a pile of tears and howls. "Tom and *my* pack answer only to *me*. I tell them what to do. No sorceress could command him." Her eyes darted around the room seeking reassurance from her pack. The lower part of her face shifted slightly, becoming longer. She began to lose control of her shape.

"I have no way to prove my words other than taking you there to see for yourself. Confront Tom and make him return with you."

"No!" The ancient man struggled to his feet. "My son's a good man. I demand truth by combat. You've killed one of our own already. Defeat our warrior and we'll know you tell the truth and our Matriarch will go with you. Be defeated and die here along with the Matriarch of the bears." He waved a gnarled stubby hand at us that was more paw than hand.

"Truth by Combat!" others around him began to chant.

"Yes, that'll tell us that you lie." Cindy growled through elongating teeth. "Your little mage against our warrior woman."

"What is truth by combat?" Alex broke his silence as the wolves began to howl.

"You fight their person and whoever wins is telling the truth." Suzzy replied softly. She turned around, faced the room of chanting werewolves and roared. They fell silent and stared at her. She turned back to Cindy whose features had stabilized about a quarter of the way to wolf form. "If anything happens to me, my bears will destroy your pack. Is this something that you're willing to risk?"

"You bring these outsiders into my house and they make accusations against the men of my pack. They claim to have killed one of our own." She growled in return. "Of course I'm willing to risk war with the bears over this. We outnumber you anyway. We have nothing to fear from your clan."

"Then let me fight instead of Alex." I said stepping between the two wers.

"No! We don't know what you are. It might not be a fair fight. Either your human fights or you forfeit. Do you think you can leave my home unscathed?" With her pack behind her, most of her fear dissipated. Their energies strengthened her resolve, making her more powerful. She stood ready to face me in her anger.

"He's a mage. Do you not think he'll be able to defeat your wolf easily? He's already killed several of your people in defense of his town. Why should your warrior woman be any different?" This could get out of hand quickly. I had to try to bluff our way out. Concern paled Alex's face.

"Oh, we've a special way to make it a fair fight. Neither his magic nor our warrior's will work during the fight. They'll have only their natural skills to draw on to defeat the other," the old man replied. "Our combat area was specially designed. We enlisted the aid of an old wizard to help, before we killed him. You see, no magic works within the ring. Whatever form our warrior enters in, is the form she must stay. Your mage has only the powers and skills he's born with to draw from. Anything of magical nature won't function in the ring."

"So you're saying that your woman won't be able to call on her werestrength or speed while in the ring?" Alex asked quietly.

"She'll have only the speed and strength of the form she enters the ring in. If she enters as human then she'll fight as human. If she enters as wolf, she'll fight as wolf." He walked toward Alex. "You'll have only the strength of your body and the power of your mind, your magic will be stripped from you. But as magic does not work, you'll not have to worry about becoming a werewolf when she scratches you, as that's also magic and will not work in our ring."

Alex nodded, and then looked me in the eye. I could see his resolve. "I accept the challenge." His voice sounded firmer than it had seconds before.

"Very well," Cindy raised her arms into the air, drawing the attention of all of her wolves. "The challenge is accepted. Prepare the ring. In half an hour we'll see who's telling the truth." She turned to us. "You may have this time to prepare. Tamela will lead you to a guest room where you may have some privacy." She returned and sat in the recliner. She tried to look like a queen in her halter and daisy dukes. The effort was almost laughable.

Tamela turned and walked toward the hallway that ran off the far end of the room. "Please hurry, there's much for me to do. This is so exciting. We haven't had a good match in the ring in a long time. Helga'll love tearing you apart," she giggled as she led us down the hall.

"Helllgaaa?" Alex stuttered. His confidence slipped a little.

"Helga Nein, she's our current warrior woman. Or at least the only one who didn't go with Tom hunting. Several of them went with him to Texas." She stopped at a door toward the end of the hall.

"May I ask which one she was?" I had an idea, but I wanted to know for sure.

"Did you see the large blonde woman as we walked into the audience chamber?" Tamela opened the door for us.

I nodded. Fear darkened Alex's eyes again. He'd seen the woman too. Her long face and pointed ears indicated that she spent too much time in wolf form. Even if she entered the ring in human form, she'd maintain a fair number of her lupine abilities.

"That would be Helga." Tamela laughed. "She's going to enjoy taking you apart, little human. You may like the boys, but Helga hates men almost as much as she does humans."

Chapter Twenty Three

AS TAMELA closed the door behind her, Alex grabbed my arm. Fear radiated from his face. I had to do something. I thought of several things that might help. I reached my thoughts out to his as I took him in my arms. *"Alex, we need to discuss this. But we have to do it this way."*

"So you have an idea of how we can deal with this? That werewolf bitch is going to eat me for a late-night snack." His heart pounded against my chest.

"Give me just a second," I caught Suzzy's eye. "Can you mind speak?" I whispered.

She nodded and placed a hand on my hand encircling Alex's waist. *"I have to be in physical contact to be able to understand everything,"* she replied, falling into our rapport. Her mental presence was like a warm fuzzy blanket or stuffed animal that you just wanted to curl up with on a cold dark stormy night.

"I need a little input here to help figure out how to keep Alex alive the next hour or so." I really needed to know what she thought was going on.

"Anything that can help. Cindy's been unstable. It seems she's gone a little further down the crazy trail."

"So she's pulled things like this before?"

Suzzy frowned. *"Yes, though Tom normally reins her in, particularly with guests. She's prone to stupid streaks, but it's almost like there's more going on here than we're aware of."*

"So you think that someone else may be pulling strings here?" That could explain a lot about an unstable matriarch. I didn't have time to deal with something like that. I didn't want to have to use magic on all

of the wolves to get Cindy's help. My best hope was to go through with the truth-by-combat trial and make sure Alex won. I could get Cindy to do what I needed with magic. But if she'd act on her own free will, it'd make things easier, especially in the form of expended energy for me. Something was telling me I'd need all the energy I could get my hands on before this was all done.

"To be truthful, I've never been around her when Tom wasn't here to keep her in line, so I can't make a good call on that one. But I know that something in these woods smells shitty and it ain't this bear." There was no chuckle in her mental voice.

"Okay, let's not think along those lines then. What do you know about this ring of theirs that has the magical blocks on it?"

"Well, I don't know about magical blocks, but I do know that the wards in the area affect a wer's ability to change. One of my clan got called up for supposedly attacking one of their guys at a bar in town. We were sure that Charley didn't do it. If Charley attacked their guy, he would've broken him in half."

My mind flashed to the heads that occasionally rolled out of J.P.'s office. You really don't piss off a bear of any kind and expect to get out of it intact.

"Anyway, they held one of these truth-by-combat things then. We came down to back Charley. That time he got to fight the guy who had brought up the accusations. Well to make a long fight short, after about three hours Charley finally pinned the bastard and made him surrender. The whole time, they both remained in human form. I thought for a moment that Cindy was going to demand death, but Tom let him live and they haven't given us much in the way of trouble since.

"We asked Charley about it afterwards and he said that he had tried to change several times just out of reflex, but something blocked him. So apparently, Cindy is telling the truth about the spells."

"But did they affect any of his natural ability? Had any of his wereabilities become natural at that time?" I knew there were ways to outwit spells if you had time and information to think them through.

"Even in human form Charley's strength was beyond that of a normal human and he was able to toss the wolf about a fair amount," She looked thoughtful. *"His stamina was also not affected. That's how they were able to go three hours. I bet psychic powers would still work."*

"That's what I'm hoping." Now if we could just boost Alex's natural psi talents enough to be effective against the werewolf in partial wereform.

"You mean if I can shut her down telepathically I could win?" Hope colored Alex's mental voice.

"Yes, but the problem is that the mind of a lycanthrope that is partially wer is a very hard thing to grasp and hold on to," I explained. *"It tends to be a very fluid thing, running between human thought and animal instinct. How is your telekinesis?"*

His shoulders sagged against me. I knew he was strong telepathically, but I had fought a werewolf in partial form before and knew it was almost impossible for even the most skilled telepath to hold onto the mind long enough to shut it down.

"Very minor, I can affect objects that are already moving, but that's about all. I know I slammed that werewolf at Geri's but I was afraid for your life, and that gave me an extra adrenaline boost."

"Not much help there." I said. *"You might be able to use the dust to your advantage if there is any. With all this snow, I doubt it. Unless they throw chairs at you, I doubt there'll be many flying objects coming your way."*

Suzzy chuckled lightly. *"They threw things at Charlie, not chairs, but rotted food. Knowing these bitches they might throw other things, but don't count on it."*

"So, my magic won't work," Alex moaned, *"my telepathy will be minimally effective on her, she's stronger and faster than I am and I'm supposed to beat her in physical combat. We need something helpful here."* Alex's mental voice was thick with despair.

I hugged him tighter and kissed his forehead. *"I have an idea I need to discuss with you. Suzzy, do you mind if we have a couple minutes of privacy?"*

"Sure, if you need any more input let me know." She wrapped her big arms around us and squeezed before kissing the back of Alex's head. *"We'll figure a way through this kiddo."* And she dropped out of our link.

Taking Alex by the hand, I led him over to the single bed that sat to one side of the room. We settled in next to one another. I figured we weren't going to be there long enough to worry about bed bugs. I looked deeply into those green eyes that I saw in my dreams now. With his face unusually pale, his freckles stood out. I ran my hand through his thick, deep red hair. I knew what would even the odds, but it must be his decision. Part of me rejoiced at the idea and part of me recoiled. I took his hands in mine, brought them to my lips, and kissed them. The fine hairs on them tickled my lips. I smiled a sad smile and stared into the green depths of his soul.

"There is one thing we can do to even the battle between the two of you, but it will change you forever." I knew my mental voice held more sorrow than I had intended.

"What?" I was surprised that there was no fear in his tone.

I paused, trying to steady myself to go on. *"You know that when a vampire shares blood with a servant, it forms a psychic link between them?"*

Alex nodded.

"Well, that's actually not a vampire exclusive," I explained. *"There are several magical races that can do that. It doesn't have to be blood. It can be most any bodily fluid, as long as it is shared. It would have been the first part of the spells we'd need to cast to bind you to me. The binding process is more than just magic. It works on the physical and psychic level too."* I paused to let him absorb what I said. *"We've already been named consorts by Suzzy. By the very nature of that, we will have exchanged bodily fluids, thus forming the link between us. This would also grant you some of my strength, speed and stamina.*

Since it's a psychic process more than a magical one, it should endure in their ring."

There was still no fear in his voice. *"What are the drawbacks?"*

"It will bind you to me, in a psychic link stronger than that of Char and Burn. You'll never be alone again and neither will I. We'll always know what the other is thinking, where the other is, what he is doing." I ran my hand across the smooth curve of his chin. He had taken time to shave at Suzzy's. The silky smoothness of the skin felt good under my fingertips. *"I'd prefer to do this with more preparations, more romance."*

"Geri always told us that when we found a life mate the link would be strong," he said thoughtfully. *"I've felt that link since the first day I saw you in my store. At first I thought it was just because you are so damn hot, but I've wanted you more than anything I've ever wanted before in my life. Geri said to go slow, to get to know you. I don't need to know you any better. I know who you are in here."* He laid his hand on my chest. *"I know what my heart, my head, and my instincts tell me about you, and I think you feel the same way."*

I gulped, and a tear rolled down my cheek. *"Yes, and I've been fighting it. I heard of life mates and soul mates before and always scoffed it off as emotional BS. But now, I know it's not. I'd do anything to keep you safe. I am half tempted to open a gate and take us far away and leave Estaben for J.P. and Geri to deal with. But even with you here, that isn't who I am. Can you forgive me?"*

He caught the tear on his finger and brought it toward his lips. *"I can forgive you, and will always forgive you. Does it matter what bodily fluids we exchange?"* he licked the tear off his finger while staring deep into my eyes as I lost myself in his.

I smiled at him, wrapped my arms around him and kissed his sweet lips. I could lose myself in his musky scent. How I wished that we could do this under different circumstances. *"No, but it takes more than one tear, and some fluids can be more fun to get than others."*

"I don't think we have time for those right now," he smiled at me. *"But very soon I want some of the fun ones."* The hopeful teasing tone

of his audible voice crept into his mental one and I caught a flash of some of his ideas about fun exchanges.

I pulled away from him slightly, remembering that Suzzy was still in the room with us. "Suzzy, I'm going to give us a little privacy for a couple of minutes."

"Sure thing, just keep it quiet," she replied huskily as I raised a sphere of darkness around us.

Being of magical nature, the sphere engulfed us in complete and total darkness. Now whoever said that darkness was cold never dealt with magical darkness. Maybe it was the heat we were putting off, but as the darkness surrounded us, it got downright steamy.

I could longer see those beautiful green eyes, but Alex's hands were in mine and our thoughts were still linked. I felt a momentary fear in the darkness and I pulled him tightly to me. He pushed slightly and we slid backwards until the bed caught us, and he lay across me. His lips found mine again. With intense passion he kissed me long and deep, building an urgency in both of us.

I ran my hands through his hair and pushed his lips tighter against mine. He gave slightly then plunged his tongue into my mouth. I nipped playfully at it as it caressed my teeth. As he passed over the top one of my canines, I bit down a little harder. His arms, still wrapped around me, squeezed tightly as his blood rushed down the back of my mouth. I licked his tongue with mine. Then I forced my tongue across his canine hard enough to make a small cut, and then explored his mouth. He sucked slightly at it to pull more of me into him before it healed.

"Together we will be," I thought the simple words of binding, while weaving a bit of magic to bind our energies together

"Together we will be," he echoed, grabbing hold of the energy I spun around us and making it his own before passing it back to me. We moved the energy back and forth between us several more times. As the blood rushed into his system, pushed along by the magic, I felt it travel throughout him. It reached into every crevice of his being. It surged within him, invading every cell with lighting speed. As it went,

it invigorated him. His arms tightened about me with strength that moments before would've been unthinkable and he ground his body into mine with a reinforced urgency, a growing need and heat.

He gasped as the link solidified and everything we both were, knew, felt and had ever experienced was opened for the other. I saw his first human lover killed in an act of hatred and felt his sorrow as he brought the killers to justice. He saw the sights of the world as I witnessed them over the past two thousand years. It'd take time for him to go through all the information he'd received.

Then he began to cry. Tears splashed down onto my face from his as he clung tightly to me. *"It's all true. Not that I doubted you, but it is one thing to be told you're two thousand years old and another to realize that you really are. All you've seen and done. Everywhere you've been, the loneliness that you've lived through."* He worked his hands free from under me and reached up for my face. I wished I could see those green eyes that I'd see every day for the rest of our lives. *"You don't ever have to be alone again. I'll always be here and I'll always love you, Tal O'Duirwood."*

There he said it, before I did. He said it. But he was right. I'd been alone a very long time. Even when I had people in my life, it'd never been like this. Previous loves never held this type of bond, this commitment for me. But all the sights in the world, all the magical text I had read, all the things I'd learned, everything that everyone ever tried to teach me, it all meant nothing to me at this point, now that I held this man in my arms. My man, the man the universe intended for me to be with forever. And woe be unto he who tries to take him from my side.

I ran my hands over his hard body, felt the contours of his muscles, and the tickle of the hairs on his arms. Again, I wished I could see those green eyes and realized that all I had to do was drop the sphere of darkness and I could. But then, Suzzy could see us and we'd no longer be lying on the bed alone. I ran my fingers lightly over his face, catching as many tears as I could. I let the love I felt for him at that minute pour out of me into him.

"I love you too."

"If you two hot studs don't stop whatever it is that you're doing in there, right now, I'm coming in. You're making me horny," Suzzy growled softly, outside of the darkness.

Chapter Twenty Four

THE RING wasn't a ring per se, it was a pit much like the pits dogfighters have used for centuries. Miscellaneous seating circled the nine-foot hole which was about twenty feet wide and thirty feet long. Based on the deep gouges that ran down the walls in places, it looked like not all of the combatants thrown into the pit were in human form when they went in. Here and there along the sides and bottom, dark stains deepened the brown of the snow-speckled dirt. There didn't appear to be a way out other than jumping or pulling your way up.

The majority of the pack was already there when Tamela led us out. They sat around in lawn chairs and on old wooden benches, dressed as they'd been in the house. Like most werecreatures, they had more resistance to the cold than normal humans. Cindy wasn't out yet, nor was Helga, unless they were some of the several wolves that lay waiting around the edge of the pit.

Tamela led us to the far end of the pit to a pair of Adirondack chairs. The entire scene was as eerily silent as snow fell softly into the dark hole. I was now glad that Alex and I had begun the bonding process. My enhancements would give him better night vision in this dark night, with the blowing snow.

We didn't have to wait long before Cindy appeared. Helga stalked at her side. The matriarch hadn't changed in the time she'd given us to prepare, but the large wolf woman beside her had. Helga stood at a good six and a half feet tall. Her face was more wolf than human. Soft blonde fur covered her tight body. Her fingers all supported long dagger-like claws, and her upper legs bowed slightly. She snarled at us, and then jumped into the pit.

Cindy walked over to her chair and sat down. "Suzzy, you can sit over here with me so you can have a good view." She motioned to the chair next to hers. "Well, mage, what are you waiting for? Get down in the pit. Helga won't wait long before she comes up out of there after you."

Alex looked at me, but now his eyes were full of confidence. "If it's a show you want." With a fluid grace that rivaled the werewolves, he jumped lightly down into the pit, careful not to land too close to Helga. I felt the magic shield around the pit as he jumped through it, but as we anticipated, it didn't interfere with our psychic bond or the strengths Alex gained from our new closeness.

Helga paced around him, sniffing the air. Her lips pulled back in almost a snarl exposing as much of her nostrils as she could while she scented the crisp air of the pit. She flexed her hands repeatedly, flashing her long, sharp claws. She watched Alex, expecting him to make the first move.

Alex stood statue still as the snow swirled between him and the werewolf. I felt him reaching out with his mind, trying to get a grasp of hers, even though I told him it was futile. Then I saw what he was trying to do, not grasp her mind so much as slide around it. He worked at it, trying to make her focus on him scatter. Unfortunately, he was used to working that trick on humans, not werecreatures, so he only succeeded in confusing her sight.

Helga shook her head and tried to focus her eyes where she knew he'd been, but he was now invisible to her. She howled and moved around in a larger circle around the ring, until she managed to get downwind of him. Unfortunately she was also behind him. He hadn't turned as she circled him. He'd focused his mind on something else. She charged him with a howl of fury.

"Alex move!" I shouted aloud as she launched herself toward his unprotected back.

He jumped up and over her using his new agility and strength. Then I saw his next move as all of the falling snow around us suddenly flew toward the pit and slammed into Helga's face, stopping her charge. He used his minimal telekinetic skill to control the only moving things he had around him. The snow coated her face, clinging to the short hair that covered it.

As he landed, Alex jumped again, this time toward Helga's back. He landed full in the center of her spine, driving her down to the ground. He landed a couple of quick blows to the back of her head. Around the ring, werewolves booed.

"Your little mage fights well," Cindy commented blandly. "If I didn't know better, I'd swear he uses magic, but then I guess you chose your consort well. He must have some psi talent in him. But don't worry, it will take more than a little psi talent to beat one of my wolves."

Helga pushed off violently with all four limbs knocking Alex off balance. He fell backward and landed heavily as she whirled around to growl at him, still on all fours.

As she crept slowly toward him, Alex placed a strong kick in her face. She slid back with a snarl and struck out with her claws. Luckily, he jerked back just as they passed so they only ripped his shirt open. He scrambled to his feet to get clear of her.

She jumped at him, trying to keep him down, but he was prepared. Alex grabbed her with his mind and slammed her into the wall of the pit. Suddenly, he pulled energy from me through our link, but the effort of moving her mass was more than he'd expected. He wouldn't have been able to do it before we linked or without an adrenaline boost; and he was trying to keep his adrenaline down now, choosing to maintain his calm instead. He moved off into the center of the pit amid a series of boos and catcalls from the audience of the little drama. Helga pulled herself out of the side of the pit and shook herself off like a dog that rolled in dirt. Again, Alex used the tiny objects that were in motion around her and gathered the dirt she cast off into a tight ball and hurled it back at her, striking her in the face. The wet dirt coated the side of her face, blocking part of her vision.

I wanted to call encouragement to him, but I was afraid I'd break his concentration. Right now, he needed all his focus as he enraged the werewolf champion. Through our link, I sent strength and love.

She swatted at her face while she charged. Alex moved with his newly-acquired speed and sidestepped her charge while landing a well-placed blow to the back of her head. She turned faster than he expected and swatted at him, catching a glancing blow off his shoulder that spun him into the side of the pit. He hit hard. I felt Alex's pain and disorientation as he struck, but it was only momentary. The crowd cheered. I wasn't surprised to see a folding lawn chair go flying into the pit and land between them. The woman who threw it glared at me from across the ring.

Helga picked it up and started toward him. He ducked under her first swing and came up with a fist in her face. She snarled and he hit her again with all of his strength. The sound of bones cracking filled the night, but I wasn't sure if they were hers or his because of the wave of pain coming from him. He shook his fist while he dashed away. I felt a sharp pain, now coming from his hand where the bones were cracked. Apparently either he didn't know his own strength or her face was a lot harder than it looked.

"That's gotta smart," Cindy laughed from her wooden throne.

I turned to Cindy. "You didn't say that weapons could be thrown into the ring!" This was trying my patience. I knew from Suzzy that these people weren't of the highest social caliber, but this was getting a little on the ridiculous side. It's one thing to half expect something like this and quite another to actually have it happen. I guess Alex should be happy they weren't throwing rotted food at him like they had at Suzzy's man.

Helga howled at him again, in pain this time. Then she threw the chair across the ring at him. She wasn't overly smart. Either that or her wolf side was becoming dominant in more than just her physical appearance. Wers deteriorated at different rates. If her mind was going, she'd be even more dangerous.

Alex grabbed the flying object and slammed it back into her. The chair's aluminum frame hit a little harder than the snow and dirt, leaving a long deep gash along the side of her head. The webbing entangled itself around her muzzle.

"I'm sorry, sometimes things fall in." Cindy smiled viciously.

"I think sometimes they do." I snarled as I turned back to the ring. I'd had about enough of these werewolves. I pulled out the dagger I always kept hidden in the small of my back. It was slender and not much longer than my middle finger, but it would be long enough.

"Alex, catch!" I tossed the dagger toward him. As it fell, the half moon emerged from behind the snow clouds and shown momentarily on the silver blade, then disappeared back into the clouds. A shiver went through me. It was as if the moon goddess, Diana, had blessed it. Alex caught the dagger in his mental grasp and it floated for a moment as he accessed my assassin's knowledge of killing. The sensation of him rifling through my brain was strange, almost like a hair stylist with heavy, clumsy fingers wrestling to get me a good cut. With a cold look on his face, the dagger flew swiftly toward Helga.

The wolves and people around the lip of the pit sat in silence, having witnessed the moon's blessing. They watched in horror as the blade sailed across the ring toward the struggling, howling Helga. We'd known this fight might be to the death, and if that was what it was going to take, Alex would be able to do it. His aim was true and the slender silver shaft sliced effortlessly through the faded nylon webbing covering the wolf's face and into her eye. She rose straight up as the blade slid home, howling in pain and anger as it pushed its way past her eye, shattering the fragile bones of the eye socket and sending bone fragments into her brain along with the blade itself. Had the blade not been silver, it wouldn't have killed her. But a silver blade to the brain or the heart is the fastest and surest way to kill a werecreature, short of chopping off its head.

Helga fell with her muzzle raised high, landing with a heavy thud on the far side of the pit as a howl of grief and dismay sounded from the werewolves. The moon appeared again as the snowfall stopped. It glistened off the blood-frothed fangs, and off the small diamond that decorated the dagger's hilt.

Alex jumped out of the pit easily and stood at my side in front of Cindy. I felt the pain setting into his hand even as my energies helped to speed the healing. It wouldn't take very long before he wouldn't even feel a slight tingle from the broken bones.

Cindy gestured to a couple of the women standing at the side of the pit and they jumped down to retrieve the body. They lifted her out with ease. Pausing to pull the dagger from her eye and hand it to Alex, they walked past to lay Helga's body at the foot of Cindy's cheap wooden throne.

Cindy looked down at the body for several minutes in silence as the pack gathered around us, their howls over for now. When Cindy looked up at us, a small line of tears ran down her face. "You spoke the truth, and it cost me the life of an old and dear sister to see that. I've turned a blind eye to the actions of my husband and the men of my pack, but no more. I shall go with you to bring back what is mine." She growled.

"I'm afraid I cannot allow that," replied a voice from the far side of the pit.

For the first time, I felt a vampire in our midst.

Chapter Twenty Five

"TAL, WHAT a pleasure to see you again. Estaben said you were now with the Coalition. I never dreamed I'd run into you way out here." Arland Dupree drifted out of the shadows at the edge of the house. I hadn't seen Arland in years, but he had one of those voices that was hard to forget. It had an old-fashioned southern twang to it. Oddly, it seemed to fit in this little piece of white trash hell I'd found myself in so far from the Mason Dixon Line.

Actually, I think it was back shortly after colonial times when Estaben and I traveled into Florida. Back then, Arland was the latest husband to Madame Cherry Vanderpeek. It was an uneasy time in the south and Arland managed to weasel and charm his way into the Madame's household. Cherry ran a very reputable entertainment establishment simply called Cherry's Place. To my knowledge, he never changed Cherry, but spent years feeding off her girls. It helped him maintain a low profile in those uncertain years.

We spent a couple of months in their lovely home while I researched some of the local shamanic magics and Estaben enjoyed the company of the growing Southern aristocracy that were building their power. At the time, Arland maneuvered himself into the crème de la crème with the locals, and he and Cherry attended more than a few formal gatherings while we stayed with them. Estaben never missed an opportunity for us to tag along. I'm loath to admit it now, but there were times I thoroughly enjoyed myself in their company.

I wasn't sure what the outcome of his presence here would be.

"Arland." I stepped in front of Alex. I realized, as I did it, that it was an unconscious attempt to protect him. "It's been a while. How's life been treating you?"

"Same as ever. So what brings you to this frozen trash heap?" His smile was sharp at the corners of his mouth. He still wore the top of local fashion. He'd have fit into the local rodeo scene with his skin-tight blue jeans, high-top boots and red plaid shirt with bolo tie, topped off with a black felt cowboy hat. Arland was no mage, but he was at least four hundred years old. Vampires who survive that long gain more than a little power. But there was some kind of magic coming off of him. Then I realized he possessed a cloaking spell of some sort, which had blocked his presence until he announced it.

Around me, the werewolves grew nervous. "Is he a friend of yours?" Cindy almost snarled. Her canines flashed as they grew with her new agitation.

"We met a while back. One of his old wives used to run a whorehouse I knew about. So how is Cherry anyway? Did you bring her with you?" This could turn ugly very easily. I had to get control of the situation. Alex silently laid his uninjured hand on my shoulder in a show of support. Having him there at my back swelled my heart.

"No, I left her in that sweaty little bordello of hers. She was about to tire of me anyway, so I left. Took her best girl with me too, managed to feed off of her for almost a year before I left her on a roadside in Virginia." Here was the predator I always figured Arland for. Like many men of his time, he preyed on people very easily and that time had been ripe with victims.

"And you show up here and now? I figured this climate wouldn't be to your liking. You always said that the heat was easier to get along with than the cold." If I could keep him talking for a little while, I might be able to figure out a way to diffuse the growing tension without unnecessary bloodshed. The wolves were on edge after Helga's death. Arland might just push them over the edge.

"Yeah vampire, why have you come onto my land unannounced?" Cindy growled at Arland as she came up to my side.

I wasn't really sure that I wanted her at my side, but I knew that for a little while I'd need to work with her. It also put here somewhere it was easier to keep an eye on her.

"Well ain't you just the little feisty one?" he laughed then. "I ken see why that big dumb hick of an alpha male of yours likes you. It seems that he and Estaben felt you needed watching. So they sent me to keep an eye on you and make sure you didn't get into too much trouble while they're busy down south. As much as I was loathe to leave the warmth of Texas, I do what I must."

"So what Tal here says is right? My man is off making more wolves without my permission?" She advanced on him, in a slow, deadly stalk.

"Should we do anything here?" Alex asked.

I shook my head while Arland laughed again. "Like a real man needs permission from a woman to do anything? Bitch, you have another thing coming if you think that's how the world runs, particularly after Estaben de'Oro gets done with it."

I knew a mistake when I heard one, and Arland had just made two. Unless Estaben had changed greatly in the years since he left my side, the male superiority idea wasn't real big in his book. And it's never a good idea to further irritate a pissed off werewolf, particularly an alpha female that just lost a gamble and a pack member. I suddenly wasn't worried about trying to diffuse the situation. Although Arland might have some useful information, the world wouldn't be missing much if the wolves shredded him. Anger leapt from Cindy to the rest of her pack. Hackles rose as they began to circle, looking for blood. In a tightly-controlled pack like this, the subordinates almost always echoed the emotions of the alphas. Cindy's anger would drive the pack after Arland.

Suzzy's large protective aura loomed up behind us. I took a couple of steps back, forcing Alex to do the same until we bumped into her. It felt safer there as the wolves moved in on the vampire.

"Hey lady, call off your wolves. If something happens to me, your men folk won't be coming back to you." His face paled a little more than normal as the wolves cut off his escape route. He was forced to step toward the advancing alpha in his path.

"They're our men folk and I'm their alpha female. No vampire can take that away from us. I'll go down to Texas and get my people. And right now, the idea of over your dead body sounds real good." Her last few words slurred slightly as she shifted further into her wolf form.

Almost on cue, a couple of the women on either side of Cindy stepped out of the circle around Arland, giving him the opportunity to break through the line. Arland used his vampire speed to get past the first clumsy, almost-staged attempts to grab him as all of the women in the circle shifted to their lupine forms. A howl went up and the pack followed the fleeing vampire as he dashed among the line of trailers that stretched out behind the ring.

"We should follow," Suzzy suggested. There was a tangible tingle as she gathered her werenergies about her. "If nothing else, we need to make sure Cindy can go with you." Then her human form was gone and a seven-foot tall grizzly bear stood where Suzzy had moments before. Her fur was the color of sunlit honey, but her eyes were the same sky blue as when she was human. She took off at a run after the hunting wolves.

I turned to Alex. "Can you see in the knowledge we now share how to shape change? We could run, but this way is more fun. And shape changing will finish up the healing of your hand." I was in the mood to chase something down right now, and if it had to be Arland Dupree, so be it. I knew that the vampire wouldn't be able to outpace the wolves for long. I was never really overly fond of Arland, and this time, I felt that he'd dug a grave he deserved to be in.

"Let's see," Alex replied, carefully touching his tender hand. He closed his eyes and the odd pulling sensation of him accessing the information we shared filled me. "Wow! Is it really that easy? I never dreamed. Shape changing is one of those things that people think is advanced magic."

I laughed. "A lot of the advanced magics are the easiest to do, but they are considered advanced because of the danger they imply. Or they might be things you need to have a certain level of maturity to use. This is one of them."

He reached into himself for the magic and brought it to the surface. Before my well-schooled eyes, he shrank in on himself and russet feathers sprouted from his skin and hair. His face flattened and became a bleached white as his lips pulled back and a bone-colored beak emerged. His shoes vanished, replaced by razor sharp talons at the end of long scale-covered legs. He blinked at me as he spread silent white wings.

"How'd I do?"

"Very nice." I replied as he turned to show his now speckled back and short tail. "You'll also need to rely on my memories of flight to do it right. Otherwise we could be here all night before you stop crashing into trees." I called up the image of a great horned owl in my mind so that I could follow his barn owl through the forest.

The wolves howled as they chased Arland across the mountainside. Suzzy's pace sounded different as she charged alongside them while Arland's fleeing steps sounded loud and clear ahead of the pack. For the moment, his vampire speed allowed him to outrun the wers, but that would soon fail and the wolves' greater stamina would overtake him. Without staying very well fed, vampires tired quickly when put to the test.

I spread my wings and lifted off the snow-covered ground and led Alex into the air. Using my memories of flying, he maneuvered very easily in and out of the trees as we sought to catch up to the wers and their prey.

"This is so cool." Alex's thought drifted to me as we wove amongst the trees.

I shared his joy at the new sensations coursing through his body as his mind sought to comprehend everything that was going on around him. I'd never been so tightly connected to anyone when they first experienced flight. It reminded me of my first time. I'd soared off the cliffs on the coast of England. It had been terrifying and wonderful. Through my bond with Alex, I relived it and it was magnificent.

"It can be a very releasing experience. I often use shape changing to get away from things. Since it's no longer safe for me to fly in

dragon form in most areas, I often use bird forms. It can be very easy to lose yourself in the perceptions of the animal. That is the big reason that this is considered an advanced magical process." True, a dragon's senses are a lot more attuned than a human's, but in most things I don't even come close to the senses of the animals. The owl forms we now wore were perfectly designed in every part of their creation to hear everything. Even my normal ears couldn't hear a mouse at half a mile as it ran through the dry leaves of the forest floor.

We broke the forest's thick cover just as the Bitter Tooth pack overtook Arland Dupree. Several of the wolves circled around in front of the terrified vampire, cutting off any more retreat. Cindy's large golden form leapt ahead of the main pack and landed heavily on Arland's back. Her weight forced the vampire to the ground with a deep thud. He gasped then screamed. We settled onto the lower branch of a lodge-pole pine above where Suzzy sat. The rest of the pack closed on their alpha as her sharp white teeth sank into Arland's shoulder. He tried to roll under her, but the movement just helped her to rip the arm deeply. A wolf I recognized as Tamela grabbed one of his feet and worried it like a dog with a rope bone. Other wolves followed her lead and within minutes, there was little left recognizable of Arland. Luckily, the vampire virus wasn't something that a wer could catch.

Cindy left the circle of the pack after they engaged in a long happy howl of success in their hunt and walked over to the tree where we'd perched. She kept her mouth open as she came toward us, catching the renewed falling snow on her tongue. She stopped next to Suzzy and the two alphas returned to their human forms together. "Your truth has been proven again. I wish your friend, who has left such a bad taste in my mouth, had shown his face before my beloved Helga gave her life to prove you true the first time."

I launched off the branch and changed to my normal form as I landed. Alex tried to mirror my move, but changed too soon, stumbled on the landing, planting his face in the light snow at the women's feet.

"You alright?" I chuckled slightly and reached down to help him stand up.

"Fine." He muttered in return. *"I'll need to work on that. You made it look easy."*

Once I had him dusted off, I faced Cindy. "I'm sorry it cost you a friend and me an acquaintance. Let's work together and try and stop Estaben before more damage is done." I offered her my hand.

She stepped forward and took it in hers as her pack closed in around us. "I go with you now, of my own free will, to help you stop this monster and bring our males back to us before they are too corrupted by his presence."

The pack howled around us.

I hoped it was a good sign as the snow picked up, shrouding the forest in a gray darkness, blocking out all light from the moon and stars. We needed a good sign.

Chapter Twenty Six

THE TRIP back to Yellow Sky was both shorter and slower than the trip out to Idaho and the library had been. I used gates for both steps. I really didn't want Cindy and Tamela, who came as her guard, to know where I lived. When this was over, I didn't want any unexpected drop-ins by the werewolf clan trying to make me pay for what they thought I caused. I've enough experience with the underbelly of the world to know how trash types worked. The way I saw it, a couple of months of licking their wounds, then I'd become the scapegoat for all of their problems and they'd be out looking for me. The less they knew about where I lived the better. I even went to the extent of making sure neither of the werewolves set a foot outside the front door so they wouldn't get a good sniff of the mountains outside. It's amazing how a keen sense of smell can find a place on just a little sniff.

At the library, we picked up Geri and the others. A small growling match ensued between Geri and Cindy until Cindy realized Geri was a mage and could easily wipe the floor with her. Happily, Geri found the spell we needed. Actually, Larry had found it in one of the more obscure pamphlets from the turn of the last century. I took time to make sure I had everything I needed in one of my portable magic bags, then activated the gate back to the house in Yellow Sky.

I was the last one though, following Alex's cute butt. His back arched and pain lanced through our link as I stepped into the tapestry. The gate momentarily twisted around us. I caught hold of the magic and forced it to stabilize. It was bent and twisted in patterns I didn't recognize. The energy fought my control. It didn't want to untwist. With a growl, I shoved at it, making it stable, if only for a second.

I stepped out of it to see Alex and the others dropped to their knees vomiting violently.

"What happened?" Alex gasped as he sat down next to his own vomit, careful not to sit in anyone else's.

I turned and looked at the doorway where the tapestry hung. Scorch marks scored the edge of the cloth. It looked like someone tried to break through or tamper with the protections I kept on the gate spell. I opened my magical vision and looked at the spells in the cloth. It looked the way safety glass windows looks when someone has tried to break in with a crow bar unsuccessfully. All throughout the magics of the gate, little cracks and twists glittered. Like a broken window that let in light, the magics still worked, but like that light, they had been twisted and thrown about. A closer look revealed that the spells most affected were the ones that served as the spacial-temporal anchors. That explained why it had fought my efforts to fix it. Someone had messed it up big time. My heart sank.

I dashed past the others as they tried to regain control of their digestive tracts. I rushed outside and looked up into the sky. The moon was only two days from full. We'd lost over a week with the gate tampering. Unless we'd lost more time than that. If it had been more than a month, we were in deep shit. It was no wonder that the intruder hadn't stayed around. We'd been gone too long. At this point, they must think we were all dead.

Alex came up behind me, his mind still reeling from the distortion caused by the gate. "What's wrong?" he asked as he put his arms around my chest.

"Someone tried to break the gate spell, or at least tampered with it. We've been stuck in the gate for almost a week now." I pointed up to the heavy moon above us, I didn't really want to entertain the idea it had been more than a month, it had to be a week, it just had to be. "We don't have a lot of time left. We must cast that spell before the moon rises tomorrow night. Tonight would be better, which means we have to find the wererats while keeping Cindy's people from finding out she's here. Then we have to be ready to move against Estaben and we still aren't even sure where he is."

Alex stared up at the moon. "That's a lot wrong," he whispered, more to himself than to me as he hugged me tightly.

Larry came running out of the house, still a little green around the edges. "Burn says she can feel Char again, but something's changed. He's stronger now and he's hungry."

Chapter Twenty Seven

ALEX AND I walked back into the hall with the malfunctioning gate. We found that most everyone had regained their stomachs, at least to some degree. Stan held Bernadette as the woman mumbled about Charles' hunger and power. Reestablishing the link with her changed twin compounded the disorientation caused by the gate. Geri knelt in front of them trying to offer comfort while Janie wrapped her arms around them, her face worried.

"Some wild ride you offer us here," Cindy growled as we approached. "Do you have any more of your magic tricks to throw us off balance? This time you took out your people as well as mine." She gestured to Tamela who was still lying in the floor, looking too nauseated to even try to sit up.

"I am sorry for your discomfort, Cindy. There are hands at work here other than mine." I walked past her to the group on the floor nearby. "Geri, if I could see you for a second please? There's a lot more going on than we know about."

"Tal, I need to calm Burn down. She can feel Char again. That's good isn't it?" A protective motherly look colored her face that under normal circumstances, I wouldn't have intruded upon, but this was hardly a normal circumstance.

"Give me a couple of minutes Geri and then I'll see what I can do for Bernadette." I glanced over my shoulder to Alex and gestured him to follow.

A couple of steps down the hall we entered the master bedroom. I wasn't surprised to find it in a much more disheveled state than when I left it. I turned to close the door when Cindy pushed her way in.

"Whatever you need to talk about to this coyote, you can say in front of me." Cindy and Geri had taken an immediate dislike to each other. They were both canine alpha females, but the fact that they were separate species didn't seem to matter to Cindy. At best, the truce they created at the library was extremely shaky. The sooner this was over and she was back in Idaho with the rest of her pack, the better I'd like it.

"Maybe you can help with this," I said as she stormed past me to take a seat on the now very rumpled bed.

"Geri, it seems that the discomfort in the use of the gate was caused by someone tampering with it. I'm not sure who, but I've a strong feeling Marcella was involved at least in spirit. The tampering caused another problem. It threw us into the future by about a week. We now have only two nights until the full moon. That includes what's left of tonight."

The look on her face said it all. "But that means we have less than a day to cast the spell, if it's going to work. It'd be better if we cast it by the end of the night. I guess we need to calm Burn for now and work on finding Charles, after we see about talking to Magenta and Cerebella. Right now, we need the rats more, I suppose. It might be safer to try and track him down by day anyway."

"Look, I have a thought on that," I said. "Can you, Alex, Larry, and Terry take Cindy and Tamela with you to find and talk to the rats while I go with Bernadette, Stan and Janie to find Charles?"

"I guess so. But is it wise to split our forces at this time?"

"Are you afraid to be alone with me, little coyote?" Cindy bared her teeth. "Or are you afraid you might need the protection of me and my guard as we go into the world you're still learning about?"

"Neither, bitch!" Geri snarled back. Cindy brought out a little more of Geri's coyote than she'd shown before. "I'm concerned for the town under my protection and I want to make sure we succeed in our task this night. It's possible Marcella may have protections around the rats even they don't know about."

I stepped cautiously between the two growling werewomen. "That's why I am sending Alex with you. With our bond, he can tap into my knowledge and be able to work with you like I was there. And if you have any questions, he can just ask me and you'll have my answer right away."

Geri shot me the same look she'd given me when Alex and I arrived back at the library with the werewolves. She sensed something that didn't please her. She didn't like the changes she saw in Alex. He pulled her aside while I reviewed the spell they found and assured her everything was fine, better than it had been, and promised a full explanation when the time presented itself for the three of us to sit down and talk.

"Alright, find Charles," Geri snapped. "If he's been changed as you suspect, then he might know something that can lead us to Estaben. I need to make a couple of phone calls to see if we can arrange a meeting with the rat ladies." She stomped out of the room. As she opened the door, the sound of Bernadette in the hall channeling the link between her and her now-undead twin came through loud and clear. It was a little disheartening. These people were so young and being put through the ringer. But, if they were going to be part of the Coalition, their lives might always be rough. It wasn't an easy time to be part of the magical community.

"You seem to have a way with the wers," Cindy smiled. She obviously enjoyed the conflict between Geri and myself. "Maybe it's a good idea if you don't go with us to see the rats." She got up from the bed and walked out of the room.

Alex came up from behind and wrapped his arms around my waist. "We'll pull this off," he whispered softly in my ear before he kissed it. Something about the feel of his arms around me gave me a comfort that I'd never felt. Somehow I felt safe and secure standing in his arms.

It had been a long time since I even thought about feeling safe and secure. I was the thing many magical creatures feared. It shouldn't be my lot in life to feel safe and secure, but I did. Right then I did. I turned around to look deeply in his green eyes. "I know. I'm just worried about the body count while we do. I want you to be careful while you go with Geri and Cindy. I don't need to tell you, I don't really trust Cindy. But to end all of this, we need her."

He squared his shoulders and flashed a bright smile. "I'll watch myself. Don't forget I've got Weasel and Topper to watch my back while I'm watching Geri's."

I kissed him, then chuckled. Trying to look overly butch, he looked a little goofy and very handsome. His warm lips comforted me, and I hugged him fiercely. "And don't forget I'm only a thought away. With our link, I can see through your eyes if I need to and you can do the same. If you come across something that doesn't look or feel right, don't hesitate to call and I'll come running."

"I know you will." He lay his head on my shoulder. "Just don't worry too much. You'll need to get to Charles. Don't put yourself at risk just so you can keep tabs on me. Keep your focus on Charles."

"I've waited so long to find you. Don't let anything happen to you if you can help it." I could almost see eternity in his eyes. I just hoped what I saw was true and not just what I wanted to see.

"Hey, you've offered me a long life. I don't plan on throwing that away." His smile held a combination of cockiness and the self-assuredness of a man who knows his own strengths and was not afraid to use them.

The strong musty smell of sweat from the fight in the pit filled me as I held him closely. I wanted him so badly. Lust rose in me and I kissed him again. He responded with a lust of his own. His hands played across my back as he pulled me tighter against him. I lost myself in his aura, his scent, his very being. The link between us flared and his love and need for me filled me. It was like a refresh splash of cold water in the middle of a desert. The astral wall between us had vanished. I eased us back onto the bed, feeling the growing pressures between us as we settled onto its cushioned embrace. His weight against my chest felt perfect as his tongue filled my mouth with its heat. He pulled his hands from beneath me and ran his fingers through my hair. I ran my hands down his back toward his belt when I felt another presence in the room as a soft growl interrupted us.

"Excuse me, but you two really do *not* have time for that now" Geri stood in the doorway with her hands on her hips and a tangible aura of anger about her. "Tal, at your age I wouldn't expect you to act like this. Alex, you should know better too. There is a time and place for everything." She turned to stomp off. "By the way, I reached Cerebella on the first call. We're supposed to be there in twenty minutes. *If* you're coming, Alex." She slammed the door on the way out.

Alex sighed the sigh I managed to hold inside. "Well, I guess we need to be on our way. I'll keep you posted. We'll finish this later." He pulled my face down to him and kissed me deeply before we rolled off the bed and headed for the door.

Watching him walk out was one of the hardest things I'd ever done. I wanted him so badly, but I knew, once this was all over, I'd have him for a very long time. A simple happy contentment surged in me as I followed them out. We both had more important things to do.

Chapter Twenty Eight

ALEX AND Geri led the others out for their meeting with the wererats. I stood in the middle of the hall in front of Stan, Janie and Bernadette, who was still lost in the reestablishment of the link with her twin and the flood of foreign impressions it brought along with it. Stan and Janie were trying to sooth her, smoothing back her sweat-soaked blue hair and murmuring soft words. I knelt down next to them and Stan looked at me with both hope and questions in his eyes.

"What can we do?" Fear for his loved one darkened his voice.

"You need to bring her back to herself enough to filter out most of the strength of Charles' mind in their link." I gestured toward the now-open door of the bedroom. "You might be more comfortable in there."

"Whaaatttt are you sugggggggesssssting?" Janie stuttered. Her young eyes were more unfocused and lost than they should've been.

"The three of you have a very strong link between you. Use that link in the way you normally use it. Take Burn to a thing the three of you share that she doesn't share with Charles. When she comes to you, filter out Charles. Once that's done, she can lead us to him and we can see if there's anything we can do for him." I sighed with impatience. Sometimes humans can be very slow on the uptake and young humans are very rarely rushed by anything other than their own needs.

Stan nodded in understanding. He stood slowly as he lifted Bernadette into his arms. Janie grasped her hand as Stan carried her toward the bedroom. Janie looked back at me as she closed the door. She looked much younger than she normally did. For her sake, I could only hope that the events that were unfolding didn't leave too much of a mark on her psyche.

"I'll be here when you're ready to go, but please try and hurry. We have things to get done quickly." I turned back toward the now-ruined gate tapestry.

I studied the magics lingering around the edges, noting where the invading magics attacked my finely-woven ancient spells. I looked carefully at them. They were many days old and fading fast. I couldn't get a definite signature from them, but they were definitely made by two different mages. One had a definite human feel to it and the other was more vampiric. I could only guess it was Marcella and the newly-turned Charles. He would've done the damage his first night as a vampire. I hoped we would be able to get him away from her and salvage him. I really didn't like the idea of killing one of Alex's friends this early in our relationship. Not to mention, I kinda liked Charles. From what I saw of him to that point, he possessed a sharp mind and lots of potential.

I searched the rest of the house. I'd missed a lot in my earlier mad dash outside and I needed to know the extent of the damage. Signs of invasion were everywhere. Most of the drawers lay open and their contents dumped onto the floor. Books lay scattered about like leaves after a tornado and I scrutinized them more closely. Sure enough, several of the more important tomes were gone, but nothing I didn't have copies of in the library in the mountains. I also checked the kitchen and the herb closet had been ransacked. Luckily, I had thought to bring what we needed for the spells on our way back, just in case of such a problem.

The computer was still plugged in and working. It didn't look like anyone had thought to take it for what might be on its hard drive. That told me a lot about Marcella. She wasn't a modern sorceress by any means. Most of the modern magic users depend on their computers as much as their ancient tomes. It also told me Charles wasn't totally under her spell. He would've thought to take the computer if he meant to find out everything I knew.

I righted my overturned desk chair as I waited for the computer to boot. It was set to pull up email at boot up, so it connected to the satellite and I received a pile of emails from J.P., and Beth.

I scanned through the new mail from J.P.. The most recent were very urgent. Estaben and his people were getting bolder in their nightly attacks on the people of Yellow Sky. In the last email, he said he was sending in backup to cleanse the town if he didn't hear from me by sunrise. I glanced at the clock on the bottom of the screen. It was close to sunrise in Scotland. I needed to call anyway.

Tasha answered the phone on the first ring. Relief flooded her voice when she heard me. She said J.P. was down briefing the back up and it would take her a couple of minutes to get him. She put me on hold.

I scanned through the other emails as I waited. There wasn't anything important there.

"Where the hell have you been? Do you have any idea how worried everyone has been since you disappeared from Idaho? Suzzy's having a conniption fit. She really likes you and that mage of yours. I was about to head to Yellow Sky myself to find out what happened and take apart anyone that had done you harm, or she was going to rip me a new one."

J.P.'s voice held a hint of anger, probably from having worried him. I could just see Suzzy demanding that he find out what happened. I'd try to call her as soon as this was all over. Before we left, she made Alex and me promise to keep in touch.

I related the situation to him, "So if you would please let Suzzy know that we're alive and working on being fine that would be great. Also tell her I'll call in a couple of days when we have this all wrapped up."

"You better or she'll have my hide tacked to her wall," he grumbled, but there was relief in his tone as well.

"So give us at least forty-eight hours before you send the cleaners in. Have them on standby if you want to, but give me that long," I felt in my bones it'd give us enough time to get this resolved. If for some reason we failed, he could call in bigger guns to clean up the mess.

There had only been a couple of times I'd seen the cleaners at work. They were methodical and more than a little bit scary. That was one of the reasons I always did my best to fix the situations I was sent out to handle. Those mages were scary on several levels.

His sigh before he answered spoke volumes for his reluctance to grant me the request. "I'll continue to have the media guys keep this low key. I've been working this Holloway guy at the local police department to death, and he's really worried about his sons. I hope there aren't people carrying tales out of there by word of mouth. I'll go ahead and have the clearing squad in Dallas, that way if it's not resolved within two sunrises they can descend on Yellow Sky within an hour of dawn and wipe every vamp in town out. Right after that, the story of a bunch of plague-carrying prairie dogs goes to the paper to explain things. It'll be the worst case of the plague since medieval Europe. We've even got some false UFO sightings planned."

I nodded even though I knew he couldn't see the movement over the phone. "Fine, thirty six hours then. I'll call you as soon as it is done. Or if there are any complications."

"Be sure that you do. I better call Suzzy...*now*."

With that, he was gone. J.P. was never much for pleasantries. I almost chuckled to myself at the thought of Suzzy keeping him in line with threats of violence to his person.

Alex reached out across our link.

"What's up?" I asked as I reached to put the phone back on the cradle.

"We're going into the rats' place. It's one of the bigger mansions just north of town. Geri said that it'll be easy to drive from here out to Weasel and Topper's dad's place and do the spell."

"That's good. Make sure you have them call home. In fact, you all should let folks know you're okay." I looked through his eyes and saw the long driveway that curved up to a house on top of a small butte that overlooked the town. The house dominated the butte, and there was no way that anyone would've been able to get there without someone from the house seeing them. It would also make it impossible for

someone using mundane means to escape undetected. *"How are Geri and Cindy getting along?"*

"They've spent a lot of time posturing and growling at one another. I've never seen Geri act this aggressively with anyone. It's almost like she wants Cindy's place in the werewolf pack."

"I doubt Geri's ever had to deal with another alpha female wer before. It wouldn't be so bad if they weren't similar species, and as Geri gets more used to handling her wer feelings, it'll get easier for her to control that side of her personality. Right now, Cindy's just too close and she's bringing her coyote self more to the surface. Not to mention the closeness of the full moon. Even a mage of Geri's training would have problems dealing with this happening so soon in their werelife. Just stay close to Geri and keep her out of trouble."

Through Alex's eyes I saw the car stop in a small parking lot filled with expense SUVs and sports cars. If I had to guess, I'd say that the wererats were doing well for themselves in the adult entertainment business.

"I hope you're right. And of course Geri isn't overly happy with me at the moment either, but I'm sure we'll get past that." I felt his shoulders shrug as he climbed out of the car.

"You and I will sit down with her when this is all over and talk to her about what's happening. She'll adjust to it and everything will get back on track." Unless I missed my guess, the doors they approached were thick mahogany. Geri and Cindy walked side by side in a stiff stride that did little to hide their animosity toward one another. To anyone used to reading body language, they both screamed personal conflict. Hopefully, the wererats wouldn't see that as a weakness they could exploit. They stopped and let Tamela knock on the door.

"Have you felt the place for magic?" I felt bad for asking, but I was still getting used to how Geri and her circle worked.

"Geri had both Topper and I scanning since we left the highway. So far, nothing more than the basic werestuff."

Though his eyes, I could tell he called on his mage sight and Geri blazed brightly in front of him, the form of the coyote looming large over her. Cindy's wolf was almost as large, but not nearly as bright. And Tamela's weresignature shone just slightly larger than her human form. He glanced around the area I could see and outside of the guys, nothing else flashed with magic.

"Good, the fewer surprises in all of this the better." Not having any other magic to deal with let me relax a bit, not much, but right then, any little bit helped. *"Let's hope these ladies are smart and Estaben and Marcella don't have their claws in too deep for them to see reason."*

The door opened slowly and a lovely young human woman stood in the glow from the lights behind her.

"Geri, Sara said to expect you and a couple of friends. Please come in." Her words came through plainly via Alex's ears. She gestured for the group to enter into the brightly lit tile entryway. She closed the door behind them before walking through the group looking each one up and down with a very schooled eye.

"So Geri, have you decided to bring your students out here for some much-needed experience?" The woman laughed lightly as Weasel and Topper blushed under her scrutiny.

"Sorry Lisa, we have other business with your mistresses tonight, but I'll keep it in mind for the future. You never know when my gang might be in need of your tender mercies," Geri all but growled.

"They can have her tender mercies, not my type," Alex told me, his loving emotions flowing to me as he followed Geri and Cindy in Lisa's wake.

Lisa led them down the short hallway to a grand entrance hall. Couches and chairs were arranged in small groupings around a marble floor. Several of the groupings held girls either alone or in groups, all talking to well-dressed men. As Alex's gaze passed over the groups, we only caught a flash of a couple of wererats among the women. All of the men appeared non-magical and human. Lisa led them through a small door on the left side of the room near a large fireplace that dominated the wall with its huge stones and heavy oak mantel.

The next room held a large desk at the far end with several wing-back chairs facing it and a pair of Queen Ann sofas on opposing walls. Behind the desk sat one of the largest women I'd ever seen. Above her hung the heavy aura of a rat; its beady-red spectral eyes glared out at the world. Long, perfectly-groomed blonde hair held small jewels braided into it. On the wall behind her, a map of the world hung with small notations Alex couldn't make out from his vantage point. Another woman, as skinny as the other was fat, lounged on the sofa to the desk's right. A few feathers had been worked into her hair, but otherwise, she was unadorned.

The large woman rose, or at least I think she rose. It looked like she made the motions of rising, but she grew no taller as she waddled around the side of the desk.

"Geri, it's been a long time," she said, her breaths nearly heaving. "I've been meaning to drop by and check on you since I heard about that incident with the coyote a while back. It looks like you are doing alright."

As she cleared the desk, I could see that she was just as tall as she was round. *"How in the hell does she make money as a whore?"* Alex asked as I felt him restrain from making a physical expression of his amazement. His eyebrows almost went up by themselves, but apparently, he'd learned enough from me to realize how much wers go by facial expressions.

I chuckled to myself. *"A lot of men find large women very attractive. I've heard it compared to riding a moped. They're fun to ride, but you don't let your friends see you do it. Besides, in some cultures, a man's wealth is judged by the size of his wife. A man who can afford a large wife is very wealthy."*

"Just promise me you won't get fat."

I chuckled again. *"I've never heard of a fat dragon."*

"Cerebella," Geri greeted her friend with a hug. Her arms barely reached around the back of the woman "You look like you are doing well."

The wererat returned the hug, almost engulfing Geri in her girth. "What can I say? Business is good, has been for a number of years. It doesn't hurt that one of my clan is on the police department and keeps the fundies from raiding the place. That and the fact that I've had most of the city council through my doors at one time or another and the ones that haven't been through have brothers, husbands, or fathers that have. So, I just rely on word of mouth to spread the word about my clean girls and the men show up in droves. Hell, I even had the mayor of Dallas in here the other day, and let's just say that he's a bigger freak than I could've imagined."

"Yeah, a real freak," the rat from the couch echoed with a giggle.

Geri turned to the other wererat. "So Magenta, has Cerebella been treating you well?"

"Can't complain. So, who's your new friend there? I didn't know you were into wolves." Her eyes were unfocused like she was in either a trance or some drug-induced haze. Her rat was almost as strong as Cerebella's, but no other magic emanated from her.

Cerebella walked back to her chair behind the desk as Cindy sat down in one of the chairs in front of it. Tamela along with Larry and Terry sat on the couch opposite Magenta.

"Magenta, dear," Geri smiled and the coyote in her flashed slightly. "This wolf is nothing more than a momentary necessity to me."

She spun and took the other chair immediately in front of the desk. Alex turned his gaze back to Magenta long enough for him to see the rat in her flinch back from Geri's predator, sinking back into the couch with a whimper, trying to disappear.

"Geri, please don't scare Maggie. You know how delicate she is after that sad incident a few years back." Cerebella chided, as she appeared to sit down. Again, the level of her head didn't change.

"I'm sorry Sara. Being a werecoyote is new to me and it sometimes gets the better of me. May I introduce Cindy Willowbranch, Alpha *Bitch* of the Bitter Tooth Wolf pack in Idaho. She's here as my guest. We've come with news and need of your help."

"I've heard of the Bitter Tooth Wolf pack. Your alpha male was here a couple of weeks ago in the company of a human witch named Marcella Bovelwood. How can I help you?" Cerebella leaned forward on the desk.

"Who was in charge when they were here?" Cindy demanded.

From Alex's viewpoint standing behind and between her and Geri, I saw that she gripped the arms of the chair hard enough to turn her knuckles white.

"It was obvious to all that the wolf was under the heel of the witch." Cerebella cocked her head and seemed to study Cindy. "Do I take it by your tone that he's with her against your wishes?"

"He was supposed to take our pack males hunting, then I find out he's here, adding to our pack without my approval," her growl was audible to all.

Cerebella made a dismissive gesture." Men, they're hardly worth all the problems they cause. That's one of the reasons I keep my beloved Magenta with me. I grew tired of them," she sighed, "and their...hunting."

She paused for a light laugh.

"Sara, may I ask what Marcella wanted from you?" Geri asked. I hoped she'd turn attention away from Cindy, who I was afraid was about to lose all control.

"Probably the same thing that she wants with the wolves. She has something planned for the next full moon and wanted my help in turning people into wers. She thought that if some of my customers suddenly found themselves furry at the full moon, it might help her cause. She talked about world domination. Now, I've occasionally thought about taking over the world, but then I realize what I have here in Yellow Sky, and find myself content with that." She shot a quick glance over her shoulder to the map on the wall.

"Gods, does she have an ego or what?" Alex muttered.

"So what did you tell her?" Geri asked to keep Cerebella talking.

"What do you think I told her? My god, do you realize what that woman hides behind an illusion? She's as big as a house, but to keep the men around her she looks like this pretty little blonde thing. I wouldn't even hire her illusionary self to service the schoolboys who come here for their first time. She obviously doesn't have much experience around wers or she would've thought to have better hygiene. I don't know how big that bitch is, but there must be spots she can't reach in the tub, because she smells. Either that or she's an undead zombie or something. I've never run into one of those, but I hear that they smell awful." It looked like the woman was about to keep going when Geri cut her off.

"So you told her no."

"Well, not exactly. I told her that my girls and I wouldn't help her. Do you have any idea what having something like that around would do for my business? But I did tell her that she could speak to any of the rest of my clan if she wanted to and see if they'd be interested. I passed the word out to the clan that they didn't have my blessings to help the fat bitch, but I wouldn't act against them if they did. I understand she found a couple of them and they've been helping her out."

"So your men are not immune to her charms either, eh." Cindy snarled. I could only hear her, but I was pretty sure there was a sneer on her face.

"Hell, I'm not sure there are any men that are immune to her charms. Rumor has it that she even has some vampire working for her. But then why would a vampire be working for a human? I thought they had enchanted senses too, so how could he stand to be around her? But then if it's a man, need I say more?" She gestured, and pointedly looked at Alex and the guys. "So Geri, are you ready to have one of my girls make real men out of your boys here?"

"Sara, I think that'll have to wait for a while. Right now I need to discuss with you what we need, if you will. Are there any wererats in town that can trace their lineage to anyone but you?"

"No, Maggie and I ate all the other ones a few years back. If it's a rat in this town it can find me as its alpha."

As Geri explained the plan to Cerebella, someone came into the room with me. I looked up at Janie standing there in the doorway. Her shirt was on, but her long blonde hair was disheveled and she smelled strongly of fresh sex.

"Burn's focused now," the young woman said. "She can find Char, but she says we need to hurry. Char's hungry and trying to find someone to feed off of."

"I'll be right there. Go ahead and go out to the garage. We'll take my Pathfinder," I replied, then turned my attention back to Alex.

"Need to go, let me know if anything happens, but it feels like this is going to work out okay with the rats."

"They found Char?"

"Yeah, and we need to hurry. Keep in touch if you need me."

"Be careful."

"I've dealt with fledgling vampire mages before. I'll be fine."

There was a mental kiss and the link slipped into the recesses of my mind.

Chapter Twenty Nine

WE LOADED into the Pathfinder. Stan, Janie and Bernadette sat in a pile in the back seat while I followed their lead across town. They directed me several miles south of Yellow Sky. Bernadette had a hard time keeping Charles out of their link. As we got closer to his location, the sensations and emotions coming from her twin grew stronger despite how Stan and Janie tried to keep her attention on them and the situation at hand. I hoped they could keep enough of her mind from being swept away with Charles that we could track him down.

As we moved away from the town toward a small group of lights on the southern horizon, I realized someone actually possessed the forethought to suggest Charles do his early feeding away from his home base. But that went against everything we'd seen up to this point in Estaben's behavior. He'd been tring to draw attention to his growing brood. Maybe this was Charles' own good sense kicking in. He knew we were looking for vampires in Yellow Sky, but I wouldn't have looked to the city south of there.

As we entered the city limits of Canyon, Texas, Bernadette cried out loudly and renewed her mumblings. Stan and Janie tried to draw her attention back and after a couple of minutes as I pulled up to the first stop light in the little town, Stan sat up and looked at me in the rearview mirror. "Near the library. We caught a flash from there. He's on the sidewalk near the library, waiting on someone to come out. He's very hungry."

"Where is the library?" I asked as I eased the car forward from the light.

"Turn left at the next light," Stan directed. "Then go down about two blocks. There'll be a parking lot on the left."

"Will that be right in front of him? I'd like to sneak up on him, if possible." Unless I was absolutely sure about what I was dealing with, I didn't like to just drive up and grab someone.

"That is my preferred method as well, that's why I suggested the parking lot," Stan replied "We'll have to go around to the other side of the building to be where we saw Char." He ran his hand lovingly through Bernadette's hair.

I pulled into the parking lot and drove far enough I could park beside a large dumpster. I stopped the car and looked into the back seat at the three of them. "I want you to stay here. Bernadette's in no shape to go, and she's getting worse the closer we get to Charles. I can handle this. Stay here, try to be quiet. I really doubt anyone will be able to see through the tinting on these windows. So as long as you're quiet, no one should bother you."

"But we could…" Janie started to object

"No," I cut her off. "I'm a hell of a lot older than you are and I've dealt with many fledgling vampires in my day. One or two of them have even been vampire mages. I'll send up magical flares if I need help."

I used my speed to get out of the car and around the corner of the building before either of them could voice another objection. The night was fairly cool with a hint of autumn. In the near future, frost would cover the ground. I stood in the middle of a college campus. I hadn't paid a lot of attention to where we went. I just assumed we were in the town square area of Canyon, but from the sign in front of me, I was on the campus of West Texas University. I continued to follow Stan's directions and pushed my senses outward to try to get a feel for my quarry. As I walked past what had to be dorms, I felt a small spell cast in a room above me. It had the feel of a love spell, simple and harmless to me, but a potential problem for the caster. With a gesture, I shattered the spell before it could reach its intended target. Then, almost as an afterthought, I causally reached back along the trail of magic and set the page in the spell book ablaze. That way the young man who cast it wouldn't stop his belief in magic, but would think twice about casting another love spell. I also gave him the idea to stop by Halfling's Hideaway soon. He had potential and might make a good addition to Geri's little crew.

As I came around the corner of the library, I felt Charles behind me. I whirled around and realized he was across the street heading the other way. A tall broad- shouldered man walked along about ten feet in front of him. It must be his intended prey for the night. From the back, I had to give him points for good taste. I fell into step with them, trying to spot a good place to ambush him. I scanned the area and spotted no other magic or magical creatures in the immediate vicinity.

The prey turned right down a narrow driveway past one of the larger buildings. Heavy shadows cloaked the drive, so this would be the best place to strike. I stepped up my pace, moving onto the thick grass to cover the sound of my footfalls. Charles did the same as he closed in on his prey. I needed to be faster to catch him before he overtook the jock he followed.

As the prey entered the shadows, bright lights suddenly snapped on. I stopped instantly before I stood exposed by the light. Charles almost slammed into the back of the guy, but skidded to a stop smoothly enough to make it look like a small stumble. I cursed myself for forgetting about motion sensitive lights that were so popular in the modern world.

Charles made apologies to the jock for almost running into him. The jock laughed and asked if he recognized Charles from class. Charles played along and the two walked off down the driveway as the jock invited Charles to accompany him to the campus pool for a late night swim. Apparently, Charles and I weren't the only ones out hunting this fine evening. I ducked back into the shadows and decided to follow and see how it played out. This would tell me a lot about how Charles was adapting to being a vampire and help me to decide the best way to deal with him.

They headed toward a large building at the far end of a huge parking lot. I paused in the cover of an immense tree and reached out for Stan.

"I've got a visual on Charles, how's Burn holding up?"

"Fine, how much longer is this going to take? We're holding out okay right now, but Hill and I are starting to get a little tired here. This isn't as much fun as it might appear." Stan's reply was tense with fear for a member of his triad.

"It's going to take a little longer than I planned. I want to see how he handles his hunting. I can learn a lot, and it'll help us decide how hard we'll have to work to save him."

"Okay, just keep in touch," Stan replied. *"Burn's settling down a bit. She's feeling a lot of lust through the hunger."*

"That matches what I'm watching. That feeling may get more intense real soon and it should be easier for you guys to handle."

Charles and his prey approached the building. *"I'll let you know something when I see more."* I took off across the deserted parking lot before they moved out of sight.

They entered the darkened gymnasium building. I flowed silently in their wake, careful not to let the doors slam and thankful neither of the two squeaked. I cleared the outer doors just in time to see a door in the middle of the hallway closing. Stealthily, I made my way down to it and listened for sounds from the other side. I couldn't hear anything. Opening the door to a locker room, I peered inside. My enhanced senses didn't feel them in the immediate vicinity of the door. I heard another door close at the far end of the room, out of my sight. Swift feet got me to the end of the row of lockers, next to the openings for the showers. The darkened room would've been too dark for a normal human to see but I knew it was empty and sped through it.

Several doors lined the wall. I paused for a moment and called on my mage sight. Anything a vampire touches is going to have a slight magical residue, so I scanned for it. Sure enough, along the upper edge of one of the doors, part of a finger smudge glowed in my sight. Charles hadn't opened the door, but he caught it before it closed on him.

Again, I paused at the door, listened for sounds from the other side and heard a loud splash. This door must lead to the pool. I stood there for a moment and wrapped myself in an invisibility shield. I hoped the lust and the hunger were strong enough Charles wouldn't detect my presence until I was ready for him. Normally I wouldn't worry about a fledging vampire detecting my presence, but I knew Charles had been well trained in the magical arts before he became a vampire. He'd be even stronger now.

Thankfully, the door opened toward me. I stepped out into the vast openness of the indoor pool. Only lights from under the water provided illumination of the scene before me. I stood there for a moment to get my bearing and let my ears draw my eyes to the source of the splashing. The two were in the pool, cavorting about like a pair of mating otters. The part of me that Alex reopened almost turned away to give them privacy. But I held fast. I needed to watch every move Charles made. I needed to be ready to intervene should the need arise to save the life of the jock who thought he found a new boy toy to play with.

I settled down to watch from the stand of bleachers along the wall next to the door.

"Hey, you busy?" Alex's mental voice whispered in my mind.

"Not really, just at this moment." I opened up and let him see what I was watching.

"Gee I never took you for a voyeur." Alex's mental laugh brought a smile to my currently invisible face.

I ignored the statement. I was old enough, it was all fairly clinical. I was studying, nothing more. *"So how's it going with the rats? Any progress?"*

"If all wererats are as crazy as these two, and David," Alex sighed, *"I can see why most of them don't last long once they've been changed. How these two have lasted is beyond me. I'll ask Geri about it later, but they've agreed to our plan. We're heading out to Weasel and Topper's father's place in a few minutes. Everyone's checked in with families and that's all good. Mom wants to see me soon. So, what's your plan with Charles?"*

"I'm trying to see how well he controls his hunger. That'll let us know if we can save him. Once I see that, I get the jock out of the way, change his memory a bit and haul Charles, willingly or not, back to the Pathfinder. Then we'll know if we need to drop him off somewhere or if we can bring him with us."

The jock climbed out of the water for a second to dive in from the side. *"Hey I know him. That's David French. I went to high school with him!"* Alex exclaimed. *"I always thought he acted a little gay. I thought he had a nice body too, but man what a little dick on the guy. Let Charles kill him and put him out of his misery."* He gave a light mental chuckle.

"It could just be the cold water," I reminded Alex.

"It could, I'm sure we'll know for sure in a few minutes."

Alex was silent for a few minutes while the two men swam together in the deserted pool. Hunger rolled off Charles. He used the lust of his body to cover it and possibly control it. It was a risky maneuver. Lust energies can hold the hunger back, but it's very easy for the hunger to overcome the lust at a peaking point. A vampire could do much more damage to their lover than they intended.

"You realize this is giving me ideas." Alex commented. He sent a stream of emotions to me, along with a few mental images.

"Not now," I laughed. *"I need to concentrate to keep this shield up so Charles won't sense me."* I had to admit to myself that I was getting ideas too. I couldn't wait for all this to be over and spend a while really getting to know Alex.

The two in the pool eased themselves out of the water and onto the towels at the side nearest to the locker room. The telling moment was quickly coming.

"For Charles' sake I hope not too fast," Alex quipped in the back of my mind.

I skillfully ignored him and carefully began to call up energies to my will. It would be a very thin line between pulling David out of Charles' clutches before he went too far and letting Charles stop on his own to let David live with no risk of becoming a vampire himself.

Their encounter became more intense and David proved it was the cold water as the hunger rose to the point it pushed against the lust battling it for control. I'd been around enough vampires I recognized the way the energies radiated out from Charles. The tinting of his own magic in them reminded me of the lack of those things in Estaben.

Charles let David take control of their encounter as he fought the hunger. He surrendered to David's lust and took it as part of his own. The hunger receded. Then, before things could go over the edge, Charles pulled David down to him. He sank his fledgling fangs into the jock's thick unprotected neck. The pain pushed David over the edge, ecstasy flooded though him and Charles took his blood.

The hunger sank back to a manageable level. To my mage sight, it was a simple red tinge in Charles' aura. Before Charles took too much, he pulled back. A slight trickle of blood ran down his cheek. David passed out on top of him. Charles untangled himself from his trick and slid back into the pool after gently laying David on the towels.

"Well that went remarkably well." I commented to Alex. *"I'd say we can definitely save Charles...as far as being a vampire goes. Now I need to find out how strong of a hold Estaben and Marcella have on him."*

"I'll pass that along to Geri and the others. We're almost out to the land. We'll start setting up and then wait for you to get here."

"We still have a couple of hours before the moon sets and that'll be the best time to cast the spell." I stood and walked carefully down the bleachers toward where Charles finished up his swim. *"I'll go talk to Charles."*

"Go easy on him."

"I'll try." I felt Alex withdraw from my mind. I decided to turn back to the bleachers and wait for Charles to notice me once I dropped my invisibility shield.

To his credit, Charles looked around quickly as I appeared on the bleachers.

"Hello Tal. I take it that you and the others survived Marcella's attempt to break your gate tapestry. I started feeling Burn a couple of hours ago. I guess that's when you got through." His voice was level, with a hint of nerves to it. "How long have you been there watching?" He went over to the pile of clothes next to where David lay, and dressed hastily.

"Long enough to see what I needed to see." I walked toward him as he pulled on his black jeans. "I see you can keep yourself from killing already. That is most commendable in one so young. You have great potential in the vampire circles."

"Thank you. Most of the vampires I've met wouldn't be happy with me for leaving him alive. They want us to either kill or turn everyone we bite. Marcella especially would be unhappy with my actions tonight. This is the first time I've been able to stop myself." He paused with his shirt in his hands and looked down at the man sleeping at his feet. "It actually feels good, knowing that I can walk away and leave them breathing." He slipped the black t-shirt over his head, pulled it down and tucked it into his jeans.

"That's what I've always heard from folks who survive well. But you're right, a lot of vampires don't try to stop or they just don't care." Unfortunately, the non-mage vampires who survived the best were the ones who didn't care about their victims and regarded them the same category that most humans saw cattle.

"So, now what do we do with him?" There was actually concern for his victim in his voice.

I took the opportunity for another test. "If it were totally up to you, if I weren't standing here, what would you do?"

He looked up, his eyes held little confidence. "My telepathy has increased since the change. I think I'd erase his memory of the details of our encounter. He would simply remember a cute trick, the pool and really hot sex. I'd have him walk himself to his dorm and go to sleep. I figure he'll sleep for a day or so and wake up ravenous."

I nodded slightly. "An excellent choice. Or, you could leave him here, but then his rest wouldn't be as sound. You show concern for your meat, which is good. Would you mind help?"

"I wouldn't mind your guidance, but I think I'd like to do this myself." He sat down next to David and put his on shoes and socks.

I stood silently, watching. Gone was the brash young mage who wanted to know everything about being a vampire. Here in front of me sat a predator in the final stages of his initial metamorphosis. Over the next few years, he'd find his vampire self, but the heart he possessed as a mortal still held sway over him. Geri taught him well. He fought the darkness that could have easily swallowed him had he given himself over to the baser nature of the vampire. I figured he'd faced his dark side years ago and learned to keep it under control. Most young mages do.

He reached over and ran his hand across the jock's large apparently-rock-hard chest before passing it over his brow. David's eyes flew open. He sat up and started pulling on his clothes. Charles smiled as he slowly stood. "Control this tight is still hard."

"It'll get easier," I tried to sound reassuring. "Do you think you'll have to walk with him back to his room, or can you manipulate him from a distance?"

Charles shook his head. "It'd be better if we go with him. I would hate for him to slip my hold and fall over on the sidewalk still asleep."

I chuckled at the metal picture. "Okay, let's go. Can we talk as we walk, or do you need to concentrate?"

"I should be alright to hold on to him and talk at the same time. I guess you want to know what Marcella and Estaben are planning. And I need to know how the others are. I felt Burn tracking me earlier. I guess you thought it would be safer for you to meet me than risk the others without knowing how I'd react. Stan and Hill are with Burn. I feel them trying to ease her mind right now."

"If you felt Burn, why didn't you come to us?" I asked, watching his face closely.

He looked down at David as he clumsily slid on his shoes. "I was already hungry. I wanted to be feed up before seeing everyone like this. Then when I felt her tracking me, I thought maybe if I led you all down here, I'd be outside Estaben's range of influence and could keep him from knowing you were back, at least for a little while."

I nodded. "Logical, and since Estaben isn't magical, a good plan. What if you were followed?"

Charles shook his head. "I doubt Marcella would care that much, she's too worried about everyone getting out there and making more monsters. The next couple of nights are key to her plan."

"I can understand that." I gestured to David. "We need to get him home."

"Yeah."

David lurched to his feet. His movements were not quite as fluid as a normal walking man. Over time, Charles would get better at manipulating someone, so eventually, he'd be able to move a victim without any evidence the person was under anyone's control other than their own. It'd take many years, but the ultimate expression of his manipulation would actually be having the person talk while under control. But even so, his control of David was better now than Alex's control of Robert Cooper had been. The vampire energies were strengthening him beyond what he realized.

"Tell you what, I'll cover the minds of any of the people we encounter along the way so they don't see anything odd." I said as we started out the door. "And yes, I need to know what you know of Marcella and Estaben's plans. The others are all fine. Alex, Geri, Weasel and Topper are off on another project while Stan, Burn, Hill and I came to get you."

"I'm glad that everyone is okay," Charles said, relief in his voice. "When I woke up, you guys were gone. The first thing Marcella wanted me to do was to help her try to destroy your gate. She doesn't have any other mages working with her. She's hoping I'll be her right hand in the magic end of all of this. I guess too much of Geri rubbed off on me. I just can't go along blindly with her plans. She's a really bitter woman. I've been playing along where I could. When she had us break into your house, there wasn't a lot I could do. I held back my magical energies, so she supplied most of the power for the disruption of the gate. She hoped you all would be trapped in there and out of her hair. That was one really nice spell you had there. I hope you'll show me how to do that one day."

"So, she's beginning to trust you?" I asked as we stepped out into the lobby.

"Well, not really." Charles replied. "I don't think she really trusts anyone. She just uses people. Hell, Estaben isn't the brains behind all of this, Marcella is. You know, like Merlin was the brains behind King Arthur. Or I think she is. Every so often it's like there is someone else pulling her strings, but I don't have real evidence on that one yet."

"Arthur was basically a figurehead wielding a mystic sword." I chuckled in memory. "Hell, that man couldn't even manipulate his own wife. The Merlin was more than the brains behind that throne, but then that's ancient history. How much of Marcella's plan is Estaben going along with? And what gives you the idea there may be someone else behind this?"

"From the sound of it, he was going along with most of it until he learned that you were here and looking for his head," Charles said, opening the gym's main door. "That made Marcella's day. She realized then that her plan of making Estaben into the big bad in all of this was working the way she wanted. At this point Estaben's expendable. If everything falls apart, she's planning to skip town and wait for the heat to die down before she tries again. But every once in a while, she changes her orders without good reason or logic. Normally it's something I don't think she should be doing, but the things she changes to are often worse than what she initially planned."

"Well isn't that classic." I muttered as we moved out into the open parking lot. I gestured to the jock in thrall. "You do know where he lives, right?"

"According to his mind, he's up in the top of the big building over there." He pointed to the south side of the parking lot. "I even have the codes to get us in. Geri taught us to be thorough." His voice had a little more confidence to it.

"So what's her big plan?" I thought I'd see if what Charles had heard matched what we had gotten from Wayne, the wolf in the bottle.

"Well she's planning on taking over the world, of course. She's going to start with Yellow Sky and then with each new full moon expand her power base exponentially. Now I haven't totally figured out how she's going to control the monsters she's making, but she seems to think that most of them will be under her control. She's also talking about something to make it so vampires can be more active in daylight. That's part of why Estaben and the others are following her."

"Yes, most vampires want to be able to move about more freely than they do," I agreed. "That'd be a leverage point. Every would-be tyrant or messiah needs a leverage point to bring in followers. That'd also explain why, until they turned you, they didn't have a vampire mage with them. By now, most vampire mages have figured out or been taught to move around more freely than non-mage vampires."

"Yeah I was going to ask you about any spells you know that might help me out."

"In time, in time." I chuckled as Charles stopped to enter the access code to open the door to the dorm.

We dropped into silence as we traveled through the dorm to David French's room. With Charles in control, he took out his key and let himself into his dorm room. Luckily in this part of the dorm, most of the older guys lived by themselves, and we didn't have a roommate to deal with—I wasn't sure I wanted to know how Alex knew that, as the knowledge trickled into my head. Charles had him undress and then slip silently into bed before bending over and giving him a soft kiss on the forehead as he released his telepathic hold of the jock.

"Let me get us out of here." Charles said, as he took my hand. I felt him call on his own psychic powers, and we found ourselves standing next to the Pathfinder, with Bernadette, Stan and Janie looking out excitedly at us.

Chapter Thirty

AFTER QUICK assurances that everyone was okay, we all piled into the Pathfinder and headed to meet up with the others. Stan surrendered the back seat to Charles and Bernadette so they could sit beside each other. As is common with twins, the two wanted physical contact to reassure themselves that everything was fine. Bernadette was overjoyed to see with her own eyes that Charles was still around and not much worse for wear.

As we drove, I continued to quiz Charles about what he knew about Estaben and Marcella's plans.

"The zombies are something that she's playing very close to her chest," he said. "I haven't seen or heard anything about how she does it. I figure it has to be something that she cast on them before they die. Maybe she has some kind of fetish or something on them."

"Well that's a good theory." I passed a small subcompact car struggling to climb the one hill between Canyon and Yellow Sky. "It'd also tell us she's been planning this for a while. Spells like that take a while to lay out and execute."

"She's not that organized. I'd be surprised if she put a lot of thought into this. But she's more in control of the situation than Estaben." Charles paused, his face in the rear view mirror got thoughtful.

"Is it normal to feel a bit of sympathy for your Sire?" he asked in a voice just above a whisper but loud enough for me to hear.

"Depends on the situation." I slowed down when Stan indicated we approached our exit. "It's more common for unwilling fledglings to hate their Sires."

Charles nodded. "I can see that. I'm fairly sure Marcella made Estaben change me. I haven't seen him change anyone else, not like the others who seem to change at least one person a night. And as soon as a new vampire is up for it, she makes them start changing people. I know that she wants me to start changing people soon. Estaben's actually been shielding me from her the best he can. He's been trying to give me more independence than most of the other fledges get. Just last night, I managed to sneak away and checked everywhere I could think to find you guys, but there was no sign of you. I didn't want to disrupt Geri's protections so I didn't go in. I went back to Estaben because I hoped I'd be in position to help if you guys made it out of the tapestry in time. I think Joe may be a bit suspicious of me, but Estaben's not."

Joe. I'd forgotten the name of the vampire Estaben created when we parted ways. "If they can trace their lineage back to Estaben then he'll have some control over them."

"She's got nothing but disdain for the werewolves," he continued. "She treats them as little more than dogs and claims it'll be simple for her to get all of them under her control once the full moon changes them for the first time. Tom follows her orders without question. I figure she has him under some kind of spell."

"If Tom's as dumb as Cindy, then it wouldn't have to be a very strong spell," Bernadette muttered almost to herself.

"If he's an alpha werewolf, he has a stronger will than most," I explained as we turned north. "With most wers, will counts for more than intelligence, especially when resisting influences."

"Right," Charles answered. "I think it's got something to do with the way most men look at her. I'd bet she's some kind of siren or something. I doubt she's had a lot of training, or at least not a lot of serious training. When we were at your place, after she disrupted the gate, she acted like your books were the most precious things she'd ever seen. I'm sorry about the gate. I did what I could not to lend much energy to that. Anyway, she actually locked herself away for a couple of days while she went over the books. I guess she called the wolves she left on guard duty back too soon. You guys made it back safe and sound."

"We could be better," Janie grumbled. "Tell you what, one of these days we'll get you trapped in a failing gate for over a week and see how you feel."

A wave of anger surged off Charles. Like a lot of fledglings, he had to learn to control his emotions better. "I said I was sorry for my part of it," he growled.

"And we understand," I interrupted before anyone else could say anything. "What was done wasn't your fault. We'll all be fine when this is over." The energy of a mental exchange going on between Bernadette and Janie tingled against my senses. Bernadette was probably telling her to back off Charles.

As we pulled onto a dirt road, I sensed the others ahead of us. I'd been in contact with Alex several times on the trip in and he said they were almost ready to cast the spell. Daybreak was only an hour and a half away. The moon would set moments before that.

It was another ten minutes across little-used dirt roads before we reached the others' cars. A large sedan was parked next to Geri's Beetle along with a dark-colored Jeep. With only minimal ground clearance, I really wondered how the sedan made it down the crater-riddled roads. I parked behind the Jeep.

Before we got out of the car, I fired up the laptop in an attempt to connect with the office, but couldn't get a signal.

"I guess even your Coalition tech can't fight the fact we're far enough out that none of the signals get through here." Charles said as he and Bernadette opened their doors.

I didn't need Stan to show me the way, but he was helpful in pointing out several spots we needed to bypass, like cactus-filled sinkholes and impassable mesquite thickets poised to provide slight delays in us getting to the circle. The terrain was the main reason there were not a lot of people in the area. Stan explained Larry and Terry's folks brought the place with the idea of a weekend getaway, but decided against that and had been unable to find anyone to take it off their hands. Once the boys started practicing magic, they realized there were several natural lines of magical energy, like streams of power, normally called ley lines, running through the land, which made it a great place to do magic. For the past couple of years, Geri and crew traveled out here to do the really big stuff, things that needed to be worked outside and somewhere they wouldn't be disturbed.

As we topped a slight rise, I saw them gathered down in a small ravine. A large fire blazed. Geri and Alex worked on laying out the circle with the help of Larry and Terry while Cindy, Tamela, Cerebella and Magenta stood to the side watching. Alex looked up as my gaze fell across him and handed a bag of salt to Terry. Geri glared at him as he took off up the steep side of the ravine toward us.

Stan, Janie, and Bernadette continued down to the others while Charles and I waited as Alex rushed toward us. He threw himself into my arms and gave me a big kiss, which I returned eagerly.

Then he turned to Charles. "You look good, considering what you've been through."

Charles nodded, looking Alex over with a knowing eye. "You do too. It seems joining the Coalition was destined to change us, huh."

Alex let go of me to give Charles a big hug. "We're here for 'ya bud. Anytime you need help through this, let us know. "

"I know, that's the thing with us, we're family, and family is always there for each other." There was a quaver in his voice. "I guess Tal's family now too."

"Ya," Alex smiled, "it's like he was made for us. Or us for him."

I placed a hand on Alex's shoulder. "Guys, we need to get down there and help Geri finish setting this up. This is going to be a long, complicated spell and we only have a little over an hour to get it cast."

Alex wrapped one arm around each of our waists, and led us to the edge of the ravine. It would have been easy to levitate us down into the ravine, but power needed to be conserved for the impending spell, so we skidded down the side of the gorge on the well-travelled path Geri and the others had worn.

I walked over and introduced myself to the wererats.

Cerebella stepped forward as I approached. "So you must be Tal of the Coalition." She extended her hand toward me.

I took the hand and kissed the back of it. The smell of her rat that filled my senses reminded me of the plague years. "Cerebella, thank you for coming to our aid tonight."

The large wererat blushed gracefully. "Anything to get that Marcella bitch out of our territory. She's giving women a bad name."

"Bad name," Magenta giggled.

Cerebella glared at her partner's outburst.

"I understand Geri has explained your role in tonight's spell," I continued, skillfully ignoring Magenta. From what I'd seen through Alex's eyes, she wasn't overly mentally stable and wasn't far from having her rat self take over entirely. Cerebella's influence was probably the only thing keeping her from turning completely. I was impressed Cerebella was as human as she was. She was the oldest wererat I'd ever met, but her human side appeared as strong as her rat side. She could've been a rat shifter, but her energies were definitely wer.

"Of course she has," the alpha rat replied. "It seems fairly straightforward. My one question that she hasn't been able to answer yet is will this spell affect the ones who have already shifted the first time?"

"According to my interpretation of the spell, the subject has to have never embraced the wereside of their existence for this to work," I explained. "If they've ever shifted, then the spell won't affect them, but other than that, it'll affect any other wers of your blood."

"It also won't affect those born wer, or shifters," Cindy added. "That is the only reason I agreed to this. I have several children at home that haven't changed yet, and you assured me they ain't gonna be affected." Like a lot of what she said, she made it sound like a challenge.

"The spell also doesn't affect natural-born wers or shifters. It relies on calling on the human side of the affected to fight off the wereside. It's sort of like giving the person magical antibodies to fight the magical infection. It kills the unborn wer before it has a chance to mature. You'll see in a few minutes." I turned back to the circle. "Now if you'll excuse me, I think I'll lend a hand getting this set up so that we can get this thing cast in time."

Geri had the altar set as I walked over to her. The bowls and knives were laid out with care in the order that they'd be needed. The candles and incense sat ready to light. I glanced around the circle, and in each quadrant, a stone pillar stood with appropriate bowls and candles. The circle of stones and salt lay around all of it, just now complete.

"It looks good," I told her, as she looked up to acknowledge my presence.

"Thanks." She replied stiffly. "We're ready, I think."

"Good. Can we talk for a moment while everyone gets ready?"

"Is now a good time?" she sounded hesitant.

"Not really, but in case anything goes wrong with this, I think we need to clear the air between us. It'll also help the magic flow more smoothly. We'll need to rely on one another in a few minutes and I don't need you hesitating because you're mad at me."

"Fine," she snapped, and then turned to walk down the ravine. "Guys, take a couple of minutes and get ready. When we get back, we'll cast this spell."

We walked in silence until we were beyond the glow of the fire pit. I knew her eyes were as sharp in the darkness as mine. The fire pit was there for the others. But glancing back, it provided a lovely effect. The glow of the fire played nicely off the red of Alex's hair.

Geri paused near a dense stand of chollo cactus. "Tal, this all moved much faster than I thought it would." If she wanted to start off on the attack that was fine. She was under a lot more stress than I.

"And you think I'm happy about how fast this thing went? I've been without a partner for generations and never had a life mate, or soul mate, or whatever term you prefer. I was happy in my solitary life, or I thought I was."

I glanced back toward the circle where Alex sat down in front of the fire pit. I felt his mind relaxing, preparing for the coming spell casting. "Now I'm afraid to lose him."

"So you bound him to you. What does that mean anyway? I've lost two of my students," she snarled.

"We'll get into that when there aren't so many ears," I replied. "I had to think of something to save his life. If we hadn't begun the bonding process that allows him to share some of my power, that werewolf would've torn him apart. We talked about it beforehand. He knows all my secrets. Trust me, he'll be fine. He'll live a very, very long life. I cherish him more than I could've thought possible."

"But I wasn't finished teaching him yet. There's still a lot for him to learn." A sharp almost frantic edge colored her words with a deep feeling of loss.

"Do you think I mean to take him away from you permanently? Of all of your students, he's now the one that's most likely to be with you the longest. In case you haven't thought about it, your werelife has extended your lifetime too. All of your students are going to get old and die before you, unless something happens to kill you before you get old."

"What about Charles?" she snapped "Your friend, Estaben, has seen to it that he'll be around a long time too."

"Estaben is just an assignment ," I said, trying to assure her. "He stopped being a friend a long time ago. The first time he changed a human into a vampire, he crossed a line and he can never go back. Now he's gone too far, and before this is all over, he *will* die. That will free Charles of any link to him."

"But will it free Charles of the curse of being a vampire?" Her voice cracked. Was this the true problem, and I was just a convenient target for her anger? Was the change of Charles the real source of her fury? Her inability to save her student tore at her.

"No, it won't revert Charles back to human," I confessed. "I'm not sure he'd want to. Some people are well suited for life as vampires. I think Charles may be one of those. He may have even asked for the change had a choice been given. I'm sorry about what happened to him. Right now, that's in the past. If we're going to prevent a whole lot of werebeings from changing into furry forms in one more night, then we need to get this spell cast. We need to work together and trust each other as we do." I held out my hands to her. "Geri I'm sorry for the loss of Charles's humanity. I would've saved it if I could. I feel he'll make good choices in the future. He still has a lot of potential. I'll happily train him and help him along the way. Also know that I love Alex very much and will do everything in my vast power to make sure he lives a long and happy life."

Geri took my hands and let me pull her into my embrace. "I've never had one of them hurt before, Tal," she sobbed. "I'm sorry I've been so mean to you since you bonded with Alex. I give you my blessings with him and with Charles." Then she broke down in tears while I held her.

Alex come up behind her and wrapped his arms around the two of us. "It's going to be okay Geri. I'm still here and I'm fine."

She grasped his hand tightly, and nodded slightly against my shoulder. Then the others, led by Charles, walked up to us. Soon we were in a big group hug with Geri and me at the center. The love they had for each other and the sense of family I'd found overwhelmed me. I found myself ready to defend all of them, not just Alex. It had been over a thousand years since I had a real family. Nothing was going to happen to my new one.

Chapter Thirty One

WE HAD less than an hour until sunrise as we broke our group hug and headed back to the circle and the waiting alpha wers.

"Charles, when the sun comes up, go to the back of the Pathfinder. When you open the rear door, you'll notice a small handle in the carpet. Pull on that it and it'll open a sunlight-proof safe box that's built into the truck. It'll keep you safe. I can let you out at sunset or you can let yourself out from inside if something happens to us in the meantime." I knew he'd need to get to safety before we finished the spell since the rising sun was the final activation.

"Thanks, I didn't like the idea of digging into the earth to get safe. In case you didn't notice, it's kinda hard out here." He chuckled, and kicked a large boulder.

The mood was lighter now that Geri had the good cry she'd been holding back. I hoped it was enough to help us work through the coming spell. For the power to flow easily, she needed to trust me. If she didn't, I could wrestle the energies we needed, but she'd worked with her students much longer than I had and knew their energies better. It'd be much easier with her controlling their energies.

"Charles, you're guardian for as long as you can. Then I guess it'll fall to Tamela. We'll need everyone else in the circle." Geri glanced around. "Up there I think would be good." She gestured to the rim of the ravine.

Charles nodded. "Tamela," he called out to the werewoman, "you're with me." Then, he started up the side of the ravine.

"Alex, take the East," Geri said, directing folks to their positions. "Hill and Burn, take South. Stan to the West, and Weasel and Topper the North." Everyone headed to their appointed positions.

Alex gave my hand a quick squeeze as he let go. I flashed him a smile. I wanted to take him in my arms, but knew we didn't have time for that now. But later, after this was all done, would be another story altogether.

Geri walked over to the altar. "Cindy, Sara, Maggie, could you join Tal and me at the altar?"

The werewomen walked cautiously over the salt circle that set the sparkling white boundary for our magic and toward the altar at the center. Cindy and Cerebella carried themselves with a similar haughtiness, while Magenta acted as if she were scared of the whole thing. I hoped Cerebella could control her when the magic began. If she broke the circle, it could get dangerous for us but deadly for the wers. The level of energies we were about to command wouldn't be easily controlled if something happened to that thin line of salt.

Geri walked over to Magenta and took her hands. "Maggie, you need to listen to me. Do you trust me?"

Magenta's head bobbed but her eyes were still wild and afraid.

"Always trust Geri. Always," her voice little more than a whisper. Somewhere she lost her giggle. Cerebella reached up and took her hand.

"You must not run beyond the edge of the circle." Geri's tone was similar to one that a parent would use with a child when they were told to hold hands. "Okay? Stay with Sara no matter what happens. Sara and I will protect you."

"Sara and Geri will protect me," Magenta babbled.

"Right dear, we will protect you," Cerebella said softly.

"Sara, if you, Maggie, and Cindy can stand over here behind the altar, Tal and I will stand in front of you. When we tell you, just extend your arms over the altar and we'll do the rest."

As the three wers took their places, a change washed over Cindy's eyes. At last, she realized exactly what was happening and came to terms with it. She nodded as she stood next to Magenta.

"Alright, guys, begin drawing up the power," Geri commanded.

The power from the world around us strengthened. The ley lines running across the land pulsed in my mage sight, looking like bright ribbons rolling across the land and sky. A strong line of air blazed bright blue directly overhead. Alex reached out with his mind and tapped into its powerful flow. Slightly beneath the ground a deeper line of blue flowed from the water line running almost parallel to the air line, Stan reached out and bathed in the energy of it. Skimming the surface of the earth, a vivid red line of fire ran through the indented section of the ravine wall that formed the fire pit. Bernadette and Janie reached into it as a team and blazed with its glory. Opposite them on the far side of the circle, a pillar of gray power surged upward into the waiting hands of Larry and Terry. Above Geri and me, the lines ran with their power, waiting.

I stilled my mind and reached out for the power surging around me and felt Geri do the same. First, I reached for the cool breezes of the air and peace and tranquility engulfed me. With but a passing thought of Alex, I grabbed for the flaming passions of the fire line. The pure burning of the energies almost took my breath away. It had been a long time since I harnessed more than one ley line at a time for any use. I took a deep breath before grabbing the rushing depths of the water line. It washed over me, and for a moment it fought against the fire I held, so I quickly felt for the earth line's stability. The earth found the balance between the four elements coursing within me. Its gentle pulse pushed back the water and fire while it sang with the air.

I opened my eyes and looked around. Before me, Geri stood enshrouded in the same energies that engulfed me. At the quarters, the gang stood aglow in the currents they'd harnessed. Fear shone in the eyes of the werewomen who stood across from us. The time to cast the spell was upon us. I nodded to Geri, sensing her unspoken request to begin.

"Let's cast the circle!" Geri's voice echoed within the small ravine. The power she held added depth and a commanding quality to her voice as it bounced off of the earthen walls enclosing us. She walked to where Alex stood facing the east, a silver Kris knife held in her hands.

She stepped beyond his pillar and stood before the circle of salt and stones that marked its boundary, then pointed the knife to the ground. "By the power of magic at my command, I cast this circle." She moved to the right, keeping the knife pointed at the ground. When she reached Alex again she raised the knife so she was holding it straight out from her body. "By the power of magic at my command, I cast this circle." Again, she moved to the right following the line of salt and rocks until she came back to Alex. She then raised the knife above her head. "By the power of magic at my command, I cast this circle." She then made her final pass around the circle.

When she reached Alex again, she carefully made her way back to the altar, making sure not to misstep and disrupt the energies that she'd spun. She then laid the knife on the altar before turning back toward the east.

Without prompting, Alex picked up the knife that lay on the stone pillar before him. It was a lovely ceremonial blade made of blue lace agate. He raised it above his head, and pointed it to the east. "I call upon the Gods of the East, powers of air. Heed my call this night. Bring us your healing breezes and the hurricane gales. Come to us with knowledge to guide our magic this dawn."

Thunder clapped and a light rose from the east. I stared in wonder as a great glowing bird flew towards the circle and settled on the rim of the ravine. Blue light played across feathers of deepest purple and lightning flashed in its eyes. Rocks tumbled down the side of the ravine, but thankfully did not cross the circle as its powerful talons sank into the dirt. Thunder rolled forth as its raptor beak opened. "I have come to your call. My magic is yours to command. Allow my wisdom to guide your hand."

In all my years, I'd never seen a Thunderbird. I thought they had all died before I came to the New World. Now I knew they were truly the messengers of the Gods.

A gasp made me turn. Cindy stared in wonder at what must be more magic than she'd ever witnessed unfold in front of her. Magenta looked like she was ready to bolt, but Cerebella kept her hands enclosed in her own.

We all turned to the south as Bernadette and Janie took up an obsidian blade entwined in their hands. They pointed it at the fire. To my mage sight, they blurred into one being. With one voice, they called. "We call upon the Gods of the South, powers of fire. Heed our call and bring your flaming energies into our circle this night. Let your passions aid the spell we cast here."

The fire pit shot sparks high into the night and a giant snake's head rose above the ravine's rim. It looked down on us with slitted eyes, its red scales flashed in the firelight as it coiled itself around the base of the fire pit and its tongue flicked in and out as it settled itself. Sparks flew as it spoke.

"You call in passion, I come in power. I will aid as you cast your spell this night." It rattled its tail and settled its head on top of its coils so that its unblinking eyes stared into the circle.

As soon as the snake settled, we all turned to the west as Stan took up a bright red coral blade. He raised it high and called out with the power he channeled. "I call upon the Gods of the West, powers of water. Bring forth your ever-changing power into our circle. Heed my call and lend us the strength of your tides."

For a moment nothing happened, then a high-pitched howl ripped through the night and a coyote appeared at the edge of the circle. Firelight danced its yellow eyes as it sat by the western pillar and smiled at Stan. "You called, student of my daughter."

Stan lay the knife down on the pillar and bowed to the coyote. "Greetings, God of Shifters. Thank you for coming to my call."

Coyote was the Trickster God of several American Indian tribes and possessed the ability to change shape to aid in his tricks. He was also associated with the element of water since his form was as fluid as his thoughts. I hadn't thought to call him into the circle since we were dealing with shape changers. My heart cheered for a moment in the hopes that his presence would aid our cause.

"But of course, student of my daughter. Your magic this night will affect many shape changers. How could I not come to lend my aid when I heard your call?" He turned to the werewomen in front of the altar."Ladies," he smiled with a chuckle. He locked eyes with Geri. She started to move from the altar, but I put a hand on her shoulder.

"Greetings, Coyote," she nodded to him but stayed with me at the altar. "Thank you for coming to assist in our magic tonight."

"Anything for one of my daughters. I heard your song in the night and wanted to come see you for myself. You have much potential. I will enjoy watching you grow into the great mage you are destined to be." He yipped once then laid his head on his narrow paws. "Please continue your casting, time grows short."

"As you wish," Geri replied. "Weasel, Topper, please complete the calling."

Larry and Terry lifted a quartz knife and pointed it toward the north. To my mage sight, their bond was not as strong as Bernadette and Janie's had been, but it was the bond of brothers. "We call upon the Gods of the North, powers of Earth. Bring your great fortitude into our circle this night. Grant us the power of your strength in the working we now do."

A deep rumble rolled through the small ravine and a large dark form took shape just outside of the fire's light. Heavy steps shook the rocks as it approached us. The form entered the light of the fire and a huge bear stood next to the pillar of the north.

"You have called and the earth has answered. My strength is here for you to use." With that, the bear sat down behind the pillar.

Geri raised her curved knife high. "We have called and the gods of the elements have answered. The circle is cast."

With her final word, the ring of salt and stone blazed brightly as the aura of magic filled the air around us. We now stood separated from the world and we were safe unless someone broke the circle.

"Now comes your part, ladies." I picked up a long white-handled knife. "Cindy , can we start with you? We need a bit of your blood and hair."

"Of course, everyone seems to want something from me these days." She' d retrieved a bit of her spirit, back from the fright of the Elemental Avatars' arrival. She extended her wrist over the bowl Geri held up to catch the blood. With a quick slash, I made a deep cut in her wrist. Had she been human, it would've been a deadly cut, but even as the blood poured down into the bowl, the wound closed, stemming the flow.

"Nice going, maybe you do have a backbone!" she replied as she pulled her wrist against her chest. "So do you mean to scalp me for a little hair?"

I smiled. "No, a small lock will do."

She snatched the knife, sawed off a small lock of her bleached-blonde hair, and handed it to me along with the knife. "Here," she growled.

I turned to the rats. Magenta looked up at me with childlike eyes. "Me first, please. My blood make pretty magic when mixed with my hair." She snatched out a small clump of red hair and dropped it in the bowl Geri offered. Then she held out her wrist for me to cut. I was a little more delicate with her and once I was done, she brought her wrist up to her mouth and sucked at the wound while Cerebella reached up and stroked her hair.

"Sara go now, not hurt as much as wolf bitch acts like," Magenta cooed as the blood stopped flowing from her wrist.

Sara held out her wrist, I quickly made the cut and her blood flowed into the bowel followed by a small lock of hair. "Here, let's be done with this, magic makes my skin crawl," she hissed.

Geri placed the three bowls of blood and hair on the altar, in the center of a large gouged-out pentagram with salt-filled groves. I lit the candles on either side of the pentagram after laying the knife off to one side. Geri picked up a pinch of wolf's bane and silver and tossed it in the small cauldron that sat just outside of the pentagram. She shook her fingers from the burning touch of silver. As we had discussed earlier, I went into a trance as Geri and the gang began a chant. "Wer Stillborn." I sprinkled a bit of silver dust into each bowl. I drew on the energies swirling around us and reached into the bowls of blood before me.

At first, I could only feel the life energies of the werewomen standing in front of me. Then the wers they created over the years gone by. I focused first on Cerebella's energies. I followed the path to her children and then worked through them to the ones they created and so on until I found the ones that had never changed into wereform. I reached for the magic Geri and her students focused in their chant and fed it along the path. The energies within those future wererats began to shrivel up and die. Alongside the weremagic, I felt another magic bound to another's blood. This wasn't weremagic, but human blood magic. Here was Marcella's hold on the wers. It allowed her to make zombies out of the ones who fell. This was how she controlled the ones who were made by her command. If I cut this magic, there was a chance she'd know what we were up to, and try to disrupt us. Then I thought of the four Elemental Gods who guarded our quarters. With a decisive thrust, I burned out Marcella's magic in each of her victims of Cerebella's line.

My work with Magenta's brood went easier. Her prodigy numbered fewer than Cerebella's and I cleansed them quickly. Cindy's wolves proved the hardest. As I reached out to them, I realized that a fair number of them had moved toward us and were less than a mile away. I also realized I wouldn't have enough time before sunrise to clear all of the people they'd infected.

I paused for a moment and reached out for Alex across our link. *"Marcella and the werewolves are coming, I don't know if I'm going to have time to finish this work before sunrise, especially if they mount an attack before I'm done. And I want Charles out of the open. Tell him to get in the truck."*

The power from the Thunderbird raced through him as he answered. *"I'll get Charles moving, and I have an idea on the sunrise problem. Just focus on clearing the rest of the people as fast as you can."*

With a clap of thunder, he broke contact and a second later, he hollered to Charles to get in the truck.

I turned my attention back to purging the magic from the victims of the wolves and Alex diverted a bit of the air energy and turn it toward another use. Then the energy of Cindy and her pack engulfed me.

Magenta and Cerebella didn't have an alpha male in their clan, but Cindy did. I'd never met Tom, but I recognized his energy from Cindy's blood. He'd been one of the first entrapped by Marcella. He fought against me as I tried to reach into his clan. In the magical world I worked, the image of the wolf appeared before me and stood in the middle of the path with his head down, yellow eyes flashed fire at me. I called my astral sword and held it between us.

Then another presence stood on the astral plane with me. I glanced behind me and Coyote stalked up to my side.

"I'll handle this." He leapt across the space to Tom, smashing into the wolf with all his force. His smaller jaws clamped shut on the wolf and his astral image vanished. The alpha wolf didn't stand a chance against the Shifter God.

"Your path is clear now. Finish your work. Your mate is about to try something interesting. I need to be there." With a yipping laugh, the God of Shifters vanished.

The moon's final glow of the night rested on the horizon. I knew I had to go on. I was concerned about what Alex was about to try, but I had to finish clearing the werewolves. Complete the spells before the rising sun hit the altar in the ravine, and the sun had begun to rise. I pushed on down the path. Cindy and Tom's pack was larger than Cerebella and Magenta's combined prodigy. I searched and began to locate the changed people of Yellow Sky. I felt the wolves coming into the area around the ravine.

Then time hiccupped and the pressure eased.

I continued destroying the infections, but it was a little tricky tracking down the ones caused by the wolves we'd already killed. It was a lot like trying to follow a river through a twisting canyon and having to jump over that canyon as you followed the path. After what felt like hours, I cleared each one and eased myself back into the reality of the circle. The chanting continued. Although the chanters were growing hoarse, the power continued to flow.

I opened my eyes and looked about. The werewolf pack had circled the ravine. They looked ready to pounce down on us. In their midst stood a tall elegant blonde woman. This had to be Marcella.

I snatched up the silver powder, sulfur powder and charcoal from the altar and sprinkled it into each of the bowls of blood and hair, then focused elemental fire. They burst into flames. With the burning of the blood, I finished the spell, effectively cauterizing the magic used on the unsuspecting populace of Yellow Sky. "So mote it be!"

Everyone stopped chanting as the fire flamed up in the pentagram, shooting toward the sky. Alex was still focusing power on something. From the look on his face it was not an easy something, either. Then it hit me. Neither the encroaching wolves, nor the rising sun were moving. The sun's rays had stopped inches from the altar. Alex had stopped time outside of the circle, or more accurately, moved the circle outside of time. He must have accessed something in my knowledge of psychic energies and figured out how to consciously use his newly-developed time ability. I dared not disturb his concentration, but I needed to use his efforts to our advantage.

"Cindy, do you think you can stop your pack if we take out Marcella?" I asked.

"I want a piece of that bitch!" she growled.

"I have no problem with that, but we don't need your wolves coming down on top of us while we take her out."

"Done, and any of them that don't listen to me, your people can take out, I don't care!" She shifted as she growled.

"Geri, we need to take the circle down and hit Marcella at the same time Alex drops us back into the time flow. The spell will complete as soon as the sun hits the altar."

"Guys, simple goodbye to the Gods called. Weasel, take over East from Alex, Hill, take West from Stan. I'll drop the circle. Stan, you and Tal hit Marcella," Geri instructed.

"What can we do?" Cerebella asked, still holding Magenta's hand.

"Get up the ravine as quickly as possible and hit Marcella physically while we hit her magically. Cindy and I will be right behind you," Geri growled. Her energies were becoming more chaotic as her coyote rushed toward the surface. She was on the verge of losing control.

I glanced over at Alex, standing in the stilled, first rays of the morning sun. Sweat covered his face. He looked ready to collapse. I gathered energies to me and prepared to lash out at Marcella, and then move to be at his side as quickly as possible. Then an idea hit me.

"Geri, grab the altar, move it into the sunlight! That way the spell completes before we take the circle down."

Geri nodded and grabbed the other side of the altar in hands already shifting to paws. We lifted it together and took two steps to the east. Energies surged as the spell completed. I glanced up at Cindy and the rats as the power rushed through them and out to the creatures destined to receive it.

The look and sweat on Alex's pale face told me he was seconds from collapse. Time to face the witch and her wolves.

Chapter Thirty Two

"ALEX, DROP us back into normal time!" I called out into the soft glow of the morning light. The gang released all quarters at the same time. As one, four voices intoned, "Thank you Gods for your presence in our circle this night. Go in peace, love and light. So mote it be!"

Geri's voice followed in quick succession. "Make the circle be open but unbroken." Her voice shattered the stillness of the morning as time began to flow again and Alex collapsed next to the pillar of the east in the wake of the Thunderbird's departure.

As the energies of the circle dissipated, I gathered them up to myself and lashed out at the witch standing on the rim of the ravine above me. Marcella screamed as my magical bolt slammed into her, followed by Stan's magical attack.

Cindy's howl of anger stopped the charging wolves in their tracks as she and the wererats in monster form charged up the side of the ravine. The wolves milled around, unsure what to do as their alpha female surged past them. The rats followed with Geri's coyote form flowing after them.

The others gathered around Stan at the altar as I ran to Alex. His breathing was shallow and his energies low. I knelt down beside him and took him in my arms. He opened his eyes a bit and smiled. He tried to say something, but I stopped him with a firm finger against his lips. Hunger gnawed at me, but I reached into the earth, drew up power and fed it to him, pulling him onto the astral plane where I could pour energy into him more effectively. Weakness dimmed his astral form. He clung to me and I bathed us in the power of the ley lines that fed the land. I pulled the healing breezes of the air to him while washing him with the purifying water and strengthening his body with earth.

The passions of fire brought numerous kisses between us. When I knew he was replenished enough to go on his own, I stopped the flow of the energy into his astral form.

"How's that?" I asked looking at his face in the astral light.

"Better. How are we doing out there?"

"We stopped the hordes of new wers from coming to life tonight. But we still have werewolves and Marcella to deal with. Geri and the others are working on that right now."

"We should probably lend a helping hand." Alex smiled

"If you insist." With that, I took us out of the astral plane and back to the chaos erupting around us.

Marcella screamed for Tom and the other male werewolves to help her as Cindy and the other females tore at her. The energy of her charms call out to them, and while they turned toward her, they were hesitant to attack their alpha. But this was Marcella's main magic. Her strength lay in her ability to get men to do what she wanted. Several of the wolves turned and began advancing on the female wers as they circled Marcella, skillfully dodging her magical leven bolts.

The power of her magics even on Geri's guys. The sorceress reached out on instinct and called men to her aid. It had been a long time since I'd met an enchantress of such power, but then she'd been getting vampires and werecreatures to do her bidding for a while now. The guys stood around the altar looking up at the battle on the rim of the ravine. No power flowed from them toward her. They'd stopped their assault. In less than a second, Bernadette and Janie shielded the men of the coven from Marcella's call. Their energies welled up around all of us, blocking her unfocused call.

One of Marcella's magical bolts hit Magenta and sent her tumbling over the side of the ravine. Her body landed with a crack and she lay still, bent over a large rock at an unnatural position. Cerebella screamed and threw herself at the witch only to have three of the werewolves intercept her and pull her down to the ground. Their teeth sank deeply into her.

I'd prepared for this. I had to take out Marcella's magic. In doing so I'd also take out everyone else's magic in over a hundred-foot radius, perhaps including my own. I had no idea what it would do to my magic, but if it caused me to lose control of my human form and change to a dragon, that would be bad. I took out a small glass ball from my pocket. It was special issue from the Coalition, only to be used in extreme circumstances. It was one of the things I grabbed before leaving home the last time.

I kissed Alex on the forehead. "I'll be by the cars. When this goes off, all magic will cease to work. I have to be out of its range." I handed the ball to him. "Throw this at Marcella when I get far enough away. The effects will last for twenty four hours. It'll be just like the pit back in Idaho."

He touched my face. "I understand. Go. See you soon," he smiled.

I kissed him tightly on the lips. The love I felt threatened to overflow, but I pulled away, shifted shape into a wolf and raced down the ravine away from the battle. I ran over the uneven ground with werewolves following close on my heels. I had to get a little further before Alex tossed that glass ball.

I rounded a bend and a large black wolf stepped out to block my path. I recognized Tom Willowbranch's lupine form from the astral plane where Coyote defeated him so I could break the spell on the others. I knew I could beat him here in the physical. But I wanted to be just a little further away. The sounds of the battle were still too close and I wasn't sure I was far enough away yet. I didn't slow down, and jumped just outside of his reach. I used a little magic and carried myself up and over him, landing on the loose stones on the side of the ravine. For a moment, my footing was treacherous and I scrambled for purchase. The wolves behind me charged up after me. It took precious seconds for the claws on my right forepaw to find a rock embedded firmly in the side of the ravine. I struggled up, throwing loose stones down on the wolves surging after me. Growls and howls erupted from below as the rocks and sand showered down on them. I launched myself over the top of the ravine with them snapping at my tail.

I paused, finally out of the danger zone. My keen wolfen eyes watched as the magic null bomb sailed out of the ravine toward the witch who struggled with Geri, Cindy and Tamela. Alex's aim was true and the ball struck Marcella in the shoulder. Alex must have used his telekinesis to make sure it hit its mark. The effects were as I had hoped, spectacular. There was no light or sound, but suddenly an enormous ancient gray-haired hag stood where a slender blonde had been.

The wolves paused and howled. They seemed to realize they were now stuck in wolf form and had no idea for how long. Now that Geri and Cindy didn't have to worry about leven bolts, they closed in on the sorceress and attacked.

The first wolf emerged from the ravine below me as Geri knocked Marcella to the ground. I turned, and from the look on Tom's canine features, he was pissed off. I growled a warning. He advanced anyway. I backed away from the edge of the ravine. I wasn't sure exactly where the null magic field ended and didn't want to accidentally slip into it during the coming battle.

I reached into the earth and called up a wall of dirt and rocks as Tom jumped toward me. He cleared the obstacle, but it stopped the others from interfering with the fight. Tom landed heavily about ten feet from me as I continued to back away from the ravine. He glanced back over his shoulder and howled as he realized I'd cut him off from his pack. His hackles went up. He lowered his head, growled and advanced on me. I knew I could easily escape him, but at this point, his pack had caused me a lot of problems. His alpha bitch had tried to kill Alex. And I really wanted to make a point so I wouldn't have future problems with this particular pack of trash.

"Marcella's down." Alex called in my mind.

Cindy's howl of triumph echoed across the plains, followed by Geri's. The other wolves answered their alpha's howl.

Tom remained silent as he stalked forward. I heard the wolves behind the stone barrier retreat down the ravine, heading to their victorious alpha. For a moment, Tom looked indecisive, but a cold light appeared in his eyes and he charged savagely.

I snarled at him, but I'm sure it looked like a smile as he rushed at me. I sidestepped his initial attack. He skidded to a stop and circled back toward me, growling louder. I bared my teeth and charged toward him. The strength of our impact knocked the breath out of me, but I recovered attack position, facing him ready for his next move. He was a strong wolf. He snapped his teeth. Rolling under him, I used my hind legs to kick out savagely. Long gouges showed in his belly as he tumbled away from me. He landed hard, but was up in a moment and advancing toward me again. I rushed him. This time he rose up on his hind legs. We crashed together. He tried to get his mouth around my muzzle, but I forced him down and sank my teeth into his right ear and twisted away from him. He howled in pain as the blood poured down his face.

The wash of blood in my mouth reminded me of my hunger. Until that moment, I ignored that I'd been running on adrenaline since getting back to Yellow Sky. I'd needed to feed since we came through the gate that trapped us. Now here was a source of nourishment. For the first time in years, I wanted to eat a higher life form, something that didn't exist in nature as prey for other species. I paused trying to get control of the impulse before I did something I might regret. Tom took advantage of my inner struggle and slammed into my side, driving me to the ground. A sharp rock dug into me. The grip on my hunger slipped and for the first time in hundreds of years, I lost control.

Even in wolfen form, I still had my draconic strength and speed. I used it. I slipped away from Tom easily as he sought to clamp his teeth around my throat. He sensed something had changed. I didn't give him time to run. I lunged into him, using my superior strength to drive him to the ground. He struggled as I lay across him, but he couldn't escape me. I held him down. He howled in pain. In moments, his cries changed to a scream of fear as I sank my teeth into the soft flesh of his neck.

I didn't want to eat him. Actually, at that moment, I did. Eating him would solve two big problems, but Cindy would probably be vindictive about it and might never stop being a pain in my side until she got revenge. He stopped struggling. There was something in all predators that when the prey stopped struggling things ease up. I was still in wolf form as I pulled back from his unmoving body. His heart still beat faintly beneath me.

I was so enthralled by Tom's still form that I didn't hear Cindy racing up behind me. She knocked me to the ground with a howl of anger. I managed to slip away from her as I came back to my senses. I resumed my human form as she stood over the still form of her mate and sniffed him.

"He's still alive, which is more than he deserves. Take him and the others and go. *Now!*"

I called a gate into existance and opened it between the land north of Yellow Sky and the wolves' compound in Idaho. "Go quickly. Thank you for your help, but go before I lay waste to your whole pack."

Cindy stood unusually silent in front of me. A couple of the wolves that were outside of the magical null area changed to human form and lifted Tom. The rest of the wolves gathered around their alphas.

"You'll be back to normal in about a day," I advised. "There won't be any lasting effects from the magic. Go in peace." Anger rose up in me, spurred on by my loss of control. I still had to deal with Estaben. I didn't want these wolves around to interfere. I was sure J.P. would just let me write them off as collateral damage, but I wasn't sure Alex would.

Geri stood just to the side of the wolves. I heard Alex and the others coming up the ravine. The gate was using up my power. "Go now, before the gate collapses."

Still silent, Cindy turned and loped into the gate with the rest of the pack behind her.

Geri nodded as everyone came over the rim of the ravine. Alex ran toward me.

"We won this one!" He cheered as he threw himself into my arms. I hugged him tightly, thinking about the way I almost killed Tom. I thought about the two dead alpha wererats. Yes, we won, but as in any battle, there had been a cost. Now all we had left was to deal with was the vampires and my backup was a group of young mages that I had just stripped of magical power, a werecoyote stuck in coyote form and a fledgling vampire whose sire was the monster I needed to kill. I needed to make a call to the office.

I kissed Alex warmly. "Yeah, we won this battle. Now, if we can just win the war."

Chapter Thirty Three

GERI INSISTED we take the bodies of Cerebella and Magenta back to their mansion, so their clan could give them a proper burial. I figured it'd be night before we heard anything out of Estaben, so I agreed. It'd also give us a chance to figure out our next move. I would've liked to swoop in and kill all the vampires by day, but with the coven mostly powerless, that wasn't a good option.

I was amazed about how quickly the rat clan rallied. Lisa, Cerebella's secretary, quickly made a couple of calls, and within an hour, most of their clan arrived at the mansion. The working girls closed up shop for the day to prepare the funeral for their madams. I took the time to find a deer and have a decent meal. Cerebella had left instructions for everyone. In her note to Geri, she indicated that Magenta had had a vision a few days before and was concerned they might come to harm from Marcella and the wolves. She left instructions to her successor on running the clan. The new alpha, Blanca Ortiz, a tall Hispanic woman with long black hair, looked over the note with tears streaming down her face, then handed the paper to Lisa as she broke down completely. Lisa scanned the letter and explained to us that Cerebella had left everything to Blanca, including her business, and wished her the best in life. Blanca's husband Julio didn't look overly happy about the announcement, but he kept his mouth shut while comforting his wife. This was the first time I'd seen the leadership of a wereclan change without fighting among the surviving members. I was impressed.

While the rats made their preparations, I called the office. I had some ideas and needed Beth to get a few things to me. She said she'd see what she could do and to call her back in an hour. When I called her back, she said she'd found everything I needed. Alex stood at my side as I opened a gate to HQ so Beth could bring me the required supplies.

Beth came through the gate with a large pack slung over her shoulder and dragging a couple of flame throwers. She wasn't a large woman in her human form, and the weapons were just awkward enough for her that they were difficult to move comfortably. Unfortunately I didn't have the energy to keep the gate open long enough to go back and forth for multiple loads, so she managed to get all of it in one haul. I didn't even feel like keeping the gate open long enough for her to get back right now.

"So this is Alex," she said, studying him for a second after setting the flame throwers on the floor. "I must say, Suzzy was right, you do make a fine couple. There are more than a few of the folks back at HQ that will be sad you are off the market now, Tal."

I hoped I wasn't blushing. "Thanks, Beth."

"J.P. said to tell you good work with the werewolves. And he still has the emergency strike force standing by in Dallas if you need them. I left the rest of the intelligence team working on the angle that there might be someone else behind all of this, but so far, we don't have any leads, or even anything that looks remotely suspicious."

"We'll just have to keep our eyes open," I said taking the pack from her. I rummaged through it checking to see if everything was there. I pulled out two bottles of light blue liquid. "Is this all they had on hand?"

"Yeah, I checked with Isabella, you know the chief alchemist, and she said that for some reason the last batch spoiled and these two bottles are from the batch before that. She says the affects will only last about an hour, so hold off on using them as long as possible. What do you need me to do?"

I took a couple of minutes and explained the plan to her.

By late afternoon, the clan had a pair of pyres built behind the mansion and the bodies of their former alphas laid on them. I stood before the pyres as the sun dropped below a nearby butte. Blanca and

Lisa said a few words to the gathered clan. Beth, Alex and the gang stood off to one side with Geri sitting at their feet. When Blanca turned and gestured to me, I called magical fire and lit the pyres. The flames burned brightly as a pair of large native drums beat a slow steady beat. Geri raised her voice in a long sorrowful howl. I intensified the strength of the fires and the wooden pyres burned quickly. By the time the full moon rose in the sky, there was nothing left but two piles of ash dancing about on the wind that had come up out of nowhere. I stood between the pyres thinking that the body count on this caper hadn't been too high, but I still had to deal with Estaben.

"You ready for the next part of the plan?" Alex asked softly from behind me.

Lost in thought, I hadn't heard anyone move, let alone come up behind me. I wasn't used to having such a close bond to another person as I now shared with Alex. I turned to face him and realized that most everyone was heading back down toward the house, moving as silently as only werecreatures and ladies of the night can.

"I'm sorry, just thinking a bit. Trying to keep everyone alive." I pulled him into my arms and kissed him lightly. I really didn't want to let him go.

"Hey, I think we have more than proven that we can take care of ourselves here," he tried to pull out of my embrace, but I held on and he didn't struggle much.

"I don't doubt that you can take care of yourself," I said. "You've proved to be an amazing man. So are your friends, but I really think that if anything happens to any of you before we put this to an end, Geri is probably going to rip me to shreds."

Alex laughed. It was a good strong laugh. "And knowing you, if something happened to one of us you'd probably let her."

I let him go. "I think you're right." I took his hand in mine and started toward the house. "Let's follow the others. We need to finish this plan."

He fell into easy step beside me. "Maybe the wererats can help more."

I shook my head. "No, they've lost enough today. I can't ask them to risk their lives for this. We have to handle this on our own. And if we can't handle this, then J.P. will send in a cleanup crew to take out all the remaining vampires, maybe even Charles."

"So, we have to make sure that we handle this ourselves." He sounded unsure, and maybe even a little scared. It was a good healthy response.

"We've taken out his wolves, his rats and his sorceress," I said, trying to sound confident "We weakened his base of power. All he should have left is his vampires."

"And all we have is you, a fledgling vampire mage, a tiger shifter mage, a coyote, and six powerless mages who have a little psi skill each and two flame throwers," Alex responded. "Do we have any idea how many vampires he might have?"

"At last count it was about two hundred." Charles added, appearing at our side.

At least he still had his magic to call on, and his psi skills were stronger than the others after his change.

"Got out of the truck, I see," I chuckled as he fell into step with us.

"Yeah, looks like you guys survived the battle with Marcella. Burn tells me that the rats didn't make it."

"Yeah, and now we are working on a way to keep the rest of us alive," Alex replied, again sounding doubtful.

"Well, we need to think fast," Charles commented as we caught up with the others.

"Does he have to find us first, or do we have to find him?" Bernadette asked as the gang turned to face us.

"He's my sire. I can feel him and he can feel me," Charles started to explain.

"And he's on his way now," Alex and I finished in unison.

"How close is he?" I asked.

"Very. Outside of a gate. We have no hope of getting away before he gets here."

"Estaben's always avoided confrontation in the past. It's not like him to seek out someone directly, particularly me. We don't have time for this." If Estaben was coming to confront me, that told me more than anything there was someone was pulling his strings.

I looked for Blanca. She stood near the back door to the house, listening with her keen werears. "Blanca, we need to talk." I waved her over.

The new alpha of the wererats came over to our little group. "Thank you, Tal. Sara and Magee would be pleased with the pyre."

"You're welcome. They gave their lives for a good cause. Right now, we have another problem. This is Charles." I gestured toward him. "He is a fledgling vampire as your senses probably tell you. His sire, Estaben de'Oro, is the head of the vampires here in Yellow Sky and the man I'm here to kill. He's on his way here and we don't have time to get away before he arrives. I'd like to help you get your people out of the line of fire."

She shook her head, her long black hair moved like a bush in the wind. "No, this is our place of power. No vampire lord is going to come in here while we stand aside."

"We don't know how many of his people are coming with him. Your clan has lost enough today."

"We could've lost more if you and yours hadn't been here to stop them. Sara discussed Marcella's proposal with us. She told those who wanted to participate they could, but not with her blessings. I saw the situation as Sara did. If Marcella's plan worked, most of the humans would be gone now, changed into either wer or vamp. That'd leave only the wer for the vamps to feed on. I don't like the thought of that. They gave their lives to stop that future. Now my people will follow my lead and stop the vampires if we must." The set of her jaw told me it was useless to argue with her.

"Okay, but will you at least offer to get the working ladies to safety before this comes down? I can gate them to my house in the city if you don't have a safe room for them."

"I'll talk to them. We have a safe room here. I'll also offer my clan the option of disappearing into the sagebrush if they don't want to stand up to the vamps." She knelt down to Geri. "I needed to tell you that David Keyon is no more. He came to me last night, barely in control of his rat side. He knew he was losing it. He was afraid you and yours were lost forever. He didn't think he could be himself any more. He asked me as the second in command to help him end it. He died in peace."

The gang was silent, but I could feel their sorrow. If Geri could have cried, she would have. Instead, she lifted her muzzle and howled a long, low, sad howl. Alex knelt down at her side and wrapped his fingers into her fur, pulling her close. I gripped his shoulders as the others gathered closely followed by the rat clan.

We stood like that, for several minutes before something brushed the edges of my senses. Charles looked up at the same time. "They're here."

I sensed a large number of vampires coming up the road. There were no lights from cars, but then, if they used their supernatural speed they could easily have run from town in the time since sundown. I guessed Estaben had brought most of his vampires with him.

Our little circle broke. "Everyone into the house." I urged as I took Alex's hand and started that way. Once into the house, I made it halfway across the sitting room before Charles called from the doorway.

"Would someone mind inviting me in?"

"Char get your ass in here," Bernadette snarled to let her brother in the house.

I saw Blanca talking to some of the ladies of the evening as the last of the rats got into the house and slammed the back doors shut.

The door bell rang.

I spotted Lisa standing near Blanca. "Lisa," I called, starting toward her.

"How can I help you, Tal?" She met me halfway across the room.

"Are you going to hide or stand and face this with the rest of us?" The gang stood behind me, Geri at my side.

"Like most of us here, I'm standing up for our home. Sara never made any bones to any of us regular girls. We know what she did to keep us normal humans safe. She and Maggie did their part. Now we have to do ours."

I liked her spirit. The spunk that so many humans show when they get backed into a corner never ceased to amaze me. It's the thing that keeps them from being swept aside by the monsters that most of them don't even realize are in their midst.

"Good. Now, I'd like to meet Estaben in the main office, but I'd prefer to meet only him. Could you please go, invite him in and bring him to us? If he insists, allow him to bring one other with him, but no more."

"No problem." She set her shoulders and started for the door as the bell rang again.

Several of the working girls left the room while I talked to Lisa, but most now stood with the rat clan behind Blanca.

"So, what do you want of us?" Blanca asked as I walked toward her.

"Have your people act normal for now. Lounge about here in the living room. If you and Julio would accompany Alex, Geri and me to the office, we'll make our impression there." I glanced at the guys behind me. "Charles, you come too. The rest of you, make yourselves comfortable out here. Try and look inconspicuous, and keep Bernadette out of sight. We don't know if Estaben knows what you look like or not. Beth, go get the stuff ready. We may need it quickly."

Blanca gestured to her people and they began to get comfortable. "Sound plan, and if things get nasty?"

"I hope your people are good with wood," I smiled and tried to sound cheerful. If there were two hundred vampires out there in the night and things got nasty, we'd have to react very quickly and be very lucky. "Let's get in our places."

We hurried into the office that I'd seen through Alex's eyes the night before. It was as impressive in real life as it had been second hand. I stood behind the desk and glanced at Blanca. She nodded her acceptance and I pulled out the leather chair out and sat, but I had to lower it a bit before I felt like I had a normal view of the room. Blanca stood at my left and Alex took up his place on my right. Concern rolled off him. I hoped that we'd walk out of this house later, mission accomplished.

"We'll do this and be fine," his thoughts rang in my head.

"Something tells me you might be right, but it might not be an easy night."

"Somehow I doubt that anything in your life is ever easy."

I almost chuckled at that as Geri sat in front of the desk. Charles and Julio sat on opposite couches against the walls. We were in position.

There was a stir in the energies of the house as a vampire crossed the threshold.

"He's in," Charles announced in a low voice.

Next to me, Blanca stiffened.

"I know," I said just loud enough for everyone to hear.

We all strained our enchanted senses to hear the footsteps as they approached the closed door to the office. Tension rose as Lisa touched the door knob, turned it and slowly opened the door.

Chapter Thirty Four

CEREBELLA WOULD never have allowed one of her doors to creak, but that just added to the dead silence in the seconds it took Lisa to open the door. Not a breath stirred as she swung it wide to admit Estaben de'Oro. My breath caught for a second when I saw him for the first time in over a hundred years. Alex's presence occupied my mind, so his noble good looks held no power over me.

In the silence of his walk toward the desk, I studied him. He strode into the room with more confidence than the man I remembered. He wore a dark blue suit that played off his blue eyes, bringing out a sharp sparkle. Like all of his kind, he hadn't changed physically in the least. But still there was a change in him. He had more presence than I recalled. It's not uncommon for vampires to gain presence as they age, but I never expected it of Estaben.

His movements belied the presence surrounding him. I imagine it wasn't noticeable to the majority of the beings that he met. He held his head high like he owned the room, but he walked like he always did when he was trying to hide something he knew would displease me. Then I saw it. A complex, multi-layered glamour lay over him. It was more than he could've done with his lack of magical skills. It was more than Marcella could've done, since all of her enchantments should've died with her. There was another hand at work here. And the enchantments were old enough, whoever had done them, had crafted them years earlier, not recently.

"Overall, not bad." Alex hid his concern behind a mental chuckle.

"Not nearly as nice as you," I replied, drawing strength from his presence.

"Hello, Tal. It's been a while." The vampire sat in the chair nearest to the desk.

"Estaben, you've attracted a bit too much attention to yourself." He was acting a bit too casual for my taste. The feeling of wrongness increased as he spoke.

He made a wide sweeping gesture with his hands. "What can I say? The best laid plans and all that."

"You vampires are a cocky lot. You cost us our alphas and all you can say is, 'the best laid plans?'" Blanca snarled from behind me.

"Hey, they had their chance to throw in with the plan and they turned us down, but that's okay. I prefer the taste of werewolf blood to wererat anyway." His body again showed a different emotion from his tone and his aura. He was more than a little bit nervous. His right hand gripped the arm of the chair at lot stronger than his left did.

"Charles. Can you look at his aura on an in-depth, almost-microscopic level for me while I keep him talking? I need to know if there's anything unusual there."

Luckily, Charles had been a good telepath and now that he was changed, his telepathic skills made it almost as easy to talk to him as Alex. None of the others had access to the magic they'd need to see what I feared was there.

"So it is their own fault? Estaben, grow up. You set this in motion. You brought the wolves here. And you've had your vampires out turning people at random across this city. The Coalition holds you ultimately responsible for what's happened here."

"So they sent you. Oh, I've heard how you've become their little assassin these past few decades. I suppose it does your ego good to feel the fear when your name's spoken. The tales of your executions are great, although how there are so many when you aren't known for leaving witnesses is *amazing*. To think that you're actually the man who nursed me through my first long years of vampiric life."

I let out a long slow breath. "To think, that you're actually one of my apprentices. I thought I taught you that all life is sacred and you shouldn't turn a human without just cause and consent."

He turned toward Charles. "Is that what you told him? That I changed you without your consent? You practically begged for it." There was almost a cruel tone in his voice. Estaben had been many things in the years I'd known him, but cruel was not one of them.

Charles' eyes focused on his sire. "Estaben, what's wrong with you? Why are you acting this way? Don't you realize that Tal's prepared to kill you?"

"There's nothing wrong with me, my son. In fact, I feel better than I have in a long time. It's like a great weight has been lifted off my shoulders." His body shook slightly, but his aura remained confident. For a moment, I wondered if he was hoping I'd kill him. More than a few vampires got tired of their immortal life and longed for release. Maybe he was trying for suicide by cop. "I never really liked Marcella, so in fact, you and the wolf bitch actually did me a favor. Now I don't have to share the glory with anyone. I can rule everything myself."

"Rule what, Estaben? All of your plans are ending now. There is nothing left for you to rule over." I was beginning to think that he was just trying to stall for some reason. But why?

"Are you looking for a small incoming thread of magic?" Charles asked.

"Where is it connecting?" I started drawing energies around me.

"You don't realize that even without Marcella—" Estaben continued, not sensing my conversation with Charles. If he was in full control of himself, he should've felt our conversation through his Sire link with Charles. "—I still have control over a lot of vampires. Then there are the others who I can and will draw into the scheme. There is a whole world out there for me to conquer. "

"Give me a second to follow it." Charles replied.

"No, where is it connecting on Estaben?" I corrected.

"The right ear."

Estaben droned on about what he planned to do and how he could do it, but I knew for sure there was someone pulling his strings. Neither he nor Marcella had been the brains behind the plan. I wasn't sure we would have time to learn much.

"Can you follow it to its source?" I asked. *"At least give me a general location where it may have come from."*

"Give me a couple of minutes, but it will mean going astral. Estaben may notice that."

"I'll try and keep his attention on me. Be quick." I advised.

I turned all of my attention back to my former lover, and student. "Do you really think we're going to be foolish enough to let that horde you brought with you into the house? This is still a home, even though the new residents are still setting up house, and they run their business from here. Vampires must be invited in and if you think that you alone can take all of us on, you are sadly mistaken." To emphasize my words, Geri growled low from her place in front of the desk.

"Tal, it's simple. You loved me. You don't have what it takes to kill me. I think I can take any of these excuses for allies you've gathered around you before your rats and magelings can stop me. And I can do it all easily since you so nicely removed the magic from those who could help you the most, like that lovely new boy toy of yours." He stared past me to Alex. "I think you might even shed a tear when he's gone."

I laughed, as much to hold his attention as from how ludicrous he sounded. "Estaben, I hate to trade threats with you, but you have little hope of leaving this room. Now it's true that we might have a bit of a problem dealing with all of your forces that are waiting at the door. But all we have to do is wait until sunrise and then hunt them down. Without the wers to protect them, all it will take is a little time to find them all. Also, should, by some chance, you manage to get out of this alive, my superiors will send in a cleansing team. They'll scour this town clean of all magical and metaphysical beasts and energies before they leave. Then other hunters will be following you and you will die."

"The Coalition isn't all that it seems. They've made their share of enemies over the past hundred years, most of which are older than the Coalition itself." He began another long rant on the evils and problems of the Coalition.

"Tal, the strand is coming from a long way off," said Charles. *"I followed it as far as the Atlantic Ocean, and can't get across it."*

"Thanks for trying." I opened up my thoughts to the others in the room. *"I'm about tired of this. I'm going to sever the puppet's strings and see what happens. Be ready."*

"Estaben, you've developed some real issues since you left my side years ago." I cut him off in mid rant. "I think I made a mistake in the jungle those hundreds of years ago, but then we were both younger and maybe you were prettier with your human naivety. Now you are just another bitter vamp." I leapt over the desk toward him, called my magical sword to hand and sliced down the right side of his face. The sword glowed brightly, but did not cut his pale flesh. He tried to dodge, but Geri leapt up and stopped him from sliding away from me. His eyes shot wide as I severed the cord of outside influence. A large pulse of energy shot down the length of the sword and into my arm. I managed to block most of it, but it still threw me backward across the desk, knocking the wind out of me.

"Tal!" Alex shouted and rushed to my side. He took my head in his hands. He looked almost comical with the concern that showed on his upside-down freckled features.

I smiled slightly as I lay there looking up into his beautiful green eyes. "I'm okay. Just a little shook up." I stood and the world spun a bit. Charles grabbed my arm to stabilize me while the room came back into sharp focus.

Estaben slumped in his chair. The outside aura had vanished from him, leaving the Estaben that I'd known for many years. He was conscious, but his eyes were unfocused and slightly glazed. The overwhelming presence that he carried into the room was gone. Now he was simply a wretched old vampire sitting in a chair.

Blanca sprang across the desk toward Estaben's unresponsive form.

"Wait," I yelled and she stopped in mid air hovering there.

"Let me kill him now or my rats will take you all. He owes us blood!" She screamed and clawed at the air, her hands shifting as she struggled.

I felt Alex strain behind me to hold her in place. Then he let out a sigh and she dropped to the floor.

"We need to find out what he knows," I said, stepping between them. "He wasn't the mastermind behind all of this, and he may know who is. We've all been jerked around big time."

This had all been a set up by someone far away. It made so much more sense than the Estaben I knew trying something like this, even with the prompting of the witch Marcella.

I turned toward Estaben. I put a hand on his shoulder and pushed him back against the chair. His eyes flashed over me and seemed to focus for a second, then glazed over again.

"Estaben, look at me." I shook him slightly.

His eyes passed over me again, stopped and cleared. "Tal, is that really you?" His voice was strained, and weak, holding none of the confidence that it had moments ago.

"Yes Estaben it's really me. I need you to take a deep breath and try to remember what's going on."

"This is bullshit," Blanca snarled, but made no move to get past Geri. "He's trying to fool us or something." I knew most wers could literally smell the truth when dealing with other wers and most humans, but that ability didn't extend to their dealing with vampires. It probably frustrated her that she couldn't tell if he was lying or not.

Estaben's eyes unfocused slightly. "It seems like a dream. The last thing I really remember was stalking this handsome young man in a club down in Houston. He led me down a dark hall. I remember following him and his tight bell bottoms into the men's room, and then I woke up here." Estaben, was telling the truth as far as I could tell, or at least the truth as he perceived it.

"Estaben, what do you remember about the vampires who are gathered outside of this house?" I hoped he might know something, even if it was something he buried inside of his subconscious.

"Are they the ones I dreamed about? It was like they were worshipping me, and there was this witch who called the wolves to come to us." He seemed to drift away again.

I turned to face the rest of those who gathered at the front of the desk. "Suggestions? He's really out of it. This also means he wasn't the one behind the whole plot to change the town into creatures of the night. The big question now is who was behind it? What do they really want? And what do we do with the two hundred plus vampires waiting outside the front door?"

Blanca sat on the edge of the desk, trying to regain her composure. Conflicting emotions played across her face. She wanted to tear Estaben apart, but was beginning to believe his story. "I've only got about fifty rats here. We're willing to try, but I don't think we can take out that many vampires without help. We can kill this one here without any trouble."

I shook my head. "No, I'd prefer that he stay alive...for now. We may need him to help us track down whoever used him as a puppet." This was going to take a lot of explaining to J.P. as well.

"But that still leaves all the vampires at the door. We can't very well go out and stake them all," Julio added from Blanca's side.

"What about fire?" Alex said hopefully. "Can you call enough mage fire to take them all out? We also have the flame throwers."

I shook my head. "I'd worry about setting the landscape around here ablaze too. In case you haven't noticed, we are in the middle of a drought right now and enough mage fire to kill two hundred vampires is bound to take out at least this house and most of the acreage around us. We'd be putting ourselves in as much risk as the vampires we're trying to kill. The funeral pyres were risky enough. This could cause the vampires to run about and set the entire area ablaze. The flame throwers are for close combat only."

Alex's wide brow wrinkled in thought. "What if we called a storm at the same time as you called the fire? You could take out the vamps and then we could douse the fire before it spreads."

I appreciated him trying to think of ways to help, but I really didn't see it working. "Alex, if all you guys had access to your magic before sunrise it might work, but you don't have it, and a storm big enough to take out the fire would be more than Beth and Charles could call by themselves."

"But there's where you are wrong. I don't need magic to call a storm. Storm calling is a family trait. So I can use my psi skills to call the storm. The rest of the guys can help by feeding me more psi energy. With Charles' new strength, we can get a storm here in no time and be ready when you are." He sounded hopeful. He needed to be of help in this and felt out of place without his magic. Through our link, I knew he thought they could do it.

I glanced down at the coyote at my feet. "Geri, do you think they can do it?"

"Yes. Charles and Beth will need to start it magically, but then Alex and the others can augment it." She replied with a yip.

I thought about it for a moment as the silence permeated the room. It might work, and right now, that was all we could hope for, short of a miracle. I didn't want to have to resort to hand-to-hand combat.

"Okay. Alex and Charles, you go get Beth and the others. Blanca, show them somewhere that they can work without disturbance; it'd probably help them to have at least one window they can watch the sky from. Then, arm your people with as much wood as you can find. You can use table legs, wooden pool cues, even chop sticks, whatever they can force through the chest of a vampire. I'll need them to run out when this all starts to catch any of the ones that I miss in my fire. See if one of your rats can operate one of the flame throwers. I believe Terry said he could handle one. They'll need to be ready to head out as soon as my firestorm ends. I'll stay here for the moment and get ready for the fire spell. Send Lisa back in when everyone is ready and she can show me to the roof."

"Sounds like a plan I can sink my teeth into." Blanca smiled and jumped off the desk.

I pulled Alex into my arms and kissed him. "Take the one of the potions from Beth and give the other one to Geri, but be careful. If it looks like you and the guys cannot get this to work let me know and we'll call it off."

He looked deeply into my soul with those to-die-for green eyes of his. "You, too. Just because you're older doesn't mean you take chances." Another quick kiss and he followed the others out the door.

I turned my attention back to Estaben, who listened quietly as we planned the attack on his followers. He looked like he tried to sink back into the fabric of the chair. "I've really made a mess of things, haven't I?"

I sighed deeply and remembered the dashing Spaniard that caught my eye as we sailed to the New World. For a short while, I'd thought we might be able to make things work long term. Compared to most human couples, I guess we had.

"Yes, this time I think you have, but it wasn't totally your fault."

"That doesn't make it any easier. I broke your basic laws many times over. If my dream is right, then I or my children have created most of the vampires threatening us now. I even turned that lovely little mage who just left here. That's unforgivable. I deserve to die." There was real pain in his voice, and as he looked at me, a scarlet tear rolled down his pale face.

"That's what most everybody wants at this point. I'm not even sure I can stop it if I wanted to. I know that you didn't do this all on your own."

"But that doesn't matter much, does it?" A surrendering tone permeated his voice.

"It matters to me." I had the sudden urge to give him a hug and tell him everything was going to be alright, but I knew it wasn't going to be. There was no way everything would ever be alright for him again.

"Are you willing to go against the others for my sake?" Estaben asked. "Would you go against Alex for me? I see how you look at him. You never looked at me with that much love in your eyes. You're going to bond to him aren't you?" More tears rolled down his face, making little trails of red over his cheeks.

"We will bond when the time is right." I had realized several days ago that I wanted Alex by my side for the rest of our lives, however long or short they may be. I was even prepared not to continue on if something happened to him. More dragons had died pining away than by knights' swords. It's just how we were.

"Do you know what I miss the most?" His voice cracked in a way I'd never heard before. "The one thing I wish I could do before I go on to my next life?"

"What?" The options were endless with most people, but with their extended life span, most vampires end up doing everything they want to do in their lives.

"I would like to walk the day, just for one day. I'd like to feel the sun shine again without fear of going up in flames."

I sighed and shook my head. "Even I can't give you the protections to go out in the daylight." He wasn't a mage. The vampires who figured out how to go into the sunlight were all mages. The spells required to block out the sun were too strong for someone to cast on another.

I started to say more, then Alex touched my thoughts. *"We're ready. The storm should break in about five minutes. That potion really kick started my magic, thanks. Geri's back to normal too."*

"Remind her, it runs out in an hour." I'd never used a supplemental magic potion before. It's supposed to give non-mages magical powers for a few hours, except this was an old batch. Seemed it was working the way I hoped it would.

"Estaben, they're ready for me. Stay here and I'll be back in a few minutes. We'll see what we can figure out."

I walked quickly out of the room. This would've been a lot easier if some outside force hadn't been manipulating him. If he'd acted on his own, he'd already be dead already by my hand. It was one thing to kill something that needed to be killed for the safety of others. But this had gone from that to killing a virtual innocent in less than an hour. Thankfully, the decision wasn't totally mine. Alex, Geri and the others, even the rats all had a say in this, not to mention J.P..

Lisa waited for me just outside the door. A flurry of activity sounded from the main room. "Blanca said to take you to the main balcony on the top floor. It's as close to the roof as we can get, but it'll

still give you a view of the crowd gathered in the front of the house."
She sounded a little scared, which was only natural. She turned and led
me through the house and up several flights of stairs to a room
appropriately decorated in deep scarlet. She pointed to the double
French doors on the far side of the room.

"I need to get back downstairs with the others," she said. Evidently,
I frightened her as much as the undead horde waiting below.

"Tell Blanca to give me three minutes and then send people out to
pick off the." I closed the door behind her, took a deep breath and
pulled out a small orb Beth had brought along with her and triggered it
with a simple thought. My magic flared up to levels I'd never reached
before. I reached down into the earth and pulled power. I visualized
the great serpent who had come to our call the night before and saw
him clearly in my mind as I opened the doors onto the balcony.

Winds from the building storm pushed against me as I stepped out
onto the night-darkened balcony. I heard the chatter and movements
from the vampires below. I knew it was only a matter of moments
before they'd feel my presence. With the mental picture of the Fire
God's avatar in my mind, I called the fire.

It may have been my own visualization, or it may actually have
been the avatar of the God who showed up, but it looked like a great
serpent of fire came roaring out of the ground. It encircled the
vampires as they stood about impatiently waiting for Estaben to return.
The ring of fire closed quickly as they tried to flee down the driveway.
Once it closed, I focused on bringing the deadly ring in on itself,
keeping my mind on the fire and making the ring burn toward its
center. I blocked out the screams of the vampires caught in my blazing
trap. It took almost all of my augmented power, but I worked as
quickly as I could. In my hand, the magical orb shattered into a
thousand little shards that fell like snowflakes into the fire below. I
sank to my knees on the balcony as the winds tried to push me back
into the room behind me. I held onto the curving railing until my
knuckles were white, calling on the last dregs of my power to control
the fire. The lawn caught fire before the storm broke.

Lightning flashed as Blanca led fighters out of the house after the vampires that escaped the fire. As the ring closed in upon itself, more of the vampires tried to clear its deadly grip. They ran off into the night as blazing comets of undead flesh. The rats reacted quickly and followed to finish them off. There were blasts from the flame throwers as Terry and one of the largest rats fried vampires while the other rats brought them down. The balcony gave me the perfect vantage point to witness the carnage below.

The rain broke just as the fire blazed up a final time, like a serpent's head plunging among the last cluster of vampires. Rain fell heavily. I stood there in the night as the cold water poured down on me, watching as the rats chased their prey into the night. I doubted that any of the vampires survived.

Standing there in the rain, an idea came to me, one that might grant Estaben his wish and give me the time I needed to talk to J.P. and get permission to let him live.

Weakly, I descended the stairs, more weary than I had been in a long time. I needed to feed again soon. I only hoped that between Beth, Charles and I, we could call up enough power to do what I now knew needing doing. I knew Alex and Geri's renewed magic would be gone before it was time, but working the idea over in my mind, I knew it was very feasible.

Alex appeared at my side as I reached the ground floor, his freckled face pale and drawn. In the shadowed hall where we stood, his red hair almost looked like blood against the pale skin. "You're deep in thought. But it's a good plan. And hey we won, didn't we?"

I had known he was okay, but it made me feel better to see him safe and sound. I pulled him into my arms and held onto him, letting his sweaty scent fill me. I'd been so wrapped up in the other things I hadn't realized how hard the storm had been for the guys to call. Alex's sweat-soaked body told me it hadn't been an easy fight, but the lightning showed they'd pulled it off and done it extremely well. I covered his mouth with mine and held him as long as I could.

When we pulled apart, I smiled. "Yes, we won." I wrapped my arm around his waist and headed back to the office where Estaben waited. "Now let's go set Estaben free."

We walked into the office and quickly explained to Estaben and everyone else what I meant to do. Geri had little debate for me and the gang all thought the idea was cool. Estaben was skeptical, but willing to take the risk if it would mean he could spend a couple of days out in the sunlight. When Blanca returned with news that her clan had run down all the vampires they could find, she was in a good enough mood to agreed, so long as she got a say in his final fate.

With all the elements in place, we spent the wee hours of the morning preparing for one final spell. As it turned out, even if it hadn't shown in her aura, Magenta dabbled in the magical arts, so everything we needed was available. It didn't take long to whip up the potion and then we stepped out onto the patio behind the house just before the sun peeked above the horizon. Gods I wanted a rest.

I handed Estaben the potion-filled coffee cup. "Now remember, there isn't going to be anyone watching you. You're on your own for three days. At dawn on the fourth day the spell will wear off. Be sure that you're in a safe place when that happens."

"Will I know what to do?" He looked down into the cup, uncertain.

"That's part of the spell, just follow your instincts and don't try to think things out too much. Now drink the potion and we'll cast the final part of the spell before the sun comes up."

He raised the cup to his lips and downed the potion, swallowing deeply. The magic we cast into it soon took effect. I reached out and put the final shape on the magic, thereby shaping Estaben. Beth and Charles added their own magic to bolster my rapidly-weakening power, while Alex and the others fed me from a psychic level. Estaben's physical form turned to jelly, allowing me to gather it up and mold it like clay. When I finished, a large gray pigeon stood on the ground in front of me. It wasn't my first choice of creatures, but other than rats, it was the only type of feather or fur I could find in the house. Changing him into another type of creature made him immune to the sun's rays so he'd be able to move about more freely.

After finishing his part in the magic, Charles disappeared into the darkness of the house without a word, fleeing the rising sun. Blanca promised him a safe room to sleep the day in.

I scooped Estaben up in my hands and he sat quietly. "Now remember, three days, and follow your instincts." Then I tossed him into the blazing light of the sunrise.

Alex stepped to my side as I watched Estaben struggle the first few beats of awkward wings and then settle into an easy flight toward the sun. My new love wrapped his arm around my waist as we stood there watching my old lover fly away.

"Do you think he'll be all right?"

"It's in the hands of the Universe now." I said softly.

As the words left my mouth, a high-pitched scream split the morning air. I glanced up and watched as a prairie flacon made a perfect dive that Estaben couldn't evade. A sharp crack rang out through the still morning air as the falcon impacted Estaben, neatly breaking his back. He fell from the sky. His spiral fall took him across the face of the newly-risen sun before he landed with a soft thud in the mud left over from the storm we called. The falcon landed atop him and began to pluck his gray feathers.

I sighed. Sometimes the Universe has a way of saying things that don't require the use of words.

Chapter Thirty Five

I COULD not remember when I last slept. After the defeat of the vampires, J.P. requested we sweep the town to make sure we didn't miss any. Beth offered to stay around a few days and help out. She, Blanca and her clan eagerly went out with Geri and her students. I decreed that we test each one before killing them. So far, we'd only been able to save one lonely housewife. As we had done with David Cooper, I arranged for her to join one of the Coalition vampires for guidance. The rest either resisted capture or had shown too much evil for me to safely let them continue roaming the night. It's been several nights since we found one, and none of us can feel any more vampire presence in Yellow Sky other than Charles. Over time, he might become the head vampire of Yellow Sky, unless someone is foolish enough to attempt to claim the territory. I don't think Geri would stand for that, and my presence would protect them all.

No one shed a tear over Estaben's death, which when I thought about it, was sad. To think he'd lived as long as he had and no one mourned him. All the lives he influenced, other than mine and Charles, were gone. I've spent long hours wondering if maybe I should've just let him die that night back in the jungle. But then I realize that I'd done what I had to do. He'd performed the task vampires existed for. He'd been a predator of humans and he performed that task very well. I guess he was what nature needed him to be. Also, if I hadn't helped him survive those first few years, he wouldn't have come to Yellow Sky and brought me here in search of him. Then I never would've met Alex.

We've all tried to find out what we could about the force that started all of the problems, but so far we've come up empty. J.P. put the Coalition's people on alert for anything that might pop up, but nothing has surfaced yet. It's like whatever it was vanished into the nether from which it came.

We called Suzzy to assure her we were fine and promised to visit soon. She'd been relieved and said she'd have a big meal ready for us when we got there.

Charles adjusted to life as a vampire, appearing to be one of those who are born to it. It took a long talk with his mother to explain it all. I promised to look after him and not let him get into too much trouble, but she's dealing with it as well as any mother could. He still hasn't told her he's gay, but then I guess one shock at a time. I met Danielle Colfax. I figured she'd handle the news just fine, particularly if she had Geri there to lean on. So, for the first time in over a hundred years I have an apprentice, well two if you count Alex.

I'm adjusting to having Alex in my life. I've spent long hours just watching him sleep in our bed. I ask myself about the future, and for the first time, I cannot see what's coming. I guess it's the Universe's way of telling me to wait and see what happens. I hate that.

Alex moved into my house in Yellow Sky. I'm renovating a bit of the house. I hadn't intended to stay here past my assignment, but Alex's life is here and I guess mine will be too, for the time being. So I bought the house. We've set up a permanent gate back to the library, so we can access it as needed. It's also nice to spend a few cool mountain nights watching the stars from the meadow that lies outside the front door there. Those evenings have been some of the best of my long life. Alex fits so perfectly with me.

I finally had a chance to figure out why my appetite increased so much. My new bond with Alex drew magic away from me during its initial forming. Now it's balanced out, but not to the point it was.

Sunrise had started. Alex went to bed several hours ago and I promised to join him when I was ready. He's a little worried about my lack of sleep these past days, but he is starting to understand that I don't need as much as he does. I'd like to spend some time dreaming. I figured out a long time ago that when people stop dreaming they stop being human. And I was tired.

The house was silent as I walked to the bedroom except for a soft snore that caught my ear as I opened the door. Alex sprawled out on his back on the bed. The sheet rode low, hinting at his nakedness under it. I paused to look over him as I have so many times these past days. In his sleep, he appeared even younger than when awake. I was alive long before his family even had a name. Did I have a right to love this young man? I realized long ago that I moved outside of normal rights and wrongs. I may be an agent of the Coalition, but I am still Tal O'Duirwood, the oldest druid and the last dragon on the planet. I am a power unto myself.

I stopped to think outside of the magical box for a moment, and looked just at the physical. I first changed in my early twenties. I glanced at the mirror Alex hung over the head of the bed and look at myself, really looked at myself for the first time in many, many years. I looked almost as young as Charles. My hair's still as full and dark as when I was human. My physique was more lean than muscular, but one thing about dragons, we don't get fat. My mind might be nearly two thousand years old, but my body was still in its twenties and always would be. Soon we'd perform the binding ceremony and Alex would stop aging, too. We really were a good match like so many people said.

Beneath his long red lashes, his eyes flicked as he dreamed. His nice, firm, hair-covered chest moved with each breath. I walked over to my side of the bed and slipped easily out of my pants, then reached down to run my hand through that dense red hair, careful not to touch his skin, just to feel it tickle my fingers. Gently, I pulled the sheet back so I could slide under. I eased next to him and kissed him softly on the lips. He murmured slightly and then returned my kiss. I laid my head down next to his to watch him as he slept, hoping I could drift off to sleep.

He rolled over, and wrapped an arm around me. "I love you," he murmured as he pulled me closer.

"I love you too," I replied as his sleepy mind swept mine away. For the first time in many days, wrapped in his loving embrace, I slept.

Don't miss Tal and Alex's continued adventures in
Dark Stars of Dallas

ABOUT THE AUTHOR

A.M. BURNS has been writing to pass the time since high school. The stories he wrote helped him deal with life. A few years ago, he started sharing those stories with friends who enjoyed them and he has started sending his works out into the world to share with other people. He lives in the mountains with his extremely supportive husband. They have a lot of critters, including dogs, cats, birds, horses, and rabbits. When not writing, A.M. spends a lot of time hiking, trail riding, or just driving in the mountains. Nature provides a lot of inspiration for his work and keeps him writing. He is also an avid photographer and falconer. Don't get him started talking about his birds, because he won't stop for a while.

Web contact info:
Website: www.amburns.com
Twitter: AM_Burns
Facebook: www.facebook.com/authoramburns
Goodreads author page:
www.goodreads.com/author/show/5134598.A_M_Burns
Pintrest: pinterest.com/mystichawker/
Amazon Author Page: www.amazon.com/-/e/B0054EVI6W

Mystichawker Press Author Page:
http://www.mystichawker.com/amburns.html

More Books From A.M. Burns:

After his family is killed by thieves, sole survivor Trey McAlister is taken in by a nearby Comanche clan. Trey has a gift for magic and the clan s shaman, Singing Crow, makes him an apprentice. While learning to control his powers, Trey bonds with a young warrior and shape shifter, Gray Talon. When they are sent out on a quest to find the missing daughter of a dragon, they encounter the same bandits who murdered Trey s family, as well as a man made of copper who drives Trey to dig deeper into the magics that created him.

It doesn't take them long to discover a rancher near Cheyenne, Wyoming is plotting to build a workforce of copper men and has captured the dragon s daughter they've been searching for. Trey and Gray Talon must draw on all their knowledge and skills to complete their quest one that grows more complicated, and more dangerous, with each passing day."

From DSP Publishing

Available on Amazon.com

And most other places books are sold.

Bigfoot hunters prowl the forests of Cripple Creek, Colorado. That doesn't sit well with Thom Woodmen-a Bigfoot-albeit the runt of his family. Being the smallest has advantages; Thom, in disguise, gets to attend high school, and he's not expected to accomplish much in life. All that changes when he comes across a distressed human in the forest.

Ben Steele is new to Cripple Creek High School, and after a harrowing experience in the woods near his new home, he quickly falls in with Thom Woodmen and his circle of friends. So what if they like to hang out with nature? Ben's got nothing better to do. Trouble is, Ben can't seem to stay out of it-trouble, that is.

However, in saving young Ben's life, Thom inadvertently kick-starts a bonding process that'll change both their lives forever. With the support of family and friends, Thom learns to accept bonding with the human boy. But with the danger overrunning Cripple Creek lately, Thom may be cut down before he can confess his secret and his love.

From Harmony Ink
Available on Amazon.com
And most other places books are sold.